Once a reporter for Independent Television News, **Gerald Seymour** has lived in the West Country for several years. His bestselling novels include, among others, *Harry's Game*, *The Glory Boys*, *Field of Blood*, *Killing Ground*, *A Line in the Sand*, *Holding the Zero*, *The Untouchable* and, most recently, *Traitor's Kiss*.

THE UNKNOWN SOLDIER

Gerald Seymour

BANTAM PRESS

LONDON · NEW YORK · TORONTO · SYDNEY · AUCKLAND

TRANSWORLD PUBLISHERS
61–63 Uxbridge Road, London W5 5SA
a division of The Random House Group Ltd

RANDOM HOUSE AUSTRALIA (PTY) LTD
20 Alfred Street, Milsons Point, Sydney,
New South Wales 2061, Australia

RANDOM HOUSE NEW ZEALAND LTD
18 Poland Road, Glenfield, Auckland 10, New Zealand

RANDOM HOUSE SOUTH AFRICA (PTY) LTD
Endulini, 5a Jubilee Road, Parktown 2193, South Africa

Published 2004 by Bantam Press
a division of Transworld Publishers

Copyright © Gerald Seymour 2004

A catalogue record for this book is available
from the British Library.
ISBN 0593 052587 (cased)
0593 052595 (tpb)

Typeset in 10½/13pt Palatino by
Falcon Oast Graphic Art Ltd

Printed in Great Britain by
Clays Ltd, Bungay, Suffolk

3 5 7 9 10 8 6 4 2

Papers used by Transworld Publishers are natural, recyclable products
made from wood grown in sustainable forests. The manufacturing processes
conform to the environmental regulations of the country of origin.

To Gillian

THE UNKNOWN SOLDIER

Prologue

'I had a life. It was not the best, not the worst, but it was a life. It was hard, a struggle, but I did not complain because it was the life that God had given me. I had happiness.'

The voice dripped. Sometimes it faded away, was lost under the noise of the combi-van's engine, sometimes it was little more than a whisper.

'I was blessed. My wife was Muna. Our son was three years old, our daughter was close to one year. They were fine children. The girl had good eyes that were the colour of the early-morning skies in summer, and she would have been beautiful. We lived in the village with my wife's parents, and four houses away were my parents. Her father had fields for goats and my father had an orchard for apples and peaches. Her father said, after our marriage, that he no longer wanted to drive the taxi, and he gave it to me. It was generous of him to give me the taxi and I thought that one day I would have enough money to buy a second vehicle and employ a driver. It was what I hoped. A man with two taxis is a man of substance.'

Caleb thought the driver talked to stay awake. The others slept. The combi-van stank from the engine's fumes, and from the oil that they used to clean the weapons. None of them had washed for more than a week. Caleb could not sleep because he was squashed tight against the driver and each time the driver twisted the wheel or reached down for the gear-stick, an elbow nudged into his ribcage and jolted him. Three of his friends had crammed into the rear seats with their rifles, the rocket-propelled grenade-launcher and the rucksack with the missiles; three more were immediately behind him, cradling the rusted old .5 calibre machine-gun taken eleven years earlier from a Russian paratroop platoon. His own body separated the Chechen from the driver, to whom only Caleb listened.

'We did not think the war would come to us. We thought the war was for the cities – for Kabul, Kandahar, Jalalabad. Once there had been a camp for the foreigners near to the village, but it had not been used for two years, and we did not think we would be a target. Why should we be? It was an early morning like any other. I had prayed in the dawn at the mosque and the *imam* had spoken to us and then I had gone to bring wood for my father and for my wife's father, and I had drawn water from the well and had washed the taxi windows and its body, and I had measured the oil, and then I had told my wife when I would be home in the evening. We were worried for our son because he coughed, but I had said to my wife that I would try in the town, in the day, to get medicine. That day my father was going to select a goat for slaughter because we were close to my wife's birthday, and my wife's father was going to cut back dead wood from the trees in the orchards. It was like any other day and the war was far away. I said goodbye to my wife and I held my son while he coughed up on to my shoulder and I kissed my girl. God forgive me, but I spoke sharply to my wife because my son's phlegm stained my shirt and that would not be good when I went into the town to hope for passengers in my taxi. I left them. I drove past the mosque and past my father's fields where his goats were, and past my wife's father's orchards, and as I went down the hill, very slowly because the road is not tarmacadam but crushed stone, I saw the trails of the aeroplanes in the skies.'

To the Chechen, who had a patch of leather fastened with elastic over his right eye and whose left hand was replaced with a chrome-coated metal claw, Caleb was Abu Khaleb. He and the other men had fought in the north and on the plain south of Kabul and then north of Kandahar, had fought and fled when disaster was about to overwhelm them, then fought again and fled again. For a week they had not rested, had barely eaten. For each of them, pressed into the combi-van – the taxi – it was hard to accept defeat. They were now on a flat plain, featureless, without trees or hills, without cover, and their destination was the mountains where, if those were their orders, they would finally stand and fight from caves, ravines and high ground . . . if they reached the mountains.

'I was driving down the hill from the village, very carefully so that the holes would not damage underneath the vehicle, and the trails from three aeroplanes were coming towards me. They were very high and I could not see the planes themselves, only the trails they left behind. In our village we knew little about the war. Everything we knew came from the *imam*, who had a radio set and who listened to the broadcasts of the leadership from Kabul, but we were far from Kabul. I remember I was angry with the dust that came up from the road because I had just washed the windows. I had no interest in the aeroplanes. It was a good morning and the sun shone . . . I thought I was blessed by God and I was thinking of the feast for my wife's birthday. I regretted that I had spoken sharply to her about my shirt.'

His head rocked, his chin drooped. Even if Caleb could have slept he would not have done. The elbow butted into his ribcage. But the taxi-driver, who used only the sidelights of the combi-van, had swerved twice on to the rough gravel beside the tarmacadam and each time Caleb had snatched the wheel, heaved it over and prevented them spewing off the road. In the Toyota pickup, with the .5 calibre machine-gun mounted over the cab, they had been at the back end of a five-vehicle convoy fleeing for the mountains. It would have been chance, luck, that the first four pickups had twisted and negotiated a way through an old roadblock of concrete-filled oil drums and had missed the coil of loose barbed wire. Their pickup had caught it. They had driven on, hearing the scraping of the tangle of wire and had thought they would lose it. They had not. The front left tyre had gone first, then the rear right. Within a kilometre the two tyres were shredded, and they were detached from the convoy, with the cold of the evening gathering round them. There had been an argument. In a babble of voices, Caleb had said they should stay by the road and the Chechen had backed him. He was the Chechen's favourite.

Four hours later, the taxi van had come down the road. Another argument when it was halted at gunpoint. They were outside the part of Afghanistan they knew, they were strangers there. Caleb had said they should use the driver and, again, the Chechen had backed him. Three hours later, and Caleb smiled ruefully at the thought of it, he knew the driver, the driver's immediate family, the driver's distant family and the driver's village. In the heat of the vehicle, he had shrugged out of his camouflage tunic – the floppy hanging trousers, the long-tailed shirt and the wool cap without a peak made warmth enough.

'I saw my friend, Omar. He had gone down the road from the village to see if there was grazing lower on the hill. He is a good man. We used to talk and take coffee together when I was not in the town with the taxi. I was slowing when it seemed as if the world exploded. The taxi was lifted up from the road. If I had not seen Omar and braked to talk to him, the taxi would have gone off the road. I would have been killed, better if I had been killed – but that was not God's will. I was two kilometres from the village, or perhaps a little more, and the noise was like thunder, but greater than anything I had ever heard before. I braked, I ran from the vehicle and lay in a ditch with Omar, my face in the water. I thought the thunder would break my ears . . . Then it was gone. When I dared to look up I saw the trails of the aeroplanes going away. But I could not see our village. There was a great cloud over it, a cloud of dust. The cloud was from the camp that had not been used for two years, right to my village and past it. The old camp and the village were underneath the cloud. And there was quiet. You would like to see a photograph of my family?'

Caleb nodded. He knew how the story would end. A wallet was passed to him and he opened it. He saw the identification card behind brittle plastic. Fawzi al-Ateh. He saw the date of birth. The driver was twenty-five years old, four months older than himself. There was the photograph of the driver – faded, in black and white, probably taken on his wedding day – but with a straggling beard and a wispy moustache. The driver's finger jabbed at the picture beside the identification card. In it, Fawzi al-Ateh stood tall beside a slight woman who wore the dark *chador* robe. Caleb could not see her face. The driver held their son against his shoulder and the wife held their daughter against her hip. He held the wallet down by his knees so that the dashboard lights lit it.

'They were all dead. My wife, my son and my daughter were dead. My parents were dead and my wife's parents. The *imam* was dead. The family of Omar were dead. A helicopter flew over in the afternoon, but did not land. We buried all of the dead that we could find, but there were still some that we had not reached but who we could smell. I think God was kind to me because we buried my wife, my son and my daughter, and my wife's parents, but we did not find my father and my mother. It was six days before help came, foreigners in soldiers' uniforms. They were Americans, and they gave money to Omar and myself. I kept my money, God forgive me, but Omar threw their money back at their feet and they beat him, then took him away in their trucks. I was left. There was me and some dogs and the goats that had been in the fields. I took my taxi down to the town. I . . .'

The spotlight blazed in front of him, its beam bouncing in the dust encrusted on the windscreen.

He saw the shape of a man, shadow thrown grotesquely forward, rifle at the hip, an arm raised high above the symmetric shape of a helmet.

Maybe the driver panicked. Maybe terror locked his foot down on the accelerator. Maybe he had never been confronted by the half-lit silhouette of an American soldier.

The combi-van surged past the soldier. For a moment it was clear of him and free.

Locked in Caleb's hand, the wallet was unseen, unfelt. There were cries, shouts of awakened confusion behind him and a claw dug into his arm as the Chechen tried to steady himself. As the van swung in the road, the sidelights caught the prone figures of men in camouflage uniforms beside the tarmacadam. Caleb heard the shouts, then the first shots hit the van.

He glimpsed the wide-eyed terror on the driver's face then – seconds later – felt the warmth as the man's blood spattered on his cheeks and in his beard.

The van, out of control, slewed off the road, rolled once from side to roof to side, then came to rest. A door careered open and Caleb was hurled across the driver's torso and head, his breath squeezed from his lungs. The gunfire went on. Bullets hammered the carcass of the van. Shouts burst in his ears. 'Watch the motherfuckers – don't go fucking close – careful, guys, careful – hit the fuckers.' Another endless rattle of firing, on automatic, raked the van. Caleb hugged the ground between the rocks that had broken his fall from the door. It was more than two years since he had heard words in that language. It was from his past, from a rejected culture. A moment of silence, then a low moan from inside the van. A final rattle of gunfire killed the moan.

He lay on the ground, his teeth chattering, his mouth filled with dry earth. The spotlight played over the van. He had seen men when they were about to die, the haunted faces of men in the trenches as the helicopters went over, men being led across the football pitch to the crossbar of the goal where a noose hung, men who followed the Northern Alliance and had used all their ammunition, all their grenades, and now faced captors who were without mercy. The spotlight's beam roved off the van and edged towards him, seemed to nestle against him, then held him. If he was to be shot, this was the moment. Did they want a prisoner? Or another corpse?

He heard the young voice, shrill with excitement: 'Sergeant, there's one alive. Over here, one of the fuckers is alive.'

He awaited the shot. The only part of his life flickering across his mind was the last two years – because the older past was forgotten.

He heard the answering shout, more distant and anxious. 'Watch him, kid, watch him close. He moves his hands, shoot him. I'm coming. Go careful, take no chances.'

Caleb was his past, and erased. He was Abu Khaleb, and that was his present. In his hand was the opened wallet with the photograph of a taxi-driver, his wife and children, the identification card of Fawzi al-Ateh. His brain, at flywheel speed, worked for his future, and his survival, and his lifeline was the photograph that almost matched his face.

Chapter One

The aircraft banked on its final circuit, then its nose went down and it started the descent.

Above him, the voice was loud, shouted over the increased pitch of the engine noise. 'I tell you, this has been a journey from hell.'

A voice barked back, 'You want to do it every week, sir, then you get kind of used to hell.'

'It's the shit bucket, isn't it? That's the smell I can't get rid of.'

'I'd say, sir, that having to wipe their arses for them is worse than the smell.'

He was ignored, might not have existed. He was as much a piece of cargo as the crates loaded with them on to the transport aircraft after he and the four others had been secured on the steel floor. It might have been four days, or five, since the journey had started. He didn't know. They had landed three times, or four, for refuelling.

Now the aircraft dived. He knew it was the last leg. If it had not been for the straps that held him he would have slid down the floor of the fuselage, then cannoned into an obstruction. He did not move, could not. He sat on a small cushion of thin foam but the floor rivets were too prominent for the cushion to protect his backside. And the cushion was damp from the urine he had leaked during the bad turbulence on the first leg. He could not move because of the strapping that held him in place, and the others. In the spiralling descent, his sandals bounced into the back of the man in front of him, and behind him feet bruised his lower spine below his fastened wrists. He was coming back as he had gone out, trussed on the floor of the aircraft. His wrists were manacled by chains, then fastened round his waist, and more chains shackled his ankles. Webbing straps that would normally have held cargo in place were looped through each elbow and back to the fuselage sides. Another strap across his chest restrained forward movement, and a last strap was woven through his legs. He wore thin bright orange cotton overalls over a singlet and pants. A gauze mask was over his mouth, removed only when they fed him, baffles were over his ears, and goggles, with tape across the glass, were over his eyes. The baffles and the mask had not been removed in the four, or five, days since he had been taken out of the camp. They didn't talk to him, not when he defe-cated or urinated, not when they slipped the face mask down from his mouth and fed him. The straps held him as they plummeted down, and with the loss of height his wrists must have bulged because the chains on them hurt more, and rubbed against the plastic bracelet on his right wrist.

'Don't mind me asking, sir, but why are we letting these bastards go free?'

'We pulled six hundred into Gitmo, and letting a few out, a very few, is good PsyOps. It's the fourth lot. They're nothing, they're use-less, they're not Al Qaeda. We demonstrate fair-mindedness – it's like giving out candy. It's about gestures, takes the heat off.'

'Is it a lottery, sir, who gets chosen?'

'You better believe it . . . Look, most of them in Gitmo are just wrong-place-at-the-wrong-time guys . . . The one up forward, he's got stomach cancer, inoperable, going home to die. Next one down, he's at least sixty-nine, and had a stroke, couldn't even lift a hand grenade. The one beside you, he's simple, was sold to us by some warlord on the take. At the back, he's half blind, can't hardly see his own hand . . . Twenty months they've been with us. Mistakes got made.'

'And this one?'

The voice was dismissive. 'Just a peasant from up-country, a taxi-driver . . .'

'If it's not a stupid question . . . If they're useless and not a threat, why are they trussed up like Thanksgiving turkeys waiting the chop?'

'Read the book. Standard treatment for the movement of prisoners. Don't ask me, I didn't write it. All I gotta do is hand them over to Afghan Security, get a signature, and that's the end of my watch.'

They moved away. He felt the aircraft level out, then through his ear baffles he heard the rumble of the wheels going down. The engines, on full power, blotted out everything except stifled cries of fear in front of him. He braced himself. It was a bad landing. The transporter hit, lurched, rose, then hit a second time, harder. The guards and the crew in the fuselage clapped without enthusiasm. They taxied, the reverse thrust dinning through the baffles, then he was jerked forward as the brakes went on.

The aircraft crawled to a stop. It was twenty months since he had been dragged on board an aircraft – at this place – shackled, manacled, blind, deaf, and flown to the camp.

The hatch ground down. The chill of the night air engulfed him. Outside, on the apron, there were raised voices. The argument developed. When he was unfastened, he could have shifted and flexed his leg and arm muscles, but he did not. Everything he had learned in the camp, twenty months of surviving there, told him that he should do nothing to attract attention. They had brought him back: his name had been chosen because he had done nothing to stir attention. He listened to the argument . . . Because the aircraft had been delayed for seven hours with maintenance problems in the port outer engine, the Afghan Security men – detailed to meet the freed prisoners and take them into Kabul for interrogation and clearance – had headed back to the city three hours ago. The base night-duty officer was not prepared to countenance the presence of five Afghan prisoners on his territory for the rest of the night: he wanted them gone, like yesterday. A telephone call had been made to the detention wing, but the cells were full. And Afghan Security were not answering their phone. And . . . He heard the night-duty officer brusquely pass the buck.

'You're going to get wheels, a driver and an escort, and you're going to take them into town and kick down the door of Afghan

Security – that's the Pol-i-Charki gaol – and you're going to dump them there. That's a non-negotiable.'

'Maybe you don't understand, Captain, but I have been with these ragheads the last four days, all the way from Guantanamo. I need a cot.'

'Don't you hear, Lieutenant? You drop these losers at the Pol-i-Charki, then you come back here and find a cot. Got it?'

'Yes, sir.'

A secondary argument started up. 'Sergeant, I'm taking these men into town. Their restraints have been removed. I want them put back on.'

'No can do, sir.'

'That is an order. Manacle them.'

'Sorry, sir. As loadmaster sergeant I have authority over all Air Force equipment. Such equipment does not leave my sight, does not leave this aircraft. Manacles, chains, ear baffles, mouth masks, goggles and cushions are air-force property.'

'Goddamnit . . .'

'Sorry, sir. Oh, and eleven hundred hours is take-off time. You better be back by then if you want a ride out. Good luck, sir.'

He knew the book. He had been in military custody for twenty months. He knew how the book was written. The arguments had not amused him and he sat bolt still with his head down. When the goggles were pulled up from his eyes he kept them closed. He gave no sign that he had understood a word of the disputes within his hearing. A vehicle pulled up, manoeuvred close to the open tail and a door was slid open. Hands lifted him up. His eyes were open now but he did not look around him. In a stumbling slide he went down the tail and the freshness of the air caught him. It was the first time he could remember scenting fresh air since he had been with the Chechen, his friend, and the others beside the long, straight road where the pickup had lost its tyres. There had been no clean air in the taxi van, and when he had been thrown clear at the ambush the stink of cordite had covered him, then the stench of the enemy in the personnel carrier, and the smell of a holding prison that was exchanged for the shit bucket of the aircraft out. There had been no clean, pure air in the camp, not even in the exercise compound.

He sucked in the air. He was to be taken to Kabul and dumped at the Pol-i-Charki. He knew the gaol: he had taken prisoners there for interrogation, men of the Northern Alliance who had fought against Al Qaeda and the Taliban – but that was long ago. Deep in the recesses of his memory, shared with the Pol-i-Charki, was a vague vision of the road from the Bagram base into the city. If he reached the Pol-i-Charki, he would be dead . . . and he had not come home to die. He was lifted up into a van with smoked windows. The driver was yawning, using his forearm to wipe sleep from his eyes. A marine was in the back with a rifle, grumpily making room for the prisoners. As the officer took the front passenger seat, the driver grinned and handed back bars of nougat chocolate. They drove away, and an open jeep followed with a machine-gun mounted on a brace behind the driver.

He remembered the base as a place of ghosts and ruins. He remembered it abandoned and looted. Without turning his head he saw new, prefabricated blocks and tent camps, then a gate topped with coiled razor wire, flanked with sandbags, guarded by men in combat fatigues. He took heart. For twenty months he had existed in a vacuum of time and information. That changed. The gate was guarded, which told him there was still the chance of hostile action on the fifty kilometres of road – through flat and featureless farming country – between the Bagram base and the capital city of Kabul. As the sentries raised the bar at the base gate, the machine-gun on the jeep was noisily cocked. They left the arc-lights and the perimeter wire behind them, and the driver switched on the radio, caught the forces programme and smiled toothily at the officer's discomfort.

It would take, as he remembered it, an hour at most to reach the outskirts of the city. His sole hope was in open country. They passed a village. The officer ignored the no-smoking sign in the cab and lit a cigarette. The driver grimaced.

If he were in the Pol-i-Charki, if he were interrogated by Afghan Security – the hard bastards of the Northern Alliance – he would fail. He would be dead. Memories of the road silted in his mind. A village, as he had known it more than twenty months before, flashed past in the headlights. Two ruined compounds, gutted in earlier fighting, were on the right. There were open fields and scrub . . . Then, if his memory held, there were trees beside the road, both sides. His fingers played with the sharp edge of the plastic bracelet on his wrist. He coughed, was ignored, and coughed again. The officer turned, irritated, and the cigarette smoke wreathed his face. He looked pathetic and cringed, then pointed downwards. The officer's eyes followed where he pointed, to his groin. The driver, too, had turned back to look.

'Shit, man,' the driver whined. 'Not in here, not in my vehicle. I'm not having him piss in my vehicle.'

The driver didn't wait for the officer's agreement. He braked hard, swerved on to the gravel, stopped.

'I take one-star generals in this vehicle. I'm not having it pissed in.'

The officer climbed out, threw down his cigarette and opened the back door. He climbed out and the officer's hand steadied him. He smiled his thanks. He went to the side of the road and knew he was watched by the men in the jeep who had the mounted, cocked machine-gun. He stepped down off the road and into scrub. He fiddled with the zipper at the front of his overalls. Behind him, the strike of a match lit another cigarette. A torch played on his back. He was coiled, tense. He did not know whether he would be able to run after four days in the aircraft and the months in the camp. If he reached Pol-i-Charki he was dead . . . He ran. The torch wavered off him as he wove. His legs were leaden. He was already panting when he reached the first of the trees. A single shot crashed in his ears. He heard shouts, and the officer's voice.

'No, don't – he isn't worth killing . . .'

He ran, panting, gasping for air, trying to kick his legs forward.

'. . . he's only a taxi-driver.'

He lost the lights and sensed the freedom. He ran till he fell, then pushed himself up and ran again.

Dawn came across the mountains, and the mountain peaks in the east made sharp funnels of sunshine. The light speared the coiled wire on the perimeter fence of Bagram – the sprawling military base, originally Soviet-built, an hour's drive west across the plain to Kabul – and slashed at the night mist, glinted on the bright corrugated-iron roofs of the repaired buildings, caught the wan faces of troopers sleep-walking to the shower blocks, burned the smoke rising in still air from kitchen stacks, lit the dull camouflage of transport aircraft parked on the aprons, then threw shadows down from the angles of the wings and tail fins of two small white-painted planes that were being laboriously manhandled and wheeled out from under shelters of canvas.

They were like toys in a man's world. Teams of men, not in military fatigues, heaved their weight against the slight wings and directed the planes towards a slip-road leading on to the main runway. They bent their heads away as a bomber careered past them on full take-off power. These two planes were different from anything else flown off the Bagram runway. Length: twenty-six feet and eight inches. Wing span: forty-eight feet and six inches. Height above the oil-smeared Tarmac: six feet and one inch. Width of fuselage: (widest point) three feet and eight inches, (narrowest point) one foot and eleven inches. They seemed so fragile, so delicate – ballet dancers in comparison with the clog-booted brigade that screamed up the runway. The planes were each powered by a single two-blade variable-pitch push-propellor capable of flying the machine at top speed of 127 miles per hour, and at loiter speed of seventy-five miles per hour when fuel conservation was necessary. What a stranger to the base, ignorant of modern technology, would first have noticed about these two planes was that unbroken white paint covered the forward area where there should have been cockpit glass for a pilot's vision. What he would not have known was that the planes, the unmanned aerial vehicles, were regarded by those who knew as the most formidable weapon in the occupying power's arsenal. They seemed so innocent in their bright white paint, so harmless, but their name was Predator.

The dawn light rested on a young man and a young woman walking quickly away from a camouflaged trailer parked beside the sheeting from which the Predators, designation MQ-1, had been wheeled out by the ground crew. They passed a satellite dish mounted on a second trailer hitched to a closed unmarked van. Marty wore baggy brown shorts and a T-shirt emblazoned with a Yellowstone Park brown bear and flip-flops. She wore jeans with frayed hems and patches at the knees, a loose plain green sweatshirt that was crumpled, as if she'd slept in it, and a pair of old trainers. His eyes were masked by thick pebble lenses secured in a metal frame, his skin was pale, his hair a mass of untidy, mousy curls. His physique was puny. Lizzy-Jo was taller, but plumper from the weight never discarded after childbirth. Her dark glasses were hooked on the crown of a wild mess of auburn hair scooped at the back of her head into an extravagant yellow ribbon. The stranger, seeing them, would not have known that, between them, they controlled the Predator.

Temperamentally they could not have been more different: he was quiet, withdrawn, she was noisy, exuberant. But two common factors bound them into their relationship: both were employed by the Agency, took their orders from Langley and were not subject to the military regimen that controlled the base; both worshipped, in their differing ways, the power and meanness of the Predator, version MQ-1. Initially, when they had been posted to Afghanistan, the Bagram base, they had existed inside the inner compound used by the Agency and had lived alongside the Agency teams, and those from the Feds, who ran the detention block behind a double inner fence of razor wire with its own sleeping, eating and recreation quarters – an apartheid cocoon for the élite that separated them from the Air Force people and the marines' units. At first they had not been part of the general life of the huge base. But the war was winding down, the Al Qaeda targets were harder to come by, and old disciplines were discarded.

The best breakfasts at Bagram were served in the marines' compound. The marines had the best cooks, the best variety of food, the best coffee. And a good breakfast would last them through the day in the stifling heat of the Ground Control Station.

He wore his ID card hooked on his belt. Hers, more provocatively, was clipped to her T-shirt between her breasts. After a sentry had checked them through the gate into the marines' compound, they joined the queue in the canteen.

In front of them, a lieutenant was bitching at a loadmaster sergeant. They listened, rolling their eyes at each other, entertained.

The lieutenant, dead tired and slurring as if he'd barely slept, said, 'I just felt such a goddamn idiot. I never figured that the little bastard was setting me up to do a runner. What am I supposed to do? Mow the little fucker down? Didn't seem right . . . He was free – useless to us, no risk, but I'd his name on the docket and was tasked to hand him over at the Pol-i-Charki. I tell you, my only piece of luck, the people that were there at the gaol, they never even read the names, never did the counting, just kicked inside the four we brought. I just felt such a fool at falling for that old trick, wanting to pee. Just some simple gook, and free – after where he's been, in the cage at Guantanamo, why would he want to run?'

'Don't worry about it, sir – I mean, he wasn't bin Laden, was he? You said just some taxi-driver.'

They dressed down, Marty and Lizzy-Jo, to emphasize that they were not military. Foul-ups in the military were always entertaining. It had made a good start to the day.

A half-hour later, with the dawn on full thrust and killing the mist, in the Ground Control Station, Marty took the Predator – *First Lady* – up off the runway, working the small computer-game joystick on the bench above his knees. *Carnival Girl*, the second craft, was back-up and would stay grounded unless needed. Lizzy-Jo thwacked her fingers on the console keys and watched as the first pictures flickered, then settled on the screens above her. The mission that day was for reconnaissance over the Tora Bora mountains to the south-west. The bird climbed, optimum conditions with light north-east winds at fifteen thousand feet. She reached across, tapped his shoulder and pointed to the central screen, which gave the real-time image from the belly camera. She giggled. 'On his way to the garage to collect his yellow cab . . . eh?'

Below the camera, clear and in sharp focus on dun-coloured scree, the figure in the orange overalls was running, but slowly. Marty grimaced – not their business. The Predator hunted meatier prey. The orange-suited figure tripped, fell, and stumbled on. Then the camera's field surged forward and he was lost.

'What do you think it's like in Guantanamo?'

'Don't know and don't care,' Marty murmured, side of mouth. 'I'm going up to seventeen thousand feet altitude, which'll be our loiter height . . . OK, OK, I suppose Guantanamo would be kind of scary.'

Camp X-Ray, Guantanamo Bay.

It was the end of the first week and he was learning. He had not failed the hardest test. Hardest was not to respond when an order, in English, was screamed in his ear. No movement, no obedience, until the order was translated into Pashto, or a gesture was made to indicate what he should do.

The numbers coming into the camp were so great that it had taken them a week to process him. Hands gripped him, pulled him upright in front of the white screen. A fist took his chin, lifted it, and he stared into the camera. The light flashed. He was manhandled again and turned so that his head was profile to the lens, and the light flashed once more. The fists took his arms and he was shuffled out through the door and in front of the desk. The chains were tight on his ankles and his arms were pinioned behind his back; the manacles were fastened to a chain looped round his waist. They put the face mask back over his mouth. A heavy-built soldier, with a swollen gut and a shaven head, gazed up at the number written in indelible ink on his forehead, then riffled through the mass of files on the desk. Beside him, a woman sat, middle-aged, her greying hair covered with a loose scarf.

'Right, boy, we'll start at the beginning. Name?'

He stared straight ahead, and saw the first flicker of impatience in the soldier's eyes.

The woman translated in Pashto.

The Chechen had said that, if they were captured, the Americans would kill them. They would torture them, then shoot them. They would rape their women and bayonet their children. The Chechen had said it was better to die with the last bullet and the last grenade than to be captured by the Americans.

'I am Fawzi al-Ateh. I am a taxi-driver. I—'

'You answer only my questions. I want only answers to what I ask. Got me?'

She translated fast.

He had been beaten at the first camp he had been brought to. He had not been allowed to sleep. Questions had rained on him, with the fists. Noise had bellowed in his ears, shrill, howling sounds played over loudspeakers. Lights had been shone into his face, and if he had slumped in exhaustion he was kicked back upright and made to resume standing. Then he had been put on the aircraft. He had not known, still did not, the destination. For a week he had been in a wire cage, in a block of cages, and if a man talked through the mesh wire to the prisoner alongside him, guards came and shouted and manhandled their victim away. There were prayer-mats in the cages, and buckets. He had learned from watching the men brought to the camp with him, and from those already there. Some had fought, struggled, spat at the guards, and were kicked for it. Some had collapsed, disoriented, and they were loaded on to wheeled stretchers, held down with straps and taken away, he did not know where to. He had been searched, had stood naked while fingers in plastic gloves had pried into his ears, his mouth and his anus, but he had not resisted. When it was hardest for him, every time it was worst, he groped back in his memory for each phrase, every word of the story of the taxi-driver, each detail and every fact of the life of the taxi-driver.

'Listen here, boy. You are a prisoner of the United States of America. You are held at Camp X-Ray at Guantanamo Bay. You probably don't know geography, but Guantanamo Bay is a military base under United States control on the island of Cuba. You are not classified as a prisoner-of-war but as an unlawful combatant. You have no rights. You will be held here as long as we consider you a threat to our country. You will be interrogated here so that we can learn the full extent of your involvement with Al Qaeda. My advice to you is to co-operate with the interrogators when you are brought before them. Failure to co-operate will lead to harsh punishment measures. At Camp X-Ray, you are a forgotten person, you have disappeared off the face of the earth. We can do with you what we want. You may think this is all a bad dream, boy, and that you will soon be going home – forget it.'

The translator's voice droned in his ear, as if it was a familiar routine, as if the words meant nothing to her.

Behind him he heard the clatter of boots, then felt something fastened to his right wrist.

'Take him away.'

He was led back to the block of cages. Flies played on his face but he could not swat them because his arms were chained. The chain at his ankles constricted his stride and the guards dragged him so that he had to hop so as not to scrape his toes in gravel. He was brought down corridors of wire covered with green sheeting. He had no comprehension of the size of the camp but from all around he heard the moaning of men whose minds had turned. He understood the muttered words of the guards, what they would eat that day, what movie they would see that evening, but he showed no sign of his understanding. He thought that if they knew he was Caleb, who had become Abu Khaleb, he would be dragged out one dawn and shot or hanged. He thought it would be as the Chechen had said: the interrogators, when he was brought before them, would torture him. His only protection was the taxi-driver's name and the taxi-driver's life – every detail of what he had been told as he had rocked in tiredness in the front of the van was protection against the fear.

He was brought to his cage. He realized the hatred of the guards. They wanted nothing more of him than that he should fight, kick, spit, and give them the excuse to beat him. The chains were taken off his ankles and from his waist, and the manacles at his wrists were unfastened. He was pushed crudely into his cage. He squatted down, huddled against the back wall near to the bucket, and a little of the wind off the sea filtered through the wire at the sides of the cage. He held his right wrist in front of his eyes. He saw his photograph on the plastic bracelet, the reference number US8AF-000593DP, his sex, height, weight, date of birth and his name.

He tried to remember everything of Fawzi al-Ateh. It was the only strand he had to cling to.

The dawn widened.

Ahead, Caleb saw a grey-blue strip, the mountains. Separating the peaks from the skies were patches of snow topped by cloud bundles. The high ground was his immediate target. He crossed a wilderness of bare ground broken by low outcrops of rock. Before capture, before the twenty months in the cages of Guantanamo – first at what was called Camp X-Ray and then the movement to the newly built and permanent-to-last Camp Delta – he had prided himself on his ability to run or travel at forced-march pace. When he had been, proudly, in the 055 Brigade with Saudis and Yemenis, Kuwaitis, Egyptians and Uzbeks, he had been one of the fittest. Twenty months in the cages – Fawzi al-Ateh, the taxi-driver – had leached the strength from his legs, had squeezed the capacity of his lungs. If he had not been at home, if he had not needed to return to the ranks of his family, he would not have been able to move at such speed across the bare, stone-strewn ground. At the training camp, the Chechen who had recruited him always made him go first over stamina-degrading assault courses because the Chechen knew he would do well and would set a standard for the other newcomers. Afghanistan was the only home he knew and the 055 Brigade was the only family he acknowledged. Everything about a life before the training camps was expelled from his mind; it did not exist. For twenty months he had been taken out for two sessions a week of fifteen minutes' exercise. His legs had been shackled, his steps stumbling and short within the constraints of the chain's length. A guard had held each arm, and his sandals had scuffed the flattened worn dirt of the circuit in the yard. In those twenty months, he had been walked the hundred yards to the interrogation block nine times. His leg muscles had atrophied, but still he ran.

He sobbed from pain. In front of another man – an instructor at the training camp, an Arab in the 055 Brigade, a guard or interrogator at Camp X-Ray or Camp Delta – he would never have shown how pain hurt him. He was alone. The pain was in his legs, in the muscles of his calves and thighs. The unworked muscles seemed to scream as he pounded forward. When he fell, many times, he scraped the skin off his knees and elbows, and blood stained the cotton of his overalls. There was no water and his throat rasped with dryness. His lungs sucked in the growing warmth of the air. The only time he stopped was when he came to a rutted track and lay in scrub near to it, with the scent of wild flowers in his nose. He waited till his heartbeat had subsided to listen for a vehicle or a man or a goat's bell. When he heard nothing, only the wind, he crossed the track and went on.

Somewhere in front of him, by the base of the line of the mountains, was the family he yearned for.

Across Afghan mountains, the Iranian land mass and the chasm of the Gulf of Oman, the same dawn rose over a limitless desert of salt flats and razor-spined dunes of ochre sand. The desert, the largest sand mass on Earth, was flanked to the north by the Saudi Arabian province of Al Najd, to the east by the oil-rich region of Al Hasa based on the refinery complex near the city of Ad Dammam and the statelets of the United Arab Emirates, to the south by the hills of Oman and Yemen, to the west by the Saudi mountains of the Asir range. Whipped by the winds, the desert sands continually moved, forming new peaks and patterns, and the great area that was a thousand kilometres wide and six hundred kilometres in depth was perpetually burned by the sun's ferocity. The itinerant Bedouin tribesmen, who alone could exist in the desert's privations, called it the Rub' al Khālī, the Empty Quarter.

The dawn light, thrown low, caught the mahogany wings of a hunting eagle. It lit the dark upper coat of a stalking fox and highlighted the tracks of the jerboas that would be food for both the fox and the eagle. It glistened the still moist gobbet of phlegm spat out by a camel that had passed two days before. The light nestled on a point of black darkness between a cleft of rocks where higher ground rose above the western section of the sands.

Other than in the few minutes when the sun came up in the east, the entrance to the cave was hidden. A man emerged from it and blinked as the sun's brightness blinded him after a night in the dim interior. Behind him, in the depth of darkness, a petrol-driven generator started up and coughed before the engine engaged. He spat out the waste between his teeth and lit the first cigarette of the day. Staring out over the expanse, he saw the single sentry squatting in a cleft below the cave's entrance, a rifle held loosely in his lap. He ground out the cigarette, then placed the butt in a small tin box; later it would go with other waste into a pit dug in the sand, then be covered up. He whistled to the sentry, who turned his head, smiled grimly, then shook it. Only the desert confronted them, not danger. He called back into the cave quietly.

Others emerged.

When the cave had first been found, when the decision had been made that it burrowed far enough into the escarpment for their needs, a compass had been used to determine the direction of the holy city of Makkah. A line was fixed in the memories of each of them as they came in the half-light away from the cave and on to a small square of beaten dirt between the rocks. In unison, they knelt. Among the five pillars of their faith was the requirement that they should pray five times each day. The *fajr* was the first obligatory prayer, at dawn. They were silent as they knelt, each man wrapped in his own thoughts, but common among them was the pleading to their God that the opportunity be given them for revenge, the chance to strike back against the embracing power of their enemy. And common among them also was the appearance of hunted men, drawn-faced, thin-bodied, exhausted in spirit.

Very few knew of the cave. A satellite telephone was inside it, but gathered dust and was not used. The generator was capable of recharging the batteries of a laptop computer but that was also left idle. Once a week, or less frequently if the security situation was difficult, trusted couriers came across the desert with messages, food and water. All of those in the cave, hunted, harried and condemned, knew that their photographs and biographies were listed in Internet sites for the Most Wanted, and they knew the size – millions of the accursed dollars – of the reward that would be paid out for information that pinpointed the location of their lair, for their capture or for their deaths.

In a few minutes, as the sun rose, the shadow of the cave's entrance would be lost.

Many hours later, the same dawn rose, this time a slow-growing light that seeped through dark gun-metal cloud that was thick enough for a second heavy fall of snow. It was the last day of their rental on the cabin and in three hours Jed Dietrich would be loading the vehicle and turning his back on the wild Wisconsin lakes. It was too late in the year to have a real hope of hooking a decent muskie but it was what he had dreamed of for the last eight months of duty far to the south. He took Arnie Junior with him and left Brigitte to pack the bags and clean the cabin. The night cold had left the first snowfall as frozen slush on the ground and the water around the pontoon piers where the boats were moored was thinly crusted with ice.

He checked his son's life-jacket, then his own, and he saw that the five-year-old child was shivering in the cold. They would not be out long but he could not have given up the year's last chance of a good fish.

In the boat, Jed smiled reassurance at his son, tugged the engine to life and sped out for deeper water, the ice crackling at the bow.

Where Jed Dietrich worked, unaccompanied by Brigitte and Arnie Junior, there was sunshine, warm water and ideal conditions for good-fighting sport fish, but recreational boats were not permitted out of harbour by the patrolling coastguards and the beaches were out of bounds to servicemen and civilians because the shoreline was covered by infra-red and heat-seeking surveillance beams. There he could only gaze out at the sea, not fish in it . . . they'd tried for more children, a brother or sister for Arnie Junior, but had not been fortunate, reason enough to have the kid with him for every one of the precious hours it was possible. He slowed the engine to little more than idling speed, tossed out the lure and let out line with it so that it would go deep. Then he dropped off the small spoon, with little hope that a wall-eye, perch or sucker would be any hungrier than a muskie, and winked encouragement at the boy. As they trolled across the lake, under the thick and darkened cloud, they talked fish talk – as Arnie Senior had to him when he was a kid – of big-mouthed monsters with rows of slashing teeth and record weights, sunken reefs and rock walls where the muskie might gather, their habits and lifestyles. The little boy liked the talk. When Jed was away, and he had only the photograph of Brigitte and Arnie Junior for company, and the phone calls when the kid seemed forever tongue-tied, he would savour the memory of these moments.

For now, Jed Dietrich was at peace. He was thirty-six years old, a HumInt specialist on the staff of the Defense Intelligence Agency.

In the sunshine, beside the clear Caribbean sea where he could not fish, the same peace eluded him.

He was tall, well-built, looked after himself, and he thought Arnie Junior would soon shape up after him, would be useful at football or softball, and would soon be able to handle a boat like this on his own. Arnie Junior was his ongoing obsession, a point of focus in a work-load that was now tedious, pointless, boring. Too often, down in the distant south, as the translator's voice whined in his ear, he thought of his kid and found his attention sliding away from his target.

Out on the water, with the quiet about him and only the child's chatter and the engine to listen to, he had felt the tension drain from him. He felt good. No matter there were no fish . . . and then his son squealed, his rod arching. They were both laughing and shouting, and reeled in a nine-inch smallmouth bass, then returned it to the water, because Jed taught his boy to respect the prey. They fished another hour. No more takes, no more bites, but it did not matter – the peace was total. They would fly down to DC and stay a few days with Arnie Senior and Wilhelmina, then Brigitte would go back to the one-bedroom apartment they rented near to the Pentagon, and he would take the feeder flight down to Puerto Rico and on to Guantanamo.

Brigitte broke the peace. She stood on the dock in her windcheater, waved and called them in . . . The holiday was over. Ahead of him were the camp, the prisoners, the monotony, the cringing answers, and the stale routine of going over ground already exhausted. The camp seemed to call him, and he turned his face away from his son and cursed softly, but the kid wouldn't have seen his irritated frown or heard the obscenity. Camp Delta dragged him back.

*

A day had passed, and a night. Another dawn, another day, another night, and then the sun peeped up.

He woke. Caleb felt the sharp tugging at the arm of his overall, jerking and persistent. Hot breath splayed over his cheeks. He opened his eyes and flailed with his hands.

The dogs backed off. They were thin but their eyes were bright with excitement, their hackles up. The teeth menaced him. He rolled from his side on to his buttocks and they retreated further, all the time snarling at him. One, bolder than the others, darted towards his left ankle and caught the skin below the hem of the overalls, but he lashed out and the heavy sandal hit its jaw hard enough for it to lose courage. Then the oldest of the dogs, fangs yellowed, fur greying, threw back its head and howled.

In the night he had seen the dull lights of the village. He had staggered to within a hundred yards of the nearest building, then collapsed. He had lain down on the dirt and stones, beside a fence of cut thornbushes, had heard voices and known that he did not have the strength to go the last hundred yards from the fence to the nearest building – and he had slept. The sleep had killed the pain that eked from each muscle in his body. If it had not been for the dogs pulling at him, Caleb would have slept on through the dawn, until the sun was high.

He could see a dozen low-built homes of mud bricks, flat-roofed, beyond a maze of small, fenced fields. The dogs watched him, wary of him, and the warning howl had not been answered: the doors stayed shut. To the side of the community's homes, separated from them, was a compound walled with stones and bricks – new, he thought – and above the walls bright flags of white and red and green fluttered from poles, and Caleb knew that it was a recently constructed cemetery, a shrine to men buried as martyrs.

If he were to find his family, Caleb needed food, water and clothes, and he needed help.

He pushed himself up but his knees gave under him and he sprawled back on the ground. The second time he tried he was able to stand. His legs were in agony, and his arms, shoulders and chest. He had no choice but to approach the village. He bent and picked up a stone, hurled it at the oldest dog, the pack leader. His decision was made: he must approach the village. In all the life he knew – two years and then twenty months – decisions had never come hard to him. He was too weak to skirt the village, to put off the crisis moment of contact. He had to trust and hope.

He knew that his arrival would cause panic. At Camp X-Ray and Camp Delta, the interrogators had told him that the power of Al Qaeda was broken, for ever, in Afghanistan, and he had believed them, and that the leaders of his family were in flight; it had been the story they told to encourage him to confess involvement and contacts . . . but he was just a taxi-driver, Fawzi al-Ateh, and he knew nothing. To return to his family he must go to the village and hope for help.

The dogs trailed him. Half-way to the village, staggering, unable to walk with a steady stride, he saw a woman's face at the window of the nearest house. She ducked away and the nearer he went to the house, the greater the cacophony of barking. A door opened.

A man, half dressed, roused from sleep, was framed in the door-way, a rifle raised to his shoulder.

Caleb's life, at that moment, hung by a thread.

He knew that in some villages the Arabs of the 055 Brigade had been detested, seen as arrogant foreigners. Now he might be shot, or he might be bound and sold back to the Americans. He straightened his back, and smiled. He spoke in the language he had learned, the language he had used in Camp X-Ray and Camp Delta, that of Fawzi al-Ateh.

He greeted the man who aimed the rifle at him. 'Peace be on you.'

The response was suspicious and grudging. 'On you be peace.'

Caleb knew the weapon. He could have stripped it blindfolded in daylight or darkness and reassembled it. The safety catch was off, the finger was on the trigger, not the guard. He stood his ground and held out his arms, scratched and scraped from the times, beyond counting, that he had fallen; he showed he had no weapon. The rifle barrel lowered, then dropped. He ducked his head, a pose of humility, but he showed no fear. Like the dogs, the man would associate fear with deceit. Quietly, Caleb asked for hospitality, shelter and help.

Without taking his eyes off Caleb, the man shouted instructions to the older child. Caleb understood him. The child led, and Caleb followed, the man behind him. The store shed was of brick, with mud daubed over it. The child opened a heavy door, then ran. Caleb went inside. He saw goats, and their fodder, long-handled spades and . . . The door was slammed shut behind him, darkness closed round him, and he heard the fastening of the door. There were no windows. Outside, the man would now be squatted with his rifle, watching the door while the child went to bring the village elders.

He sat on a carpet of hay and the goats nuzzled against him. They might kill him and bury his body in the village's rubbish tip, or sell him, or they might help him.

He slept.

Later Caleb was woken by the sound of the door scraping open. He staggered out into the brilliance of the sunshine, and sat cross-legged on the ground in front of a horseshoe of the village men. The oldest men were in the centre. He told his story. They might hate the Arabs of Al Qaeda, they might have fought alongside them. He spoke the truth as he knew it. His voice was soft, gentle and without hesitation. Their faces were impassive. As he spoke, a helicopter flew high overhead. His presence endangered the village. The village would have wealth beyond the dreams of any of the tribesmen if they sold him on. From the moment he held out his right arm and showed them the plastic bracelet with his photograph on it and the name of Fawzi al-Ateh, and the reference US8AF-000593DP, he knew he was believed. He was tall for an Arab, but had swarthy coloured skin, and in his time in their country he had learned their language well. They listened, were spellbound, but it was not until the end of his story, when he ducked his head to show he acknowledged that his life lay in their hands, that he knew he would not be shot or sold. The oldest village man came to him, lifted him, then walked him to the cemetery.

A year before, fighters had been killed a day's walk from the village, caught on foot and in the open by helicopters. The younger men of the village, with mules, had brought their bodies here. They were buried with honour . . . The fighters were *Shuhadaa*, martyrs in the name of God. Their bodies lay in the cemetery, their spirits were in Paradise.

That afternoon a messenger left the village with the name of Abu Khaleb carried in his mind, along with the name of the Chechen, to travel into the mountains to the encampment of a warlord.

That evening a kid was killed, gutted and skinned, and a fire was lit. Caleb was fed and given juice to drink.

That night, his orange overalls were thrown on to the dying fire and they burned bright. He wore the clothes of a young man from the village.

That week he was the protected guest of the village while the elders waited for instructions on how the journey to return Caleb to his family could be achieved. And he did not know how long that journey would be, or where it would take him, or to what fate – but he knew that he would make that journey.

Chapter Two

Caleb's body and face were flooded by the light. The men around him scattered.

The week in the village had passed quickly. He had rested, then he had worked at his strength and gone into the hills above the village to exercise his leg muscles and expand his lungs. He had eaten well and had known that the villagers used precious supplies of meat, rice and flour to feed him. When he had left the village, armed men had accompanied him; he was never out of their sight. The code of these people, he knew, was *pukhtunwali* and it had two principles: the obligation to show hospitality to a stranger, without hope of a return favour, was *malmastiya*; the duty to fight to the death to protect the life of a stranger who had taken refuge among them was *nanawati*. Twice in that week, formations of helicopters had flown high above them. Once, in the distance, he had seen a moving dustcloud and thought it would be a fighting patrol of the enemy's personnel carriers. The tribesmen had stayed closer to him – they would fight to the death to save his life because he was their welcomed guest. An old man, blind, sitting astride a donkey led by a boy, had come to the village in the afternoon of the seventh day with the answer to the message. On that last night in the village, they had feasted again, used more of their precious stores. No music and no dancing, but two of the older men had told stories of the fighting against the Russians, and he had offered his of the fighting against the Americans. The fires' flames had lit them, and the old man, the blind traveller, had recited a poem of combat that had been listened to in silence. He had realized at the end of the last evening, the fire dying, that all eyes had been on him, and he had seen in the shadows the furtive movements of the women and knew that they, too, watched him. He had been given a robe of pure white and he had stood and lifted it over his head, over his shoulders, and had let it fall so that it enveloped him. He had not known his own value to the family, but the village men recognized it, and the women, and they stared at him as he stood in the robe while the fires' last flames showed their awe of him. Each of the village men came to him, hugged him, kissed his cheeks. He was the chosen one.

The next morning, the old man had taken Caleb a half-day's walk from the village. At a point where a path into a mountain pass climbed away, he had held Caleb's hand in a skeleton's grip. Tears had run from his dead eyes, and he had left him. He had sat for an hour on a rock, then watched the little column of men and mules emerge from the pass. A few words spoken, a few sour gestures, and he had gone on with them. For nine days he had been with them as they led him with great caution away from the village and to the west. They hugged the foothills, but had also gone higher where the night air was frosted. From the beginning he had known what cargo they guarded in the bulging sacks strapped to the mules' backs. He could smell the opium seeds. They were villainous men, he had seen no charity in their faces. They carried curved knives at their waists with which they could have mutilated him. From the moment of their reluctant greeting, Caleb had doubted that they acknowledged the code of *pukhtunwali*. They shared food grudgingly, they did not talk to him or show any interest in his identity. If he had fallen back he did not think they would have waited for him. He had never complained, had never lost the pace of the march, had never feared them. But on the eighth day he had seen the slightest softening – an extra morsel of dried meat, beyond his own ration, had been tossed at him during the evening halt, and a water-carrier just filled in a mountain torrent had been passed to him; later, an extra blanket had been thrown in his direction as he had lain between rocks trying to shelter from a fall of sleet. He sensed, that last night, he had won their respect. When the grey light under the sleet's clouds dipped, he saw that the four of them watched him, as the villagers had – as if something set him apart. He did not know by whom he was set apart, or for what reason. That ninth morning he had sensed the tension among them. In the afternoon they had gone more slowly and one of the four had been a quarter of a mile ahead, the furthest distance at which his shrill all-clear whistle could be heard. That evening they had cocked the rifles in readiness, and had told with new nervousness of the dangers ahead as they came close to Iranian territory. With the greatest suspicion they had approached the frontier where the rendezvous was to be made to which they had been paid to bring him, where there were frequent and heavily armed border patrols. They had been in a gully, going slowly so that the mules' hoofs would be quieter, when the light had snapped on and caught them.

Caleb raised his hands. The beam reflected off the white robe, now stained with sweat, mud and the blood from scratches on his arms.

A voice called to him from behind the beam's source – first in Pashto, then in Arabic, he was given the instruction to come forward. Caleb could not see beyond the light. He walked and kept his arms high. Behind him he heard the retreat of the men and the mules. The voice had authority – the command beat off the gully walls around him. In front of him he should hold out his right arm so that his wrist should be seen. The light licked at the plastic bracelet, and at the photograph, and caught the print of the taxi-driver's name. He was pulled forward and ordered to lie down. He lay on the stones in the track. There was a final command, in a language he did not know. At the edge of his vision, he sensed the light's beam move on, rove further away . . . Then the machine-gun started.

The tracers spewed over him, bursts of six, seven shots, then a moment's pause, then more firing. There were two answering rounds, the detonation of one grenade from a launcher, and silence. The machine-gun replied. The men who had escorted him for the last nine days were trapped between the walls of the gully. Caleb wriggled his body so that he might make a pretence of burrowing down into the stones and dirt of the path. Boots came past him, a brisk march of power, and he heard the final execution shots that would have finished the men and put the mules beyond further pain.

The boots came back behind him. A fist clamped into the back of the robe and he was hauled to his feet. His right arm was snatched and he felt fingers on the plastic bracelet.

'You are welcome.' There was no care in the voice.

Not as a reproach but as a matter of fact, Caleb said, 'They treated me with respect, with courtesy, they shared their food with me. They brought me.'

Now he saw the man who welcomed him, an officer in neat uniform with a polished belt. Attached to the belt was a holster. He smelt the cordite. The officer was dapper in build and on his upper lip was a trimmed moustache. By the markings on his shoulder flaps, Caleb thought him at least a major, perhaps a colonel. The officer led him past the troops to two lorries and a Mercedes car with smoked windows. A driver snapped out of the Mercedes and ran round the back to open the rear door. The officer flicked his finger for Caleb to follow him.

The Mercedes pulled away.

Bumping on a dry track, in low gear, they left the gully and headed into flat lands beyond. A packet of cigarettes was offered, but Caleb declined. The officer lit a cigarette, then kept the lighter's flame burning. His delicate fingers lifted Caleb's wrist and he examined the plastic bracelet. 'Who is Fawzi al-Ateh?'

'He was a taxi-driver. He is dead.'

'You took his name?'

'I did.'

'You were brought, with his name, to the American camp at Guantanamo.'

'Yes.'

'The interrogators at Guantanamo did not break your story, that you were a taxi-driver?'

'They did not.'

'That is remarkable.' His laughter fluttered across Caleb's face. 'So, I consider two possibilities. You defeated the best of the interrogators at Guantanamo. You were released to spy. I hang spies, I am a good friend of those who defeat Americans . . . What I immediately like about you, you do not ask questions without invitation. I invite you.'

'Why were they killed?'

The voice hardened. 'They were not killed because they were traffickers in narcotics, criminals, they died because they were witnesses. It is a mark of the importance with which you are regarded that they were condemned – I do not know who you are, why you are so valued. They saw your face.'

'So did the villagers where I stayed for a week.'

The cigarette was ground out. The officer put back his head and his breath relaxed. Caleb thought that within minutes he would be asleep ... He thought of the village and the trust of its men. Anonymously, the name of the village would be passed by this officer to American agents, and bombers would circle over it and death would rain down from the high skies – because there they had seen his face. He thought of the blind old man and he prayed to his God that the old man, who had been unable to see his face, would live.

'Where are we going?'

The officer murmured, 'You are going where you will be of use, if you are not a spy.'

'I am a fighter.'

The Mercedes took him far into Iran, and the night was nearly spent when they reached a high-walled villa where heavy gates of steel sheet opened to take him inside.

He was a bloodstained step closer to his family.

Night lay on the far-away desert. The moon was up, pitted with stars' patterns, and the quiet was total.

Two camels, one ridden by a Bedouin, moved on the desert sand, going fast and away from the escarpment and the cave's mouth. A message had been brought and a reply sent.

Far at the back of the cave, by candlelight because the generator was switched off at night to conserve fuel, a man worked at the interior of a new Samsonite suitcase – described on its sales tag as an 'Executive Traveller' – that had been purchased seven weeks before at the open market of the Bir Obeid district of San'ā, capital city of Yemen; at the frontier roadblocks, the soldiers had laughed raucously when they had found a shiny new suitcase being taken home by a vagrant tribesman from the desert and had let him pass and head away into the Rub' al Khālī. The man working on the suitcase, positioning the circuitboard behind the case's lining, ignored the quiet conversations around him. He had the knowledge gained from a university degree in electronic engineering in Prague. His eyes ached in the dim interior. He knew nothing of where the suitcase would be taken when his work was finished, but he had been told by the Emir General, who coughed near to him because his chest was inflamed, that the man who would carry the suitcase had begun his journey to reach them. He had also been told that the hazards of that journey, which still lay in front of that man, were huge.

But time was short – all in the cave knew it. They were hunted, they were in retreat. Time ran like sand through their fingers.

'Hello – I'm told you're Dr Bartholomew. Is that right?'

He was standing at the edge of the room, more of a voyeur at the party than a participator. He had not noticed her approach. He seldom joined the spirit of a party, preferring to remain at the edge, listening to conversations but not contributing to them. His glass was close to his hand but set down on a set of bookshelves. He had slopped the Saudi champagne when his arm had been jogged, leaving a stained ring on the wood. He cared as little about the ring as he cared for Saudi champagne. It was always served early at Riyadh's expatriate parties – a mix of apple juice, American dry ginger and fresh mint leaves; cucumber slices floated with the ice cubes. He could have gone to a party such as this one every night of the week if he had chosen to, could have mingled with the familiar crowd of aerospace workers, oil men, medical people and their wives, and the nurses who were there for decoration. The talk around him was the usual numbingly tedious crap – the rental price of compound villas, the quality of the local workforce, the heat, the cost of imported food. He hadn't noticed her coming.

'Dr Samuel Bartholomew, or Bart to the many who know me and the very few who love me.'

He realized she had trapped him. Against the wall he had been a free agent at the party, now he was confronted. A hi-fi system played loud music, as if the combination of its beat and the alcohol-free champagne would stimulate the guests into believing they were enjoying themselves . . . She was different from the nurses and wives.

She blocked any escape and her posture, with her feet a little apart, almost intimidated him. And it was an interruption. As he always did at the parties, he had been listening hard for little morsels of information. He sucked in trifles of indiscretion, was a carrier of tales and confidences, and his hidden existence was the sole pleasure he took from life: it gave him power. He was forty-seven years old. He had been christened Samuel Algernon Laker Bartholomew – his father had taken two weeks' holiday a year, one for the Guildford cricket festival, one for the annual Oval Test match, and his third given name came from the cricketer who had done something to the Australians in the year of his birth. As a schoolboy, with pudgy jowls and a slack stomach, he had detested organized sports. His maxim, then and now, was not to run if he could walk, not to walk if he could ride. Others at the party would jog on the pavements round the compound walls in the early morning before the heat became intolerable or would work out in an air-conditioned gymnasium. His late father had believed that cricket gave a man a code of decent disciplines for life – he would have turned in his grave if he had known his son traduced the trust given him.

'I'm Bethany Jenkins.'

'Pleased to meet you, Miss Jenkins.'

Bart always used old-world manners ... It was the start of his third year as a general practitioner in the Kingdom. He acted as a link man between patients with real or imagined symptoms and the expensive foreign consultants at the King Fahd Medical City, or the King Faisal Specialist Hospital and Research Centre, or the King Khalid Eye Hospital. He passed them on and received a cut of the fees, smoothed the way and was rewarded. He was losing the drift of a conversation to his right: two men from a British company's aerospace software division in earnest talk about the failure of in-flight radar in the Tornado strike aircraft sold to the Air Force. He tried to refocus on the conversation, but her hand was held out.

He shook it limply, but she held his hand too tightly for him to ignore her.

'I've booked an appointment with your secretary for a couple of days' time. I'm up from the south, going on to Bahrain tomorrow, a bit of shopping, then I'm coming to see you before I go back down.'

'I'll look forward to it, Miss Jenkins.'

There didn't look to be much wrong with her. She was different from the other women in the room: she was tanned hard, her legs and ankles, arms and wrists, her face below the cropped blonde hair weatherbeaten from winds and sun. Late twenties, he thought, but an obvious outdoors life had aged her skin. The other women in the room fled from exposure to the sun, anointed themselves with protective creams when they had to go out, wore headscarves and carried parasols. And she was different also in her clothing – the other women wore cocktail dresses, but she was in a blouse that was clean but not ironed and a shapeless denim skirt that hung on her hips. She was stocky but he thought that there was no flab under the blouse and skirt, only muscle. Other women wore gold chains, pendants and bracelets bought in the *souk*, but she had no jewellery.

'Mind if I say something, Dr Bartholomew?'

'Bart, please – feel free.' He'd lost the conversation on in-flight radar failure. He smiled sweetly. 'Please, say what you want to, Miss Jenkins.'

'OK, Bart.' She looked directly at him, one of those wretched people who had no disguise. He detested honesty. She reached out and picked up his glass, took a handkerchief from her skirt pocket and wiped the base, then rubbed hard at the ring on the bookshelf.

His grin was as limp as his handshake. He disliked women who fixed him in the headlights of their eyes. He was the rabbit. He shuffled. The Tornado people had split and moved on. He was fearful of women, particularly those who seemed to strip him down, leave him naked. It was a long time, so long, since he had been close to a woman – then there had been tears, his, and arguments, hers, and the overwhelming sense of private failure. He did not know where Ann was now, where she lived with the children, and the shield he used to safeguard himself from that failure was that he did not care.

'You don't look like a man who enjoys being a guest of the Kingdom.'

It was an extraordinary remark. She knew nothing – nothing of his past and nothing of his present . . . He frowned, then downed the contents of his glass and slapped it back on to the bookshelf. 'It is, Miss Jenkins—'

'I'm called Beth.'

'It is, Miss Jenkins, almost a privilege to be a humble part of this fulcrum of the sophistication and technological excellence of Saudi Arabia. Actually, I hate the bloody place, and all who sail in her – yourself, of course, excepted.'

Her eyebrows arched. She laughed richly, as if at last he interested her. She followed with a flood of questions. When had he come here? Why had he come? What were his hobbies? Where did he live? How long was he staying? His answers were staccato. He deflected her with responses that were rude in their brevity, but she seemed not to recognize it. He was frightened of close questioning. In the expatriate community he avoided the endless discussions about family, work conditions, terms of service, anything that might expose the lie with which he lived.

'You don't want to mind me, Bart. Where I live, down south, I don't get too many chances to talk to people. It's like one of those monasteries with a vow of silence.' She touched his hand, was smiling . . . Then rescue came, of sorts . . .

He hadn't seen Wroughton arrive, hadn't seen him among the guests. Wroughton's fingers pulled at his sleeve, his head gesturing towards the door. No apology at the interruption, but Edward – Eddie to his female friends – Wroughton never apologized, wouldn't have bloody known how to. Bart blundered away from the young woman, followed Wroughton into the hall and down towards the kitchen.

Wroughton leaned against the wall. Then his finger poked in a tattoo on Bart's chest. 'You cut our last meeting, Bart.'

'I was busy.'

'You don't cut meetings with me.'

'Just pressure of work.'

'I waited two hours, wasted two hours.'

'And I hadn't anything to give you.'

'Then just pedal a bit bloody harder.'

'Sorry about that, Eddie.'

'*Mr Wroughton* to you. Got me?'

'It won't happen again, Mr Wroughton,' Bart whined.

'Listen to me – I don't want to be fucked about here. It's not pleasant, believe me, but I have you by your shrivelled little balls, and I will squeeze and I will twist and—'

'What I just heard, there's problems on the in-flight radar of the Tornado aircraft they've got.'

'Which squadron?'

'Don't know.'

'Jesus, you're a useless piece of shit. Have you been listening? You're going to have to do better or I'll be squeezing and twisting.'

Wroughton was gone.

Bart stood in the corridor and gasped. Little spurts of breath bubbled on his lips. He mopped the sweat from his forehead. When he had composed himself, when his breathing was regular, he went back down the corridor. The noise from the room bayed at him. His host barked in his ear, 'Not got a glass, Bart? More champagne? Or are you going to hang around for a bit and have something better?' A nod and a wink ... Bart smiled weakly. He was looking for the hostess. A guest, a woman in a bright floral dress, tried to intercept him and he started to hear her query on the best preventive tablets for diarrhoea, but he slipped her his card, pointed to his surgery number and moved on. He saw Bethany, Miss Jenkins, her hand easily on her hip, talking to oil people.

The hostess said, 'Not going yet, Bart, surely not? It's just warming up.' He said he had a call-out, embellished the excuse with a casual mention of septicaemia, and thanked her for a wonderful party, quite lovely.

Bart drove the mile back to his own compound, and his own three-bedroomed villa, which cost him the *riyal* equivalent of twenty-two thousand pounds in annual rental and which he could comfortably afford. In the daytime he used a chauffeured car but at night, a short journey through light traffic, he drove himself. The security men at the gate recognized his Mitsubishi four-wheel drive, waved to him and let him through. Two more parties were blaring out over the compound lawns. He let himself inside the darkened villa. Nothing of his life adorned his home, no pictures, no photographs, no ornaments, no mementoes from his past. Even the cat, the sole centre of affection in Bart's life, mutual love, couldn't help him escape from the place he hated.

Wroughton left. He knew he had the whispered reputation of a sexual goat, but he would not have made a pass at the nurse with the ghastly accent, Falkirk or East Kilbride. His conquests were with wives mature enough to maintain discretion. The reputation was never proven. He headed for his bachelor apartment in the diplomatic quarter. As the station chief attached to the embassy, Eddie Wroughton was allocated an armour-plated Land Rover Discovery with bullet-proof windows, but the plates inside the bodywork and the reinforced glass beside him, through which he looked on to the deserted road, would only have been noticed by an expert.

He despised men like Samuel Bartholomew; one of the hardships of his life as a senior officer of the Secret Intelligence Service was the requirement to deal with first-degree scum. But against the hardships there were purple moments when he gloried in his work. Saudi Arabia was a class posting, interesting intellectually, challenging and, above all, a stepping-stone to greater things.

He always left an expatriate party before the alcohol was served. He left before the 'champagne' was exhausted, before the home brew was offered, or the 'brown tea' was poured – usually ostentatiously – from a china teapot, most often Jack Daniel's but sometimes Johnnie Walker and always taken neat. It would have been bad for his career, probably terminal, if a party he was attending where alcohol was available was raided by the *mutawwa*, the zealots of the Committee for the Propagation of Virtue and the Prevention of Vice. He always went home early . . . If he needed to drink, the bottles were in the sideboard of his apartment's living room, premises protected by diplomatic immunity, and in the safe of his embassy office.

Few knew him. Only the wives he bedded, the most valued of the agents he handled and his one friend in the Kingdom's capital could have passed a serious judgement on Eddie Wroughton. He appeared a caricature of an Englishman abroad and he played to that super-ficial image. Day and night, at work, at the ambassador's dinner table, as a guest of the princes of the ruling family or on a field trip out of the city, he wore a cream-coloured linen suit that was always pressed and creaseless, a brilliant white shirt, a knotted silk tie and burnished brown brogues. He wore dark glasses, indoors or out, in the heat of the sun or the cool of an evening. Few knew the strength of those eyes and would have recognized in them traits of character.

They were bright, ruthless, glinting, mocking. They were cruel . . . He was a clever man, and knew it.

In his apartment's kitchen, in the microwave, he heated himself a curry for one, then washed his hands.

With regard to Samuel Bartholomew he had two distinct certainties: he dominated him, and at some moment in the future the domination would pay off, big-time. The microwave bleeped. He knew the doctor's history, had read it in the confidential file sent to him when the wretch had arrived in Riyadh. He served his meal and took it on a tray to his favoured chair. He thought the man pitiful, knew what he had done in Palestine, thought him beneath contempt – but potentially so very useful, one day.

Al Maz'an village, near Jenin, Occupied West Bank.

It was only the end of the first week and already he had played his part.

Bart stamped out of the wooden hut and jumped down from the doorway on to the thick gravel that made a path across a sea of mud. He turned, held up his medical bag and waved it angrily at the man now leaning against the door jamb. It had been his first meeting with the Shin Beth officer, his handler. 'You know what? I'll tell you what. You dishonour the human race. Your behaviour is simply beyond the pale,' Bart shouted.

His handler lit a cigarette, threw the dead match down on to the mud, and gazed back at him with indifference.

'And I'll tell you something else – and wipe that smile off your arrogant little face. You are a fucking disgrace to your nation.'

He rather liked the handler. He'd expected a man manipulative and brusque but he'd found instead a sensitive, frail young fellow, perhaps fifteen years younger than himself. Would he like coffee? How was he settling into the village? Were the signs good? Was he trusted? Could anything be done to help him? The handler, Joseph, worked and slept, cooked and ate in the hut close to the checkpoint. Of course, Joseph wore military uniform with the same insignia flashes as the troops controlling the checkpoint.

'I'm going to report you for gross obstruction. As a UK national engaged on humanitarian work, funded by my government, I can raise a storm. I hope that storm lands on your disgusting little head. Stopping a doctor of medicine going about his work shames your uniform. You see if I don't make waves.'

In the hut, over coffee, Bart had been shown photographs of local leaders of Islamic Jihad and Hamas. He had pored over the map of the village and its satellite communities. He had a good retentive memory. Joseph's briefing on the local security situation had been excellent – calm, detailed and lacking in political rhetoric. Joseph was professional . . . He'd had pictures, in a threadbare-covered album, of the aftermath of suicide attacks on Haifa buses, Jerusalem's market and Tel Aviv's cafés, but Bart had already been shown similar albums in Tel Aviv and in Jerusalem where this stage of his journey had begun – and from the start of that journey he had never had the chance to refuse, to step off the treadmill. As he walked away, crunching over the gravel, the rain spattered on him, and the mud seeping through the stones caked his shoes.

'Don't forget my name! It's Sam Bartholomew, you bastard,' Bart shouted over his shoulder. 'But you'll wish you'd never heard it by the time I'm through with you.'

The soldiers had finished searching his car – he heard the door slam. By the time he reached it the rain had soaked what hair he had left, ran down his face and dampened his clothes. A corporal, scowling, held open the car door for him, but Bart shouldered him aside, as if he refused to accept any belated courtesy from a member of the Israeli Defence Forces. Standing in the rain, perhaps forty Palestinians were held up at the checkpoint. It had taken Bart twenty-five minutes apparently to be processed at the roadblock, but it would take the Palestinians half a day to go through if they were lucky, and half a day to be turned back if they weren't. Their faces, men, women and children, had been sullen when he had emerged from the hut. But they had heard his abuse, and those who understood it translated for those who did not. As he climbed into his car, decorated with red crescents – the Palestinian equivalent symbol to a red cross – on the side doors and on the roof, there was a ripple of applause, and he saw little rays of pleasure break on their faces. It was as intended. He drove away.

His head slumped. His eyeline was barely above the rim of the dashboard. He was trapped, he could tell himself, he'd had no option. If his father had learned to where his son had sunk he would have strangled him, but his father was dead. He drove on towards Jenin where he would go to the clinic, make friends and collect what few of the basic medicines were available. He cut his father out of his mind, and the need for medicines, so that he could better remember the map he had been shown and the photographs of wanted men . . . Joseph had told him that he must beware of self-doubt, that he should not hate *himself, that above all he should not entertain the luxury of conscience. If Joseph had only known, Samuel Bartholomew's conscience was long gone.*

They reached the quayside at Sadich. The map shown to him told Caleb they were on the southern extremity of the Iranian coastline. The dark seascape in front of him was the Gulf of Oman. He felt a raw, drifting excitement because he was about to take a further step in his journey.

The officer spoke in Arabic: 'You are, my friend, an enigma to me. I cannot think of the last time that a man surprised me. You have achieved what I would have believed an impossibility, a confusion in my mind. I call you "my friend" because I do not know your given name or the name of your father. I am given tasks by my government that are of the greatest sensitivity, and trust is placed in me for the reason that I have a reputation for delving into the secrets of men's minds, but after eleven days in your company I have failed. You are not a taxi-driver – and I consider also that Abu Khaleb is only a temporary flag of convenience. Before I pass you on, who are you?'

It was certainly not a town, barely a village. They had left the Mercedes and the driver in the car park beside the building for the co-operative that boxed fish and put ice into the boxes before the lorries came. At the quayside there were trading dhows, fishing-boats and a little flotilla of a half-dozen launches with large twin outboards, all poorly lit by the high lights. The wind came in hard and sang in the rigging stays of the dhows, and rocked the launches at their moorings. Caleb gazed at the sea, did not respond to the officer's question, as he had not for the past eleven days and nights. Some of those days had passed fast, some slowly. Some of the nights he had slept, for others there had been no end. He had been questioned by the colonel inside the locked, shuttered villa, but for most of the hours between meals he had watched Iranian television and had used the weights and the rowing machine offered him; he had alternately rested and built his strength. He imagined that messages had gone ahead, that answers had been received, but he did not know where the messages had been sent, or from where they had been returned. What he had learned, in those long days and longer nights, was that his importance and value to his family were

48

confirmed further – as they had been during the time he had waited in the village in far-away Afghanistan. The sea's blow whipped his long robe and the importance gave him pride – not that he would boast of it.

'Do I need to know your true identity? No . . . but I like to have the loose threads tied. There is your accent. The Arabic I speak is from Iraq. I learned the Arabic of Iraq from prisoners of their army captured in the fighting on the Faw peninsula – but I do not know Egyptian Arabic or Yemeni, Syrian or Saudi. I tried tricks on you . . . You remember the morning I woke you with a shout, an order, in English, but you did not respond? At lunch, two days ago, without warning I spoke to you in the German language. Five days ago when we walked in the garden, it was Russian . . . You are a man of great talent, my friend, because you did not betray yourself. You have no name, you have no origin – I think that is your value.'

He looked out beyond the breakwater of heaped boulders, beyond the navigation light raised on rusted stanchions, and he saw the whipped white crests of the incoming waves. He felt the chill of the wind. At the villa behind the walls and the steel-plated gate, the robe had been taken from him and laundered. Now the wind plastered it against the outline of his torso and legs.

'And you have no history – perhaps because you are ashamed of it, perhaps because it is irrelevant to you, perhaps because you are in denial of it. You appear in Landi Khotal, on the Pakistan side of the common border with Afghanistan, some four years ago, a little less, and there is nothing before that, only darkness. You frustrate me . . . You are recruited, trained, placed with the 055 Brigade, captured, and by deception – I promise you, I admire the deception – are freed. Word is passed that you have escaped the Americans, and instructions are given at the highest level that you should be moved on – your worth is weighed in gold. It is not my business, I know, I only carry out instructions given me in great confidence, but you are a man of value. I do not know who you are or what your history is, or what it is hoped you will achieve. I tell you, in great honesty, my friend, when you are gone I will wake in the nights and that ignorance will be like a stone in my shoe.'

On the quayside's rough concrete, men were working in the faint light to repair nets, and others were climbing down the quayside ladders to the launches. He heard the deep-throat roar of the outboards starting up.

'They cross the Gulf to the Omani shore – they go empty and come back with cartons of American cigarettes. We permit the trade. It is useful to have a route out of and into the country that is not observed . . . You have to go, my friend . . . Time calls. May I say something more? . . . I am certain of you. If I had doubted you, I would have hanged you. I do not understand your motivation, your commitment, but I believe in its steel strength. You will strike a great blow against a common enemy – I do not know when or where, but I am satisfied that I will have played a humble and insignificant part in your strike, and I will listen to the radio and watch the television and when it happens I will be happy to have played a part . . . May God go with you.'

The officer put his arm on Caleb's and they walked together towards the launches.

'The war goes badly. There have been setbacks. Have regard to the power of the enemy and its machines – only the hardest man can succeed . . . You look at the men who will carry you across the Gulf, and they will have seen your face. Have no worry. They will return with cigarettes, they will be taken by the Customs police and they will go to gaols in the north. They cannot betray you.'

He stood above the ladder. Five of the launches were already edging out into the harbour behind the breakwater; the last was held against the ladder.

'You have seen my face and I have seen yours. My friend, already I have forgotten you, even if I wake in the night, and I have no fear of your betrayal. You will never again be captured. You will taste sweet freedom or sweeter death. God watch you.'

Caleb went down the ladder. He felt the night close round him, and the cold.

'What the hell, man, I was asleep. What time is it?'

Marty blinked at the ceiling light.

The duty officer who manned night-time communications in the Agency's corral stood over him.

'The time is about ten minutes after the Best and the Brightest have finished a good lunch in the senior staff diner at Langley. An

50

excellent time, they believe, to fuck with the lives of low-rank foot-soldiers. Local time, if you need it, is ten after midnight. Read this, Marty, and inwardly digest . . . Seems clear enough, even for a pre-tend pilot.'

Marty worked the sleep from his eyes, reached out and took the offered sheet, and read. He read it again. The duty officer was raking round the little room with its low ceiling and hardboard walls. He read it a third time, like he hoped it would go away but it didn't.

'Shit . . . Who's seen it?'

'George – well, he's the one who's going to have the headache. I felt he should be first.'

George Khoo, the Chinese-born mission technical officer, was responsible for keeping *First Lady* and *Carnival Girl* maintained and operationally ready. Down the corridor, through the thin door and the thin walls of the rooms, Marty heard a door slam, then boots hammering away, and he heard a shout of protest at the disturbance. George wouldn't have cared, not now he'd been given Langley's orders.

'So, what did George say?'

'That's a real nice picture, that is, pretty cool . . . Nothing I'd care to repeat.'

There was a framed photograph of his parents outside their cabin in the hills up north from Santa Barbara. But the duty officer was staring in fascination at a big picture in a gold-rimmed frame, Marty's pride and joy. He'd seen it on the Internet, offered by a firm in London, and it had arrived at Bagram six weeks back. The legend under it was 'The Last Stand of the 44th Regiment at Gundamuck, 1842'. It showed fourteen Brit soldiers clustered in a little circle, rifles raised and bayonets fixed; a couple of them had sabres drawn, and plenty more Brits were spread round the group, dead or wounded, and the tribesmen were coming up the hill towards them. It didn't seem that the Brits had a single round left between them. Behind the tribesmen were snow-covered mountains. It was by William Barnes Wollen, born 1857, died 1936.

'That is a really cool picture.'

Marty grunted and pulled himself off the bed. It was the first picture he'd ever owned and it had cost him seventy-five dollars for the print, ninety dollars for the frame and $110 for shipment, but it had survived the transportation. In front of the men who were going to die, and knew it, an officer stood, sword in one hand, a revolver in the other, straight-backed like all Brits were supposed to be, and he wore a suede coat with fur lining. Under the coat the gold-decorated flag of his regiment was wrapped round him and worth defending. The officer, Lieutenant Souter, had been spared because the Afghans thought him too important – he had the flag – to castrate and kill, so he'd been ransomed. Marty had done research on the Internet, but he didn't tell the duty officer.

'Has Lizzy-Jo been woken up?'

'Thought I'd give that pleasure to you . . .'

The duty officer left him. Marty swigged water from his bottle and spat it into the sink, then unhitched his robe from the door hook.

He knocked on Lizzy-Jo's door, heard her, went in. She sat up in her bed and didn't seem bothered that her pyjama top was open.

Marty said, 'We're being moved. We're pulling out in the morning, heading to Saudi Arabia, don't know for how long . . . George – God, and I wouldn't like to be near him – has gone off to get the birds in the coffins. The plane to lift us is being readied.'

She heard him out, then told him to switch off the ceiling light and turned to the wall. He went out. Only Lizzy-Jo could go back to sleep in the face of such crazy intrusion into the routine of their work – it would have taken an earthquake to frazzle her.

As the night ended, the flotilla broke formation. Five of the launches veered to the south, his carried straight on. The parting was at speed and the farewell shouts, the other crews to his, were drowned in the engine noise and the hull beating on the swell of the waves. He watched until the wakes of the five were gone, then subsided again into the corner of the low cabin where he'd wedged himself. He had been sick twice and his shoulders were bruised where he'd been tossed against the forward bulkhead of the cabin and its side wall. The crew were two kids in jeans and windcheaters with long hair. He wouldn't have talked to them if they had wanted it, but they didn't. He was as much a piece of cargo as the cigarette cartons they would bring back. He assumed they had been paid generously by the intelligence officer for transporting him and had no suspicion that when they returned to the harbour on the southern shore of Iran they would be arrested, then left to rot in prison cells. Above the engine he heard the shout. The one at the wheel had his hands cupped at his mouth, then pointed. He saw the excitement on the kid's spray-soaked face. He peered through the cabin's porthole.

He saw the great hulk.

A tiny bow wave parted as the aircraft-carrier edged towards the launch. It was grey against a grey sea and a grey sky. He saw its massive power. The other kid passed him binoculars and he steadied himself, elbows on the ledge below the porthole, focused and looked. The image danced before his eyes. He saw sailors on the decks walking as if they were in a park, like in Jalalabad or by the zoo in Kabul. He saw the aircraft stacked at the edge of the deck, some with their wings folded back. The kid at the wheel jerked them away from a closing course and he dropped back into his corner. They would have thought, walking on the aircraft-carrier's deck, that their power was invincible. He held his head in his hands.

Crossing the Gulf, wearing the white linen robe that had been given him, Caleb sensed the complexity of the plan to move him closer to his family. He had come to the village, pathetic in his weakness, and now – out on the sea and speeding towards a distant landfall – he understood the great effort made to return him to the family.

It lay as a burden on him, which only he could carry.

Chapter Three

The launch knifed into the surf of the shore and surged as if on a
collision course with the beach. The final quarter of the sun balanced
on the ridges of distant hills. Caleb watched the approach from the
cabin's porthole. All through the journey across the Gulf the kids had
not spoken to him and they had not fed him. His only contact with
them had been when a canvas bucket filled with sea-water had been
dumped at the entrance to the cabin. He had realized its purpose and
rinsed out the vomit from his robe, then had used his hands to clean
the cabin floor. Much of the time they had watched him but when he
had looked up from his place against the bulkhead they had turned
away their eyes as if they understood that – unarmed, alone – he had
carried danger to them . . . As the sun fell below the hills, Caleb failed
to see any movement on the shore. Three or four miles to the right,
when they had been further out at sea, he had seen what he thought
was a fishing village, but as they came closer it had disappeared.

Abruptly, the kid at the wheel swung it. Caleb was thrown across
the floor. His shoulder thudded into the far wall and spray drenched
him through the cabin's open door. On his hands and knees he
crawled to a hard chair that was screwed down, and held tightly to
it. Then the kid who was at the controls throttled down the two

outboards, allowing the waves to carry the rocking launch nearer to the beach. The kid at the wheel jerked his head, gesturing for Caleb to come out of the cabin. He could barely stand, and he used the chair, then the edge of a table and the doorway to support himself. He could see the beach where the surf broke, and he heard the little ripples of sound as the sea ran on sand and shingle, then fell back. Fast, they had him by the shoulders and arms and propelled him towards the launch's side. Not only was he no sailor, he had never swum. He did not resist.

They had had time to learn every contour of his face. They could have described the shape of his nose, the cut of his jaw, the colour of his eyes.

He could have told them the fate of four men who trafficked opium who, also, had seen his face.

They lifted him up, his stomach scraping on the launch's side.

He told them nothing.

Had they stopped, pulled back his head by the hair at the last moment and looked into his face in the dying light they would have seen the harshness of his features – but they did not.

Caleb was pitched over the side. He saw the twin grinning faces, and then he went under. The shock of the water forced air from his lungs. He went down, into blackness. He was scrambling with his feet, kicking, and the salt water was in his mouth, his nostrils, and the pressure on his chest was leaden. His feet flailed into the sea bed.

When he broke the surface, gasping and coughing, the launch was already under full power, arrowing away from the beach. The limit of his memory was the few days in Landi Khotal and the wedding party – before that there was nothing, the same blackness as when he had gone under the water, and after that there were memories of Afghanistan and more memories of the camps at Guantanamo Bay. Nothing in that cut-short memory told Caleb how to swim. He was a man who could fight with skill, with resolve, a man who could trek and endure the confines of a prison cage constructed to destroy a prisoner's soul, but he had never swum. He lashed at the water. The thrashes of his legs and arms, and the power of the waves, pushed him towards the beach. He felt no guilt that he had not told them of their fate. His mind was as cold as his body in the water. His feet hit the bottom. His sandals had stayed on. He stood at his full height and the waves broke against his back. He waded towards the shore. When he was clear of the water, Caleb sank down on his haunches, then rolled on to his back and little pebbles pressed into his spine.

Above him, a low shaft of moonlight came off the water and covered him.

His life, as he knew it, had begun at a wedding party on the outskirts of the town of Landi Khotal and before that there was the same darkness as when he had gone down into the water off the launch. He had no wish to clear the darkness because older memories threatened him. On his back, looking up at the stars, he saw the man with the eyepatch and the chrome claw, always watching him. He had felt then that the one eye was never off him. The party had drifted on and food had been eaten, and when the evening had come, the man with the eyepatch and the claw had sat beside him. Lit by hurricane lamps in which moths danced, he had seen the scars spreading out from under the eyepatch and up the wrist to which the claw was strapped. It had been the start of the journey of Caleb's life.

A light flashed in the trees, winked at him.

His sandals slithered in the sand. He went towards it. For a whole minute the flashes guided him but when he reached the debris left by the tide's highest point the light was killed. He blundered forward in darkness and wove between tree-trunks. Thorns caught at his robe. His clothes were sodden and the cold of the coming night swaddled him . . . Caleb was not ashamed of fear. Since the wedding, he had been afraid many times. The Chechen had said that fear was unimportant, that the control of fear was the talent of a fighter . . . If he was to return to his family, he must take every step on trust.

He trudged through the trees. He pulled the robe clear when it snagged.

Caleb had control of the fear because the camps at Guantanamo had hardened him. He was a survivor . . . He passed a palm tree's trunk. His arm was grabbed and the light fell on the plastic bracelet on his right wrist. Then his arm was loosed. The fear was gone.

In the low light, the farmers approached the corpse with caution. They had walked up from the track, among the rocks, because they had smelt the stench of the body. The track ran from the Yemeni town of Marib across the border, and on north-east to the Saudi town of Sharurah. They had left their donkeys and sheep by the track where a bullet-scarred car had burned out. They came to the corpse. The head had been cut from the neck and the hands from the wrists. Flies crawled over the torso, and already some of the flesh had been torn away by foxes. Holding his shirt tail over his nose, one went close enough to the body to reach out and check the pockets, but they were empty, and when he pulled up a sleeve there was no watch. The farmers circled the corpse and threw stones on it until they had made a cairn to cover the body. Then they ran, leaving the smell and the stones behind them.

'Is that right, we let some out?'

'Just five, only five . . . It was about pressure, image. So, what's the big deal? It was five guys, why does that matter?'

Across the desk, the supervisor glowered at him. To Jed, he looked drawn, stressed in the neon strip-light washing over his face. It highlighted the strain at his mouth and the sacs below the eyes. If Jed hadn't gone down with the headcold he would have returned to Guantanamo a week earlier. By the time he had gone back with Brigitte and Arnie Junior to the apartment near the Pentagon, the headcold had been streaming out of his nose, he'd had a raw throat and a hacking cough. He'd delayed his return to Gitmo. He held the list of names in his hand. The days that Jed Dietrich, in his time with the Defense Intelligence Agency, had called in sick could have been counted on the fingers of one hand. It had hurt him, a conscientious man, to be back late off leave, and the winnowing guilt fuelled his show of temper.

'It matters, Edgar, because two of them are on my work list.'

'The hell it matters – and, as I said, pressure and image played their part. Those factors may not figure at your level, Jed, but they do at mine. Coming across my desk is pressure to improve the image of this god-forsaken place. So, we let a few out and the pressure eases, the image improves. Now, it may be the end of the day but I still have a shitload of work to do.' The supervisor grinned cagily. 'And I imagine, Jed, you'll want to look after that cold of yours. Get your feet up so you don't lose any more time here.'

It was dismissal. His supervisor had fifteen years on Jed and three grades of superiority. Perhaps because the headcold had tired him, perhaps because the connection out of San Juan had been late, perhaps because victories at Camp Delta were in short supply, Jed persisted.

'Shouldn't have happened, not names on my list. They shouldn't have been released, not without consultation. Did they just come out of a hat?'

'For God's sake, look at that.' The supervisor waved at his piled in-tray. 'I have work to do.'

'Did you authorize the releases? Was it your decision?'

To a few colleagues, Jed Dietrich was dedicated. To most colleagues he was a plodder. He liked things done right . . . He had nearly, almost, cleared two of the names on the list but 'nearly' and 'almost' were not good enough for him. A frown clung to his brow. He knew the way it would have worked out in his absence. The Bureau and the Agency had authority; DIA was down the ladder, bottom rung.

Jed said, 'The blind one, I don't have a difficulty with him, but this guy – Fawzi al-Ateh – he was unfinished business.'

'What are you trying to say?' the supervisor menaced him.

'I'm just saying that it's not professional. It's crazy to clear a guy, Edgar, when interrogation hasn't run the full road.'

'You're on a roll this morning.' The supervisor's smile was grim. 'It's not crazy, it was an order.'

'I thought about him.'

'Did you? Well, let me say it – when I'm up for vacation I won't be thinking about any of them, about anything to do with this place. He was just a taxi-driver . . . Lighten up. Forget about him. All you need to remember is that he's gone. This is your new roster.'

The supervisor handed Jed the printout of his interrogation duties for the coming week. Jed held it in one hand; in the other was a list of the five names of men released when he'd been away from Gitmo. The first week of his vacation, the names and patterns of the questioning had drilled in his mind; by the time he'd reached the cabin in Wisconsin overlooking the lake, they'd been scrubbed out. But on seeing the name on the list, the itch and irritation had returned. He must have been scowling.

'Damnit, Jed, didn't you get any fish up there?'

He stood up and went out into the evening air. The *Maghrib* prayers were being broadcast over loudspeakers. Beyond the wire fences, flooded by the arc lamps' light, he heard the murmured response of six hundred men, a droning cry, like the swarm of bees. He passed the interrogation block, his workplace, where ceiling lights blazed, and came to the prefabricated wood building that was his work-home. He hated the place because, here, even little victories were hard to come by. In front of him was the concrete building – not of prefabricated wood – where the Agency and the Bureau were installed: they took the cream of the prisoners; they weeded out the best from which bigger victories might be squeezed. They were the kings of Gitmo.

In his cubicle, barely wide enough to take a single outstretched boat rod, long enough for a single float rod for bank angling, Jed studied the roster for his week's interrogations. There were names he didn't know, which would have been passed down to him because other interrogators had finished their Gitmo posting. There was a rhythm and routine at Camp Delta that added merely to a sum result of failure. He swore . . . Later, he would sign himself out at the compound gate, take the shuttle bus to the ferry and go across the bay to the main Marine Corps base. From his sparsely furnished room he would phone Brigitte and he'd tell her everything was dandy, fine. But first he had work.

His fingers hammered on the computer console. The message was to Defense Intelligence Agency at the Bagram airfield in Afghanistan. Could a check be run on Fawzi al-Ateh, ref. no. US8AF-000593DP? Could a report be sent back on the return of Fawzi al-Ateh to his community? Had he been quizzed on the reasons for the request, Jed could not have responded with any coherence. Might have been merely pique that he had not been consulted. Might have been a feeling far down in his gut.

It would be a month, if he was lucky, before Bagram replied. He sent the signal.

The marine eyed him as if he was an intruder and not welcome.

Eddie Wroughton smiled back, left his opinion, like flatulence hanging in the air, that the marine corporal's hostility was of no concern. The messenger from the front desk of the embassy left him at the gate. The suite of offices used by the Central Intelligence Agency was high in the building. The outer walls had been strengthened, the windows were shatter-proof, and the inner doors were steel-plated. The marine watched over the grille gate into the suite. Wroughton gave his name and flashed his passport. Before the marine could telephone for instructions, Juan Gonsalves had bustled from an inner room. The gate was opened. Wroughton was admitted. His name went into the ledger. They embraced. Gonsalves led Wroughton through an open-plan work area, the territory of the juniors and secretaries. Eyes followed Wroughton, echoing the hostility of the marine corporal. Precious few of the embassy's own American staff, seldom even the ambassador and no other non-nationals, were permitted access to this inner sanctum where Riyadh's heat and dust could not penetrate. The air-conditioners purred. What Wroughton knew, Juan Gonsalves didn't give a shit. Eddie Wroughton was the only foreigner allowed into the heartland of Agency territory. They went past a desk and a junior bent forward awkwardly to hide his papers. A secretary flipped the button to blank her screen. They walked on. Wroughton wore his linen suit and ironed white shirt, his tie knotted over the button; Gonsalves had faded jeans low on his ample hips and his shirt tail had worked out of the belt. They were opposites but they had mutual trust because they fed off each other, and they shared a common enemy. It was, however, an unequal feast.

Eddie Wroughton's greatest problem in his Riyadh posting was bringing sufficient food to the table. Too often – and it nagged him – all he had was a fistful of crumbs. He was led into a side office.

The room was a mess. Wroughton knew there had been an inspection team out from Langley three months before, and he presumed that his friend had made an effort to shift chaotic heaps of files off the floor, the table and chairs, to have the coffee-cups and wine glasses washed and laid to rest in the cupboard, to clear away the fast-food packaging, to put a cover sheet over the updated Most Wanted photographs, to keep the safe locked – but it was now twelve weeks since the team had gone home and standards had slipped again. His own office, in the British Embassy, was presided over by an assistant, who was prim and elderly with her hair netted tight in a bun above the nape of her neck.

She kept the room pristine, as if she feared provoking his criticism.

Wroughton stepped carefully between the files, removed a box of papers from a chair, selected the least dirty coffee mug, held it up and gazed into the crowded depth of the open safe. Above him, when he sat down, the faces of the Most Wanted stared down malevolently, some with a Chinagraph cross daubed across their cheeks with the date of their capture or death; the majority were still unmarked. A plate with a half-moon of pizza abandoned on it lay beside Gonsalves' steaming kettle. Coffee was made and an old biscuit tin passed to him. Dominating the Most Wanted photographs was the image of the First Fugitive. A long face topped by a white cloth that hid the hairline, bright, sparkling eyes, a prominent nose, a range of uneven but white teeth, a moustache that came wispily past a laughing mouth to merge into a straggling beard of which the centre was greying and the extremes were dark. Around the throat was a buttoned-up brown overshirt. Above the First Fugitive's head had been written in a juvenile hand, ' "The death of the Martyr for the unification of all the people to the cause of God and His word is the happiest, best, easiest and most virtuous of deaths": Medieval Scholar.' Wroughton was thinking of the men who had climbed on to the passenger aircraft less than three years before and was wondering if they'd known those words. Gonsalves slumped in his chair, tilted it, heaved his feet on to the table, scattering papers, and slopped his coffee.

'OK, Eddie, can I shoot?'

'Fire.'

Gonsalves languidly gestured to the Most Wanted and the First Fugitive, sipped his coffee, then shot.

'They are screwed. In trouble. Hunted. They have problems. They are in disarray. They are looking over their shoulders. Not capable, right now, of the big hit. They are hurt. But—'

'But they are intact, Juan.'

'But they are intact. Bull's eye, Eddie, right in the inner circle. So, in retreat a commander looks to find a new defence line, somewhere he can hunker down and—'

'And regroup, Juan.'

'Afghanistan is finished for him. Pakistan is hot and difficult for him. Iran is—'

'Iran is quietly co-operative, useful as a transit and short-time hideaway.'

'Iran is not a place for a long-term base camp. Chechnya, forget it. Somalia and Sudan are past history for him, the game's moved on. We're hearing talk from elsewhere . . . What do you know, Eddie, about the Empty Quarter?'

Eddie Wroughton could have said that what he knew about the Empty Quarter was that it was empty, could have said that it wasn't a part of Saudi Arabia to which Juan should take his Teresa and the tribe of children for weekend camping, could have said anything facetious – but didn't. When he fed from his friend's table, he cut the smart-arse quips.

'I've flown over it, of course. I used to have that major in the Border Guard, you'll remember him, but he's posted up north now. I know precious little about it.'

'It isn't SigInt, and not ElInt, and it's most certainly not HumInt, it's just rumour. I did some reading anyway. Except for some mountain in the Himalayas, right on the peak, the Empty Quarter seems to be as remote as you can get. It's a huge area, like the name says, but I have confirmation there have been no satphone links out of there, or radio, and—'

'There wouldn't be, unless they're suicidal.'

'—and all I have to go on is a rumour of couriers passing through northern Yemen and heading up to the border, and people coming back. Three days ago it got kind of interesting.'

A story from Gonsalves was like water spilled on linoleum, it meandered but it kept going. It did not sink quickly into sand. Without the morsels of Agency information Wroughton's own work would have been harder and his future darker.

'We don't have people in north Yemen, not on the ground, but we have the Yemeni military we've trained. Three days ago, our liaison officer in San'ā was brought a cardboard box, like it was a present, the sort of size box you'd put groceries in. There were guys standing around and giggling, and he was invited to open it up. There was a head, severed, and two hands, all sawn off with a knife, and there was some squidgy sort of shit – I mean it. A guy had approached a roadblock, had seen the military, had jumped out and left his vehicle, then run for cover in the rocks. They did well, the military, but not quite well enough. Before they shot him, he was seen to swallow something – OK, OK, he's dead. So, what they did, Eddie, was they disembowelled him. They got into his upper intestine, down the bottom of his throat, and they got out a scrap of chewed paper, what you'd use for home-made cigarettes. Then they took off the head and the hands – you understand, for identification. I think our liaison guy's putting in for counselling, maybe for a transfer. I mean it, they slit his stomach and got out his tubes, then cut into them. Christ, we got some allies . . . What was left of the paper went back as an image to the laboratory at Langley, but we can't break into whatever writing there was. All we end up with is a courier carrying a message so tiny it might not have been found, so important it was worth swallowing and dying to protect it, and we don't have identification and there's no databank in Yemen that could match the fingerprints off the hands. The other thing – earlier, the roadblock military had seen a small camel train waiting down the track, nearer to the frontier. We trained those boys well, they're bright and keen. As soon as they'd filled the cardboard box they skipped back up the road to where the camels had been and two Bedouin. The sound of shooting carries a long way across those hills and the sand – no camels, no Bedouin. What do you think?'

'I'd say that's promising, maybe interesting.'

'What we're doing, Eddie – this is between you and me, this is between friends or it'll be my head in the next cardboard box – is we're going to put some toys down in the Empty Quarter, we're—'

'Big kids' toys?'

'You could say that. Anything you hear—'

'Top of my agenda. Your toys, what's going to be their status with the locals?'

'Fifteen of the hijackers came out of here. They're bankrolled from here. The families of the Twin Towers are serving writs here for punitive damages. Then there's the war, the *Angst*. I wouldn't trust any last one of the bastards. They get to know the sum total of damn all. I'd appreciate your help. What we're saying is, the indications are that the Empty Quarter might just be a good place to regroup.'

Eddie Wroughton was escorted out and the marine corporal slammed the gate after him. He remembered his one flight over a desolate, heat-baked wilderness. His step was jaunty – God, he fed well off the Agency's table.

The swollen fingers, where the flesh bulged over gold rings, took his hand.

'Don't look into my face,' Caleb said. 'Don't remember me.'

The man's head dropped, as if he took a point of focus for his eyes on the dirt and gravel at the centre of the intersection of the two tracks, but his slug-thick fingertips moved over Caleb's hand and on to his wrist. Clumsily, they unravelled the cloth, then the wrist was pulled gently forward and the head twisted to look down at the bracelet. In a soft voice, the man recited Fawzi al-Ateh's name, and the reference number given at Camp Delta. Caleb's wrist was let go. The man walked, with a waddling stride, back to his car, and bent to retrieve something from the safe box under the passenger seat.

He was a parcel and was passed on. A van with smoked windows had met him at the Omani shoreline and driven him inland. He had sat in the back, at the side, away from the field of vision of the driver's mirror. He had been left at a roadside near to a town, Ad Dari, on the far side of a mountain range. Traffic had sped past him until a Japanese four-wheel drive had ploughed on to the road's dirt shoulder, scattering dust over him. Through the open window his wrist bracelet had been examined. He had been driven away, again in the back seat, and taken beyond the wadi Rafash. He had been dropped off at a cross-point where trees in leaf threw down a sweet pool of shadow. He had waited there an hour, or more, and then the Audi had come, and the grossly overweight man had levered himself out and come to him.

The plastic bracelet from Camp Delta was his identification, as important as the pass-code numbers used by the guards when he had been brought from the cell blocks to the interrogation compound.

The man's robes flapped loose in a light wind. He carried back a small but heavy silken pouch, whose neck was held tight by a woven thong. He had forgotten himself and had stared momentarily at Caleb, then remembered and ducked his head. He gave the pouch to Caleb.

Caleb squatted down. His robe, dry from the sun, starched from the salt water, was tight between his thighs and made a basin in which to empty the pouch's contents. Gold coins cascaded on to his robe. They shimmered in the light. Caleb counted out a fortune in money, then carefully replaced each coin in the pouch, and put it into the inner pocket of his robe. The man looked away studiously, up the empty roads.

His voice was soft, like spoken music. 'I do not know your name, stranger, or what is your business, or where you go. You are a person held in extreme value by your friends ... May God go with you, wherever he takes you. As a *hawaldar*, I have no eyes and no memory. You do not seem to me to be from Oman, you are too tall and too heavily built, and I do not think you come from the Gulf. I deal in transactions of cash – ten dollars or a million dollars. I do not require your name because I do not need your signature. *Hawal* is the name of the trade. In our tongue, in Oman and the Gulf, it is a word that means *trust*. There is no trail of paper. I say you have received the money and those who are your friends will believe me. The trust is absolute. Rather than betray you, I would go to my grave. Rather than betray those who have sent you the money, I would cut out my tongue.'

He looked down into Caleb's face. The sincerity was there, and loyalty. He seemed to drink in the features of Caleb's face, to gorge himself. He crouched beside Caleb. 'I tell you, my young stranger, that the intelligence agencies of the Americans and the British hate, detest, loathe, the system of *hawal*. Money transfers are made, coded signals, and they cannot suck up the messages into their computers and so identify me, you and your friends. They blaspheme in frustration. The links are secret and you should have no fear.'

Caleb leaned forward and kissed the man's cheeks. He saw the admiration in the man's eyes and was confused.

'May God go with you, may your destination be Paradise. The poet Hasan Abdullah al-Qurashi wrote: "Glory in life is complete for the one who dies for a principle, for an ideal, for a grain of sand." I have admiration, beyond bounds, for your courage and for your willingness to sacrifice yourself. I know you are of great importance – were you not, the effort to move you would not have been made. It is my privilege to have helped you. You are like the bright star in the night, the brightest.'

The man pushed himself up and went to his car. The dust spewed behind him as he drove away.

At the crossroads, where the tracks met, where the shadows lengthened, Caleb sat, his head bowed. After the vehicle had disappeared, the quiet was broken only by birds' chatter. With each step he had made since he had run from the road between the base and the prison, he had sought only to return to his family. But each man he had met, who had moved him on, had shown the same fascination, awe of him. Why?

Far away, a dustcloud careered off the northern track and came closer.

Was he already marked with death? Had the family chosen him for death? The words were hammer beats in his head: 'Glory in life is complete for the one who dies for a principle, for an ideal, for a grain of sand.' The poet's lilt had gone.

An old, dust-coated pickup stopped, then reversed and sped bumpily away. He was taken north, and sat close to a bleating lamb between two hobbled goats.

Bart worked late. The surgery was in a side-turning off the Al-Imam Abdul Aziz ibn Muhammad street. The glass-faced block was easy to find, half-way between the Central Hospital and the Riyadh museum.

He reassured the German banker that his stomach pains came from ulcers in the lower gut, not from bowel cancer, prescribed the necessary remedies and showed the grateful man to the door. The banker would pay his receptionist, and the fee would be generous. No expatriate was using his own money: it was either from an insurance policy or from the company employing him. The banker wrung his hand in thanks at the diagnosis, then headed for the receptionist and ferreted in his pocket for either his cheque book or his wallet with the credit cards. Bart smiled balefully after him, then closed the door. He washed his hands at the sink, then stared out of the window, through the slat blinds, at the evening traffic. In the morning, the reward for his diagnosis, not a life-threatening tumour but a simple ulcer, would be electronically moved to a numbered, nameless bank account in Geneva, then its trail would scatter via Liechtenstein and Gibraltar to the Cayman Islands ... It was his nest-egg – but where would he spend it? He assumed that, one day, when Wroughton had no more use for him, he would be cast off and allowed to drift away, but he did not know where he would eke out his last days. Then, wherever, he would be alone at the mercy of a conscience. Oh, yes, Samuel Algernon Laker Bartholomew had a newly developed conscience: in the nights it gnawed at him – he would wake sweating – and in the days it stabbed him. He dried his hands. His buzzer went.

She was shown in by the Malaysian nurse.

Bart beamed. 'Good evening, Miss Jenkins. I hope you haven't been waiting too long.'

'It's Beth, remember? No, not too long.'

'How was the shopping in Bahrain?'

'Bought a couple of pairs of jeans, some smalls, some pasta, a new pair of sand boots. Oh, I read a bit, swam a bit – crashed out, really. It was just good to feel the sea.'

Her voice, Bart thought, was money – educated money and class money. She was one of those young women, he felt, who had only certainties in her life, for whom things happened because she wanted them to. There was about her that same confidence he had seen at the party. She was, he recognized it, a little breath of freshness in the daily routine that cocooned him in the sealed consulting room.

'Good, glad it worked out,' he said vacantly. 'Well, how can I help you?'

'I'm hoping you can't help me at all.'

She was rocking on her feet, staring back at him. She might have been gently mocking him. She wore the same skirt and the same blouse as she had at the party. He wondered if she had stayed for the 'brown tea', but doubted it. She didn't look to Bart to be the sort of expatriate who needed slugs of Jack Daniel's or Johnnie Walker for survival in the Kingdom.

Bart said, 'Very few people come to see me merely to indulge in conversation.'

She laughed. 'Sorry, sorry – I've been here just short of two years. I've never had a check-up. I live down south and I'm the only woman there. The quack's used to dealing with men falling off drilling platforms. I just wanted to make sure I was all right before going back. I hope I'm not wasting your time.'

'Very wise, a check-up. You're not wasting my time. Anything that's worrying you?'

He was glad he hadn't to ask her to strip: her directness frightened him. He took her blood pressure. He listened, through the material of her blouse, to her heartbeat. Women who caught his eyes and held them had always frightened him – Ann had, and the senior partner in the practice at Torquay, and his mother. Her blood pressure was good and her heartbeat was fine. He tapped her chest, poked her a little with his finger and felt the solid wall of her stomach muscles. Nothing wrong with her reflexes. The stomach muscles told him she was as strong as an ox, and he saw that her biceps bulged against the cuffs of her short-sleeved blouse. He went through his check-list. Menstrual problems? She hadn't any. Pains in the kidneys? None. Ten minutes later, he stepped back from her. 'Nothing to worry about.'

'Thanks, it was just that I don't know when I'll next be up here, in civilization.'

Something about her disarmed his caution, as it had at the party. The examination finished, the nurse had left them.

'Not that I wish to contradict you, Miss Jenkins, but we have differing ideas about civilization. I would think you have to be fresh out of a cave to regard this place as civilized. In my book the construction of glossy buildings, wide roads and an extravagant spending power bordering on the obscene do not add up to civilization. The culture here is of corruption – it's a society of skimmers, fixers and intermediaries, one bloody great family freeloading off the oil resource. I'm here, like every other expatriate, to feed the greed.'

She asked, with that inbred directness, 'So why do you stay?'

Bart blanched. 'We don't all have options, Miss Jenkins,' he stammered. 'Right, any problems and you don't hesitate to call me. Oh, if it's not impertinent, how did you hear of me?'

'I was down at the embassy, logging in with the new people. I was talking to one of the second secretaries and asking him about a doctor, a check-up. Another chap wandered up to us, must have heard what I was asking for. He gave me your name.'

'Oh, I must thank him. It's always good to know the grapevine works. Who was he?'

She paused, seemed to trawl in her memory, then smiled. 'Got it. Wroughton, Eddie Wroughton. That's who you should thank.'

Bart stiffened. She had made him reckless. He hardly knew her, but she had weakened all the defences he arrayed round himself. 'He's a parasite. He feeds off people. No, I'm wrong, he's worse than a parasite. Wroughton is as poisonous as a viper.' He caught himself. 'Have a good journey back, down south.'

Later, when his waiting room was empty and the nurse and receptionist had gone, he looked through the papers she had filled in. She was twenty-seven years old. Her handwriting was like her personality – bold. He rather hoped he would never see her again. Her address was a post box, c/o Saudi ARAMCO, at Shaybah. He knew where Shaybah was, and that little morsel of knowledge comforted him – he would not see her or hear of her again. He rang for a taxi. It seemed to him that when he'd touched her, her chest, muscles and organs, he'd touched danger – and when he'd looked at her, into the sparkle of her eyes, he'd looked into the depths of danger.

Before the sun had dipped far away to the west over the Asir mountains, the pilot had called Marty and Lizzy-Jo forward, had parked them in a jump-seat and the co-pilot's and had given them the bird's eye view. They had flown over the desert, and the map, devoid of recognizable features or the green of vegetation or any sign of habitation, had been on Lizzy-Jo's knee. The red sand, lit by the falling sun, had been scarred only by the dune formations, and what the pilot called their 'slipfaces', and he'd talked about 'crescentic dunes', 'star dunes', 'fishhook dunes' and 'linear dunes', and had identified all the strange and naturally made shapes at twenty-eight thousand feet below them. And he'd pointed out the *sabkhas*, the salt-crusted playas of sand between the dunes. He'd told them, his dry Texan voice clear in their headphones, that the Rub' al Khālī covered an area of – close to – a quarter million square miles, and that trying to map the dune features was time wasted because they moved, prodded and reshaped by the winds. He'd said that, right now, down there and under the sun's blaze, the current ground temperature was well over 100 degrees Fahrenheit. Three years back an F-A18 Hornet, overflying the Rub' al Khālī, had gone down out there in the middle of nowhere and a sandstorm had prevented helicopters with long-range tanks getting in. The rescue party from the Prince Sultan airbase at Al Kharj, on the northern fringe of the desert, had finally reached the wreckage using Hummer four-wheel drives, and had been too late. 'It was like the sun had burned him to death, dehydrated him, taken every last drop of juice out of him, and he was a trained guy, and the last day he'd been alive it was reckoned the temperature had hit one hundred and forty degrees, ma'am.' Then, the light had gone and they'd started a gradual descent.

'You folks drive the Predator?' The pilot was on manual but found time to talk. He wanted conversation: the UAVs were in their coffins behind the bulkhead, with the Ground Control Station and the trailers on which the satellite dishes were housed. Perhaps he thought that a young man with distorting spectacles, tousled hair and short trousers didn't look like any pilot that he, a military man, had ever known. Or perhaps he thought the young woman in her short skirt didn't seem like any sensor operator he'd ever met.

'What we do, as with all Agency business, is rated as classified,' Marty said.

'Just asking – don't mean to put my nose where it's not meant to be.'

Lizzy-Jo said, 'He's the pilot for what we've got, MQ-1s. I sit beside him and do the fancy stuff – telling the truth, there should be two of me but the guy who's supposed to be—'

'Lizzy-Jo, that's classified,' Marty snapped.

She ignored him. '—supposed to be alongside me is down at Bagram with amoebic dysentery. We have to make do.'

The pilot was almost old enough to be Marty's father. 'Where have you flown, son?'

Marty said that he had flown at Nellis, Nevada, for his training, and out of Bagram, and he looked defiantly at the pilot. At Nellis there had been veteran pilots, and at Bagram from the USAF, and they'd all been spare with words but had not hidden their contempt at his age and appearance. Flying for them was a killing game when the Hellfires were on the pods under a Predator's wings. For Marty, flying was as intellectual a task as working the machines in a kids' arcade. He scowled and waited for the sarcastic retort from the pilot about his inexperience. He didn't get it.

'Perhaps ya'll know all this – in which case you'll say so. Feel the turbulence? That's standard here. We have big winds over the dunes, forty knots or fifty. What I heard, Predator doesn't like winds.'

'It can cope,' Marty said.

'Can't even take off if cross-winds exceed fifteen knots,' Lizzy-Jo said. 'And it's pretty difficult to get decent imagery on screen if it's rough up high.'

'The winds are bad, and then there's the heat over the sand. When you're up we find there's a density-altitude barrier, it's what the heat does. Even if there had been no sandstorm when we were trying to get that Navy pilot at the downed Hornet, the helicopter people were not keen on flying. What I'm saying is, it's difficult territory for aviation. It takes understanding. Nothing moves, nothing lives, you could call it a death trap. It's one hell of an unfriendly place down there, it's—'

The pilot broke off. He was holding his stick tight. The co-pilot came behind Lizzy-Jo and told her to vacate the seat. He replaced her, strapped himself in, and reached across to lock his hands over the pilot's, helping him hold the stick and fight a wind powerful enough to throw the big transporter off line. The pilot didn't loosen his grip on the stick but gestured to his left with his head.

Lizzy-Jo tugged at Marty's arm and pointed port side of the cockpit window.

The darkness below them was broken by a spasm of light. The first light they had seen since the sun had dropped. Not a prick of light in the Rub' al Khālī until the brilliance that the aircraft now banked towards. The light was like an inland sea and around it was a wall of blackness, then nothing. Coming closer, the lights broke their solid formation and Marty recognized runway lights, road lights, compound and perimeter lights and buildings' lights.

'God,' Marty said. 'Is that it?'

'That's it,' Lizzy-Jo said. 'That's our new home. How long you sticking around for?'

The pilot grimaced. 'About a half-minute after your offloading is completed, I'll be powered up.'

They went down. The wind shook them. The pilot was good and feathered them on to the runway. They taxied, but the pilot didn't cut the engines when he'd braked. Far at the back they heard the metal scrape of the tail being opened.

The pilot sipped from his water bottle, then smiled at them. 'Take my word, this is hell on earth. I hope what you're going to do is worth the effort.'

Marty said, 'Any mission we are sent on is worth the effort—'

Lizzy-Jo cut in, 'We don't know what the mission is, but I expect someone will tell us when it's convenient for them.'

They went back into the fuselage and gathered up their gear. Two bags for her, one bag and his framed print for Marty. He was subdued. Everything the pilot had said about wind turbulence and heat played in his mind. He was sort of nervous.

They walked down the tail and George Khoo already had the maintenance team at work. They carried their bags to the side and dropped them, but Marty held his picture under his arm. The coffins were rolled down the tail on their trailers.

The pilot was as good as his word. In a half-minute after the last of the gear had been offloaded, the engines were revving to full power.

They walked towards the dirt at the end of the runway, where within a half-hour George had started to supervise the erection of a tent camp.

They were off the track when, without warning, the pickup swerved to the left. The lamb screamed and a goat fell into Caleb's stomach, then kicked with hobbled hoofs to be clear of him. Ahead there was a single low building – no village, no huts, no compound walls. Caleb crawled to the pickup's tail and jumped. On side-lights, the pickup left. The moon's glow fell on the building. There was a sliver of brightness at one window and another under the door.

Caleb clenched his fist and hammered on the wooden planks. He called out his old name, the one the Chechen had given him.

A bolt was drawn back, scraped clear of its socket. The door whined open.

Caleb went in. On an earth floor at the centre of the room a hurricane lamp threw out a dull light and the stink of kerosene. Beside it there were three plates with meat and rice on them and on one a half-eaten apple. Beyond the lamp's light, in shadow, stood a pile of olive green wood packing-cases but he could not read the writing stencilled on them. There were crumpled blankets, discarded cigarette packets, boots caked in old dirt and . . . From the deeper shadows, a shaft of light fell on a rifle barrel, aimed at his chest. As he slowly, and very carefully, raised his arms, the barrel tip of a weapon was pressed hard into the back of his neck. Then he heard breathing close to him and smelt the breath behind him. Away from the rifle there was a scurrying movement and then the lamp was lifted. A man held a hand grenade, the pin gone from it, in one hand and the other held the lamp.

In Arabic, Caleb said, 'If you drop the grenade or throw it at me everyone in the room is killed, me and you – you should put the pin back.'

He heard a little giggle of nervous laughter from the side, where the rifle was. The man put down the lamp, then fumbled in a trouser pocket and replaced the hand grenade's pin. Caleb saw the face of the man, old, tired and thin . . . The weapon stayed against his neck, but Caleb's right arm was wrenched down. He felt the cloth strip taken from the plastic bracelet. The light was lifted. His arm was released and the weapon dropped from his neck.

Each in his own way, the three men gazed at him. One slipped a pistol into the belt of his trousers. One stacked the rifle against the wall. The elder one grimaced and dropped the grenade into a coat pocket. Then they were eating, but still they watched him – not with awe or fascination, not with wonderment. Their glances were of rank interest and they seemed to strip him bare to the skin. It was as if each weighed his appearance against the value given him. It was, he understood, the first contact with the outer layers of his family. They gave Caleb their names, but spoke indistinctly because they were all eating as if food was scarce. He thought the elder one who had had the hand grenade called himself Hosni; the one with the rifle was Fahd. The man who had held the pistol against his neck and who had examined his wrist said his name was Tommy. They wolfed the food until the plates were clear, then wiped the plates and sucked their fingers for the last of the rice and sauce. Caleb sat at the side in the shadow, leaning against the stacked crates, and his stomach growled. He could have given his own name, or any name, but did not.

Caleb asked, 'Where do we go?'

Tommy cleared his throat and spat with venom at the floor. Fahd laughed shrilly, as if in fear. The elder, Hosni, said, without expression, 'We will be in God's hands. We are going into the Sands.'

Chapter Four

He was shaken.

Caleb had not slept well. The coughing, snoring and wheezing had prevented it.

Fahd stood over him, pulling at his shoulder.

It was still dark inside the room, but the light outside pierced the window where the plywood cover did not fit.

At the moment he was woken, Caleb had been in a restless dream world that nudged him to the limit of his memory, took him to the chasm, but would not let him step over into the void.

Hosni stretched and Caleb heard his joints creak. Tommy sat on his blanket and, without purpose, ran his fingers through his cropped hair as if that were his waking ritual.

They went outside for prayers. Fahd took the line for them and sank to his knees. The others followed. The first low sunlight caught the tips of the wadi's low boundary hills, and far beyond them was the Holy City, Makkah. He had said in the first training camp – near to Jalalabad, 'La ilaha illa Allah, Muhammadun rasoola Allah.' In old language, from back before the memory's void, he had known he said: 'There is no true god but God, and Muhammad is the Messenger of God.' He had said, facing the shooting range and the obstacle course, that he believed the Holy Qur'an to be the literal word of God, revealed by him, believed that the Day of Judgement was true and would come as God promised, accepted Islam as his religion, would not worship anything or anyone except God. He said the prayers taught him, and watched the others. Beyond his dream, where his memory did not go, there was no God. Hosni prayed quietly, as if it were a time to gather personal dignity. Fahd rocked forwards and backwards and his face contorted as if man's inability to match the demands of his God made an agony for him. Around Caleb were the whispers, mumbles and cries of devotion. He thought Fahd was the zealot, and marked it in his mind. There had been zealots in the trenches, and they were dead. There had been more zealots in the cages, and they were driven to insanity. Did Caleb believe the words he spoke soundlessly? He could not have answered. The prayers finished as the sun caught their faces.

He sat in the dirt against the mud wall and watched corridors of ants come to him, crawl over his ankle and pass on.

He was told they would move in an hour, was told transport would come.

The dream returned. Staring into the sunlight, his eyes were closed.

The dream was clear . . . the wedding. A veranda of wood planks in front of a small villa with white rendering on the walls, a garden with flowers, dried-grass lawns with chairs and rugs scattered among shrub bushes. Sharp in his mind. The bride was Farooq's cousin. The bridegroom was Amin's second cousin. Caleb was the Outsider. A feast. A celebration. Welcomed because he was the friend of Farooq and the friend of Amin, shown the hospitality that was true and warm. A feeling of liberation because he had made a great journey – but his memory no longer accepted where he had come from, from what he had been freed. He had been watched by a man sitting on a bench back from the veranda, among the shrub bushes, and who was dressed in a black turban, a long-tailed black shirt and loose black trousers. Guests came to the man and spoke quietly into his ear, and all who came near him ducked their heads in respect, but the man's one eye was fastened on Caleb.

He was only aware of the attention focused on him there, at the wedding party. He did not know that that attention had lighted on him when the message had come from far away to the town of Landi

Khotal that Farooq and Amin were bringing their friend to this distant corner of the North-west Frontier of Pakistan. Could not know that, from the hour of his arrival, he had been observed, followed, tracked and noted. Neither could he have known that the interest he created in the days leading up to the wedding was sufficient for a message to be sent across the border into Afghanistan. What was learned of him, and relayed in the message, had been enough for the man with the eyepatch and the chrome claw to have travelled to witness him at first hand at the celebration. A hawk's eye was on him, and he was in ignorance of it.

Once, when the bridegroom carried a tray of glasses filled with apricot juice to the man, the claw had hooked his elbow and pulled him lower. A question had been asked, the claw pointing at Caleb, and the bridegroom had answered it. Two lambs had been killed for the feast, and a kid. Only the remnants turned on the spit over the fire of cut wood, but the scent of the meat drifted in the smoke to Caleb's nose – and the man watched him. As the dusk came, younger men drifted away and while Caleb struggled to be understood by the relatives from the village of Amin and Farooq, there were shots beyond the garden. The man came towards him. Farooq whispered in Caleb's ear that the man was from Chechnya, a hero of the war with the Russians, but Caleb knew nothing of any war. The man was at his side and reached down. The claw caught Caleb's arm and lifted him. No smile, no greeting, no warmth. Farooq had tried to follow, as if anxious about his friend, but had been waved away. The man from Chechnya led him to the fence that marked the extremity of the cultivated garden. Four men were there, with rifles. They fired. The targets were a lentils can at the base of a dried-out thorn tree, and further back one that had held cooking oil wedged between stones, then far beyond, a fuel drum. Some bullets shook the targets, some caused little dust spurts near to them and the whine of ricochets. The man and Caleb could not speak, had no common language, but another came to Caleb's side and, with a guttural accent, translated the hero's words and Caleb's answers.

'Do you shoot?'

'I have never tried and no one ever showed me.'

'It is a gift from God, not taught. A man who shoots is a man who respects himself. Do you have respect for yourself?'

'I've never done anything of value to get respect.'

'A man who shoots well is a man who can fight. A fighter has supreme self-esteem. He is valued by his friends, trusted by comrades, loved.'

'I wouldn't know—'

'You would not know because you were never given the chance to be valued, trusted, loved . . . I was given such a chance.'

'To shoot?'

'To fight. I learned it close to here, against the Soviets. We ran, they followed us. We ran further and still they followed. We hid among rocks, they lost us. We were quiet as mice, they went past us. They stopped. We could shoot at their backs. We killed all of them – we killed all of them because we were fighters and born to it . . . and then we were valued and trusted and loved. Does my story frighten you?'

A great plunging breath. 'I don't think so – no.'

'It is precious to have self-esteem. Would you look for it?'

The breath hissed from his lungs. 'Yes.'

Caleb was given a rifle. He had never held a firearm. The translator had slipped away. He was shown, the sign language of the claw, how to hold it. The four men had stood back. Only Caleb and the Chechen had been at the fence. The whole hand had adjusted the sight. He had fired. The rifle stock had thudded against his shoulder. The can had toppled – his breathing had been steady. The sight's range had been changed. Caleb had seen the cooking-oil tin dance in the slackening light – his squeeze on the trigger bar had been constant. The sight had been altered. The fuel drum had rocked – he had lowered the rifle and turned to receive praise. On the Chechen's face he saw grim approval. Away beyond the garden's fence, far above the targets, a hillside was spotted with boulders, cut with little ravines, and at the summit was a precarious hanging rock. The Chechen had the rifle and pointed the barrel at it.

Caleb had understood. He had dropped off his suit jacket and loosened his tie. He had torn the seat of his suit trousers on the barbed wire as he had gone over the fence. He had run. He wore shiny shoes, polished for a wedding, that slipped on the rock surfaces, gave him no grip. At first there had been shots above him. He had hugged rocks, had crawled into the clefts. The firing had become less frequent. His suit trousers had ripped at the knees, his shirt was sweat-soaked, dirt-smeared. He had reached the top, bright in the last of the sun. Exhilaration had swamped him. He had stood on the hanging rock, his arms outstretched, in triumph . . . and he had come down, sliding, stumbling, and making little avalanches of stones. The dream had been near to the waking moment when Fahd had killed it. Since the scenes of the dream he had never again worn suit trousers, a suit jacket, a clean shirt with a tie, polished shoes. He was a chosen man. At the fence, when he reached it, the Chechen's claw had gripped his shoulder and held him close, and he had known that – an Outsider – he was a man respected, and wanted. Through that evening he had sat at the feet of the Chechen; Farooq and Amin had not come near him. In the morning, before dawn, he had left with him. He was the Chechen's man. It had been the start.

He was called. The dream was finished. He was the member of a family, and there had never been a family before.

He helped Fahd lift the boxes from the back of the building's one room.

They grunted under their weight, and their bodies were close as they struggled with each through the door.

'What do we call you?'

Caleb said that he had many names – did a name matter?

'What was the first name you were given?'

Caleb said that it had been 'The Outsider' – but he had been told the name did not mean he was without trust.

'Then you are the Outsider, not from a grouping or a faith or a tribe, but held in value. If it had not been for that value we would not be here. We call ourselves by the names of our enemies, better to remember them.'

The box was set down. 'Who is your enemy?'

'I am Saudi. Fahd was the king when I was blessed by God and received into Al Qaeda. His wealth was grotesque – it was twenty thousand million dollars. When he went on his holiday to Europe, he took three thousand servants with him. He allowed the infidel soldiers into the Kingdom, the crusaders of America. He is a hypocrite, an idolator, an apostate to permit the Americans in the Holy Land of the Two Cities.'

'And Hosni?'

'He is Egyptian. His enemy is Hosni Mubarak, who follows the

Americans, is their paid servant, who tortures and hangs the true believers.'

In the room, Hosni folded the blankets, had washed the plates from the previous evening's meal, had prepared a breakfast of bread and fruit.

'And who is Tommy's enemy?'

'Do you not know about Iraq?'

'I know nothing about Iraq since I was taken to Guantanamo.'

'Do you not know what happened in Iraq?' Fahd's voice whistled in astonishment.

'We were told nothing in Guantanamo,' Caleb said simply.

'You did not know the name of Tommy Franks?'

'I have not heard that name.'

'Let him tell you.'

Tommy did not help them but sat on his haunches in the sun, cleaned the weapons and did not look at them. There was sour concentration in his eyes. They set down the last of the boxes.

'Are you here – and Hosni and Tommy – because of me?' Caleb asked.

'Because of you we waited here for twelve days.'

She had taken the early flight down from the King Khalid International airport at Riyadh, claimed by the Kingdom to be the most perfect in the world, and had arrived at the oasis of steel and concrete before the heat had settled on the sands around it. She had dumped her shopping in her two-room bungalow, changed, and had kept running. Beth had been ten minutes late for her first class of the day.

A blackboard behind her, workers from Saudi, Yemen, Pakistan and the Philippines in front of her, she taught English language. The majority of her pupils were older than her. They were engineers, chemists, construction managers and surveyors, and the English she taught them was not that of polite conversation but would enable them better to scan manuals and technical work. The workers were the cream of the Kingdom's oil-production personnel; the site where they brought up extra-light crude from one hundred and twenty-five wells was called the most advanced in the world, and was praised as the most ambitious.

They were good students, determined to learn.

Other than the three nurses in the medical centre, Beth was the only woman at Shaybah. Standing before her class, she wore a long, plain dark dress that hid her ankles, the shape of her body, her wrists and her throat; a scarf covered her hair. If it had not been for the patronage of the province's deputy governor, she would not have been there . . . but she had that patronage. In Riyadh, Jedda, Ad Dammam or Tabūk, it would not have been acceptable for a lone woman to teach men – or to drive a vehicle, or to eat and use the library in the compound's club – but the pioneering site at Shaybah, deep in the Rub' al Khālī desert, was beyond the reach of the *mutawwa*. The religious police of the Committee for the Propagation of Virtue and Prevention of Vice had no remit at Shaybah, and it was known throughout the compound that Beth had the patronage of the deputy governor. The job, teaching English oil-extraction language, allowed her to pursue the love of her life. The love was in the study of meteorite geology and far into the sand dunes from Shaybah, but reachable, was the meteorite impact site at Wabar, considered by scholars to be the most remarkable on the earth's surface. The job and the patronage enabled Beth to fulfil her passion.

Apart from the nurses, Beth Jenkins was an only woman among some seven hundred and fifty men. The compound was two hundred and fifty land miles from the nearest habitation. The living accommodation, offices, the club, the high-rise constructions of the gas-oil separation plants, the towers of piping and the airfield covered forty-five hectares of desert. Production exceeded half a million barrels per day. Shaybah was the jewel in Saudi ARAMCO's crown. The statistics were daunting: 30 million cubic metres of sand had been moved; 638 kilometres of pipeline carried the extra-light crude to the refineries in the north; 200,000 cubic metres of concrete had been poured; 12,500 tonnes of fabricated steel had been shipped in to make 735 kilometres of interconnecting pipes. Beth thought herself blessed to be there. The men she taught came and went, worked short spells away from their families, took the shuttle flights out whenever they could, griped about the harshness of the climate and the conditions. Beth did not complain.

She would have said that she wanted nothing more of life. She would have claimed she could hack the heat and the isolation.

She would have refuted the mildest suggestion that she was isolated. She would have been perplexed to know that she was described, behind her back, as brutally rude and aloof. Away from the classroom, in her little bungalow where her clothes were strewn, she kept her books and study papers on the Wabar meteorite site, all she cared for. One day, Beth Jenkins would write the definitive paper on the site where black glass and white stone had rained down with the explosive force of a primitive atomic detonation on to what science called an 'ejecta field'.

She had the class reciting, in unison as if they were the kids way back at an Ascot convent school, the phrases 'proven reserves', 'API gravity', 'gas compression plant', 'well-head', 'stabilization and separation' and . . . She looked out of the window. The haze was thickening. The runway that linked Shaybah to the world outside was indistinct and hard to focus on. At the far end, deep in the haze, there was a small collection of tents and vehicles, two satellite dishes mounted on trailers and wide canvas awnings. She had not seen them when the flight had come in, had been asleep till she was rocked awake by the landing. Momentarily, she wondered why they were there, at the extreme end of the runway, by the perimeter fence. Then she began to set the work for her students to be done before she next met them.

They filed out. Another class came in.

No, she was not alone and inadequate. Yes, she was blessed.

The queue failed to move. Bart hissed, moved his weight from foot to foot, whistled his frustration through his teeth, coughed, but the queue did not shift. He needed a new *iqama*. It was renewal time for his resident's permit. He had with him the one that was about to expire, his driver's licence, a certificate from a colleague of a satisfactory eye and blood test, the document confirming employment by his local sponsor at the hospital and a further fistful of bureaucratic crap. In front of him, beside and behind him, corralled in a narrow corridor flanked by ornate rope, was a collection of the foreigners who took the Kingdom's shilling and were treated for their efforts with all the respect shown to a dog with mange . . . God, he loathed the place.

But there was no way round the queues, no avoidance of them.

The key word was *patience*. Bart knew all the stories of expatriates who had filled in their forms and sent a minion down to the ministry to avoid the queue. The bastards at the desks always found fault and sent them back. The highly placed and low-ranked had learned that the only way to get a resident's permit renewed was to stand in the damn queue.

Around him the need for *patience* would be muttered in a dozen tongues – in Arabic and German, Urdu and Dutch, Bengali and English. A few, the more important, had bodyguards, who idled in the chairs away from the queue. Bodyguards were a barometer of the deterioration in the security situation in post-war times. Bart paid only lip service to security in daylight hours, but would not have walked a street at night, certainly not in the areas where the Kingdom's new reality of economic depression had spawned beggars and the women who raided refuse bins for food scraps.

The servants of the Kingdom, bought with petro-dollars, shuffled and wheezed, and watched the painfully slow progress towards the counters.

At the end of the queue there were four desks. Two were occupied by men in the traditional flowing white *thobe*. On his head each wore a *ghutrah*, held in place by rope, the *igaal* that, in former times – when they were all in the sand and not in concrete and glass follies – was used to hobble a camel; now they rode, not on a camel's back, but in Chevrolets. Men worked at two desks. The other two were empty. Why were the desks not taken when the queue stretched back to the bloody door? Bart boiled. Some of the expatriates occasionally wore a *thobe*, and thought the gesture impressed their hosts. Did it hell! The days when expatriates were the chosen élite of the Kingdom were long gone – there was even talk that income tax for expatriates might be introduced. They were not wanted, only tolerated, and they were made to queue.

But that day God favoured Samuel Bartholomew, Doctor of Medicine. Five hours in the queue, patience rewarded, and at the head of the queue just before the break for lunch.

He produced an oily smile, presented his papers, remarked in his passable Arabic what a delightful day it was outside. He was good at doing lies: his life was a lie. He had done lies well since childhood. The son of Algernon Bartholomew, accountant, and Hermione (née

Waltham) Bartholomew, housewife, he had told the lie often enough about a happy childhood in a loving home in a rural village near the Surrey town of Guildford, and maintained the lie of contented boarding-school life. At the school, about as far away in the West Country as they could afford to send him, put him out of their sight and out of their minds, he had learned the law of survival: never explain, never apologize, never trust. Poor at games, unloved and lonely to the point of tears, he had comforted himself with lies. It served him well. As he walked back down the line, the stamp on his renewed *iqama*, a little smile spread on his mouth.

Caleb saw it but could not hear it.

The argument was about the boxes. He sat on one. On the old olive-green paintwork was the stencilled legend: *Department of Defense – FIM-92A. (1.)* There was a date, seventeen years back, when he had been a child, now blacked from his memory. He knew the weapons loaded into the boxes, had handled one briefly in the training camps, had felt its weight on his shoulder, and had seen one fired in the trenches, but he did not know its workings and guidance system. There were six boxes and they had created the dispute. Caleb sat with Hosni and Tommy, and watched the argument between Fahd and the farmer. Away to the right, barely visible, was a village with surrounding irrigated fields, clumps of date palms and lines of bright washing. Further up the watercourse, taking no part in the argument, a man and a boy squatted beside the legs of six camels. There were three more camels with Fahd and the farmer, and the price for them was contested.

Six camels were sufficient, just, to carry a guide, his son, Fahd, Tommy, Hosni and Caleb, with food and water, to their destination. But the six camels could not also carry the six boxes. For that more camels were needed. The farmer had more camels, and a price for them. Fahd had to have the extra camels but bridled at the price – the farmer was a 'thief' and an 'extortioner'. Each time he was insulted the farmer moved away and Fahd had to chase after him. They had been more than an hour, sitting with the boxes, in the full heat of the day. Caleb stared at the camels that were needed. He said, 'Why is it him who negotiates?'

Hosni shrugged. 'Because we are close to Saudi, because he is

Saudi, because he speaks the same language, because that is his job.'

'But he fails.'

Hosni picked up pebbles, threw them down. 'Each of us has a responsibility in this matter. It is Fahd's.'

'Why not you?'

Hosni sniggered, as if the question were an idiot's. 'I am from Cairo, from a city. I know nothing of camels. As a child I played at the Gezira Club. Camels were for peasants. I would not know a good camel from a bad camel, a lame one from a whole one. I do not take responsibility.'

'Why not him?' Caleb eyed Tommy.

Hosni snorted. 'Where he came from, what he did, he would only have seen a camel from behind the closed window of a Mercedes saloon.'

'Where will the guides and the camels take us?'

'Into the Sands and across them.'

'What are the Sands?'

The Egyptian shuddered. He was the eldest among them. He had frail, bony shoulders and there was no weight in his arms or at his stomach. His check jacket, which was torn at the elbows and frayed at the cuffs, hung loose on him, and his beard was sparse and untended. Caleb assumed the Gezira Club, in Cairo, was for the rich and he thought the Egyptian had made great sacrifices and had given up comfort in the name of Al Qaeda, and that the sacrifice had weakened him.

'You will find that answer.'

'And what is across the Sands?'

When Hosni spoke the breath wheezed in him. 'Across the Sands, if we can go through them, are the people who wait for us, who have called for us. Especially they have waited and called for you.'

'Thank you ... Why do we not shoot the farmer and take his camels?'

'Then all the village knows we have been here. They make a blood feud against us. They send for soldiers and police ... Then we are dead, and you do not reach those who wait for you.'

Caleb thought it a good answer. He stood and stretched, and the heat bathed him. The weight of the pouch was in the inner pocket of his robe. He walked away from Hosni and Tommy. He went to the guide who sat as if uninterested, and his hand ruffled the hair of the child, and he said that the child was a fine boy, a boy to be proud of, and he asked if the camels were capable of the journey. The guide nodded but did not speak. Caleb went back down the watercourse to the farmer, Fahd and the hobbled camels. He led Fahd a few paces away, so that their voices would not be heard by the farmer, and told him to go and sit by the boxes. He looked into Fahd's eyes, into their brightness and fury. He gathered his strength, took hold of Fahd's hand and pushed him away, back towards the boxes. They had not yet started out on the journey – a journey that made Hosni shudder – and Caleb knew he would travel with an unforgiving enemy. Fahd stumbled away from him.

Caleb sat beside the hobbled hoofs of the camels and smelt them and he stroked the leg of one. Then he took the pouch from the inner pocket and on a flat rock he spilled out all of the gold coins that the *hawaldar* had given him, on trust. He told the farmer that he wished to buy the three camels and he asked the farmer to take what coins they were worth. A fortune lay close to the farmer's gnarled, calloused hand. Sunlight danced on the coins. Trust counted, trust showed friendship. The hand hovered over the coins, pecked at them, lifting and dropping them. Trust. The farmer took three coins, then gazed up into the impassive face confronting him. He took three more coins, smuggled the gold into the pocket of his trousers, then reached out his hand. Caleb took it.

In his life, as far back as his memory took him, it had never been hard for Caleb to lead.

He retrieved the remaining coins from the flat stone and dropped the pouch back into his hidden pocket. The farmer kissed him and started to remove the camels' hobbles. Caleb waved for the guide to come to him.

An hour later, with all the camels loaded, they started out.

Camp X-Ray, Guantanamo Bay.

He squirmed back into the recess of the cage.

Each day, others had been taken. Hours later, as long as a day later, some had come back shivering, some had been pitched into the cage and had huddled with their heads bent on to their knees; some had wept or cried for their mothers – one had spat at the guards when they returned him, had been dragged away again and rechained. Caleb had not seen him since.

He had waited his turn, and the fear had built.

Three men and a woman crowded into the cage. They were huge in their uniforms and they towered above him. The chains were for his ankles, waist and wrists. Hostile faces, reddened by the sun. He seemed to read in all of them, but most particularly the woman, that they wanted him to fight. He thought he had been in the cage for three weeks but on a few of the days, as dusk had gathered and the arc-lights had brightened, he had forgotten to scratch the little mark with his fingernail on the back concrete wall to mark the passing of that day.

The fear was bad, worse than the shock of capture, worse than the beatings or the disorientation. The fear held him as the big hands, and the woman's, reached forward, seized and heaved him to his feet. Up to now, they had only taken him out of his cage for the first processing and photographing, for weekly exercise and showering – but he had been exercised and showered the day before. The fear caught in his stomach and he knew the little routine that he had learned was broken. The chains were tight on his ankles and wrists, and further chains were linked to the one that circled his waist. Then he was blindfolded.

They took him out.

He was a taxi-driver. The fear was in his mind and his body. He was Fawzi al-Ateh. The fear made his bladder burst. The wife of Fawzi al-Ateh, and the children, his parents and hers, had been killed by the bomber that made the trails in the sky. The warm wetness ran down the inside of his legs and he heard the sneering laughter. He was from a village in the hills above a town where he drove his taxi.

He was taken into a building. The blindfold stayed on. His feet were kicked apart. He was pushed forward, a blow in the small of his back and his fingers took his weight against a concrete wall, and when his feet wriggled closer to the wall to relieve the weight the boots hacked at his ankles to drive them back. His weight was between his toes and his fingers. A screeching sound filled his ears. He was a taxi-driver. The sound blasted into him, penetrated his skull and his mind. He was Fawzi al-Ateh. He could not escape the noise and the pain grew in his fingers and toes. The sound blistered him, but again and again he repeated silent words that alone could save him. He fought the wail of the noise. He did not know for how many hours he stood against the wall.

Then silence.

Then a new voice drawled, 'All right, hand him over.'

He tried to fall but hands caught his overalls and he was propelled back up, and he took the weight again on his toes and fingers and his bladder again burst.

'Give me your name.' The demand was in English. He felt each grain of the concrete against his fingertips. He bit his tongue.

'I said, give me your name.' Arabic. He closed his eyes behind the blind-fold and bit harder on his tongue.

'What is your name?' Accented Pashto, as if from a classroom, not spoken with the softness of the people he had known.

'I am Fawzi al-Ateh.'

'What is your occupation?'

'Taxi-driver.'

'Where are you from?'

He named the village, the town, the province. The Pashto of the questions was poorly phrased, as if the interrogator had learned the basic language on a brief intensive course. A little of the fear was lost. Everything he had learned in the van, he told. He stumbled through his answers. A pause. He heard water poured into a glass, then it was drunk.

The voice said, the same drawled English: 'You never know, with these ragheads, whether they're lying through their teeth or whether they're snivelling the truth. Give him another dance, and I'll call him back – give him some more. Victim of circumstance or a killer – how do I know? God, get me a beer.'

A door closed. The noise started again. At least twice he fell, and each time he was hoisted up, and he could smell the breath and the sweat on the men who lifted him and threw him back against the wall. The noise wailed around him and he could not shut it out.

A second time, the questions were asked. They were in Pashto, and he cherished the little victory.

Slumped, held up by their fists, unable to swing his shackled legs, he was taken back to his cage. He had told his whole story. He was Fawzi al-Ateh, taxi-driver, he had been driving at night and alone when his combi-van had been seized by armed men. He had never seen those men before. He had driven them at gunpoint. If they had not been so tired or if they had known that part of the province, they would have killed him and driven themselves. The cage door was opened and he fell inside. Some had shivered, some had huddled at the back of the cage, some had wept and some had cried for a loved one . . . Caleb lay on the mattress and slept.

Because, for the first time, he had lost a little of the fear and was able to sleep.

The white-painted Cessna, twin engines, circled once then levelled out for a slow approach.

Marty watched it yaw in the headwind. The same wind, blowing in his hair, threw up a screen of sand from the edges of the runway. Everything the pilot had told him on the transporter was seared in his memory, though he didn't believe the Air Force flier would have realized how deeply he'd drunk in the information. Cross-winds, heat making a density-altitude barrier, and upper turbulence had all played in his mind overnight; he'd barely slept. Lizzy-Jo had: she didn't take responsibility for keeping *First Lady* and *Carnival Girl* up and operational. Lizzy-Jo was back in the Ground Control Station, would be checking out the camera and satellite systems after the journey. Behind him, he could hear George Khoo lecturing the ground crew under the slung tarpaulins as the wings were bolted back on the fuselages of his girls. He watched the landing, saw the Cessna waver before it set down. Here, at this oil dump, he would have no wise head to feed off when he flew the girls. At Nellis or at Bagram there had always been a veteran pilot to take into a corner and quiz about conditions. That he had been awake in the night was the mark of his anxiety. The Cessna taxied.

He went to the door of the Ground Control Station. He rapped the door.

'Lizzy-Jo – the head honcho's down.'

A man climbed awkwardly from the Cessna's hatch. He was big, bloated, and his shirt-tail flapped out of his trousers in the wind. He was unshaven, was mopping his forehead already in the few short yards he had walked across the Tarmac, and was clinging to a brief-case, as if it held his life savings, holding it against his chest. He came towards the little ghetto of tents, awnings and vehicles that George Khoo had made in the night at the extreme end of the runway. George worked the men hard, and the noise had disturbed Marty nearly as much as the worries about flying conditions.

'You Marty?'

'Yup, that's me, sir.'

The man looked at him quizzically. It wasn't said, but the man gave him the feeling that he had expected Marty, the pilot, to be ten years older, or fifteen – not looking like a student just out of high school; it was the way he'd been looked at by the other Agency guys and the Air Force men when he'd first pitched down at Bagram. He was getting used to it, but it still annoyed him.

'I'm Juan Gonsalves – God, flying's a bitch. We were tossed around like rats in a sack. Wish I could do your sort of flying.'

'What is my sort of flying, sir?'

'Just sat in a cabin, air-conditioned – no air-pockets and no turbulence ... Hey, I'm not suggestin' you don't do the real thing. Look, where can we talk, where are there no ears? I mean *no* ears.'

'There's people at Ground Control. Back in the tents, there's people sleeping, sir. I'd say there's no ears right here, sir.'

Marty waved expansively around him. They were a hundred yards from the tents and the awning shelters where the wings of *First Lady* and *Carnival Girl* were going on to the fuselages. The sun was high, at the top, and his shadow was around his feet. Lizzy-Jo came out, hopped down the steps. He introduced her and Gonsalves broke off from the mopping to shake her hand, then took a map from his briefcase, spread it out on the dirt and put small stones on the corners.

'You been in this sort of heat before, Marty?'

'No, sir.'

'We're lookin' at one hundred and twenty degrees. Christ, do you know what pisses me off, Marty, more than the heat?'

'No, sir.'

'It's being called "sir". Call me Juan. I may not be prettier than you, son, but I am your superior. Funny thing is that great temple, our mutual employer, has given you a job that I can't do, and me a job that you can't do ... so today, that makes us about equal. Nice to meet you, Marty, and how d'ya do, Lizzy-Jo? What else you need to know about me is that the love of my life is Teresa and our kids, and the hate of my life is Al Qaeda. I'd like to say I live and sleep Teresa and the kids, but I don't. I live and sleep Al Qaeda. Each time we nail one of those A-rabs, I get a hard-on ... Nothing personal, you know, it's not that anything has happened to anyone I know, but it's the obsession that rules me. What I say to anyone who raises an eye-brow, thinks I'm a freakin' lunatic, is "If we don't throttle that organization right now, then we'll sure as shit end up on our backs with their boots on our throats," that's what I say.'

Marty gaped at the intensity. The sweat now ran on the man's face and he squinted as the sun came back up off the dirt and the map. His thinning hair was plastered wet. Gonsalves pressed on: 'I am a technophobe and an intelligence officer. I do not own a power drill but I understand the cell-system intricacies of Al Qaeda. In my house, Teresa has to change the lightbulbs, but I know the way the mind of Al Qaeda works. And don't ever try to blind me with the science of your machines. I don't care . . . Let's do the map.'

Marty saw that the nails were short but still had dirt under them, and the first two fingers of the right hand were nicotine-stained. The hand splayed out and passed over the map of the southern quarter of Saudi Arabia.

'What I predict, and here's where I'm gonna stick my neck out, is that this is the next big war zone. Forget Afghanistan, most par-ticularly forget the stuff in Iraq, you're looking at the new ballpark. It is the Rub' al Khālī, which is the Arabic for "Empty Quarter" – it is what the Bedouin simply know as "the Sands". It's bigger than you or I can comprehend, amigo, it is as hostile as anywhere on the good Lord's Earth . . . You see, it's where I'd crawl to if I'd taken a bad punch and was down and the count had started, except I'm going to beat the count, and I want the bell, I need to hunker down in my corner and get my breath and focus. I'd go to the Rub' al Khālī. It's where I'd be, and I'm confident I know their minds . . . Believe me, it's where they are, and I bet my shirt on it.'

He grimaced.

'I don't take everyone at Langley along with me. They still want paratroops and mountain forces and Rangers tramping in the Pakistan tribal lands and the Afghan mountains, but I say that's history. What I say is, they're right here right now. They are wounded, hurt, as dangerous as a maimed bear. They are supplied by couriers, they have no phones and no electronics . . . And do you think I can call on the Saudis for help? Hell, no. First off, they're suspicious of anyone telling them what to do, second, they're not capable of doing it, third, man, they're so insecure, I tell them nothing and they tell me nothing ... Well, I beat on the temple's door often enough for the Langley people to get freakin' sick of me, you know, they want to shut me up. Get me nice and quiet, so they sent you.'

'What are we looking for?' Lizzy-Jo was subdued and staring at the expanse of the map now covered by a film of sand.

'Wish I knew.'

Marty said, 'We have to know what we're looking for. It's one mother of a playing field, more map boxes than we've ever tried to cover. We have to know.'

Age, tiredness seemed to lodge on Gonsalves' face. Marty craned to hear him better. He spoke as if he knew what he said was inadequate. 'Well, not wheels ... not big groups in caravans ... not on roads because there aren't any – there's only one track that goes nowhere ... Small groups, maybe three or four guys and three or four camels ... out where nothing exists ... A pinhead in a dump truck of dirt ... Maybe the camels are carrying gear, maybe they aren't. People where they shouldn't be. This is not a refuge for low-life but for the leadership – they must send and receive messages and retain control. Only a very valued few will be summoned to their hole in the ground, people they need to see ... Can't help any more than that.'

Lizzy-Jo said, 'We'll give it our best shot.'

He pushed himself up and shook the sand off the map, then folded it and made a mess of that, gave it to Marty. He told them what their cover would be, and he said he'd get down again as soon as was possible but meantime he'd speak each day. Gonsalves started to walk back to the Cessna, his head down, as if he knew he'd failed to convince. He stopped. 'It's good, this equipment you've got?' He waved his arm airily at the birds under the awnings.

Marty said, 'We got the best. If they're out there then we're gonna find them, sir.'

Lizzy-Jo said, 'Our two, *First Lady* and *Carnival Girl*, are the oldest UAVs the Agency has deployed. They're nearly ready for a museum. This cries out for Global Hawk or for an RQ-4. We've got MQ-1 – that's the way it is.'

Marty savaged her with his glance.

Gonsalves didn't pause, ripped at him with his hoarse voice: 'But you've brought Hellfire?'

Marty nodded. 'Yes, we've brought Hellfire.'

'Then let's hope you get to use it . . . Any last questions?'

Marty said softly, 'What sort of guy do you think is gonna come to this shit hole?'

'The man they need. The man that can hurt us most, with gear.'

Gonsalves went to the Cessna, clinging to his briefcase. They watched the plane take off and fly away low over the sands that were without end. Neither Marty nor Lizzy-Jo spoke. There didn't seem anything sensible to say. Then she punched his arm and said she'd go make some coffee.

The new idea of the director general, the new broom, was to expose senior officers at the London headquarters building of the Security Service to external opinions and to encourage more lateral thinking. Michael Lovejoy sat in the auditorium's back row; he always chose a back row when he had not volunteered. Behind his folded newspaper, his study of the crossword interrupted, he yawned – but he listened as he scanned the clues.

The psychologist, from a north-east English university, gripped the lectern tightly. 'What we have to understand – a disturbing and unwelcome truth but nevertheless a truth – is that terrorist leaders have a better understanding of "profiling" than the people charged with countering political violence. On your side, ladies and gentlemen, you look for obvious and naïve stereotyping – not so with your opposition. They – in particular Osama bin Laden and his lieutenants – have refined a skill in identifying young men of varying social backgrounds and economic advantage who are prepared to make supreme sacrifices for a cause. They look for men who may be willing to die, may want to die as a price for the attack's success, but whether suicidal or not will drive home that attack. We are fond of using the word "brainwashed" about our enemy. It is inappropriate and erroneous. They are patient and work by gradual progression to the stage where a man is prepared to crash an air-liner into a public building, plant a bomb in a crowded concourse, carry a suitcase filled with explosives and lethal chemicals or microbes into the heart of a city. They lead him towards that goal. They do not hurry. They set ever greater hurdles for him to climb – and all the time he is wrapped in the familial culture. Isolated in training camps or in a wilderness of desolation, he loses contact with any world other than that which is close to him. The family becomes the only society he knows, and he will develop intense pride in that association. They are better at spotting the right man than you are.'

There was a little sucking intake of breath in front of Lovejoy. He was an old hand with the Service. Insults no longer disturbed him. The psychologist had his interest – and fifteen down, 'The patrician of Coriolanus', eight letters, went unanswered. It was only the newspaper's quick crossword.

'You look upon the terrorist groups, and Al Qaeda specifically, as parasites that lure young men into their ranks. You have the catch-all word of "loner". I imagine you search through your Special Branch files looking for these "loners". Friendless and inadequate boys, who are impressionable, drifters, and therefore may easily be drawn towards commitment to terrorist outrages, are your targets. Have you done well? I don't think so . . . Al Qaeda has stood a quantum leap in front of you. "Loners" may be satisfactory as foot-soldiers, good enough to wash the plates in Afghanistan, but quite inappropriate for the war that I guarantee stretches for years ahead of you. Look for a simple stereotype and, please believe me, you will fail.'

The psychologist paused, gazed balefully at his audience, then sipped from the glass of water on the table beside the lectern. Lovejoy imagined irritated frowns settling on the foreheads of the younger generation who had taken forward seats: the profiling of loners was taught as a creed in D Branch. He thought he rather liked the cut of the academic.

'I've taken up most of your lunch-hour, and I know you're busy people, but may I leave you with a final couple of thoughts? A retired soldier recently wrote to me and his notepaper was headed, along with his address, "A beaten path is for beaten men." The stereotype of the "loner" is a beaten path, and if you follow it you will be the beaten men and the beaten women. I urge you to look elsewhere. Where? For quality, for ability, for the best – because it is those young men that the lieutenants of bin Laden search for. Imagine, also, the excitement of being a part of that select fugitive family, picture the personal self-esteem, conjure up a sense of the adventure and purpose. No, no, I promise you, the young man who can damage us, wound us to the quick, revels in that excitement – his true religion – and in the adventure that life brings him. Thank you.'

As quiet, polite applause rippled in front of him, Lovejoy wrote 'Menenius' in fifteen down.

The watercourse was far behind them. They had climbed and scrambled up a steeper slope and now, on the summit, the wind whipped them and their shadows splayed out beyond. The sun sank.

Fahd prayed. He cried out, as if for help, and his eyes were closed, as if the view ahead overwhelmed him. The Saudi was tall and gangling and he seemed to plead to his God, as if God alone could save him. Beside him, the guide knelt, the boy at his side. Tommy made no pretence of worship but had his old army boots off, and his socks, and massaged his feet. He moaned. Hosni did not pray but sat on a rock by the camels, who shredded the feebly growing thorn-bushes. Caleb sat close to the Egyptian and thought he had not heard such passion in prayer since the first days at X-Ray and Delta when despair was greatest.

He gazed in front of him.

'How far do we go?'

'Only the guide knows – perhaps a thousand kilometres.'

Caleb said, 'It's late to ask it, but why don't we drive?'

'Where there are roads for a vehicle, there are blocks and checks. The military has blocks and checks ... They wait for us, for you, those who have called us, in a place of death where there are no roads, no eyes to watch for us. It is a place of death but also a place of dreamers and fools.'

'Are you a dreamer?'

Hosni said, in a murmur, 'I think I am a fool.'

The guide collected together the camels, and Tommy hurriedly pulled on his socks and his boots. They went down the hill's reverse slope, past a cairn of stones that was the border. Ahead of them, limitless, stretching towards dusk's infinity, was the desert that was made red gold by the sun. Caleb saw the Empty Quarter, where his family waited for him.

Chapter Five

Rashid, the guide, was at the front and walked beside the lead camel. The Egyptian, the Saudi and the Iraqi rode, then came the baggage camels with the tents and the water, and they were followed by the three camels that each carried two of the boxes. At the back, walking, were Caleb and the boy, Ghaffur.

It was the third day since they had entered the desert.

The sun beat down on him. The heat pierced the *ghutrah* that wrapped his head and wound round his mouth and jaw. It burned his exposed cheeks and nose, and the reflected brightness devilled in his eyes . . . and the boy talked. In his ears was the soft singing of a light wind, the muffled strike of the camels' hoofs in the sand and the groaning murmurs of the Saudi. They left behind them a trail of broken sand, indented with hoofmarks and footprints, but even the gentle wind had the strength to shift loose sand into the little pits they had made. When he looked back, as far as he could see, their trail was already covered, lost. The boy questioned him as thoroughly as had any of the interrogators at X-Ray or Delta. Ahead of them, what he saw, through squinted eyes, was an endless sand-scape to the horizon. Caleb set himself the target of each horizon, a dune ridge that met a sky that was without a single cloud, and when that horizon and ridge was reached another faced them. The treble pitch of the questions was like a fly's attention, distracting but not irritating, and he ignored it as he would have ignored a fly at his nose.

Who was he? Where had he come from? What was his purpose? Why did he travel? They might have been the questions of interrogators. Then he had hung his head and had quietly repeated the life story of the taxi-driver. Now he swatted the questions away with a smile or a grin that was hidden by his *ghutrah*. They skirted the higher dunes where they could but some were so vast that they could not be avoided and then Caleb and the boy helped to drag the stumbling, sliding animals up the lee side where it was steepest, and on the way down they would let the camels loose so that their angled legs danced awkward steps as they careered down. On top of each dune, driven by the winds, were razor ridges that made slight avalanches when broken. Mostly Caleb looked at his feet because then he did not see the horizon and had less sense of the pitiful slowness of their progress and the distance to the next dune's top . . . It was only the beginning. Last evening they had stopped at a well, and the camels had been allowed to drink their fill, and he had heard the guide, Rashid, tell the Egyptian that this was the last well on their route. That morning, after prayers, before the sun's heat had gathered, they had left the well, which was merely a little box of mud bricks with a dead wood beam across it and a rope stretching down to a hanging bucket – the water had been brackish, stale, foul: he knew because he had sipped it, then spat it out. His own questions played in his mind and mirrored the boy's. Who was he? Where did he come from? What was his purpose? Why did he travel? He could not have answered them.

They halted in the middle of the day – not for food or to drink, but to pray. They had eaten and drunk before they had left the well and would not do so again until they stopped and pitched tents. By walking at the back of the caravan, with the boy, Caleb had distanced himself from his unchosen companions. The last evening, before they slept, Fahd had told him briefly, with a sneer, of the disaster to Iraq, the fall of the regime, that American tanks had driven at leisure through the wide avenues of Baghdad. Then Tommy's glance had settled on Fahd and the story had been left unfinished . . . In front of him, astride the camels and perched on the humps, they all suffered. The Saudi would yell out his pain, and twice the Egyptian had tumbled into the sand. Rashid had lifted him up without sympathy, then thwacked the camel's back to get it moving again. He sensed, constant in his mind, the resentment they held for him because they had waited twelve days for his arrival.

They climbed, scrambled, descended, and each in his own way would have prayed for another of the salt-crusted flats that made plateaux before the next line of dunes, and the heat was unforgiving . . . and it was only the start. The questions had started again, the piping voice demanded answers.

'No,' Caleb said. 'You shall answer me.'

'What?'

He saw the triumph on the boy's face: a response had been won.

'How long do we travel?'

Mischief lit the boy's face. He grinned. 'How fast can you go? And the others? I think we go slowly.'

'How many days?'

'The camels drank this morning.'

'How many days can the camels travel after they have drunk?'

'For eighteen days.'

'Is eighteen days enough time?'

'How fast will you go?'

'What happens after eighteen days?'

'The camels die,' the boy, Ghaffur, said, and his eyes sparkled. 'But we must have water.'

'How many days can we live without water?'

'Two days, then we die.' The boy's smile wreathed his face.

'Has your father been on this route before?'

'I do not think so. Not with me. He has not said it.'

More questions bounced in Caleb's mind. All had the same core. How did the guide, Rashid, know where he was going? What markers did he use? What pointers guided him? They were unspoken. They had barely started, it was only the beginning . . . On every camel goats' stomach skins bulged with drinking water. Two days after that water was exhausted, they would die of thirst, and after eighteen days the camels would die. Caleb had not seen anything that told him men and beasts had gone this way before. The sands were pure. There were no tramped trails where hoofs or feet had been, and he did not think there was any possibility, however remote, that a vehicle could have ploughed through the soft, shifting sands of the dunes. Twice, in that morning's march, the guide had stopped and looked ahead, had seemed to sniff at the air, and his concentration had been total. The first time he had veered towards the right, a sharp, angled turn, and the second he had gone to the left, a softer turn. But the boy said his father had never been here before. He realized it: their lives depended on the instincts of the guide who strode ahead of them, led them further into the sand wilderness.

Caleb asked, 'Does anyone come here?'

'God is here.'

He walked faster. The straps of his sandals were making blisters on his heels. He saw nothing that supported life, only the dunes – no track, no bush or dead wood, no trail. If he had not been important then the challenge of crossing the wilderness would not have been given him, but he did not know why he was important ... He walked faster but his legs were leaden and his mouth cried out for water. The boy gambolled beside him, mocked him.

He staggered. The boy caught his arm, but Caleb angrily pushed him away, and the horizon was blurred by the sweat in his eyes. He seemed to see, in his mind, the bones of the dead who had exhausted their water, and the bones were stripped white by the sand and the wind. He blinked, then wiped the sweat savagely from his eyes. He had stared into a trap of self-pity, as men had done at X-Ray and Delta.

He screamed and the sound of it soaked into the dunes' walls and the cloudless sky.

He checked his list for the day – three interrogations.

They would all be dross. The Bureau and the Agency ruled in Joint Task Force 170, and the DIA ran a poor third, bottom of the heap. In his cubicle, Jed had scanned his overnight emails – nothing that couldn't wait – then turned to the files of the three men. The Bureau and the Agency worked the prisoners who stared at the ceiling and soundlessly repeated Holy Qur'ān verses, or fed out the disinformation snippets, or gazed back at the questioner with silent contempt. The Bureau and the Agency had the big-time game of trying to break into the silence or the lies, and that was good, stimulating work. The men given to the DIA were the no-hopers, the unfortunates on the edge of nervous collapse. In the morning he would see a Kuwaiti, who said he was an aid worker in Jalalabad. In the afternoon, an Afghan would be brought in who said his father had given offence to a tribal chief in Paktia province and the chief had therefore denounced him. In the early evening, across the desk there would be a German passport holder from Tunisia who claimed the Pakistanis had handed him over when he was only an Arabic language student. It was pitiful.

By now, any benefit of Jed Dietrich's vacation was eroded. He wouldn't have told his father, Arnie Senior, but the work at Guantanamo bored him. A few times, he felt compulsive anger towards his targets, the men he faced, but the army's interrogation manual was clear cut on the boundaries he must not cross: he was permitted to use 'psychological ploys, verbal trickery, or other non-violent and non-coercive ruses'; he was warned that 'the interrogator must have an exceptional degree of self-control to avoid displays of genuine anger'; and absolutely forbidden was the 'use of force, mental torture, threats, insults or exposure to unpleasant or inhumane treatment'. Maybe if he had responded to that anger and kicked shit out of them, life at Guantanamo might not have been so dreary. It would not happen . . . He supposed that what kept him sane, what kept a man buying a lottery ticket, or what kept a guy out on a rainy day walking mud fields with a metal detector, was that something – one day – might just turn up. He started to read the case notes of the Kuwaiti who claimed to have been doing charity work in Jalalabad.

A clerk brought the signal to him.

He signed for it, watched the clerk close the door, and read it. He hadn't really the time to ponder on it, not if he were to get the Kuwaiti done in the morning. He read it a second time. He bit at his lower lip and dug his fingernails into his palms, but couldn't beat the frustration.

From: Lebed, Karen. DIA, Bagram.
To: Dietrich, Jed. DIA, Camp Delta, Guantanamo Bay.
Subject: Fawzi al-Ateh. Ref. US8AF-000593DP.
Hope the sun's shining and the swimming's good. Concerning the

above individual – no can help. Afghan national Fawzi al-Ateh did a
runner (exclaimer). He escaped from USMC escort en route Bagram-
Kabul. A mess (double exclaimer). Subject should have been collected
*by Afghan Security (yeah****yeah****) but incoming flight was delayed*
and they'd gone home – believe me. Subject pleaded nature call and was
allowed out of transport, but didn't drop his trousers, just ran.
Anyway, why the query? Wasn't subject cleared for release? Subject's
home village is not accessible to us unless in battalion strength, bandit
country. Low priority means follow-up assessment is not possible. OK,
OK, so he went home early. Wishing you a happy day.
Best,
Lebed, Karen

He winced. Ever since his supervisor had told him of the taxi-
driver's release, the irritation had come to him in spasms. It was not
a tidy wrap-up. He could go back in his mind to the first day of the
vacation, up in the cabin by the lake, when the faces across his desk
had been clear, clean images. He had identified something enigmatic
about that subject: a tall young man, softly spoken, never shaken in
his story. All the others who pleaded innocence, as the taxi-driver
had, had tried to prove their non-association with Al Qaeda by
naming men they'd 'met' or men they'd 'heard of' who were in the
055 Brigade, or men they'd 'seen'. This one, the taxi-driver, had never
met an Al Qaeda member, never heard of one, had never seen one. It
was such a small point, so trivial, and by the second day on the
Wisconsin lake he'd forgotten it. It would not have resurrected in his
mind if the Bureau and the Agency had not walked, in big boots,
over his supervisor . . . It had made a niggling suspicion. He filed the
signal.

He went to work. He walked between the block where his office
was and the block used for interrogation. He could see the beach. The
wind came off it. It should have been a place of beauty, but it wasn't.
It was a place of fences and cages, of howled misery and failure. He'd
complained, more than five months back, to Arnie Senior about the
numbing tedium of the interrogation sessions – but Arnie Senior had
done his draft time in the Central Highlands of Vietnam where
questioning was 'robust': 'Take 'em up in a chopper, three of them,
get up to a thousand feet, make two take a hike and then ask the third

some questions. Never fails.' Arnie Senior's eyes had glazed over, sort of manic, and Jed had never again talked about his work to his father.

The translator was from Pittsburgh, second generation American, Syrian stock, and Jed disliked him, didn't trust him. The translator lounged and pared his nails. The chair opposite the desk was empty; they waited for the Kuwaiti to be brought in. Jed had talked three times to the taxi-driver, sitting in that same chair. He had found him co-operative and word-perfect on his story. Each time he'd done the oldest of tricks, what they taught at the training of interrogators, go back suddenly over a fact given an hour before, but every time the taxi-driver's story had matched and the trick hadn't caught him. Truthful, and he wouldn't have admitted it – not even to Brigitte – he'd rather liked the young man, and the story of the family's death from the bombers had kind of hit him . . . He looked up.

The chained prisoner, between the guards, was shuffled into the room. His thoughts of the taxi-driver – where he was and what ground he walked – were shut from his mind.

He looked into the pleading face of the Kuwaiti.

The birds soared.

She flew the peregrine, the *shahin*, he flew the saker falcon, the *hurr*. They were high, specks in the sky.

Beth and her host, the deputy governor, were out for a day's sport, with four vehicles and a retinue of drivers, falcon-minders, and servants to pitch an awning when they broke for the picnic; there were bodyguards with rifles, and a tracker from the Murra tribe to bring them back to Shaybah if the GPS system failed. She would have preferred just her and him, one four-wheel drive and the two birds. It could not be: the deputy governor, a prince of the Kingdom, required such a following as a symbol of his rank.

The birds, high enough over them to make her arch her neck and struggle to follow their flight, searched for prey.

Had they been alone, two persons in the wilderness of sand, she would have experienced what she loved: the solitude, the quiet and the serenity. The desert captivated her. Lawrence had written, three-quarters of a century before, that 'this cruel land can cast a spell', and she understood him. She was captivated by the emptiness and the infinity of the horizons. Its imprint, she knew, would mark her mind for the rest of her days.

She watched for the diving stoop of the peregrine, waited for it to spy out a bustard that would be condemned.

They were a dozen miles off the road running to the north alongside the pipeline; the meteorite impact site of Wabar was a hundred and twenty miles to the west. The deputy governor would have been apoplectic had he known that she went alone to the ejecta field, had found a route for her Land Rover. He believed she only travelled there when he authorized drivers, a back-up vehicle and servants for the camp she must have, with a cook, a tribesman from the Murra, and troops from the Border Guard; with that crowd she felt constricted and watched, unfree. She had no fear of the desert that Lawrence had called 'cruel'. Once a month, Beth slipped away on her own to walk among the black glass and the white stones, to map and examine them, and once every second month she took the deputy governor's deputed escort. She had been told by a Bedouin trader who had come to Shaybah of another place, south of Wabar, where the glass and stones had fallen from the heavens, and had been given landmarks, perhaps a place where no human foot had ever been. She would be there, alone, with the quiet – if her Land Rover could get her there.

The birds searched, had not yet found a prey below.

She was there because she had written the letter to the Saudi Embassy in London, and had requested a visa for scientific research of meteorite impact sites. She had, of course, exaggerated her academic qualifications and egged-up her field experience. Her mother and father had lectured her that the Kingdom was not responsive to foreigners, intruders. Three months later she had whooped when a positive response had dropped through the letter-box, signed in person by the deputy governor, instructing her to go to the embassy where a visa would be issued to her. Everyone she knew in London said it was a miracle that she had won admission to follow her studies.

The birds came down, but not in the dive to strike.

Their flight back to the cluster of vehicles was frantic and in fear. Above them, distinct and threatening, an eagle hovered. The sport was finished: no bustard would be taken. The peregrine and the saker falcon would not fly again if an eagle dominated the sky. The picnic was laid out and the birds shivered in fear in their cages. She watched the eagle, felt its presence, a killer over the sands, danger where before there had been none.

He followed the example of the guide, Rashid, and the boy.

He must have the respect of Rashid. Caleb had seen, looking up the length of the caravan, that when Rashid glanced back there was no respect on his features for the men who rode the camels.

He stopped, bent, and unfastened the buckles of his heavy sandals. He let his bare feet sink into the sand, then hitched the sandals' straps to his waist. He took the first step. He must have respect, he was driven to find it. The heat of the sand scorched the flesh on the soles of his feet, the grains clogged between his toes. The second step, and then he was climbing a dune's lee slope and each step set fire to the skin under his feet, which was pink and protected between the calluses and the new blisters, but his grip was better than it was with the sandals; his toes dug into the loose sand and he did not fall. The burning ran from his feet to his ankles and up to his thighs. Caleb gasped. His teeth locked on his lip. He would not cry out. They tumbled down the dune's reverse slope. He fell but did not scream as the pain surged.

The boy, Ghaffur, was gone. Caleb was alone, abandoned by the caravan's stampede down the reverse slope. He scrambled to his feet. He saw the boy sprint, sure-footed, past the pack camels and past the camels on which Fahd, Hosni and Tommy clung, as if for their lives. He plodded after them, the gap growing and the pain burning. The boy reached his father at the head of the caravan and tugged at his father's sleeve. Rashid seemed to listen to his son, then turned. Tears welled in Caleb's eyes. His bare feet gouged into the sand. He saw, through misted eyes, the moment of disinterested contempt on Rashid's face, heard faintly the cough and the spit, then Rashid resumed his march at the caravan's head.

The next dune line was at least a mile in front. It was as if bulldozers had scraped off the sand bed, scalped it down to a surface of grit and chipped stones. Rashid led the camels on to the new ground. The boy waited for him.

Each step on the burned grit and the sharp stones was rich agony.

The boy waited and watched him.

Caleb's own craving for respect made him hang the sandals at his waist. If, now, he dropped the sandals to the ground, slipped his feet into them and refastened the buckles, he could not win respect. The vista stretched ahead of him, and he started to count numbers to divert his mind from the shoots of pain.

The boy's gaze wavered between Caleb's wet eyes and his feet. He thought the boy understood.. The boy's feet were hardened as old leather and Ghaffur stood and waited for him. Caleb counted each step. He came closer to the boy – and the distance to the end of the caravan and the last bull camel carrying two of the boxes had widened. He reached the boy, still counting, and passed him and kept on walking and each step hurt worse.

'What do you say?' the voice piped.

'I am counting.'

'What are you counting?'

Caleb grunted, 'I am counting each step I take.'

'I have never heard of such numbers,' the boy said, and shook his head.

He counted the next number . . . and realized. The pain and the heat, the grit and stones under his feet had pushed him beyond the chasm that was the limit of his memory. He cursed softly. An old language had seeped into his mind, his past. He stamped on the memory and walked on.

Caleb endured.

At the base of the next dune line, where there would be soft sand, Rashid had called a halt. Fahd prayed, but the Egyptian and the Iraqi squatted in the shade of their kneeling camels. Caleb reached them.

Tommy sneered, 'What do you wish to be, a soldier or a peasant?'

When the Saudi's prayers were complete, they went on. The boy stayed close to him, eyes never off him, because the boy had heard the evidence that the life of the Outsider among them was a lie. Who was he? The boy's question had, almost, been answered. Caleb was able to hold the pace that Rashid set.

The traffic was fierce.

Lunatics hurled cars, vans and lorries around Bart's chauffeured saloon. His driver, a favourite with the expatriates at the compound, was slow to anger and seldom treated the roads as if they were stock-car circuits, manoeuvred among the hazards with caution, was a byword for calm, and therefore was in demand. They had just left the supermarket, on the northern edge of central Riyadh, where Bart had filled a trolley with meals-for-one. It was always a risk for an ex-patriate to drive himself: a foreigner was inevitably considered to be in the wrong at an accident scene. A European foreigner could be milked for rich pickings if a Saudi was injured or his car dented: no access to a lawyer, and no help from the embassy. He sat in the back of the Chevrolet, believed the company's sales pitch on the strength of the vehicle, and was relaxed.

He was going shopping. The supermarket had merely been his first call, and his last call would be the English-language bookstore, but next in line was the Pakistani-staffed men's clothes emporium. There, at least, he would be treated with courtesy, made to feel valued – and so, at their prices, he damn well ought to be. Little luxuries had come late in life to Samuel Bartholomew: none at home as a child, none at school where pocket-money allowances were grudgingly paid by his father, none as a student in London. He was looking for a couple of ties, silk, and a couple of shirts, best Egyptian cotton.

Bart's student years and the pre-qualification studies had been an endless miserly existence. Nine years in all, and always his wallet had been light. Through pre-clinical and clinical, through his pre-registration year with six months as a hospital house physician and six more months as house surgeon, and during the final three working as junior scrote at a general practitioner's surgery in east London and back again into a south London hospital, he had suffered un-relenting penury. The legacy of it was that today's purchase of shirts and ties had importance. Being able to shop when the mood took him was, even now, a small sign of personal achievement.

The traffic wove and schemed around them. The blast of horns and the roar of speeding engines was filtered in the air-conditioned interior.

Ahead, over the driver's shoulder, he saw a Land Rover Discovery pull up to the kerb. A blonde woman, quite young and European, stepped out and kids spilled from the back.

He could see the nape of a young man's neck tilted back against the driver's headrest. An Arab, holding a plastic bag, paused by the near side door, hesitated on the pavement.

His own driver was slowing: the traffic-lights in front were against them. Around his car he heard the scream of brakes. God, worse than castration for these people would be the loss of their vehicle's horn. The Arab crouched, was hidden by the Discovery, and when he stood again he no longer held the plastic bag.

The lights changed, and suddenly the Arab was running.

The driver saw nothing, concentrated on the surge of the traffic towards the junction. The plastic bag was half under the rear door of the Discovery. There was a waft of cigarette smoke through the front window on which a tanned elbow rested.

Bart knew. Every three months, in batches, expatriates were summoned to the embassy for sessions with the security officer, and Eddie Wroughton would usually slope in, unannounced and without introductions, and stand at the back as the security officer briefed the audience of bankers, accountants, surveyors and defence-equipment engineers on precautions that should be taken, where the no-go areas were and the dangers. During the war, when Al Jazeera and Abu Dhabi TV had pumped out, twenty-four/seven, images of destruction and mutilation in Iraq, expatriates had been advised to stay at home, keep off the streets and boycott work. Now the families were back, but 'Care should at all times be exercised', the security officer had said, at the last briefing Bart had attended. Usual routes should be varied and vehicles should not be left on the street; it was sensible to check under a car each morning. Bart understood what he had seen. He sat rigidly upright in the back of the car.

They passed the Discovery.

He said nothing. He saw the young man lounging, relaxed, in the driver's seat, waiting while the wife and kids browsed in a jeweller's shop. Through the plate-glass front of the shop, he saw a flash of the young mother's hair and the kids beside her. His own driver accelerated. Then they passed the Arab, sprinting, and his *thobe* billowed against his legs as he ran. His face was close to Bart. He seemed to be reciting, his lips moved as if in prayer, his eyes were behind spectacles, his cheeks were clean and his moustache trimmed – he was like any other of the young men who paraded the pavements and hospital corridors, and sat behind ministry desks. His driver was picking up speed. The Arab was lost from Bart's view. He had swivelled in the back seat, inside the constraint of the belt, and looked back at the Discovery, could just see the young man's face: first posting abroad, making the sort of money he could not hope to match back home, living in a villa with servants and a pool for the kids, and . . . The Discovery was a hundred yards behind them. They went through the junction.

He could have turned his head away, looked instead over his own driver's shoulder, but did not.

He saw the flash, its blinding light.

He saw a door come off and cannon across the pavement into the glass of the jeweller's window. Then a bonnet. The Discovery seemed to be lifted up, and when it came down the duststorm gathered round it. There was the thunder. His driver braked. Every vehicle around them braked. They were spewed across the road, jamming it.

Bart imagined . . . His own driver swung his body and lifted the medical bag – black leather and embossed with the initials S.A.L.B. – off the front seat and was passing it into the back . . . Bart imagined the blood spurting from severed arteries, legs amputated because they always were in a vehicle explosion, a head crushed against a shattered windscreen. Hardly turning from what he watched, Bart pushed away the medical bag. He imagined the young woman frozen in the jeweller's shop, cut by glass, and the kids clinging to her legs. He imagined the quiet groans of the young man in the Discovery, as the pallor settled on his face, because death from vehicle explosions always came later, in Accident and Emergency. He knew it because he had seen it when his life was a greater lie.

He faced his driver, who still clung to the medical bag, which held the morphine and syringes that killed pain when death was inevitable. What he should have done, what he had practised and become expert at before moving to the Kingdom, was debridement. If there had been the smallest chance of saving life, there in the road while the patient groaned in shock and pain, he could have cut out the wounds and lifted clear with forceps – they were in his bag – the worst of the blast's debris: plastic from the dashboard, cloth material from the seating, clothing, old techniques developed by Napoleonic surgeons and still valid.

'Drive on,' Bart said.

Amazement and confusion wreathed the driver's face. Bart was a qualified medical doctor, had passed the exams and been inducted as a member of the Royal College of General Practitioners. He had sworn the oath named after the father of medicine, Hippocrates, to follow the ethics and duties required of him. He was, he knew it, dirt ... Did he care? So much of his life was betrayal. He did not care. 'Don't get involved, don't get caught up' was the mantra of expatriates in the Kingdom. 'Don't put your nose in because no one'll thank you and you'll get it bitten off instead' ... Fuck the shirts, screw the ethics, fuck the ties and screw the duties ... The oath had been sworn too long ago. He hated himself, and disgust squirmed in him.

'Where to, Doctor?' the driver asked.

'Back to the villa, I think. Thank you.'

When the traffic moved, when the sirens were in the road, they drove away.

Bart had justification to hate himself.

Al Maz'an village, near Jenin, Occupied West Bank.

The patient had acute diarrhoea.

He had been called by the patient's father. It was now four months since he had been embedded in the Palestinian community, and trust for him was growing.

Bart was escorted into the bedroom. In low light other members of the family ringed the walls, but only the mother was beside the bed where the girl lay. Four months before, the smell would have made Bart retch; he was used to it now. The mother held her daughter's hand and spoke soft, comforting words to her.

What astonished Bart was that the whole of the village was not laid out prostrate with acute diarrhoea. That part of the village was a shantytown of homes thrown together with corrugated iron, canvas and packing-case boards. No sanitation or running water. When he had left his car he had seen that this corner of the village used an open sewer.

The girl was pale and weak from dehydration. He had learned already that hospitalization was not an option for the shanty's community. At home – at what he still thought of as home – there would have been an express ambulance ride to the Royal Devon and Exeter. He was not at home, and likely never would be. Clean drinking water, care and love were the best that the girl could hope for. He had the water, and the parents would give the care and love. From the father's description of his daughter's symptoms, Bart had known what to expect, and had brought with him four two-litre bottles of Evian water, and he told the mother how much should be given by spoon to the girl and how often; he made a point of urging her to wash the spoon in boiled water. There was a picture of Arafat on a wall and, near to it, another of a young man with doe dead eyes and a red cloth band tight round his forehead. Bart never talked politics in the village, never talked of the struggle of Arafat's people, never passed comment on the martyrdom of the suicide bombers. He did not have to. The whole village, the shanty area and the homes round the central square, knew of his bitter denunciation of the military at the roadblock outside the village. He was the worm in the apple's core. The door at the back of the room was open. Beyond it was a cooking lean-to with a table and bowls for washing, and a stove threw off the scent of damp, burning wood. It was not warm enough for rain, not cold enough for snow; the weather was driving wet sleet. What blankets they had were piled on the girl's bed, and he thought the other children and the parents would sleep cold that night, if they slept. The girl was a waif, reduced by the severity of the diarrhoea, but he smiled warmly and predicted she would be fine. At the back of the cooking area there was another door and from it came the draught.

The main door, behind Bart, which opened on to the mud alleyway where the open sewer ran, creaked open and the wind was carried inside. He saw the mother look up and flinch. Bart did not react. It was what they had told him: he should react to nothing, however minor and however major: to react was to betray himself, betrayal was death. He was saying when he would next visit, at what time the next evening. He heard the boots. The mother had flinched when the first man had entered, but her face lit with brief relief, traced with concern, at the sight of the second or the third. Bart saw a smile glimmer on the face of the sick child. Three young men crossed the room, and the last momentarily hugged the father and grinned at the girl; the third would have been the son, the brother. The face of the third young man was on the edge of Bart's vision: a good face, a strong face, a fighter's face. Bart talked about the next visit, and the need for quiet for the girl, as if that were possible in the shanty where the families were crushed together – refugees from the destruction of inner Jenin when the tanks had come in seven months before – and he had the mother's hand in his, as reassurance for her. The three young men went through the cooking area and outside into a small yard with a shed of nailed-together plywood and planks. They disappeared inside it. He recognized the face of the son, the brother. The last time he had seen it had been in a photograph album, front on and profile, monochrome, with a serial number written underneath it.

The mother clung to his hand. Did she believe him? Could the decline of her daughter be arrested?

He smiled back his best smile. 'Trust me.'

He left them.

Do nothing that creates suspicion, they had told him. 'If you make suspicion, Bart, you will be watched. If you make the smallest mistake when you are watched, you condemn yourself. A condemned man is a dead man,' they had told him. He had lingered at the outer door with the father, had held his arm tightly and had remembered the features of the face of the father's son. He had gone to another patient, who had the symptoms of hepatitis, an old woman, and to the home of a small child with post-traumatic stress syndrome, and then he had driven to the roadblock.

He shouted at the soldiers, Israelis the same age as the three young Palestinians, bawled at them as they ordered him out of his car. 'Oh, yes? What are you looking for this time? The way you behave is criminal.'

He was quickly propelled into the hut – larger and warmer than the one in the yard of a home in the shanty part of the village. Joseph made him coffee.

When the coffee had warmed Bart, the album of photographs was retrieved from a safe. He had a good memory, excellent recall. Within five minutes, after eight pages, he had identified the young man. Joseph was expressionless, did not congratulate him and did not tell him what importance the young man was given. Did Joseph admire his agent, or did he consider him scum? Immaterial, really – neither the admiration nor the contempt of the Shin Beth officer would have freed Bart from the treadmill he walked on. Joseph took him to the door.

Back out in the street, Bart shouted, 'Just you wait, your time will come. Justice will catch you. You are as much a criminal, in wilfully obstructing a doctor of medicine, as any of those Serbs at The Hague. I wonder, after what you do, how you can sleep at night – no decent man would sleep.'

He drove away through the chicane of concrete blocks, and the sullen eyes of soldiers tracked him.

*

Marty took *First Lady* up for the first time from Shaybah.

He could not see her as she sped along the runway: the windows of the Ground Control Station looked out over their tent camp. The Predator, MQ-1, needed sixteen hundred metres of runway to get airborne. Lizzy-Jo called the variants of cross-wind, but they were inside what was manageable – hadn't been the day before.

The first flight since she'd been unloaded from her coffin and put back together would be an hour, not a lot more, but they'd get to the ceiling of altitude and go on maximum speed and loiter speed, and they'd run *First Lady*'s cameras and infra-red systems, all the gear. They'd check the satellite link to Langley and that the Agency floor in Riyadh had a real-time picture. The lift-off was fine. The forward camera showed the perimeter fence disappearing beneath them, and then there was the sand, only the sand. His place was in the Ground Control Station with the joystick in his hands and the screens in front of him, but where he'd like to have been was outside with his hand shading his eyes, watching her go. She was the most beautiful thing he knew. Back at Bagram, Marty had always wanted to know when the other Agency birds, or the USAF MQ-1s, were going up. Like a bird, such grace . . . Worst thing he'd known was a ride on a Black Hawk and seeing, below the helicopter, the wreckage of an Air Force Predator that had gone down with on-wing icing; a broken bird, shattered, scattered among rocks. His bird, *First Lady*, had a maximum operational radius of five hundred nautical miles and an operational endurance time of twenty-four hours, but for the first flight they'd do little more than an hour with close to seventy-five nautical miles covered.

Lizzy-Jo talked first to Langley. Yes, they read her well. Yes, the pictures were good. She switched to Riyadh.

They'd taken off away from the control tower, and away from the cluster of office buildings and accommodation blocks. The control tower had had to be informed of their presence and of all their flight movements: it had a vaguely worded sheet of paper from the Prince Sultan base up at Al Kharj: test-flying, evaluation of performance in extreme heat conditions – the bare minimum.

The zooms on the belly camera showed wide landscapes, then blurred till they refocused on the individual rims of dunes. Marty thought the place had beauty, but the pilot's talk still hurt him. The guy who'd parachuted down from the Navy's Hornet had done what was right, stayed by the wreckage and died of thirst and heat stroke. He reflected that beauty did not have to be kind: there could be dangerous beauty. She'd found a bush, a bush that was ten feet high and maybe six feet across, and he had *First Lady* at twelve thousand feet and climbing at a ground speed of seventy-three nautical miles per hour. Lizzy-Jo had a bush to show to Riyadh. On the screen, the bush was clear and all of its branches and most of what leaves it had.

'That's cute,' she said, into the bar microphone over her mouth. 'There you are, Mr Gonsalves – fantastic! Life is up and running in the Empty Quarter. Wow . . .'

The voice came back over Marty's headphones. 'Incredible, I've never seen that before. Extraordinary. You could recognize a man, one man. I am in awe . . .'

But the wind, at that altitude, caught *First Lady* and tossed her, like she was a child's model, and the bush was lost and the picture, for all the gyroscopic kit, rocked and wavered.

'Correction, I *was* in awe – is that the wind?'

Marty said, 'It was the wind, sir. Understand me, I'm not making excuses here, but this will not be an easy place to fly out of.'

'It's where we are, you are. Can't base in French Djibouti, too long a range. If it was at Prince Sultan, we're telling the world, a hostile one, where we are and what we're at . . . It's about security. You got to live with the wind. You got to learn to fly with the wind. Security is paramount. They have a saying here: "You want to send a message, then tell it – and swear her to secrecy – to your daughter-in-law." You don't talk to anyone outside your perimeter and, most certain, you do not permit anyone entry. You draw as little attention to yourselves as possible. It's like these people, who hate us, have their ears down on the railtracks. I tell you, believe it, security counts . . . But you can fly there, no problem, right?'

Marty said, 'We can fly here.'

Lizzy-Jo muttered, 'I'm not about to promise how effective we'll be.'

Marty said, 'Don't worry. We'll get the show on the road.'

'I got a meeting – thanks, guys.'

Marty chipped, 'You didn't tell us when you were down here – if we get a target, what's the status?'

'You'll have Hellfire on the wings when you go operational. I'm running late for my meeting . . . If I'm right in what I'm predicting, and it's a courier route, then you track, but if you're at the end of your fuel load and can't stay and track, then a target is "shoot on sight". Adios, amigos.'

The static burst in Marty's headphones. He threw the switch and cut the link. He felt the excitement and looked at her. Lizzy-Jo winked a big brown eye at him. *Shoot on sight*.

They had all prayed, even Tommy.

Caleb thought it a mark of the brutality all around them that when they had reached the stop point of the day, with the light going down on the dunes, they had made a line and sunk to their knees. Then he and the boy had gone foraging, and left Rashid to build the night camp and hoist the tents.

It amazed him. On the whole of the day's march, he had seen no wood – nothing that lived and nothing that was even long dead. The pain had throbbed on the soles of his feet even as the sand had cooled and he had been self-absorbed by his discomfort and his pursuit of respect. Three times, where Caleb had only seen ochre sand the boy crouched and scrabbled with his hands like a burrowing rabbit and had triumphantly produced dried-out roots.

The roots were brought back, broken and lit. Rashid used the old ways – worked his hands under the smallest and narrowest of the stems, sliced a flint across the blade of his knife, again and again, until the spark made smoke and then flame. The fire darkened the desert beyond the small circle of its light and the outline of the tents.

Caleb watched. He had much to learn.

Where the fire flared, Rashid scooped a hole under the widening embers, not seeming to feel pain. He had a metal bowl filled with flour and he sprinkled salt on it, then sparingly poured water on to the flour and kneaded the mess to little shapes. When he'd worked them and was satisfied he put the shapes into the hole and pushed sand over them. Their eyes met.

Rashid, the guide, stared at Caleb's feet. Caleb tried to read him. Was he impressed? Rashid had the face of a wolf. Under his headcloth, held loosely in place with rope, his forehead was lined and wrinkled, his narrow eyes savaged what they lighted on and his nose was as prominent as a hook. Thin lips were above and below yellowed, uneven teeth and around them a tangle of hairs made the moustache and beard. No comment was given. Rashid moved on, hid his feelings. There was no sign of respect.

When the sun had gone, before the moon was up and when the blackness cloaked them beyond the little fire's range, Ghaffur took the bread from the hole, shook off the sand and passed each of them two pieces. Rashid measured the water ration, poured a cupful. They ate the bread, drank from the cup and passed it back. Then they were given three dates. Caleb held them in his mouth and sucked until the stones had no more fruit on them.

He said quietly to the Egyptian, 'What are you doing here? Why are you with me? What is my importance?'

Hosni smiled and the shadows of the fire crackled across his face. He blinked and Caleb saw the opaque gloss on his eyes.

'In the morning, perhaps . . .'

Inside the cool of the tent, the pain at last ebbed from Caleb's feet. He knew so little. If the memories had crossed the chasm, he would have known more. He slept dreamlessly, his mind as dark as the night outside the tent.

Chapter Six

The scream pierced the morning air.

Startled, Caleb looked around. He saw the guide, Rashid, loading the boxes on to the pack camels, with his son, Ghaffur. Fahd was clumsily folding the tents. Hosni kicked sand over what was left of the night's fire that the signs of it might be hidden.

The scream was terror, from the depths of a man.

He saw the Iraqi, Tommy. Tommy had never, not since they had set out into the desert, helped with the loading of the boxes or with folding the tents, as if that were beneath the dignity once belonging to him. Tommy had walked away after they had eaten the last of the bread baked the evening before. Once the work to move off had started, he had walked fifty paces, or sixty, from the camp and had squatted to defecate. That completed, he had sat apart from them and watched them as if he were not a part of them.

The scream shrieked for help.

As Caleb saw it, the Iraqi sat with his hands out behind him to support his weight, his legs stretched in front of him. He was rigid, as if not daring to move, staring down at the skin between his boots and the hem of his trousers.

The guide was the first to react. Rashid ran with a short, scurrying stride towards Tommy, and Ghaffur followed. Hosni looked into the distance, at the direction of the scream, but seemed unable to identify its source. Fahd scrambled to catch the guide but when he was at the Bedouin's shoulder, he was abruptly pushed away. Caleb went slowly after them, but hung back.

He looked past Rashid, gazed at the Iraqi. He stared at the eyes, which were distended, he raked over the chest and the open jacket and on to the trousers, still unfastened, and around the groin, then on down to the trembling ankles. Caleb saw the scorpion.

The sun, not yet high, fell on the scorpion's back, identified each marking on it. It was small, would have fitted into the palm of his hand. Its head was hidden in a fold of the trouser leg, but the tail was clear. It was arched over its back, and below it was an angry reddening swell with a puncture hole at its centre.

Tears rolled on Tommy's cheeks, his lips quivered. The scorpion was still, but the tail was up, poised for a second strike, and Caleb could see the needle at its tip. Rashid allowed only his son, Ghaffur, to come forward.

The man and the boy were at either side of Tommy's legs. Each knelt, then each edged slowly towards the legs, until they were within a hand's reach of the ankles and the scorpion. Caleb heard Rashid murmur to the Iraqi, but could not hear what he said. Then he spoke, with great gentleness, to his child. Caleb saw Ghaffur, so slowly, rock backwards and forwards, as if he prepared to strike with the speed of the scorpion. Father and son kept their bodies and heads low, almost to the sand, so that their shadows did not pass over the legs and the scorpion.

The father did not tell the son when or how, had trust in him, as though he knew his son's reactions and movements would be faster than his own, he would make a better strike than himself. The trembling spread from Tommy's head to his chest and hips; if he could not control it, if the creature were further disturbed, more venom would be injected into him.

Ghaffur's hand flashed forward.

Caleb gasped.

The finger and thumb, delicate, slight and unprotected, caught the tail half an inch from the poison tip . . . and then the boy was grinning and holding up the writhing little creature. The Iraqi seemed to have fainted. Ghaffur marched with the scorpion first to Fahd, who flinched away, then held it in front of Hosni's dulled eyes, then brought it to Caleb. The scorpion thrashed and its pincers, limbs, body and head crawled against Ghaffur's hand; small spurts of venom came from the needle tip. Caleb saw, momentarily, the pride on the father's face before the mask slipped back. The boy took the knife from his belt and, with a slash as fast as his strike had been, he cut the tail from the body. The scorpion fell at his feet, writhing, then the boy threw the tail and its tip carelessly over his shoulder.

Rashid used his fingernail to stroke the bitten wound.

The yellowish body and legs and the darker pincers of the scorpion were still, dead in the sand.

Rashid's fingernail stroked towards the centre of the swollen place, where the pinprick was, pushing the venom back from the extremities and towards the hole.

Rashid barked an instruction at his son.

Caleb followed Ghaffur. The boy returned to the camels, bent close to them and started to refasten the hobble ropes.

'What does your father say?'

'My father says the man is not fit to travel, that we will lose half a day before he is well enough to move. My father says we have to wait until he is stronger . . It is bad.'

'You did well with it.'

'Where you come from, are there no scorpions?'

Caleb grimaced, was guarded against the question. There had been scorpions at X-Ray and Delta, only once had a guard been bitten, many scorpions in the corridors and cages and the guards had stamped their heavy boots on them or the prisoners had flattened them with their sandals. He lied: 'I have never seen a scorpion before.'

The boy shrugged. 'It is easy to kill them . . . but we may lose half a day and that angers my father.'

Away across the sand, near the dune wall, Rashid had torn a strip of cloth to a bandage width and was binding it round the Iraqi's shin, just below the knee. He began again to stroke his fingernail across the swelling.

Caleb went to the Egyptian. 'We will lose half a day's march.

We cannot move until he has recovered. It was a revolting creature.'

'Any snake is revolting,' Hosni said, with bitterness.

'Yes, any snake.' Caleb stared at the dulled eyes, and knew.

'I did not see it well, I stayed back. I saw the boy take the head off. Was it a viper?'

'I don't know snakes,' Caleb said. 'Last night I asked you – why do you travel with me? Why am I important?'

'Important? Because of where you come from. Think on it, where you have come from. They tell me you are not a believer – to us you are the Outsider. That is what you have to consider when you ask of your importance. Can you admit it, where you come from?'

'From the 055 Brigade – from Guantanamo.'

'And before you were recruited?'

Caleb took sand in his hands and let the grains fall between his fingers. Before the wedding and his recruitment was the darkness he had imposed. He remembered arriving in his suit, with Farooq and Amin, at the celebration after the wedding, and remembered the way that the Chechen had watched him, then set tests for him; everything before was in blackness. The next morning he had left – and he could remember it clearly – Landi Khotal before dawn; he had been told by the Chechen that he should forget his friends, Farooq and Amin. A pickup had taken him through the border and through the last of the narrow passes, and he had been brought to Jalalabad, and then straight on to the camp. At the camp, two days later, two postcards had been given him. The reverse pictures on the postcards had not been shown him, but he had read the words 'Opera House' and 'Ayers Rock', and he had written two bland messages that he was well – and on each he had written a name and an address, but the name and the address were now erased from his mind. A small, tired smile played on the Egyptian's face.

'You are the Outsider, you are separated from us – I am not offended. To us, the Outsider is the most valuable. He can go where we cannot. He has access where we do not. He can walk unseen where we are noticed. Who are we? Lesser creatures. What use do we have? Small, nothing that is strategic. We will watch you go, and we will pray for you, after you have disappeared into darkness, but we will listen to the radio and will hope to learn that the trust given you was not wrongly placed.'

Once the Iraqi cried out, the only sound against the whisper of the Egyptian's voice and the restless grunting of the hobbled camels. Hosni's fingers, stubbed and wrinkled, came and touched Caleb's face and they moved across his features, as if discovering them, ran over his nose and his chin, through the hairs round his mouth, and it was a long time before they dropped away.

'Don't go all shy on me – what did your Miss Jenkins have to say for herself?'

Eddie Wroughton always varied the meeting-places with Samuel Bartholomew: a bookshop, a museum, a hotel lobby . . . The hotel was sumptuous, fitted to the highest specifications of carpets on marble flooring, lighting and furnishing. He'd ordered the orange juice, which was garnished with lemon slices, but Bartholomew hadn't touched his.

'She paid for the consultation, didn't she? Strong as a good bay mare, I'd have said. So, what did she say?'

Opposite him, Bartholomew sat hunched, pudgy head in pudgy hands. There was a cool, comfortable temperature in the lobby, but Bartholomew sweated.

'Come on, come on . . . all right, I'll remind you. She is friendly with the deputy governor of the province, friendly enough to be allowed to live down there – what's his pillow talk? Didn't she gossip just a little? Such a wonderful consultation-room manner you have . . .' Wroughton leached sarcasm. 'Surely a few minor confidences were exchanged as you poked round her. While she had your disgusting fingers crawling over her, surely there was some gossip. Be a good chap, cough it up.'

He knew he frightened the man, that he was supine. At the age of forty-one, Wroughton was young to be station chief at so prestigious a posting as Riyadh. His last two overseas bases had been in Sarajevo and Riga, but now he was top league. There was one overriding catastrophe in his life, a cloud that darkened the sun's glory: he had no money. He lived off his salary, spent cash only on what could be seen, was a pauper behind the privacy of his front door. There was no investment portfolio ticking over in London, only a rabbit hutch of an apartment on the wrong side of Pimlico. His poverty was kept as hidden as his sharpness and intelligence: playing a wealthy dandy, a buffoon, did him well . . . But the irritation at the lack of personal money was only battened down by his workload. He lived for work.

'I don't push business your way out of the goodness of my soul. I expect payback. Miss Jenkins is down there in the sand, a place where a saint wouldn't survive. Didn't you pedal a bit faster, just a little? She's unique where she is, might just be the most interesting corner of this whole hideous place – she goes out into the desert. Got eyes in her head, hasn't she? What did you talk about? Her menstrual cycle?'

Money, promotion, status in the Service, had never mattered to Wroughton's father, or to his grandfather. He was from a dynasty – not a financial dynasty, but a dynasty based on the precept that a grateful population must be allowed to sleep safe in bed. His father had done time in Moscow and Prague during the Cold War; his mother had been in Library, sifting, filing and annotating, until his birth. His grandfather had been seconded to MI5 after the Dunkirk evacuation, and then had had a good war turning the agents the Abwehr parachuted in and having them broadcast back misinformation; his great-uncle had hunted down war criminals after VE Day, and enough to have filled a small bus had gone on the dawn walk to the gallows. All through his childhood, at Sunday lunches, the glories of intelligence and counter-intelligence had been preached. No chance he could have gone elsewhere. He had been groomed as a youth for the Secret Intelligence Service. To Wroughton, Bartholomew was more pathetic than the agents his father had run behind the Iron Curtain, more pitiful than the turned Germans who saved their skins, more disgusting than the hanged butchers.

'I sometimes think you forget your situation – do you? If we cut you adrift, then slip the word round, you're a gone man. Those nice little accounts, earning a low rate of interest but safe – the nest-egg for the future – can each have funds withdrawn at the pressing of a button. We have any number of people who specialize in that. Didn't you know? With your history, a quiet word from me, and your future is sleeping under cardboard beside Waterloo station. Just that I some-times think it's necessary to remind you . . . If she ever comes back to you from that trackless wilderness, make sure she's pumped dry – there's a good chap.'

To reinforce it, emphasize his argument, Wroughton manoeuvred his right foot's brogue, then kicked hard against Bartholomew's left ankle. Wroughton had never believed his mother had liked him, let alone loved him, or that his father had respected him. On the day of his first induction interview at the Service, his grandfather had offered him the stern advice that he should look in the City for employment, but Eddie Wroughton had never flinched from meting out punishment to this repellent man. Most of his work was in the sifting of publications, less of it was in mixing with the Saudi élite, as they liked to be regarded, a little of it was cohabiting in the gutter with scum. Bartholomew was scum. The best of it was with Juan Gonsalves, his friend. The best brought the praise from London, the certainty of advancement and the probability of an augmented salary.

'If she comes and sees you again with as much as a pimple on her sweet little shin, then you gut her and fillet her, and you damn well learn something of what goes on down in that bloody place. Don't snivel. Plenty goes on there, and she'll know it. I don't think you're big on scruples, so it shouldn't be too hard.'

He kicked again, then stood. He looked down on Bartholomew.

From his pocket, Wroughton took a slip of paper. A name was written on it, and an address. 'Go and see her, take the time. Give her a bit of tender and loving care, what you're so good at. And learn something – what she saw, what, if anything, was shouted out, any warning or any denunciation. Then report back – course you will.'

'Where'll you be?' The voice squeaked from between the hands.

'Away for a couple of days, then I'll hear from you ... All that perspiration, it makes you look old and revolting. Do something about it ... You haven't finished your juice. It's thirty *riyals* a glass, don't waste it.'

Wroughton smiled sweetly at the concierge who held open the outer door for him. He had no conscience as to dealing out a bully's blows at Samuel Bartholomew. From his childhood days at the Sunday lunch table he had learned that the relationship between handler and agent should be master and servant: no emotion, no affection, no relationship. Like dogs, they should be at heel and obedient.

*

Lack of engine thrust had grounded *First Lady*. The four-cylinder Rotax 912 push engine was playing delicate. George wanted time on it, half a day.

They'd already had *Carnival Girl* up once, but she was back-up – so, George would have his half a day, and Lizzy-Jo could kick her heels.

She had her problem.

It was not a problem to be discussed with Marty, most certainly not with any of the rest of the team. Marty was in the tent beside the Ground Control Station, was by the fan that circulated stinking hot air, had his feet up and was reading back numbers of *Flight International*.

'I'm going to go find a shop,' she told him, but he was too absorbed with the magazine and last year's articles to respond with anything more than a grunt.

'I need to look for a shop,' she called to George, and he looked up from the engine pieces and nodded.

'I need to do some shopping, won't be long,' she said to the armourer, who sat facing the space left in the barbed wire coiled round their perimeter. He wore a multi-pocket khaki waistcoat that concealed his shoulder holster and the Colt. He had a baseball cap low over his face, and he shrugged.

There must be a shop.

The encampment was at the extreme end of the runway. Beyond their own wire was a single strand fence, then the desert, and set in the sands in the near distance were the landing lights of the strip. Half-way up the strip, on the far side, was the cluster of buildings that she presumed were the accommodation blocks for the workers: there would be a club, a gym, a clinic – and a shop.

She walked briskly. As a New Yorker, she walked everywhere briskly. The temperature on the thermometer hanging from the support pole of her tent had shown 98° Fahrenheit, in shade. For decorum, local sensibilities and that crap, she had a blouse over her T-shirt and she'd slipped on long loose trousers and had a headscarf over her hair. She skirted the end of the runway, looking up to check there wasn't an incoming flight that might, if the wheels were down, have taken her head off.

Selfishness had brought Lizzy-Jo to Shaybah. The electronics expert was a selfish woman; she had made a career out of selfishness ever since the Air Force had sent her on the sensor operator's course. She had been with Predator from the start.

At the far side of the strip, she turned and started out on the long tramp to the buildings – she could have taken wheels, but the restrictions on their movements away from the encampment would have meant the fullest of explanations about her problem to the armourer and to George and Marty . . . Her problem was not theirs.

She'd done Air Force time, then seen the recruitment notice posted by the Agency for UAV personnel. She'd left the Air Force and been taken on by the Agency, and then the selfishness had ruled. Rick had been with her at the Air Force camps, and Clara, but the Agency didn't do married accompanied. Rick sold insurance now in North Carolina, and last year had been his company's Salesman of the Year in the state; his parents looked after Clara. They'd divorced while she was at Taszar, Hungary, doing sensor operator for flying over Kosovo, a long-range divorce that spared her meetings in lawyers' offices. And she was not, it was her justification for selfishness, a natural mother. What Rick wanted out of life was to sell death benefits to customers; what she wanted was to find pictures on *First Lady*'s cameras.

The heat shimmered on the dun-painted buildings ahead, and the sunlight burst back from the buildings' windows, and behind them was the city of pipes and containers, cranes and stacks.

She had seen that Marty had his old Afghan war picture propped against the metal cupboard beside his cot; Lizzy-Jo had a small tent to herself, woman's privilege, and beside her bed a collapsible side table with the picture of Rick and Clara – she assumed that Rick had a picture of her beside his bed. Not that it mattered to her. She wrote to them, not more than a page, every three or four months, birthdays and Christmas, and once a year she wrote to her own people in New York; her own people, she knew, didn't hold with divorce, were fervent Christians, and disapproved of her abandonment of Clara. It was tough shit, for all of them. She wanted to be with the Predator team, and reckoned the eighteen months of Operation Enduring Freedom, out of Bagram, had been the best time of her life. She didn't regard herself as selfish, just as professional. It mattered to her.

She was closer. Lizzy-Jo could make out what she thought

was a recreational building, fronted by a veranda. She hit her stride.

There was a sign for a shop, and she followed its arrow.

She walked inside and the air-conditioned cool punched her.

She followed the shelves, wove among men – some in robes, some in slacks and shirts – who carried wire baskets or pushed trolleys. There was food, frozen trays, vegetables and fruit. Confectionery – chocolates and boiled sweets. Clothes, for men. Toiletries, for men, and cosmetics, for men. Juices of every shade and taste. Stationery and software. Music DVDs and compacts . . . Then she found the chemist's section. Headache pills, sunstroke creams, insect repellents. Eyes were on her. When she met them, they dropped or turned away, but she felt that as soon as the eyes were behind her again they fastened back on to her, clung to her.

But the problem had to be answered.

It was part her own fault, and part the Agency's. The instruction to travel and the take-off from Bagram had given her too little time. Too many of the few hours available between the order and the flight out had been taken up with downloading the computers and checking the loading of the gear; they were her computers, her gear, and she had fussed over them, not permitting the technicians free range over what was hers – and she had not been to the base shop.

She joined the queue to the cash desk. The man in front of her, robed, edged away from her, pushed against the man in front so that a distance might be between her and him. Oh, sweet Jesus . . . At the cash desk an older man, a dish-towel over his head, a moustache and fat jowls, repeated in a strident voice everything asked of him by his customers.

She was next to the head of the queue. The customer in front of her paid for a bag of fruit and a tube of shaving soap. She said it again, to herself, and she could feel the sweat on her back. The cash-desk man looked up at her, then averted his eyes.

Lizzy-Jo said it out loud, like she would have done in a New York drug store. 'Do you have tampons?'

'Tampons?'

'That's what I said. Tampons. If you have them, I can't see them.'

'Tampons?'

'It's a pretty simple question – what your wife . . .'

The cash-desk man shook his head, a great rolling movement.

The voice behind Lizzy-Jo was crisp, clear English. 'No, they don't.'

Lizzy-Jo spun. Eyes dropped, swivelled, fell from her. Six back in the queue was a woman, younger than herself, and she caught the grin like it was contagious. 'They don't have tampons?'

'No – not a great call for them here. Look, why don't you wait outside, or by the door? I'll sort you out.'

Lizzy-Jo went past the younger woman and saw that her basket contained an insect repellent spray, an anti-inflammatory cream and sunblock.

So, Lizzy-Jo met Beth, who took her to the club. They sat out on the veranda and were shaded by a table parasol. They drank iced lemon juice, and she learned that Beth Jenkins was the only woman resident with the run of the Shaybah oil-production works.

'And I'm assuming you're with those little aircraft. I saw one take off, a pretty little thing. Why here?'

Lizzy-Jo said quickly, too quickly, 'Just test flights, performance evaluation in heat over desert – mapping.'

A little frown puckered the young woman's forehead: she would have thought there were about a million and ten places that were easier for that evaluation, and a hundred thousand and ten places that were more of a priority for mapping. The explanation was not queried.

'Anyway, can't stay. I've an English literature class, my top group. We're doing Dickens, *Oliver Twist*. They like that, bestial English society, makes them feel good. Got to go. How long have I got? You desperate?'

'Not now. I will be by the end of the week.'

'I'll drop some by . . . Don't worry, my tongue doesn't flap, I won't see anything.'

As she walked back along the side of the runway strip, Lizzy-Jo reflected that she'd made a poor job of the security of the mission, but maybe just once security took second place. Tampons counted. She reflected, also, as she turned at the strip's end, that a young woman who took a stranger for a drink when she was short of time and late on a class commitment was lonely – not alone but lonely. Lizzy-Jo didn't do loneliness, but the thought of it frightened her.

George and his technicians had the casing back on the engine, and were standing back from *First Lady*. The light caught the forward fuselage, clean and virgin. She remembered the words loud in her headphones. 'Shoot on sight.'

They had lost half a day. Worse than the hours lost was the water used. Caleb watched the pot brought to the boil. And more of the withered dry roots that Ghaffur had kept the fire alive with. Rashid took the sodden plants from the pot, clasped them in his hand and seemed not to feel any pain as the scalding water seeped between his fingers. The plants were slapped on Tommy's inflamed ankle, the Iraqi cried out, then rags were bound over them. Tommy writhed. There was no sympathy from the guide. Caleb sensed Rashid's concern: what to do with the water? Wait for it to cool? More time gone. Throw it on to the sand?

'What is that?' Caleb asked.

The reply was curt. 'It is ram-ram.'

'Is it an old cure?'

'What my father would have used, and my grandfather.'

'Tell me.'

'We learn from the Sands. There are lizards. They are not bitten by the snakes, not bitten by the scorpions. We watch and we learn, and we hand down what we know. The lizards eat the ram-ram plant, and they roll in it, wherever they find it. It is a protection against the poison.'

It was said matter-of-factly, without feeling. First the majority of the venom had been drawn out by the stroking fingernails, now the poultice would extract what remained. Old practices and old times. At Camp Delta, when the guard had been stung by the scorpion alarms had rung, medics had charged to the scene, an ambulance had come with the siren wailing, panic had been alive, and within two days the guard had been returned to the block. That was the new way, but the old way of Rashid had been quiet, calm and competent.

Rashid swung his foot, kicked over the pot and the water momentarily stained the sand. Then he shouted for Ghaffur to pick up the pot and stow it. The guide lifted Tommy on to his shoulder, carried him to the kneeling camel and heaved him on to the saddle on the hump. Again Tommy cried out, again his pain was ignored. The caravan moved on. The wisp of smoke from the fire was left behind them.

Caleb walked beside Hosni, who rolled on his saddle. Twice Caleb reached up to steady the Egyptian; it was not a journey for a man of his age. The question welled in him. 'What is the first thing that I should know?'

The voice wheezed, 'You should know your only loyalty is to your family, us and those who wait for you.'

'And the second thing?'

'Your duty is to your brothers, us and those who wait for you.'

Again he put the question. What should he know?

'You have no nationality, it is behind you. None of us has a country. We are the rejected. Tommy would be taken by the Americans, or their puppets, and would be put before a military court or a sham court of their stooges, and he would be executed . . . Fahd, if he were arrested here, would be tortured by the police, then taken to the square in Riyadh in front of the Central Mosque and beheaded. I, if I were held, would be flown to Cairo and if I survived the interrogation I would be hanged in a prison. And you, you would be . . .' Hosni's voice died.

'What would happen to me?'

No answer. The question was ignored. A new fervour came to the Egyptian. 'You are a jewel to us. Men will give their lives that you should live . . . Is that not enough? At a chosen time you will go back where you came from, or to America. You will be the servant of your family and your brothers, and you will resurrect your memory. You will strike the blow that only you are capable of . . . Enough.'

Hosni's eyes, as if they hurt or disappointed him, were closed.

Caleb dropped back.

'If only he'd come with me,' she sobbed. 'If the silly bugger had come with me, he'd have been all right – but he didn't. He wasn't interested.'

Her behaviour, the anger in it, was predictable to Bart. He knew the pattern from road accidents back in Torquay, and from his time as house physician in London. Melanie Garnett's outburst was what he would have expected. If he'd been called out earlier, just after it had happened, he would have heard a horrified description of the bomb detonating under the Land Rover Discovery.

'No, he wasn't interested in that necklace. He said we were saving money, were supposed to be. We're only here for the mortgage – God, what other reason would anyone be here? He didn't have the guts to tell me I couldn't have it so he stayed in the Discovery.'

Clearest in Bart's mind was the image of the man at the driving-wheel, elbow out through the open window, and the puff of his cigarette smoke. She was a fainter image, blurred behind the glass of the jeweller's shop. He wondered where the children were now – oh, yes, they'd be round at a neighbour's, with the Lego out on the tiled floor. Yesterday there would have been the horror, today would be the anger, tomorrow the guilt. The anger was easier to deal with . . . Even if he had stopped, done his duty as a man of medicine, he would not have been able to save the man.

'He wanted to save for a mortgage so's we could live somewhere posh when this three years of hell was over – somewhere like Beaconsfield or the Chalfonts. And it killed him. Damn him! I mean, what's a three-bedroomed semi in Beaconsfield worth? Worth getting killed for?'

An older woman shared the sofa with Melanie Garnett, widow. She would have been a long-term matriarch of the expatriate society, and knew her stuff. She was doing well, made a soothing listening post with her shoulder, and didn't interrupt . . . Ann would have interrupted. Ann never could keep her mouth shut. Bart examined her. He murmured little questions, not to calm her but to pump information from her. What had she seen? What had she heard? Had there been any threats? Nothing, nothing, and no – nothing seen, nothing heard, no threats. It would be a negative report to Wroughton but he had asked the questions. While he took her pulse and heartbeat, he looked around him. The furnishings were sparse, the decorations minimal; the sense of a home was missing, except for the heap of toys in a corner and children's books on the table. He looked for signs of the familiar expatriates' scam, alcohol boot-legging. Then there would have been flash opulence, but there wasn't any . . . Ann would just have bought the bloody necklace, charged it to his card, and the first he would have known of it was when she wore it. He could blame everything on Ann. The size of the mortgage, the scale of the overdraft, the fees for the private school that the kids had to go to, the two foreign holidays a year, and the remedies he'd sunk to were all down to Ann . . . His mother had come to the wedding, been barely civil, but his father had not. His mother had told him, in a stage-whispered aside, well into the reception, that Ann was common and unsuitable and that her relatives were plainly vulgar – and, thank the good Lord, Hermione Bartholomew had not lived long enough to crow at him that she had been right. In the Kingdom, all the deaths of expatriates by bomb or bullet were put down to alcohol turf wars; this one would be too, but Bart knew better.

He prescribed diazepam, a maximum of ten milligrams a day, two tablets. From his open bag, he took the bottle and counted out sufficient to last three days. He should have felt, beneath the professional exterior, serious sympathy for Melanie Garnett. What had she done to deserve an encounter with a bomber? She was without blame. He was almost shocked at his reaction, as near to being shamed as was possible for him. He put the tablets into an envelope and scrawled the dosage on the label.

'I really wanted that necklace – wasn't a crime to want it. If he'd come with me . . . if he'd come with me just to look after the kids. He didn't come with me, the kids were arguing, and he's dead. What I hate about him, the last I saw of him, properly saw of him, he was all stone-faced and getting his fags out. Not a kiss, not a "love you", not a cuddle, but looking sour. That's the last I saw of him, damn him.'

To his mind, rebellion was alive in the Kingdom and soon, pray God, the whole stinking edifice would come down. Bart had always been good at learning lines but, then, his talent was to play a part – the part of a liar. Against the weeping anger of the widow he was able to recite in his mind, perfect recall: 'My name is Ozymandias, king of kings: / Look on my works, ye Mighty, and despair!' The towers of glass and concrete, airports and luxury hotels, wide highways and people of such mind-numbing arrogance were floating on oil, and the edifice was crumbling. A bomb here and a shooting there, work for the executioner in Chop Chop Square, a frisson of fear eddying into the palaces. Each time he read of, or heard of, an atrocity a little raw excitement coursed in Bart. 'Round the decay / Of that colossal wreck, boundless and bare, / The lone and level sands stretch far away.' He hoped, damn it, that he would still be there to see the decay come to fruition, be able to scent it.

'His mother's on the flight tonight. What am I going to tell her? If her precious son hadn't been so bloody mean to me, his wife, he'd still be alive. Do I tell her that?'

Tomorrow would be worse for the widow. She would have his mother there, organizing her, and she would have her guilt. Post-traumatic stress syndrome would crucify her with guilt. If she had not wanted the bloody necklace, her husband would be alive, her kids would have a father. The guilt would churn like a whirlwind in her mind – poor little cow. Ann had never felt guilt, even when she had brought him to his knees. He went into the kitchen, where a maid cowered, poured a glass of water and carried it back into the room. The matriarch slipped a tablet into Melanie Garnett's mouth, then gave her the glass.

Bart waited until she was quieter, then left. Out in the compound, spied on by the neighbours, the sliver of independence deserted him. He walked to his car, preparing what he would say to Eddie Wroughton. He was in fear of Wroughton, and knew it. He flopped into the back of the car and the driver took him away. He was as pliant as putty, and he knew no route for escape, no track that could free him.

He fumed, but his experience of recent years had taught Eddie Wroughton to mask fury. Had he shouted abuse at the Omani police-man, he would have lost him.

He had been driven a hundred kilometres or so west of the capital to Ad Dari, a trading town *en route* to the interior. He should have been at the police station, in an interrogation room. Instead, he was shivering – with anger and from the cold – in the refrigeration room of the hospital mortuary. The British staffer in Muscat city was green, so lacking in experience with the Secret Intelligence Service that Wroughton – on hearing of the arrest – had caught the first available flight from Riyadh.

The man he should have been questioning, with relish and vigour, was now a corpse, frozen solid. Death had come in a spasm of pain that the refrigeration plant had preserved. The attendants hadn't even closed the man's eyes, which were wide and staring.

'Cardiac arrest, there was nothing we could do,' the Omani intoned.

Yes, there bloody well was. He could have been properly searched on arrest, had goons in his cell and his hands manacled behind his back.

'The autopsy will be tomorrow,' the staffer intoned emptily, like he thought it was his failure. 'Don't know what they'll find.'

Wroughton could have reeled off a list of poisons, right for self-administration, that were quick but painful while they did their work.

He turned away. He had no more need to look down at the trolley and the body. The man was late fifties, or perhaps early sixties, but his age would be confirmed over coffee in the policeman's office. His name and occupation were paramount, particularly the occupation, which had brought Wroughton scurrying off the plane. His last sight of the man was his fat fingers and the width of the two gold rings, one on each hand, over which the flesh bulged.

They walked along the corridor towards an office.

'It was a rumour, Mr Wroughton, from information we received. We acted on it immediately,' the police officer said, ingratiating and ashamed. 'We heard that this prominent *hawaldar* had travelled a few days ago up-country. He was a wealthy man, prominent in his trade, and he had gone to a place where there is only poverty. We said, and I discussed this with your young colleague, that he must be arrested immediately.'

The staffer flinched because now the blame was shared ... Wroughton understood. The western members of the Financial Action Task Force regularly and predictably targeted the Gulf states for the movement of money that benefited Al Qaeda. There had been a gesture of action, and the action had led to catastrophe. The *hawal* system was the nightmare, money moving without paper or electronic trace. And big sums were not needed – an investment of $350,000, wisely spent on flying lessons, simulators and cheap motels, would cost the Americans $200 billion, for the rebuilding of the Twin Towers and the economic losses post the hijackings. What was required was money to follow, to track. Breaking into the *hawal* networks was as big a priority as existed in Eddie Wroughton's life – and the man was dead, the bastard was a stiff. Guilt was proven. A man who took a pill after only cursory questioning was a man harbouring a big secret, a man who would die rather than face in-depth interrogation.

'I'm sure you did the right thing,' Wroughton said, without charity.

There would, of course, be mobile and landline telephone records to work on, but he doubted they would show up anything beyond inconsequential dealings.

They sat. The first coffee was poured into a thimble cup. He sensed a nervous energy building in the staffer. They talked of the *hawaldar*'s connections, his links, they hacked at his Special Branch file . . . It was nearly an hour before the staffer's energy burst out.

'There is something else you should know, Mr Wroughton. An American Navy helicopter came in here recently with a CasEvac. A crewman needed facilities they didn't have on board the carrier. I met the navigator off the helicopter. He just told a silly story – we were talking smuggling. You know, cigarettes going from here to Iranian fishing villages – fast speedboats. Maybe it wasn't much of a story.'

'Well, if it's "silly", keep it short, please.'

'Yes, of course. The navigator explained how they regularly track the speedboats, keep them on radar – because of suicide attacks. They were following this formation when it broke. One speedboat detached from the main group and took a line that was going to bring it close to the carrier. The navigator's helicopter was put on immediate intervention alert. It was all armed up, missiles live for firing. They didn't have to take off. The single speedboat headed away, and they tracked it. It went right in to the Omani coast, then up the shoreline and rejoined the others. On the return trip there was the same number of them as with the original formation. Have I explained that? Well, it was the day before the rumour put the money-lender up-country, where there was nothing for him that we can identify. I thought you ought to know.'

Wroughton didn't thank him, did not praise him. He hid the increased pulse beat in his heart.

He asked for a map. It was spread across the table. He asked where the speedboat from Iran had hit the Omani coast, and he made a cross at that point with his pencil. Then he asked where rumour had put the *hawaldar* up-country, and he made a second mark. Could they, please, bring him a ruler? When the ruler was given him, Wroughton made a line that linked the coast and a road junction, took the line on and traced it right to the Saudi border.

He was in a good humour. The corpse and the frustrations were forgotten. He told the police officer and his staffer what he wanted from the morning, and at what time they should leave. In the privacy of his hotel room, Wroughton would manage a large drink, damn sure, he would study the map and dream of what the line told him.

The guide, Rashid, had set a forced pace. Caleb had thought, when they came to the dune wall, rising in front of them, an almost sheer slope, that they would rest there for the night. The sun was low, the half-light treacherous. Soft-spoken, but harshly, Rashid gave his orders. His son sulked, but obeyed. Only Tommy was the exception, but for this one evening only. The camels were unloaded. The waterskins and the crates were lifted down from them. Two at a time, Rashid led the camels up the near vertical slope with their hoofs kicking for, and failing to find, a grip, and Tommy scrambled after him on hands and knees.

Fahd carried waterskins. Hosni struggled with food pouches.

One at a time, Caleb and the boy took the boxes. With ropes, they dragged them to the dune's ridge line, gasped for air, were glowered at by Rashid and went back down for more. There was no encouragement from Rashid, only contempt at his thin and bloodless lips. Three times, Caleb heaved a box to the ridge, then slid back down the slope. The last time he went there were no more boxes at the base of the dune, but Hosni was there with the last two of the food pouches. He did not think Hosni saw him until he was beside him. Caleb lifted the last two pouches on to his shoulder and snatched at Hosni's hand, put it against the belt of his robe and felt the fingers tighten. They went up together – it was family, they were brothers. He would not have done it for Fahd, or for Tommy, only for the Egyptian. Twice, on the last climb, the dune's sand cascaded away from under his toes and he fell back, cannoned into Hosni and felled him. Twice he picked himself up, each time realizing that the fingers still gripped his belt, and they went back up. He took Hosni to the ridge. He flopped, and Hosni collapsed beside him. Only a quarter of the sun was left and the desert, darkening, stretched away beneath them. Below, at the base of the gentler slope of the dune, Tommy held a tangle of the camels' reins, and Rashid was loading the boxes on to their backs.

They started down.

Rashid, again, set the pace.

The boy, Ghaffur, was beside Caleb. Caleb walked, dead, saw nothing. He did not know from where the boy found the cheerful laughter.

'Look, look.'

The boy had hold of his sleeve, tugged it for attention, then pointed.

Thirty yards from where they walked, to his left Caleb saw the crazily formed white shapes. In the half-light, he could not identify them, but the boy dragged on his arm and led him from the path made by the camels' hoofs.

'You see them? Yes, you do.'

He could make out the backbones, skulls and ribcages, half buried in the sand. The leg bones were covered where the sand had drifted, but the four sets of bones were clear. Flattened empty skins lay on the ribcages, the same size as those holding water that Fahd had carried up the dune. The black leather of the skins lay on the bones' whiteness.

'Shall we find the bones of the men?'

'No.' Caleb pulled himself free of the boy's hand.

'If the camels died, the men died – don't you want to find them?'

'No,' Caleb grunted over his shoulder.

'After the camels died, the men would have finished their water. At first they would have hoped another traveller would find them. But when the water was finished, and no traveller came, the thirst would have destroyed them and they would have tried to walk away. Their bones will be near here.'

Against his instinct, Caleb turned. The darkness was coming fast, but the bones were highlighted.

He heard his own voice, breathy, anxious. 'Do we have enough water?'

'Only God knows.'

They hurried to catch up; the light of a small fire guided them when they could no longer see the camels' trail. Caleb felt the pain in every joint of his body. He sank down. Water was passed to him, his

134

measured share. He drank it down, the last drop, then scraped his tongue round the mug's sides. He imagined travellers who had finished their water and on whom the sun had blazed. Every joint of his body was alive with pain.

He waited to be fed, huddled by the fire under which the bread cooked, and felt the cold settling on him.

Chapter Seven

The heat drained life, energy, from Caleb. The sun was not yet high but still scorched him. Rashid made no allowance for weakness, offered no encouragement, no reassurance, but he had slowed the pace. Even Ghaffur had lost the cheerfulness and stayed close to his father. The camels trudged on but the spring in their stride was gone. Tommy preferred to walk in a camel's shadow rather than ride and be unprotected from the sun.

An hour back, they had passed a little square of baked black sand – where earlier travellers had made a fire – but there was no trail of hoofprints or footmarks, no sign of when they had been there, a week or a year before.

Caleb retched, and dizziness forced him to cling to the straps holding the boxes on to the camel's side. He thought he would fall.

He was the back-marker. If he fell, would any of them know? Would they walk on and not realize he had fallen? They did not look back. The camels would not have cried out if he had fallen. Two more hours, at least, before the stop for the *dhuhr* prayers. Each step was harder, each stride fractionally shorter. The sun, rising, towered over him.

Abruptly, he was lifted.

The sand was caked round his eyes, hard like concrete from the tears, but he saw it.

Away to his left, level with him, was a patch of green. Living, luscious, wet green confronted him. It seemed to call to Caleb. If he let go of the strap, started out over the sand, went to the left of the struggling column, kept going, then the green and the coolness of it would be closer. He heard the ripple of water falling, and smelt it, and he saw the waving of branches heavy and bowed by leaves . . . It was not Afghanistan. In his mind he saw jumping, dancing pictures. He clutched the strap and his head rolled. The green of a park and the shrieks of kids kicking a ball, a fountain of old stone where the water spiralled up then fell back into a pool filled with the debris of potato-crisp packets and . . . Caleb gripped the plastic bracelet, held it so tightly that his fingers hurt with the pressure against its edges. As he squeezed his bracelet, he closed his eyes and the sand's crust pricked them. He shut it out. There had been a green grass park where the kids played football in the rain; there had been a fountain to an old queen on whose head and crown the pigeons crapped, and the water from the fountain came down on a filthy pool. He obliterated it. Only when the memory of the park and the fountain were gone did Caleb loosen his hold on the bracelet and open his eyes.

He walked on.

The mirage was broken, the delirium was beaten, the memory was dead.

He forced his stride forward, faster and longer. They would have returned for him if he had fallen. They were there because of him, because of his importance.

The column stretched ahead, and he followed. He thought he had glimpsed his weakness, and that sight hurt him.

'I'm sorry, ma'am, but I can't admit you.'

The bar was across the entrance and the man stood in front of it. He looked as though his mind was made up. Beth leaned through the open window of her vehicle and gave him a sweet smile, the one that usually opened doors or gates, raised bars.

'It's only a package that I promised to bring round for Lizzy-Jo.'

The man stood in front of the bar, his arms folded across his chest.

She could see the bulge under his waistcoat. The small white-painted aircraft had glided along the runway an hour earlier, then lifted off. It had climbed slowly and had headed out over the Rub' al Khālī. The heat was coming up and she had lost it over the dunes, in the haze.

The man said, with studied and insincere politeness, 'Then I'll see she gets it, ma'am.'

She persisted. 'It'll only take a minute. I'd be grateful if you'd tell her I'm here.'

'No can do, ma'am. But, rest assured, she'll get it, the package.'

He came to her window and reached out a hand. She had wanted, damn sure, to look around the site, hear about it. The bar was not about to be raised. The woman, Lizzy-Jo, was not about to be called from whatever work she did. The man was not going to shift. The combination of the barbed wire, the compound at the end of the runway, the aircraft that flew without pilots and the bulge under the man's arm all tickled her imagination – OK, to hell with it. She snatched up the plastic bag and thrust it through the window. He took it, nodded with courtesy, and turned his back on her, as if she was so unimportant in the order of his day that he'd already forgotten her.

He was back down on his chair and the way he sat, chair tilted back, the bulge was unmistakable. By his feet was a sports bag that she thought was long enough to hold a rifle with a folded stock. She gunned the engine, made the sharpest of fast three-point turns. She scraped up a dirtcloud with the tyres. In her wing mirror, she saw the cloud cloak him. She paused before pulling away. He emerged from the cloud on his chair and he didn't wipe his face or curse her – he merely ignored her. She drove off.

Back in her bungalow, she started to pack what she would need. From the bedroom, standing on tiptoe at the window, she could just make out the distant compound. The irritation had grown. She should have been focused, totally, on the trip she was embarking on. Everything else should have been cleared from her mind. If the Bedouin traveller had spoken the truth, had recognized the stones and the glass, had given her the correct direction and landmarks, she would be walking the next day on an ejecta field where no man or woman had ever set foot before. She had a checklist of clothing and equipment that should guarantee her survival. If the Bedouin's description of the scale of what he had found was correct, if the single stone and the piece of black glass he had brought her were samples of a greater scattered mass, then the paper the deputy governor had commissioned her to write would make her a scientist of proven worth.

Beth could, of course, have gone out into the sands with an escort – drivers, a cook, servants to pitch her tent, and guards – but an escort would have killed the exhilaration of the solitude.

Too many times, Beth broke away from her checklist, dropped the sheet of paper on the bed, returned to the window, stretched up and peered at the vague shapes of the distant tent tops. And the sun beat down on her bungalow's little patio beyond the window, and on the roof of her Land Rover, and no wind rustled the palm trees' fronds.

Camp Delta, Guantanamo Bay.

When the prisoner was half-way down the corridor, Caleb recognized him.

It was six days since they had been taken out of the cages at X-Ray, shackled and blindfolded, had been pushed on to buses and driven to the new camp. They had been led down new corridors and had smelt the new concrete and new wire, and they were closer to the sea. When the chains were off, and the blindfold, Caleb had studied the new cage. Under the high grille window, through which the sea wind blew, there was a basin with running water, and beside it a squatting lavatory with a tap for flushing. There was nothing temporary here. They were out of the converted cargo containers, and these blocks had been built to last.

He knew the man.

He had seen the Emir General only once. Surrounded by his bodyguards, the Emir General had visited the second training camp to watch the recruits go through the assault course, with live firing. This man, with a lean, hungered body and eyes that never rested, had been on the left side of the Emir General. He had seen the man again a week after the bombing had started. Caleb and others of the 055 Brigade had been manning a checkpoint and a convoy of pickups had come through. The side rear windows of the third pickup had been curtained, but the convoy had stopped and the Chechen had climbed inside it. The bodyguard had stood at the back and a machine-gun was mounted on the cab roof. They had exchanged remarks,

Caleb and the bodyguard, nothing talk, then the Chechen had left the pickup, and the convoy had gone on.

The cage beside Caleb's was unlocked. There were two more guards than usually escorted a prisoner. The bodyguard was pitched inside. At X-Ray they were moved every fourteen days, and put into cages where there were strangers on each side of them. Caleb understood: they did not allow relationships to build. The guards came in after him and two held batons threateningly as the prisoner's chains were taken off. They seemed to expect him to fight, seemed to want him to. The man gave them no excuse. They left him. Caleb thought they went reluctantly, cheated.

He sensed this was a prisoner of status.

The guards now came down the corridor every two minutes. Before the bodyguard's arrival it had been every ten or twelve. But everything about them was predictable. Caleb sat against his wall, and the bodyguard lay on his bed, both in silence and ignoring each other, until prayer time. The guards did not come down the corridors in prayer times, did not spy on them. When the call came on Delta's new loudspeakers, the bodyguard knelt and faced the direction where they were told the Holy City was, his shirtsleeve pressed against the wire. Caleb came close. They were both kneeling. Their words were soft-spoken but were not the words of the Holy Book.

'Where have you come from?'

The bodyguard's head did not turn. 'From what they call the "cooler", the isolation cell. I speak to a brother, encourage him, then I go back to the cooler. In a few days they take me from the cooler and put me in another cage. I speak more encouragement, then I go back to the cooler. If I stay in one cage I may damage the chance of a brother.'

'The chance of what?'

'Of freedom. They know my identity. I am a prize for them. Who are you?'

'I was at the training camp, I saw you. I saw you also at a roadcheck we had, outside Kabul. We talked.'

'With the rocket-launcher, at the block. On the assault course at the camp. Each time, you were spoken of . . . What do they know of you?'

'I am a taxi-driver.'

'Who can denounce you?'

Caleb murmured, 'All the men I was with, and the Chechen, were killed when I was taken by the Americans. When I am interrogated, I tell them

140

that I, alone, survived, I am a taxi-driver. I do not believe they know any-
thing else of me.'

'And you are strong?'

'I try to be.'

Caleb had to strain to hear the bodyguard. 'Make a promise for me.'

'What do I promise?'

'If you are ever freed, you never forget. You remember your brothers. You
remember the martyrs. You remember the evils of the crusaders.'

'I promise I will never forget, will always remember.'

There was a great calm about the man. He was thin, without a dominat-
ing stature, and his face was unremarkable, but his eyes burned.

'And you will fight. Whatever the barriers put in front of you, you will
cross them. You will walk through fire. You will fight.'

The prayers ended. The guards tramped down the corridor. The body-
guard did not speak again, neither did Caleb, and they sat as far apart as the
cage confines allowed. When food was brought, when the mosquitoes buzzed
close to the ceiling lights, when the bodyguard's cage door was opened, he
lashed out with his foot and caught the knee of the guard carrying his tray
from the trolley, spilling the food. More guards came. Twice he was
cudgelled with a baton, and he was blindfolded, then dragged away.

Caleb felt the new strength. He was no longer frightened. He was
toughened, hardened by the encounter. He was a taxi-driver, but he had
given his promise.

It broke quickly, without warning.

Silence, then raised gasping and exhausted voices.

Caleb scraped the crust of sand from his eyes. The Saudi, Fahd,
high on his saddle, lashed his foot at Tommy's shoulder, toppling
him. When Tommy stood again, Fahd worked the camel round so
that he could return to kick again; he aimed for Tommy's head, but
missed; the effort almost made him fall from the saddle. Tommy had
hold of his leg and was trying to drag him down, but he lost the grip
and sagged back.

A blade flashed.

Tommy had the knife. Fahd watched it. Tommy edged closer, the
knife raised, ready to strike.

The guide, Rashid, came from behind Tommy and, with the speed
of a snake's hit, snatched at Tommy's knife arm, held it, then twisted

it behind Tommy's back, until the man's face grimaced in pain. The knife was loosed. As it fell, Tommy smashed back with his free arm and caught Rashid on the upper cheek. The arm was twisted tighter and Tommy dropped to the sand. Rashid bent to pick up the knife, took the reins of Fahd's camel and led it to the front of the column. The march resumed.

The boy was beside Caleb. 'Do you understand?'

'What should I understand?'

The boy's face creased as if in anguish. 'He hit my father. He struck my father. Because he hit my father, he is dead. Nothing else is possible.'

'But your father walked away, he did not kill him.'

'He will, at his own choosing. It was the worst insult, to hit my father.'

Caleb asked the question heavily: 'What did they fight over?'

The boy said, 'The one called the other a murderer of the faithful. The other called the one a coward and a fool. It is what they said, and now the other is condemned.'

Caleb pushed the boy away, gently but with tired firmness. He thought death now trudged with them. His anger blossomed. Where they travelled there was no beacon of hope. Life did not, could not, exist. The sun burned and crushed them. Madness had made the argument. Impossible difficulties weighed them down, and now they had the new burden of the argument, and one of them was condemned.

He could have howled with his anger.

Most days a wrapped baguette, tuna and mayonnaise, with a can of Coke in his office passed for Jed Dietrich's lunch. He took the chance of the midday break to write up the assessment of the morning interrogation – increasingly fewer observations seemed relevant – and to prepare for the afternoon session. The secretary for Defense had called the men he questioned 'hard-core, well-trained terrorists'; the attorney general had said they were 'uniquely dangerous'. But neither the secretary nor the attorney sat in with Jed. There were six hundred inmates at Delta, and maybe a hundred of them were 'hard-core' and 'dangerous', and the Bureau and the Agency had care of them. Jed never saw them.

He binned the wrapping from his baguette, drained the can, wiped the crumbs off the table. As the minute hand climbed to the hour, the knock came on cue.

The prisoner was brought in.

Jed doubted he was even a 'foot-soldier'. God alone knew what questions he would find to put to the man. The prisoner, the file said, came from a small town in the English Midlands, was of Bengali ethnic origin, was one of the five per cent for whom anti-depressive medication was prescribed by the Delta doctor, had been studying Arabic and the Qur'ān at a religious school up the road from Peshawar, and had gone into the net, had been handed over by the Pakistani intelligence people, who probably felt they needed to show willing and make up a quota number. If Jed, the fisherman, had pulled this one out of a Wisconsin lake, he'd not have bothered with a photograph or the scales, would have chucked him straight back – he had never been to England, had no knowledge of the 'Midlands'.

Jed was aware of a growing swell of opinion outside the States that demanded either for criminal charges to be laid against prisoners or for them to be freed. He was as aware that the courts back home had claimed no jurisdiction over Camp Delta. It was not his business, he had no opinion. Had he gone out of his room for lunch and discussed it with enlisted men he would have found total indifference. The Agency and Bureau men wanted every last one of the prisoners locked up in perpetuity. The Red Cross people, had they ever owned up to their true feelings, would have condemned Delta, would have criticized the concept of the camp, but he didn't go out to lunch.

None of the British ones had been brought to Jed's room before.

With a British prisoner, at least there was no requirement for an interpreter. Translators destroyed the chance of an interrogator displaying his skills.

The man shuffled through the door. Well, not a man – more of a boy. The file said he was twenty-three years old. He would have been twenty when he was captured, would have had his twenty-first birthday inside a Guantanamo cage . . . Jed thought of him as a boy. The chains were taken off, and the guards stood back. The man sat down. He put his hands on the table top – it was orders that a prisoner's hands must be visible at all times when he was un-shackled. The hands shook. Jed reckoned they would have shaken worse if it had not been for the anti-depressants . . . God, was this guy, categorized as an 'unlawful combatant', the real enemy?

He went through what had been asked of the man in previous interrogations. Why had he gone to Pakistan? Whom had he met in Pakistan? What had he been taught in Pakistan? Who had funded his studies in Pakistan? Had he ever received military training? Had he gone into Afghanistan at any time? The answers were the same, word for word, as they had been at every interrogation. He had the transcripts in front of him, and the pages were signed by the interrogators. Sometimes Jed let the answers run; sometimes he interrupted and his tone was savage; sometimes he smiled and softened his voice as he put the question; sometimes he doubled back. As the boy was denying ever having been in Afghanistan, he returned to the funding of the studies. Jed never caught him out, no discrepancies in the story, but far down in his mind a thought was developing.

He couldn't place where it came from. Whom had he met in Pakistan? Had he ever received military training? He felt the stab of recognition.

Jed paused. He collected his thoughts. They had been chaff, a jumble. Most of his concentration had been on the questions he'd asked, a little of it had been on his family and on the week gone by. He cut away the chaff.

He sat for a full minute in silence. He watched the fingers writhing, and the breath come in little pants, and let his instinct rule.

Jed's voice was gentle, in English. 'Friend, do you speak Pashto?'

The faces of the two guards were impassive. He had used the word 'friend'. The guards would talk about that afterwards. Guards hated the prisoners. Guards knew that any fraternization with prisoners was forbidden, would lead to a flight out without their boots touching the Tarmac. Guards knew that a brigadier general, Camp Delta's commander, had been summarily fired and that 'defense sources' had claimed he was too 'soft' with the regime he'd ordered. In Delta, signs – printed by the ICRC – told detainees their rights, and had been posted with the authorization of the brigadier general. When the brigadier general had visited prisoners' cages he had greeted them in Arabic, 'Peace be with you.' He'd been sacked . . . but an interrogator had the freedom to call a prisoner 'friend'.

The man across the table, the 'friend', nodded.

In English, because Jed didn't speak that language: 'Would that be good Pashto, or only a little Pashto?'

'I can speak in Urdu . . .'

'No, no.' Jed leaned forward. 'Do you have Pashto?'

'Some, a bit, there were Afghan people in the college. I . . .'

Jed used his hand to gesture that the answer was sufficient. He used his desk telephone to call the central office. He requested the immediate presence of a Pashto interpreter. There was doubt as to whether one was available. He did not raise his voice, but it carried enough menace to the clerk. He dropped the 'request', replaced it with 'requirement': a Pashto interpreter to his room immediately – not tomorrow, not in half an hour. In a drawer on his side of the table the tape-recorder turned, and microphones were built into the table, on his side and on the prisoner's. He opened the drawer and stopped the tape. He waited. The quiet clung in the room. The man opposite sat bolt upright and still, except for the motion of his hands. Jed wrote, in a fast long-hand scrawl, answers he remembered. The answers were not verbatim, but as he recalled them. Ten minutes later, when the interpreter came into the room, he passed him the two pages, now thickly covered with his handwriting. He asked the interpreter to translate them, on paper, into Pashto. Again there was silence as the interpreter crouched at the table and wrote down the translation.

He could not be sure where this would lead him. When the translation was complete, the pages in Pashto were laid in front of the prisoner and Jed switched on the tape-recorder. The prisoner was asked to read aloud.

His host had put Bart at the end of the line.

They had been down to the paddock to inspect the first race's runners, then had climbed back to the stand. They made a party of eight and they waited for the start of the five thirty-five at Riyadh. The banker did the book. No Tote or William Hill or on-course bookmaker, the banker wrote down their little bets. Ten *riyals* or twenty *riyals* were the flutters. No money would change hands in the stand, no winnings or losses would be paid over in public, but rewards and debts would be settled at dinner at the defence-procurement man's villa.

Most of the row of seats in front of Bart was empty, and the row behind him only sparsely filled. Not like the old days, before the war in Iraq: then the whole stand would have heaved with expatriates. 'Terrorism threat' and 'personal security' were the catchphrases of the day. Only the diehards remained. He did not own binoculars and struggled, when he looked down the course to the start, to see the quartered shirt and cap that he was backing, and he listened to the talk in the row stretching away from him. Here, at least, indiscretion was possible.

'What I say is, the place is cracking up. I think it's terminal.'

'Take the servants, there's a new impertinence. I'd call it dumb insolence.'

'More to the point is Saudization – is that a real word? You know what I mean. They're stuffing lazy incompetents into jobs they can't handle.'

'I never go out at night, not now, not even with a driver. This used to be the safest city on earth, not any more.'

'Dreadful what happened to young Garnett – such a sweet girl that Melanie, beautiful children.'

'It's all become so dishonest, corrupt. The ethos is almost criminal here now. I . . .'

They were off, away in the distance the small shapes of the horses, and the smaller ones of the jockeys. Bart could not make out his horse and he didn't bloody care. He had not been invited because his host particularly liked him: one day he might be useful for a late-night emergency call-out.

It all came back to Ann. He wondered where she was, whether she was still shagging the owner of the Saab franchise showroom, how the kids were . . . Ann demanded private schools, two holidays a year that weren't package. The debts had mounted: unopened envelopes carrying final demands had littered the Torquay house, and the mortgage payments were in arrears. By 1995 – yes, he could remember the date, clear as bloody crystal – she'd started the taunting that he hadn't the balls to stand up to the practice partners and demand they offloaded private patients on to him. He'd faced ruin, and he'd faced her goading . . . Then Bart had responded. In April that year he had come to the solution to the ills. Josh, a right little weasel, had been in the consulting room and had sown the seed. Josh was an NHS patient, there to have his face patched up after a beating. Josh was a dealer. Josh left an address in the bed-sit land at the wrong end of the town. Josh had a roll of banknotes in his hip pocket, a fat wad. Josh paid up on the nail, cash on delivery . . . and Bart had delivered. Morphine alkaloid tablets were the currency for which Josh paid cash, and heroin and cocaine. Any patient on Bart's books who was terminally ill, or any patient with chronic pain from a back injury, could be prescribed the morphine tablets – and always, from the spring of 1995, he prescribed big. The bathroom cabinets of his patients bulged with the bottles of morphine tablets . . . And when there was a death, or when a back's pain was relieved, he collected what was left and took it away. Josh had the left-over tablets, and the cash from the roll of notes in Josh's hip pocket began, by the late summer of 1995, to dent the piles of unpaid bills. So simple . . . Heroin and cocaine were used to help, quietly, those on their way when life had little more than a fortnight to run. Relatives were grateful for the release of their loved one from suffering. Bart called it the Brompton's Mixture: a gin or sherry cocktail with the addition of liquid heroin or powdered cocaine; when he signed the death certificate, and before the undertakers called, Bart cleared the unused excess. The partnership with the little weasel, the bastard, Josh, might have lasted for ever – not for a mere eighteen months, until the catastrophe.

There was no betting slip to tear up at the races in Riyadh. His prediction had been correct: his horse was last over the line. Again, the conversation down the line of seats clamoured, as if the race had been a minor diversion from the main business of gossip and complaint.

'I really don't know whether we should all get out, cut and run. But what I reckon – back home – no one wants to employ a banker of my age.'

'That Al Qaeda, it's a cancer, and Iraq's taken the eye off the main ball. We're all targets now, that's what I feel.'

'If the Kingdom collapses we're in deep trouble, about as deep as you can get. We keep bags packed, we're all ready to go, but if it happened suddenly, without warning, how would we get to the airport? Who'd protect us? And can you imagine pitching up at

Heathrow with just a suitcase each? That's assuming we got to the airport.'

'It's all so unfair. What do you think, Bart? . . . Bart, I'm speaking to you.' The banker's wife tugged his arm, peered into his face.

He jerked his mind away from Josh, the tablets, the cocktail and Ann. 'Isn't it more dangerous crossing the road in Riyadh?'

'Is that all you've to say about the security situation?'

He was emboldened. 'If you want my opinion, Al Qaeda's power is overstated.'

'Have you plans for a quick bolt, Bart?'

For emphasis, Bart smacked a closed fist into the other palm. 'No, I have not.'

It was a lie – of course he had a permanently packed case. Whether he would ever use it was another matter. Would Eddie bloody Wroughton – the marionette tweaker – ever permit its use? He had nowhere to go without Eddie bloody Wroughton's sanction.

'I have no plans to run. Al Qaeda's threat is probably minimal. A few fanatics in the desert or up in the mountains, chewing dates, suffering from amoebic dysentery. I don't rate them, no.'

Shocked into silence, the other guests in the row shuffled their feet and examined their racecards. Bart thought of nobody but himself – himself and Eddie Wroughton.

The host's wife chipped in, 'Well, that's enough of that. I think it's time we went back down to the paddock.'

The dung was dried, desiccated.

The line drawn on the map had served Eddie Wroughton well. At each village close to the pencil line they had stopped and Wroughton had stayed in the vehicle, forcing the police officer to go among the mud-brick homes. The routine had led them to the last village, then on to the single isolated building. There had been signs there of recent use, and the fire that had been lit. He'd photographed the interior, then the new bolt and the new lock on the inside of the door. No shepherd or goatherd would have sealed a window so thoroughly, then lit a fire inside, or would have used a new lock and a new bolt on a shed door. They had gone on, following the pencil line on the map, using ever rougher tracks.

The toe of his brogue brushed the top of a dung stool, which fell away as powdery dust. But he worked with the toe until he had exposed the stool's underside, where there was still dampness. A week, a little more perhaps, but not a month. From the dung, he decided that more than half a dozen, fewer than a dozen camels had been there, had waited, had defecated. Near to the riverbed there were tyremarks but on the dirt track; Wroughton could not have said whether they were a week, a month, or half a year old. Away to the right there was a cluster of buildings from which cooking smoke spiralled, and there were irrigated fields. That community would be centred on a well. The police officer had been there and had come back with his head down, as if he felt ashamed to report back that his questions had met a wall of silence. If he was given time, if Wroughton had allowed the police officer the time to take two of the older men away from the village and drive them to the cells at the station back down the road, the questions would still have gone unanswered, so he did not permit it. The wall of silence denied that strangers had been there within the last several days. Tribesmen and farmers, his experience of the hardship of their lives told him, did not respond to inflicted pain.

Slowly, taking his time, Wroughton gazed around him. His eyes were shaded by his dark glasses and he could look out over the ground from which the sun reflected. When he was satisfied with what he had drunk in, seen nothing that interested him, he turned and began again. He looked for the mistakes that men made. A discarded wrapper, a ground-out cigarette filter tip: men who thought their precautions were total always made one mistake. Most of Wroughton's life was dictated by paper: paper accumulated on his desk, was spewed out by cypher machines and his computer. From the paper mountain came clues to the identity and relevance of the prey he hunted, but only rarely. He turned again, stared up at the high ground on the right side of the riverbed, and saw the movement.

Horns moved, then ears, a head and then the goat was gone from a ledge above the right side of the riverbed.

Wroughton looked hard at the ledge and saw that it reached precariously to a patch of green and yellow grass, and that there were more goats. According to his father, grandfather and great-uncle, the best work of an intelligence officer was in close-quarters observation

– they might not have thought him suitable to follow them, not thought he could hack it as a career, but he had remembered. Where there were goats there would be a boy. He had left the villagers to the police officer, but this was for himself.

He scrambled up the loose stone. He clung to the branches of little sprouting bushes that grew from rock crannies. His best brogues were scraped, his linen suit was dust-smeared and his pure-white shirt was sweat-soaked, but he reached the ledge. Never looking down, he edged along the rock wall to where a small plateau opened out. On it, extraordinarily, there was grass. Perhaps a tiny spring dribbled water from the upper rocks. There were goats, and a boy was sitting on the grass among their excrement. He caught his breath. The occasions when excitement had gripped him were rare enough for him to count on the fingers of one hand. The boy watched him as he composed himself. He spoke in Arabic, with the gentleness he would have used to his friend Juan Gonsalves' children.

Twenty minutes later, Eddie Wroughton left the plateau, came back along the ledge, then started the descent to the riverbed. To break his fall, he snatched at the little bushes, slid on his backside in an avalanche of dust and stones. Those who had bought camels from a farmer had not looked up and spied a goat high above them. His suit jacket was torn at the elbows, his trousers at the knees and seat. It mattered nothing. The boy had seen the men and their voices had carried faintly to him. They had been strangers. The camels had waited in the riverbed and had dropped their dung while an argument had raged over the price of the three more camels needed to move boxes, six boxes. Ten of the twenty minutes with the boy were taken with his questioning, so softly done, over the size, shape and colour of the boxes. Five of the twenty minutes concerned the detail of the features and physique of the young man who had closed the negotiations.

Unrecognizable to those who knew him, unwashed and his clothes not changed, Eddie Wroughton boarded the last flight of the day out of Muscat. At the back of a near-empty aircraft, he thought of the centuries-old trail that had been the route of the frankincense traders half a millennium before. His pencil had traced a line beyond the watercourse, over the hills, into the Empty Quarter. Nine camels, a guide and his son, four men and six crates of weapons were now on the trail. He had much to be cheerful about, but pride of place went to the boy's description of a young man unlike any Arab he had seen before.

On the screen, the image of the Land Rover flashed for a moment, and was gone; then the camera was tracking over sand again.

Lizzy-Jo didn't point out the Land Rover, painted blue with two vivid green stripes running diagonally up its sides and over its roof. Marty was doing a banking left turn. She did not want to disturb him while he made the manoeuvres to bring *First Lady* on to the line-up for landing. She'd been in the Land Rover, been driven from the shop to the club in it – where she'd been lectured about meteorites; Lizzy-Jo grimaced. Marty was hunched over his stick, and his eyes, magnified by the thickness of his lenses, squinted in concentration. The former Air Force pilots for whom she'd done sensor work in her first days with the Agency had flown the newer Predator MQ-1s like they'd have driven cars on a quiet country road up-state, but Marty always had the look on him that it was life or death.

He made a good landing.

She always clapped when he brought *First Lady* or *Carnival Girl* down. It was her routine, had been since the first time they'd flown together out of Bagram. The sound of her clapping reverberated in the Ground Control Station. He blushed, as he had the first time. She reached over and squeezed his upper shoulder, as if she could loosen the tensed muscles.

He taxied her back. He cut the pusher engine. They had flown *First Lady* for eight hours, covering some six hundred nautical miles. The camera had photographed sand and more sand and nothing but sand: flat sand, steep sand and sloping sand. On the workbench, between them, was the big map with the squares on it and she put a Chinagraph cross over two more. There were six squares now with crosses on them, and ninety-four without. The big man from the embassy had talked of thousands of flying map boxes, but that was because he did not understand the Predator's capability. Lizzy-Jo had divided the desert into a hundred squares. Her eyes ached from gazing at the screen. She stood and arched her back.

She opened the trailer door. The heat blasted into the air-conditioned interior. It blanketed her, seemed to suck the life from her. A plastic bag lay, roasted, on the step. None of the ground crew was permitted entry to the trailer. She looked inside, then let out a little whoop of gratitude, and thought of the Land Rover the camera had seen. She murmured her thanks – then ran for the toilet.

Five minutes later, she wandered back towards the trailer. She passed the awning where George and his team already had the engine cowling off *First Lady*. He called to her: 'How did she go?'

'Good.'

'No thrust problem?'

Marty was on the top step at the trailer door and answered for her: 'No problem, she was sweet. Eight hours today, twelve or thirteen tomorrow – don't reckon Lizzy-Jo and I can take more than that.'

Lizzy-Jo said, 'Yes, we can do twelve or thirteen tomorrow, then maybe take *Carnival Girl* up the day after and—'

George shook his head decisively. 'Not tomorrow, not thirteen hours or one. The forecast's a fucker. You're not going anywhere tomorrow. Better believe it – nowhere.'

She and Marty went to the awning. The forecast printout was given to them. The orders were strict, about as strict as they could get: a Predator should not be hazarded in extreme weather conditions unless for vital operational necessity. There was no argument. She was perplexed. She thought of the Land Rover picked up by the camera as it headed away from the Shaybah compound and into the emptiness. She held the package of tampons under her arm and murmured to herself, 'If the forecast was that bad, why'd you think she'd be driving off into that nowhere?'

The camel roared and swung its neck. Caleb was behind Tommy, who was against the camel's flank, as if clinging to its body's shadow. The camel's movement threw Tommy clear and water spilled from his mouth.

More water cascaded on to the flank of the camel. Its great tongue flailed to catch the drops. Ghaffur shrieked for his father. Rashid ran back, the camel snorted and Tommy crouched down.

The truth came to Caleb. The Iraqi had not walked beside the camel for its shade: he was there because his head was against a goatskin of water. They were all fighting exhaustion: all their heads were down, their feet and the camels' plodded. They knew nothing of the water being stolen, but the camel had smelt it. Perhaps, as Tommy sucked at the neck of the skin holding the water, a little had dribbled from his mouth on to the camel's flank. For days the animal had not drunk, was slowly using up its reserves from the well at the start of the Sands. Water, clear, clean crystals of it, fell to the sand. Enough for one cup, or two, then for three cups and more . . . The camel's neck was arched round as its tongue tried in desperation to reach the drops.

Rashid plugged the skin's neck, then retied the loosened thong round it.

He said nothing, but his gaze on the Iraqi confirmed that Tommy was condemned.

Caleb thought at least two days' water had been lost from the slack skin. The sight of it had worsened the dryness in his throat.

At the night stop, the Iraqi sat away from them. Only the boy went to him with food, uncooked bread because there were no roots for a fire, and the measured cup of water, but Fahd and Hosni sat with their backs to him.

As the darkness fell, Caleb crawled away from the others, went to Tommy and sat beside him. His voice croaked, 'You were called a "murderer of the faithful". Who did you kill?'

There was defiance, almost pride. 'I was the hangman. At the Abu Ghraib gaol, the gallows were mine. I could hang three men at a time, or three women. First I was the assistant, then I was the hangman, then I was the supervisor. I hanged the principals of the Shi'a who rebelled in 1991, and I hanged the agents of America in the north in 1996. I hanged men or women who were spies, who plotted against the regime, who told jokes that mocked the President. I could hang them so that death was instant, or hang them so that death was slow – it depended on the order I was given. There was always a note on the execution order that said how it was to be. The scaffold was my place, it was where I worked. In the morning I would dress in a clean uniform, always clean and pressed, and my driver would take me to the prison. Some days I was idle, some days I was busy. At the end of each day I went home to my wife and my children.'

The voice softened, a little of its guttural quality left it.

'After I had hanged the Kurds who followed the CIA's in-structions, in 1996, I left the Abu Ghraib, the prison in Mosul and the prison in Basra, and I was given a new posting. I became a security officer for the Republican Guard's Nebuchadnezzar Division. I gave up my ropes, my pinions and my hoods, left them to the men I had trained as my assistants. In the division, I was the officer who said nothing and heard everything. If there was doubt about a man's loyalty, I sent him to those men who had been my assistants. Then came the war. Then came Tommy Franks. Then came the disaster. I fled. I took my wife and my children and drove them by back tracks to the Syrian border. I was one of the first to go. Later the route was closed. Now my wife lives in a two-roomed apartment at Aleppo, and my children, and they have citizenship, and they will never see me, or talk of me, again. If I had stayed in Iraq, if the Shi'a or the Kurds, or the families of officers and guards in the Nebuchadnezzar Division had caught me, I would have been hanged from a lamp-post or from a tree.'

The voice quavered.

'Don't have the arrogance to judge me. I looked into the eyes of men, put the hood on them, the rope, worked the lever. Could you? *Can you?* I don't know at what time or in what place you will look into a man's eyes, or a woman's, or a child's, and pull a lever. It is why you are chosen . . . It is why you walk with us in this God-fuck place, in secrecy so that your safety is preserved. If you judge me, then you must judge yourself. I will go back to Iraq and kill Americans, a few . . . You will look into hundreds of eyes, perhaps thousands of eyes, the chosen man . . .'

The voice dropped. The defiance and pride had fled.

'Thank you for sitting with me.'

Chapter Eight

It hissed on to them, swept in with a sudden force that devastated them.

The storm burst over the dune wall beyond the caravan's pitched camp. In the dawn's half-light, the wind surged over the rim. The warning of its coming was brief, a few seconds, then it hit them. Caleb was outside his tent, had slept only fitfully, was stretching and massaging his leg and shoulder muscles, facing the first peep of the rising sun, when he heard the whistle of sound, as if a tyre's valve was released. He turned. The cloud of sand careered over the dune and buffeted him. He rocked, could not stand, sank to his knees. For a moment he stared at the cloud that followed in the wind's wake, then the grains were in his mouth and nose, and pierced open his eyes. If he had not already been down on his knees, he would have been felled by the wind. The noise deafened him. The sand scraped the skin on his upper cheeks and round his eyes, his wrists and ankles, and ripped at his robe. It came in waves that seemed to belt the breath out of him. Caleb twisted away from it and snatched at the loose sand to prevent himself being carried away by the gale.

A tent went past him, chased by bedding.

He heard the screaming of the Saudi.

The camels, hobbled, struggled to escape the wind's force but could not.

Another tent followed the first. Its canopy was caught, and it floated, then sank, raced over the sand's surface, was lifted again and ripped. After the bedding went the cooking pot and plates, the mugs from which they drank water, and clothing. A rucksack ran with the wind.

Through slitted eyes, Caleb watched the destruction of the overnight camp as the pieces billowed away from him. Tommy howled abuse at Rashid. 'You are a fool, an idiot. Did you not know it was coming? Were you not paid to know?'

The camels tried to flee the gale and the thickening cloud now blotting out the sun. Caleb heard their shrill bellowing. They could not run: their hobble ropes held them. They skipped, fell, rolled, and their long legs thrashed before they could stand again. Watching them, Caleb realized the scale of the catastrophe that had hit the caravan. While the others had still slept, Rashid and Ghaffur had begun loading the camels. Some had the crates already fastened to their backs, others had the water bags and food sacks roped to their flanks.

Caleb forced himself up, was tossed forward and tumbled, then crawled towards the two shadowed figures in front of him going in wavering strides after the camels.

Without the water they were lost. Bones in the sand. Without the camels they were lost. Bent double, Rashid and Ghaffur were in pursuit of the camels. On his hands and knees Caleb followed them. Sometimes the cloud of whipped sand was too dense for him to see them. Sometimes he could see them clearly, father and his son, staggering after the camels that carried the water bags. The camels that carried the crates were ignored. Water was the lifeblood of travellers in the desert. Whenever he stood, thrust himself up, Caleb was immediately tossed down on to his face, and ate the sand grains. He called out to them that he was coming, following, but the distance between them and him widened.

The wind came with a new force, stronger, hitting harder. Its cry blasted at his ears, and the grains scoured his body. He did not know for how long he crawled. He could no longer see Rashid and Ghaffur, or the scattered camels. The darkness spread over him. The only light in his mind was that of the whitened bones of a camel's ribcage.

It was gone as suddenly as it had come. His eyes were closed, the sand was loose under his hands and knees. His robe fell back over his buttocks and thighs. The sun, as harsh as on any day before, beat on his face and eyelids.

Caleb wiped the sand from his eyes. He stood and was not felled by the wind. The sun blazed at him. The cloud was in the far distance.

Stone-faced, eyes glinting in anger, Rashid came towards him leading three camels, with two more following. Away to the guide's right, the boy brought more. Two water bags, deflated and empty, lay in Caleb's path. He saw Ghaffur bend and pick up another, heard the triumphant cry that signalled that the binding on the neck had held.

Caleb called after Rashid, 'How much have we lost?'

There was a snarl in the reply pitched over the guide's shoulder: 'Too much. We have lost too much.'

The storm hovered at the horizon.

Caleb found a crate lying nearly buried. He scraped the sand from around it, snatched up the fastening rope and dragged it after the guide, his son and the camels.

Wretchedly, at the campsite, they searched for what could be retrieved. They had lost water, a quarter of what had remained, and food that would have lasted four days; one camel had broken a leg. Caleb had turned away as Rashid's knife had flashed and Ghaffur had held the long hair above the beast's throat. They had lost a day of the march. When Caleb found Hosni, the Egyptian was on his stomach, his eyes pale and watering. The lower part of his body was buried in sand and his shoulders shook with a never-ceasing convulsion.

All that morning, as the sun's heat grew, Caleb helped the guide and his son search for the remnants from the campsite, but they found no more filled bags of water. When the sun was high, Caleb was beside the boy. 'Is it bad?'

'My father says there are too many men for too little water,' the boy said simply.

George Khoo took charge. The accommodation tents were streaming from the barbed wire of their inner perimeter fence; the clothes and bedding had gone further and were held by the barbs on the fencing at the extreme end of the runway.

He had fretted all night because of the forecast. Every hour, on the hour, his pocket alarm had bleeped on the flooring beside his camp bed. He'd not undressed, had not even shed his boots. His only concession to the night had been to leave the laces loose. For five minutes in each hour he had paced restlessly round the tethered awnings that sheltered *First Lady* and *Carnival Girl*, then had gone back to his bed. He'd lain on his back, stared at the tent ceiling and waited for the bleep to sound again. He'd been lucky. The first strike of the storm had been while he was hunched on his camp bed, gathering the strength to slide off and go to make the inspection tour.

It had come in a numbing shockwave, with a suddenness that would have paralysed another man into indecision.

On his orders, barked against the wind and split with expletives, the twin sets of wings had been taken off *First Lady* and *Carnival Girl*. They had been dumped without ceremony. Then the awnings had been dropped to hang loose on the fuselages of the two aircraft. Ropes had been hurled over the awnings. Each man, and Lizzy-Jo, had been given an instruction, shouted at a volume and passion that frightened them more than the storm. Some hung on to the ropes. Others, with Lizzy-Jo, clung to more ropes that straddled the roof of the Ground Control shed and the trailer with the satellite dish. While their possessions, few enough of them, raced to be snagged on the perimeter wire, they held the ropes against the wind.

George Khoo heard them cry out, yell, swear, and he ignored their fear. He thought it was like combat – but there was no enemy, no hostile incoming. One, on the same rope as Lizzy-Jo, pumped blood – a chair had struck the guy across the forehead close to the left eye. He would have been knocked half-unconscious, but his grip never wavered on the rope; neither did Lizzy-Jo's, nor the others'.

George had not known before a storm of this ferocity. Nothing like it in Chicago, the Windy City, where he'd been reared. Or at Nellis where he'd been trained, or at Bagram. He moved, best as he could, among them and each time he came back past them he blasphemed worse, ridiculed their efforts and cursed harder. He was, near as made no difference, double the age of the pilot, Marty, and a full fifteen years senior to Lizzy-Jo, and he felt for each of them as if they were his kids. His own kids were back in Chicago with their ma, and their ma's ma.

Without George Khoo's bullying aggression they would not have come through, would not have held on to the ropes till the palms of their hands were rubbed raw and bleeding.

Because he thought of Marty and Lizzy-Jo as if they were his kids he suffered and cried for them, and cheered with them. If *First Lady* had turned over, had gone in a rolling spiral towards the perimeter crushing the real-time cameras and the infra-red sensors then good-bye, damn double fast, to the mission. George Khoo knew responsibility for failure was never dumped fairly by the Agency. Failure was failure – no excuse permitted. Failure had a smell that made a man's gut turn. Failure stank, was cruel. If the aircraft went, the shit would rain down, buckets of it, on Marty, the pilot, and on Lizzy-Jo, the sensor operator.

And it went on by.

The wind dropped and the sand haze cleared. If he was weak they were all weak. He snapped orders. Guys to go get the tents and awnings back off the perimeter wire. Guys to go get the wings fitted back in place on *First Lady* and *Carnival Girl*. Guys, Marty and Lizzy-Jo, to go get the electronics tested in Ground Control and the satellite link. Guys to get some breakfast made. Guys to get medical treatment readied. Guys to go get . . . He felt so damn tired and so damn old, and he hadn't the time to think he'd done well.

And he told the armourer to go get the Hellfire missiles checked. He looked across to where the tents had been and saw Marty who seemed to probe in what debris was left there and he saw him lift up the picture that was his pride and joy. Even at that distance George could see that the glass, small miracles, was intact and a big smile creased the kid's face.

George Khoo's gruff cruelty melted. Lizzy-Jo stood apart from the team clustered inside and outside the Ground Control. He saw her wipe her hands on her trousers, just pyjama trousers that she'd slept in. She was gazing out over the desert and her eyeline seemed to follow the disappearing tail of the storm. There was new blood on the trousers where her hands had wiped. God, they were good kids, all of them.

He stood behind her.

Lizzy-Jo said, distracted, 'Hey, you know, there's a girl out there. A really nice girl. I needed some tampons, and she sussed some out for me. She drove out there and I never saw her come back before I turned in. She's out there, in that storm – no way she'd have escaped it . . . Sorry, George, I know it's not your problem, I know, but – listen – she's all alone.'

It had been like the white-out blizzards she'd known in Scotland and Norway.

She sat on the sand, the small of her back against the top of the near front wheel casing of the Land Rover.

No tears, of course not. Beth Jenkins could rage at herself and she could be contemplative about the future, but she would not weep. She had precious little to sustain her and tears would have eroded what little was left. The sand on the near side was banked to the wheel casings; on the driver's side it was higher . . . It was madness to have gone out into the desert without leaving a note in her bungalow giving detail and map co-ordinates of her route and destination. She had no satellite phone and she had no classes for three days, and she was often away and it might be four days or five before she was missed, and a week or more before a search was mounted . . . In her rush to be away from the bungalow she had not done the most fundamental, bloody obvious task of consulting the airfield control tower for the weather outlook.

She was marooned. She had been driving on full headlights, guided by her GPS, had been threading between the dunes and using salt-baked flats and was, she reckoned, within eight miles of the site of the ejecta field she had been told about. The four-litre plus engine had coped, just, with the ground terrain – until the storm had hit when she was about to kill the headlights and use the natural light of the dawn. God, and it had hit. The wind had seemed to shake the Land Rover's heavy frame and the sandclouds had overwhelmed the wipers. She'd had the sense to turn and manoeuvre the vehicle's tail towards the oncoming storm – about the only clever thing she'd done. She might have gone a hundred yards before the traction was lost, the cab had filled with sand, insinuated through closed doors and windows, and the pedals were covered. A minute or two after the wheels had started to spin, going nowhere, the engine had cut out. She had sat in the cab until the storm had passed.

When it had gone, Beth had prised open her door – had to put her shoulder to it – and she had slid and stumbled round the Land Rover. At the back the sand had banked high over the tail door. She couldn't see the rear wheels. At the front only the tops of the tyres were visible. She had lifted the bonnet and seen the coating of sand over the engine parts. She had then crawled into the back of the Land Rover and scrabbled through the film of sand to retrieve her shovel.

With the sun climbing and the temperature rising, Beth had dug at the sand round the forward wheels for two hours. It had been a Sisyphean labour. For two hours, with the temperature above forty degrees, Beth had dug away the sand from the near front wheel, and each shovelful she'd chucked away had been replaced immediately by more soft dry sand rolling into the cavity she had made. The tyre was still hidden. Two hours had achieved nothing. Then she'd drunk water. She'd loaded enough, she reckoned, for three days. Half of what she'd loaded was now drunk. And even if she had been able to clear the sand from round one wheel, down to below the axle, there would have been three more tyres needing to be exposed – and even if she had been able to get all four tyres free of sand there was the engine, which would need stripping down and cleaning. She sat against the wheel casing and the sun was too high for the vehicle's body to give off shade.

Beth Jenkins understood what would happen to her.

One distant day, a dried-out, clothed body would be retrieved and shipped home. A stone would be put over a grave. *Bethany Diana Jenkins. 1977–2004. Failure, idiot, life cut short through arrogance. Spinster.* She thought of boys and young men, and love she had not known. She had told herself, often enough, that her work was more important than searching for love. Plenty of time for love later. Now there was no more time . . . She had never met the man she could love, never would. Other young men, introduced by her mother, from Guards regiments and City broking firms, had faded from her side when she'd enthused about the rocks she studied. Guards officers and City brokers weren't big on granite, volcanoes and meteorite glass – their eyes glazed and they sloped off to hunt elsewhere. She had been left, too many times, mid-sentence . . . Love had never been offered.

The sun baked on her.

She would drink the water, what was left. She would not hoard it. She would not fight for life any more than patients in Intensive Care who knew nothing of the drugs in their bloodstream and the tubes in their veins.

Beth had her arms tight across her chest and the sun seemed to suck the moisture from her body. The sweat seeped and she hugged herself as if that might give her an image of love.

Another lunchtime, and the programme of lectures continued. Michael Lovejoy's packet of sandwiches, bought from the mid-morning trolley, awaited him on his desk. His newspaper crossword was frustratingly held up by the complications of five down: 'Groucho on Ike', three, four, six, seven and seven letters. And, not that he would have shown it, the lecturer interested him, diverted him from the clues.

They had a Russian from Counter-intelligence – flown in from Moscow – young and bright, with a flawless command of spoken English, and he came with enough good baggage to make waiting for the prawn and coleslaw worthwhile. 'The kernel of what I want to say is that we can too easily be blinkered when we seek out the snake with the intention of decapitating it. We look too easily at the obvious and then we are surprised when the television news in the morning confronts us with the newest atrocity . . . and do not ever forget that we bleed in our cities from the same atrocities as you do. Too readily, you, ladies and gentlemen, and we in Moscow and St Petersburg and Volgograd, attempt to target the Muslim that we can classify as a fanatic – and the bombs continue to kill and maim our innocents. Take my advice. When you stand and look for the Muslims whom you believe carry the Holy Book in one hand and an explosives charge in the other, stop, consider, then turn a hundred and eighty degrees. Face the other way. Consider, what do you now see?'

Four seats down from Lovejoy was the military historian, retired from the Army, and from a Strategic Studies think-tank, now doing time with A Branch on surveillance; a mild-looking senior citizen in a checked sports jacket was unnoticeable in a public library or on a crowded train.

'What do you see? At first you see nobody. No Muslim, no fist clutching a Holy Book, no finger on an electrical circuit switch. Are you looking in the right place? You are confused. You do not wish to take my advice, but you hesitate. Men appear – but not the right men. They are people like yourselves, and like myself. You see white faces. You see Caucasians and Anglo-Saxons. Not robes and beards but suits and clean-shaven cheeks. Let me take you back to an inexact analogy, but that will point to the direction in which I travel. I believe I have the names correct – Omar Khan Sharif and Asif Muhammad Hanif, whom you had never heard of before they crossed into Israel through the most stringent border checks on the border with Jordan, journeyed across Israel to the Gaza Strip, left the Strip and went to Tel Aviv for reconnaissance, then put on the 'martyr warriors'' belts and attempted to kill Jews in an Irish bar. What was most significant in this inexact analogy? They used British passports. They claimed the protection of Her Britannic Majesty – not Egyptian passports, or Saudi, or Moroccan, or Algerian, but British passports. That is my starting point, and that is where you will not look if you are blinkered. I will take it further.'

Leaning across, without apology, Lovejoy tapped the arm of the historian, passed him the newspaper and rapped his pencil on the clue to five down . . . Khan and Hanif were still Muslims even if they did carry British passports.

'Believe in the unbelievable, that is what I urge you. What if the men recruited by Osama bin Laden and his lieutenants, or the multitude of pilot organizations that swim with that shark, were white-skinned and had no links to the Faith of Islam? Where are we then? They carry British or American, French or German passports, they dress like you and me, they speak with our accent, and they have access. A young man, well dressed and clearly recognizable as one of you, one of us, carries a shoulder-bag containing a laptop. Why should he be denied entry to any crowded public building? Why should he be stopped when he goes down an escalator into a subway or Underground station? Why should he be prevented from reaching the front row of a crowd that greets a prominent figure? Why should he be regarded with suspicion? I hear, ladies and gentlemen, your silence. I do not hear your answers.'

Men and women sat statue still. But, from the corner of his eye,

Lovejoy saw the historian writing busily . . . So what do we do? Lock everyone up who is too young to be in a care home?

'He does not have to be a Muslim, does not have to be recruited in a mosque, does not have to be Asian. All that is required of him by the shark is that he should hate . . . Don't ask him to debate the subject of hatred because he is unlikely to give you a coherent response. Somewhere, in his psyche or his experience, there will be a source of hatred. He hates you and me and the society we serve – he holds us in contempt. He is the new danger. A radioactive dirty bomb, microbiological agents or chemicals in aerosol form may be built into the laptop. He is real, he walks among us, his power over us is devastating. How to stop him? Do I have the answer? I regret I do not. Can he be stopped? We have to believe it or we face disaster. I am sorry if I detain you, but I have only one more thing to say.'

The newspaper was passed back.

'My final thought is positive. I ask whether this man, one of us, a mutation from our own culture, suffused with bitterness from an actual or imagined wrong, believes in the seventy virgins awaiting him in Paradise. Is he a martyr? Does he plan to commit suicide or to survive? We cannot know . . . My own feeling is that he would wish to attack and live to watch the results of his revenge. We have more chance of stopping a man who wishes to live. I offer a trifle of comfort. Thank you for hearing me.'

As the Russian stepped back from the lectern, Lovejoy read the note scribbled in the newspaper's margin. 'It wasn't a Groucho original: he lifted from a Senator Kerr of Oklahoma.' Then, as subdued and stifled applause rippled around him, he noted the answer to five down. *The only living unknown soldier.* He shuddered. How appropriate – the 'unknown soldier' who was 'one of us'.

He went for his belated sandwich lunch. 'One of us.' That would make him chew the prawns and coleslaw with thoughtful preoccupation.

Caleb sat, hunched, on one of the boxes. By mid-afternoon, with the skies clear and the sun baking the sand, the storm would have been a memory, a nightmare, but for its consequences. The camels, still traumatized, stayed close together, body to body, as if fenced within a wire corral. Rashid and Ghaffur had been on three separate expeditions away from the destroyed campsite to search for the remaining stores and possessions that had been scattered. After they had returned from the third search, Caleb had expected that Rashid would load the animals and order them to move; he thought there were at least three hours of daylight left, and perhaps they could move further during dusk and the early night. The guide gave no explanations. His sour face, the thin hostile lips under his hooked nose, seemed to forbid interrogation.

When they were small figures, Caleb heard a little whoop of delight, and saw Ghaffur hold up a metal mug. Hosni slept, prone on the sand. Caleb heard Fahd's slithering approach over the loose sand; the temperature would have been a hundred degrees, and the wind was now minimal. When Caleb turned to face him he saw that the man shivered. They were all older, wiser, frightened. As the Saudi was about to drop down beside him, Caleb stood.

'Come on, we have work.' He said it brusquely, an instruction that was not for discussion.

He saw the man's face fall.

'Yes, we have work,' Caleb rapped.

The response was shrill. 'Do you now tell me what I should do?'

'I am telling you.'

Caleb took Fahd's arm, gripped it, and led him to the heap of stores and bedding, tenting, water bags and sacks that had been retrieved by the guide and his son. At first, the Saudi stood beside Caleb, arms crossed and idle, as Caleb crouched and started to sift, separate and pack. Suddenly, as Caleb's arm was outstretched, reaching for the last of the plates and stacking them, Fahd reached out and snatched at his wrist. His fingers fastened in a bony vice on the plastic identification tag. 'You were at Guantanamo?'

'I was.'

The fingers stroked the photograph , the printed name, Fawzi al-Ateh, and roamed over the identification numbers.

'Then they released you?'

'After nearly two years they released me.'

'Why? Why did they free you?'

'Because they believed me.'

The Saudi freed his wrist. He stood above Caleb and gazed down at him. His shoulders and arms still shook and his lips wobbled with the shiver. 'People more notable than me, more intelligent than me, have chosen you for a strike that will bring fire, pestilence against the Americans and the allies of the Americans. They have chosen you, but it is still to be decided as to whether you are trusted. Hosni says you should be trusted because you were clever and deceived the Americans at Guantanamo. Tommy trusts nobody – Tommy says that the constant purpose of the Americans is to put informers, spies, among us. Myself, I do not know whether to trust you or not to trust you . . .'

Caleb said quietly, 'Whether you trust me or not, you can help me pack what is here.' He pushed the pile of sand-covered bedding to Fahd's feet. 'Shake it, fold it, stack it . . . Should I trust you?'

The mouth of the Saudi puckered in anger. 'You are the Outsider, I am not. I have no home other than where the Organization takes me. I have no family other than the Organization . . . The Organization cares for me, and God cares for me. God is . . .'

'Can you not walk away?'

'I am hunted. My picture is in the police stations of the Kingdom. If I am taken alive, pain will be inflicted on me, and with the pain will be drugs. I pray to God, if I am taken, that I will be strong and will not betray my family. At the end of the pain, if I am taken, there will be the executioner and the executioner's sword. I have a degree in mathematics, I could have been a teacher . . . but I worked as a gardener. I was a gardener in the Al-Hamra compound for Americans. I cut the grass and watered the flowers, and I would be shouted at by the supervisor if I left a weed in the earth. I did the work of Yemenis and Pakistanis. Because I believed in the Organization, and in God, I did the work of a foreign labourer – and I watched. I was behind the wall and the guards. I used the grass-cutter, the hose, the trowel and the broom, and I watched. I counted the guards and remembered their weapons. I saw where the important Americans lived. I worked late into the night, cutting and watering, weeding and sweeping, and I watched. When martyrs drove two vehicles into the Al-Hamra compound last year they used the map that I had drawn for them. They died, they are in Paradise, but others lived and were taken. They were tortured and they did not have the strength – they betrayed the names of many. I have been told my home was raided, my parents were abused. That is why I cannot leave the Organization. If I am taken, my future is the sword.'

'I trust you.'

Fahd shook the sand grains from a sleeping-bag, then carefully rolled it. Then he lifted a blanket and flicked it out. 'I am condemned, and Tommy, and Hosni. We are all dead men . . . What I regret, I will never be able to make as great a strike as you, the Outsider, who are blessed . . . Because you are blessed, you are also condemned.'

The sand flew in Caleb's face. He blinked.

The guide and his son walked back towards them and each had again gathered up another armful of the campsite's debris. Rashid gave them no praise for sorting through the heap. When the camels were loaded, and the sun finally dropping, they moved.

Caleb was the back-marker. His face was set and sombre. He had waved away the boy and walked alone in the last camel's hoofmarks.

The patient swung her legs off the examination couch and smoothed her skirt. The patient's husband eased up from his chair.

From the basin where he washed his hands perfunctorily, Bart intoned the details of the only acceptable recipe for acute depression, nerves and stress. Good old diazepam. Where would he be without diazepam? Up the bloody creek, no paddle. He could have told them to go home, get on the big freedom bird at the airport, head off for Romford or Ruislip or Richmond, but they wouldn't. The expatriate community was down to the hard core since the bombs at the Al-Jadawel, Al-Hamra and Vinnel compounds had thinned out the foreign community. Those who stayed, who could not face life in a London suburb where they'd struggle for work and be without servants, swimming-pools and fat-cat salaries, were now prisoners inside the compounds, their lives dependent on the alertness of the guards at the gates. A few, those who had been with him at the races, pretended life was unchanged; the majority cowered in the custody of their homes, and were reliant on the diazepam he doled out.

It was all about money for them . . . Beside the basin, the window gave him a good high view down the street. The wind tore at the white robes of men on the pavement below and creased the black robes of women against their bodies. A damn storm was up. The trouble with storms was that they carried sand. It would be all over his vehicle, that was always the worst thing about storms coming up off the desert . . . All about money. Bart knew about money, the absence of it.

At six twenty-five in the morning, they'd come. Two oafish uniforms, a plainclothes constable with the weary look of a man close to retirement, and a gimlet-faced woman who'd identified herself as a detective sergeant and who wore an unflattering black trouser suit. At six twenty-five in the morning, he'd had a patrol car and a saloon in the driveway, and every one of the bloody neighbours would have been parting the curtains, lifting the nets and gawping. Ann knew nothing. Ann had hissed, stage-whisper, as they'd filed into the hall, 'What have you done?' She'd had her dressing-gown wrapped tightly round her as if she was about to be raped. Ann only knew that there were new carpets in the hall, holiday brochures on the dining-room table, and school invoices in the office desk with 'Many Thanks for Your Prompt Payment' stamped on them.

'Done nothing,' he'd murmured. 'Go in the kitchen and make a pot of tea.'

He'd led them into the lounge. Did he know a Josh Reakes? Yes, he had a patient by that name. Did he know Josh Reakes was a dealer in class A narcotics? No, he did not. Would he be surprised to learn that Josh Reakes had named him, Dr Samuel Bartholomew, as a principal supplier? Yes, he would, and it was a damned lie. He had kept with the denials, stuck with them. He learned that Josh Reakes, arrested the previous evening, had named him as the source of the morphine alkaloid tablets, liquid heroin and powdered cocaine that had been found when he was strip-searched. Deny, deny, deny – his word against a contemptible little rat's; a baseless allegation that was poor thanks for his efforts on behalf of one more of Torquay's addict population. They had a search warrant for the house and another for the surgery. They went through the walnut-veneer desk – bank statements and income-tax returns. Each time Ann had come into the living room, between feeding the kids and getting them ready for school, she'd looked like an ally of the police, squinting at him with suspicion. The best thing he'd done was give her the housekeeping in Josh's cash, so the carpets, holidays and school fees came out of the bank account and were laid against his salary . . . Then down to the surgery. A full waiting room for him to tramp through with his escort. Into the records of the quantities of morphine alkaloid tablets, liquid heroin and powdered cocaine he'd prescribed, and then he'd realized they were trawling and had no decent idea of how to prove that the terminally ill who'd been given Brompton's Mixture, or the back-ache sufferers, had left excess supplies for him to collect.

He'd brazened it out. The word of a professional man against the word of an addicted yob. He'd known he was on solid ground when the detective sergeant had snarled through her pasty little lips: 'I'll bloody get you, Bartholomew. You are a fucking disgrace – a doctor who is a mainstream supplier. I'll get you sent down, see if I bloody don't.'

They'd taken him down to the station, hands on his arms like he was a criminal, and he'd dictated a statement of innocence – and known they believed not a word of it.

By the time he was freed, seven hours after the wake-up knock, his partners had met and revealed to him their considered opinion that he should leave the practice, not the next week and not the next day but within the next hour. Within a month, the day after he had again been interviewed at the police station and the day before he was due to be grilled in London by lawyers of the British Medical Association, Ann and the children had moved out of the family home and into that of the guy who had the Saab franchise up the road from Torquay. He was unemployable in the United Kingdom, friendless, and soon divorced; the house was sold and nine-tenths of the proceeds had gone to the mortgage company. But he had to have food in his stomach, a shirt on his back and a glass in his hand, and in the profession's journal he'd seen the advertisement . . . If he'd thought what had gone before was the steepest downhill tumble, he had been so wrong.

If they had only known the truth of his life, the patient and her husband might have felt sorry for him. He counted out thirty diazepam tablets, bottled them and wrote the dosage on the label. He was more trapped, incarcerated, than they were. He showed them out. All their problems were money, but Bart's were far beyond that level of simplicity. He closed the door after them.

Al Maz'an village, near Jenin, Occupied West Bank.

Bart braked.

If he had not slammed his foot on the pedal, crushed it against the floor, had not swerved and come to a grinding halt as he emerged from the side turning, he would have run straight into the armoured personnel carrier. There were three more behind the one he had missed colliding with.

They rumbled down the street, but the machine-gunner on the last swivelled the mounting and kept the barrel aimed at him until they were gone. He sat behind the wheel and the sweat poured off him. Outside the four-wheel drive it was cold enough to freeze the sweat. He could no longer see them but he heard the racing whine of the carrier's tracks and the street was pitted where they had been. Where had they gone? He knew. Down that street a patient, a child, was suffering from acute diarrhoea, and in the patient's home there was a back kitchen and a yard beyond it. In the yard there was a shed . . . Jesus. He heard gunfire. He sat with his head in his hands and tried to blot out the sounds that crashed in his ears.

After the gunfire there were the explosions of grenades.

Men and kids were running in the street in front of him. More shots. He was recognized. More explosions. His door was opened, he was pulled out by a clutch of hands and his bag was snatched off the seat beside his. He was propelled forward. Across the street in front of him an armoured personnel carrier was slewed and the same machine-gun now traversed on to him. That day he was wearing, over his anorak, a white sleeveless jerkin with a red crescent symbol at the front and a red cross on the back. His bag was pushed into his hand. From beside the carrier two shots were fired into the air. The crowd stayed back but Bart advanced. The barrel of the machine-gun was locked on him. There was a shout, first in Hebrew then in English. He was to stop or he would be shot. He was alone in the street. Behind the armoured personnel carrier there was sudden movement. Soldiers burst from an alley dragging what might have been a sack of grain, but the sack had legs and a lolling, lifeless head. Bart saw the head, only for an instant, as it bounced on the street's mud. The engines revved, the troops jumped for the rear doors of the carriers, and they were gone.

Screaming filled the street. He saw a brightening bruise on the mother's cheekbone and blood dribbling from a cut on the father's forehead. He wondered if they had tried to block the troops' entry, or whether they had attempted to hold on to the dead body of their son and been beaten back with rifle butts. God might forgive Bart, no other bastard would. He reached the door and the crowd had thickened behind him. He did what was necessary, bathed the bruise and staunched the cut, and all around him was the wailing of misery. He realized it: he was a trusted as a friend.

Three hours later he was at the checkpoint, and while his vehicle was searched methodically, and while the pretence was made that he was questioned in the hut, he drank a mug of strong coffee.

Joseph said quietly, 'I don't think you are a military man, Bart – as a man of medicine you are a man of healing and peace – but, I promise you, what we do is for the preservation of peace. Terrorists are the parasites that feed off people. We have to destroy those parasites or there can never be healing. You saw a body. The body was defenceless. You saw but you did not comprehend. He made the belts and the waistcoats that are used by suicide bombers. You have seen the buses that are destroyed, you have seen the markets where they kill themselves, you have seen the cafés where they detonate the bombs. He was good at his work. What you have done, Bart, is save lives. Sometimes a suicide bomber kills maybe ten, but it has been as high as thirty, and for every death there are five more innocents who lose their sight, their limbs or their mobility. Because of you, many innocents have been given the chance to live a whole life. You should feel good, you have removed a major player in what they call their armed struggle. I salute you.'

He did not want to be saluted or congratulated. Some time, on the decision of others – and it had been promised him – his life would begin again, but only when others permitted it.

Bart swallowed hard. He blurted, 'I saw him. I was in the house. Surely there will be a security investigation. How was it known he would be back at his home, that he was using his home? I was there. Too many people know I was there. What about me?'

Joseph smiled and his hand rested in reassurance on Bart's shoulder. 'We take great care of you. You are a jewel to us, so precious. Have no fear.'

He left his coffee half drunk. He was pitched out of the hut and his feet slithered in the mud. When he had his balance he swung and shouted at the troops by the hut door. He was watched by the Palestinians who waited for processing at the checkpoint and he heard the applause, the fervent clapping. Some chanted his name.

He drove away.

They talked of the complicated and intricately webbed world they inhabited.

'You're not bullshitting me here, Eddie?'

'You can count on it. I was there. I found the prime eyewitness. He wouldn't have known how to lie. The body of the paymaster, I saw it, on the slab. It's about as far from bullshit as you can get.'

They were at the kitchen table. Juan Gonsalves and Eddie Wroughton shared the table with his children, their crayon-coloured drawings, and pepperoni pizza fresh from the microwave. The children ate and drew, Teresa tried to separate sheets of paper from the food, Wroughton talked and Gonsalves scribbled notes. Separated from his work, Gonsalves could laugh, but he never laughed when he worked. Wroughton understood the pressures now lying on the shoulders of every Agency man in the field: the disaster of failed intelligence analysis before 9/11 dictated that every scrap should be written down, passed on and evaluated. The life of a Langley man who ignored a warning was a cheap life. The pressures on Wroughton were lightweight, he thought, by comparison.

'The caravan was a Bedu, his son and four strangers. I don't have the exact number of camels, but they carried enough water and food for a long trek into the Empty Quarter. They are important enough to be using about as remote a piece of the border to cross as there is. No Omani or Saudi border patrols, and camels rather than trucks and pickups.'

'Who'd walk, or get camel sores, when they could ride in a vehicle?'

'People of exceptional value. For the Organization it would be a major setback if men of that value were intercepted on either side of the border.'

Theirs was a good friendship, that was Wroughton's belief. Most politicians in London deluded themselves they had a special relationship with the White House . . . but, here, on the Gonsalves kitchen table, the relationship was indeed special. Wroughton's report of his journey up-country in Oman was now being studied in London; in a week, when desk warriors had rewritten it, the revised report would go in the bag to Washington; in another week, the report would be passed to the sister agency at Langley; a week later, after further revisions and rewriting, a version would be sent in cypher back to Riyadh and would land in Gonsalves' office. The real relationship, between two dedicated professionals, was across a clutter of crayons and paper, and was dictated above a babble of excited kids' voices.

172

'He said quite specifically that the camels were loaded with six packing cases, crates, whatever – they were painted olive green, military. Dimensions are estimated but seemed to be the eyewitness's arm span, both arms. Machine-guns wouldn't be in crates. The weight of the crates is a handicap going into the Empty Quarter, so we are looking at something that cannot be exposed to the elements, also that requires cushioning.'

'What are we talking about?'

'I'd reckon we're talking armour-piercing or ground-to-air missiles. If I had to bet I'd say we're talking ground-to-air. Try Stinger.'

Gonsalves grimaced.

'I did some work on it today. You shipped, with your typical generosity, some nine hundred Stingers into Afghanistan; the mujahidin downed an estimated two hundred and sixty-nine Soviet fixed wing and helicopters using them. At the end of the war, when the Soviets quit, two hundred were unaccounted for, still out there. Your people tried to buy them back but went empty-handed. They can blow a military plane out of the skies or a civilian air-liner . . . What we don't know is shelf life. Eighteen years after their delivery, are they still functioning? Have they degraded? Don't know. My own view, what it's worth, the crates aren't the problem. The problem's bigger. I think the men matter, the four strangers are the priority.'

Their greatest difficulty, as counter-intelligence officers, was to sift the relevant from the dross. Mostly their trade relied on the electronic intercepts of conversations sucked down from satellites, gobbled by computers, then spat out as raw verbiage. Wroughton and Gonsalves called it 'chatter'. Their bosses called it ElInt. But this was the rarest commodity they dealt with: the word of an eyewitness.

'Right, four men are being taken across the Empty Quarter in conditions of the greatest secrecy – they matter. The eyewitness is definite there was an argument over the price of the camels. Then one of the men intervenes. He assumes authority. He is young. He is tall. He does not fit in physique and build – the eyewitness notes that. He is different in his features from the others – wears their clothes, but is different. A young leader, with authority, that's what I have – but that's all.'

All of the best material, high grade and rare, was exchanged across the kitchen table. The kids liked Wroughton. He drew the pencil out-lines for them to colour in better than their own father, and after the meal they would go out into the floodlit yard where he would pitch a ball at the eldest kid, and do it better than Gonsalves, and later he would read to the kids in their beds and they liked his accent better than their mother's. In London and Washington there would have been coronaries and fury at the closeness of the two men.

'Juan, they are regrouping down there, pulling in new men, new blood. I can smell it.'

'Kill her.'

Caleb's head was down as he climbed the dune. He saw the sand, loose, slide through his burned toes. Beside him the camel struggled. He had hold of its rein and helped it steady itself. They went up together. The voice was Tommy's.

'I say it, kill her.'

He looked up and the low sun bruised his eyes. They were all at the top of the dune and were silhouetted in the dropping light. Their shadows, and those of the camels, fell down the dune's slope towards Caleb. He heard only the Iraqi's voice.

'Because she has seen us, kill her.'

They seemed not to hear him behind them. They gazed ahead and below. Caleb reached them. He pushed past Hosni and Fahd, past the boy, who turned and faced him, wide-eyed, past the guide, who was clawing at the baggage on his camel and had his hand on the rifle. He was at the shoulder of Tommy, the executioner. He looked down.

'Because she has seen us, can identify us, kill her.'

She was standing. The sun back-lit the gold of her hair, which was tangled and sweat-streaked. She wore a dirtied blouse of soft colours, faded jeans and heavy boots. Her hands, face and clothing were stained with oil. She looked up at them, rocking as if she no longer had the strength to stand erect. There was a calm about her, like an indifference. She did not flinch from Tommy . . . and Caleb saw the Land Rover wedged in the drifts of sand. He wondered what faint, minuscule, mathematical chance had thrown her into their path.

'If you won't, I will kill her.'

The guide had the rifle. With a fast, clattering movement of his hands, he armed it. Caleb looked into Rashid's face, saw the hesitation. Furrows lined his weathered forehead. Caleb understood. It was the way of the Bedu to offer help, aid, whatever was in their power, to a traveller in distress. It would have been the way of any villager in Afghanistan . . . He had been offered help, aid, when he had crawled towards the village. Deep memories stirred. They came from beyond the chasm he had fashioned to block them out. The words croaked in his throat: 'We would break the culture of the Sands. We would dishonour ourselves.'

Tommy laughed at him and spittle flew from his mouth. It rested wet on Caleb's face. 'Culture, that is fucking rubbish. Dishonour, what is that? You won't, I will.'

'She has seen a caravan pass by. She has seen nothing . . .'

They would have known, all of them, that his words were empty. In turn they sneered derision at him.

Caleb ignored them. Rashid had the rifle. He fixed Rashid with his eye. He held the eye. He did not blink, did not waver. He stared at Rashid. He would listen only to Rashid . . . He himself was the chosen man. He was the one for whom the rest struggled in the Sands. Was he not worthy of trust? Rashid broke, looked away, then began to replace the rifle under the bags on his camel's flank.

Caleb said to Rashid, 'You are a fine man, a man I love . . . Go, till it is too dark to go further. Light a fire. There I will find you.'

They went. After a splutter of argument, on which Caleb turned his back, the guide led them in a deep half-circle around the woman, as if by her glance or her presence she might poison them. Caleb watched them go. When the sun first touched the horizon's dunes, when he could no longer see them, when his body ached with tiredness, hunger and thirst, he went heavily down the slope towards her.

She was reaching into her hip pocket. 'Are you going to try to rape me?'

As she spoke, in clear Arabic, her hand slipped to a position of defence. Against the dirt and the oil smears on her blouse Caleb saw the clean shape of an open penknife blade.

'Are you going to kill me?'

'No,' Caleb said. 'I am going to dig you out.'

Chapter Nine

In the bone-crushing, muscle-numbing exhaustion, he felt freedom.

Caleb had dug through the last of the sunlight, through the dusk, through the time the desert was bathed in silver. He had cleared the wheels. From the time she had given him the short-handled shovel he had not spoken a word, as if talking would further waste his energy, and she had seemed to realize the silence's value. He had used the roof boxes from the Land Rover to make a wall beside the wheels so that when he threw aside a shovel's load, the sand did not slip back into the cavity he dug. Each wheel was harder to clear; with each wheel his strength seeped and his tiredness grew. She could not help him. When each wheel was freed, he let her ram down the next box into place for the next wall, and she brought him the water that sustained him. She had watched him through the dusk and the night, only darting forward to drag the boxes into position and to bring him the water.

The boy had come back in the night, had sat apart from them and had minded his own camel and Caleb's.

For those hours, digging and gasping down the water given him, Caleb had known a new freedom. Links were broken, burdens offloaded. He was no longer a recruit in the training camp, no more a member of the 055 Brigade, was away from the trenches and the bombing, was distanced from Camps X-Ray and Delta, did not live the lie, was not travelling to rejoin his family. The sense of freedom burgeoned.

She had had a torch, and in its light Caleb had stepped over that chasm of his memory. He had raised the bonnet over the Land Rover's engine then fastened it upright. With his fingers and then using his headcloth – the *ghutrah* – as a whisk, he had cleared the surplus sand that covered the parts. Since the wedding and his recruitment, he had never taken that step into his past, never shown his knowledge of the working parts of a vehicle's engine. She had rummaged in a bag for a clean blouse, ripped the soft cotton material into strips and passed them to him. A strip for the filters, two strips for the carburettor, a strip for the pump, strips for each part of the engine that sand grains had infiltrated. When the torchlight had guttered, the moon had fallen, he had worked by touch, from memory.

The freedom would not last. With the coming morning he would resume his march to return to his family.

At the end he had used the short-handled shovel and, with what little remained of his strength, he had battered the blade against the wood of one of the boxes until it had fallen apart, then he had placed the wood lengths, four of them, hard against the revealed tyres, for a valuable yard of traction. He had sat in the driver's seat, had turned the key and pumped the pedal. The engine had caught, then he had switched it off.

He had climbed up to the crest of a shallow dune, had collapsed on to the sand, and begun to erase the memories. Without the memories, Caleb was an Arab, he was returning to his family, was a man who hated, was a chosen man. Behind him he could hear the quiet sounds of the restless camels and the soothing voice of the boy. She was beside him and he knew he must guard himself or the memories would swamp him, and with them came weakness.

Her questions were a torrent.

'Who are you?'

'Where are you from?'

'Where are you going?'

The questions were asked in Arabic. He stared up at stars losing lustre, at a moon losing brilliance. He felt the cold of the night, the pain in his legs, arms and shoulders, the emptiness in his mind. She crouched over him. It must have been the last strip from her ripped blouse, and the last of the water, that she used to damp his forehead and his mouth. He could smell her, not perfume from a spray but her sweat. Her fingers moved over his skin and his lips. He had been frightened to talk for fear that his language would slip and betray him.

'You are not a Bedu – too tall, too strong. Where have you travelled from? You knew the engine of the Land Rover – where did you learn it?'

He had the last of her blouse strips, the last drops from the water container, and the last of her sandwiches – hot, curled and dried out in the past day's heat – and he had thought he was going to vomit but he had swallowed hard instead.

She was closer to him, lying back. She lapsed into silence but her fingers played patterns with the hairs on his right arm. Old senses stirred in Caleb, pulses beat. The fingers worked over his forearm, then came to rest on the material that covered the plastic bracelet. They stopped there, as if it were a barrier. The bracelet was exposed, then the torch snapped on and its failing beam was on his wrist. Caleb writhed away from her, but she had hold of his wrist and tried to work it into the beam. She was strong-muscled, not dainty. They wrestled, but he had his arm under his body. She loosed him, knelt beside him. The beam moved on. It caught the soles of his feet. He heard the shocked gasp, then it veered on again and shone full into his face. He hit her arm, suddenly, surprised her and the torch fell away.

She sat back, reached out and switched off the torch. 'Time to talk.'

He looked away.

'Who are you?'

'You don't look into my face. You don't read what is on my wrist. You don't know me, please, and you forget me.'

She was laughing. 'He speaks, has a voice. The mystery grows. A voice that is not Saudi, not Bedu, feet that are raw. Who are you? I am Beth Jenkins, teacher and geologist. I work at the Shaybah oil-extraction plant. I am twenty-seven years old. I was in the desert because I had been told of a meteorite site never studied before. I have no satphone and I am out of range of any mobile link. I have left no note of where I am, it would be days before a search was started and then they would not know where to look. There – you know all about me. Now, what about you? You saved me from dehydration and death, or from a rifle and death. At Shaybah there are Arabs of all nationalities, but you I cannot place. Your feet tell me that for the first time in your life you are walking without shoes or sandals. Why? Because of my debt to you, I have the right to know who you are.'

'You never saw me. The storm missed you. In the morning you go on and you never remember me.'

Sitting close to him and cross-legged, she said, 'Those men with you, because I saw their faces, wanted to kill me, would have. I heard you. Know that I thank you.'

'And you never remember me – I am forgotten.'

No reply.

Her warmth was near to him. He felt the pain loose its hold on his muscles. A great calm came to him. Her breathing was slowed, regular. She slept. Had he moved clumsily he would have woken her. She knew everything of him. She knew that he wore a plastic bracelet on his wrist as if it were a convict's tag, that he crossed the Sands in secrecy, that his identity was hidden, that his business was worth killing to protect, that his accent separated him from the region, that the scars, blisters and welts on his feet meant he was a stranger and an Outsider. He heard, from the base of the dune, the boy's hacking cough, the sounds of the camels stirring and their grunts as they spat. If he moved he would break the spell of her sleep. She shifted, without waking, and her head was on his chest, her throat on his shoulder. His hand moved. His fingers touched her throat. They ran on her throat from the windpipe to the back of her neck until they tangled with her hair. She could drive back where she had come from and she could go to a police post or an army post. She could betray him. His fingers were on her throat. She slept and was without defence. He moved his fingers from her throat. She slept because she trusted him.

The first shaft of the sun hit him.

He heard the boy whistle for him.

With great care, with gentleness, Caleb lifted her head and drew his arm clear, then lowered her head back to the sand. Her eyes did not open. He edged back from her, scratched at his face, shivered, then pushed himself up. The boy, expressionless, watched him. He left her and slid away down the dune.

Caleb took the camel's rein. They walked briskly, leaving behind him the woman and the Land Rover. The boy led him. He had gone fifty paces, sixty, and the slight warmth of the sun nestled on his back.

The shout was clear behind him, burst over the sand: 'Thank you. You saved my life and I thank you. If it is ever possible I will repay you.'

He did not turn but he cupped his hands and yelled, at the plateau of sand around him, 'You never met me, I was never here . . . You never saw my face.'

They walked on.

The boy said, 'The Iraqi would have cut her throat. My father would have shot her.'

'But he did not.'

'You made a softness in my father. I think it is because you are different from us – my father cannot explain it. None of us knows you.'

'What have you been doing? Lifting too many ammunition boxes?'

Bart stepped back from the couch and peeled off the rubber gloves.

'Not ammunition boxes, no.'

The patient was mid-forties and overweight, a former Logistics Corps man, had risen to warrant officer and had looked for better remuneration than an Army pension would offer. They talked across each other.

'What I'm thinking is a hernia.' Bart's face cracked with his general practitioner's smile, comforting.

'You don't get those SANG guys to lift anything, not if they can wriggle away and get someone else, some other idiot, to do it. It's been CS-gas cartridges mostly, and plastic bullets, more than live stuff.'

'I'm going to pass you on to a consultant specialist, but I'm pretty sure that the pain and the lump mean an inguinal hernia.'

'Most of what we're doing with SANG, these days, is riot control and crowd control.'

'I expect you were worried about prostate cancer, with the swelling and the symptoms. That I can most definitely rule out – so it's not been a bad day for you.'

At the basin, gloves off and binned, Bart scrubbed his hands while the former warrant officer, now on the training programme for the Saudi Arabian National Guard, spilled out the detail of his daily work.

Only when he'd finished saying anything useful, when he'd come off the couch, zipped up and belted his trousers, put his sneakers back on, did Bart start to hurry him.

'Convalescence isn't bad, two weeks till you can drive after the operation. No heavy lifting during that time. Actually, it's the anaesthetic – if you have a full one – that governs recovery time. I'll make all the arrangements, fix an appointment and, please, leave my receptionist with the details of your cover policy . . . It's been a real pleasure to meet you.'

When the patient had gone, having grinned and pumped Bart's hand in gratitude, he sat at his chair and made his notes. Nothing about an inguinal hernia. Everything about the National Guard's current training schedule, yes: all classified as top secret, all closely guarded by the leaders of the Kingdom. Good stuff, the best he'd had for at least two months. He was a kept man, Wroughton's toy-boy. He had been a kept man since he had answered the advertisement, had been accepted for employment on the basis of his severely edited curriculum vitae, had flown to Cyprus, paying his own fare, and had taken a taxi that had cost a small fortune to Nicosia. Ann behind him, and the kids, all of them the responsibility of the bastard with the Saab franchise, and the divorce papers signed. A new start and a new beginning in the sunshine. He hadn't crawled into the water, he had jumped. In the last month before he flew out of the UK, with no for-warding address for the sour-faced detective sergeant in Torquay or the pompous creep of a solicitor from the British Medical Association, he had begun a crash course in the Russian language. What he'd read, there were more Russian banks on the island of Cyprus than anywhere other than Moscow. There would be Russians with heart problems, liver problems, kidney problems, and there would be British tourists with sunstroke and alcohol poisoning. Piece of cake, on his feet at last.

After a good dinner and an excellent sleep, having shaved care-fully, then dressed in his best suit and a sombre tie, he had walked from his hotel to the block where the practice he would join worked from. Kept waiting twenty-five minutes, no coffee and no biscuits. Left to cool his heels before a harassed man, with a face that said death was visiting, had called him in. 'I regret, Dr Bartholomew, that the offer made in writing to you no longer stands. We have a considerable reputation on the island that my colleagues and I will not sacrifice.' A moment of leaden silence while the man looked at the floor and Bart had gaped. A letter was passed to him, headed 'British Medical Association'. It gave close detail of a police investi-gation into the illegal sale of class A drugs, as yet incomplete, and a BMA inquiry, as yet not concluded. The man shrugged, then almost ran to the door to open it. 'You understand, Dr Bartholomew, that no alternative is open to us.'

He had gone out, dazed, into the sunshine. His head had been bowed, so he had seen the cigarette tossed down on the pavement, then crushed under a polished shoe. A voice had said, in flawless pedigree English, 'What I always say, those days you wake up and the sun shines are those when you go out without an umbrella and the rain starts pissing down. Know what I mean? Raining now, isn't it? Let's go and have a drink and see if we can roll the clouds back. Come on.' He had been led and he had followed, as any kept man would.

When the notes were complete, Bart rang Wroughton to fix a lunchtime meeting, then buzzed for the next patient.

Beth stood where no man or woman had stood before. She should have felt a thrill of exhilaration, should have wanted to jump and cheer and punch the air.

The memories of the night trapped her. She stared around her, then began to walk forward. The crater was in front of her. What she had been told to find was a high wall of sand, the highest in that part of the desert, and four hundred paces from the right side of the wall was the perfect circle of the crater. It should have amazed her that her Bedouin informant could be so exact in his description of the place and, without a GPS, so certain of the route she should follow. She had driven only eleven point three miles from where the storm had caught her, and after four – when doubt was settling – she had seen the wall that towered higher than any others. The crater was a dozen strides across, its rim clear to see, and there were other, smaller, circle shapes near to it, and a scattering of dark grey stones.

The crater had a raised lip. Five hundred years before, or five thousand, or five million, a mass of rock had hurtled down from the heavens. Having burst the atmosphere it had detonated on impact. The entry heat would have melted the external parts of the rock, leaving them as blackened slag, fusing the iron ore that was its signature, and creating intense heat sufficient to turn sand to glass. There would have been, in that part of the Sands years before, the equivalent of an explosion by five kilotonnes of TNT. Perhaps there had been people close by, perhaps the desert had been as empty as now, but anything living within hundreds of metres of the ejecta field would have been killed. Her mind, mechanically, made calculations and estimates of the size of the meteorite, while her thoughts were on the young man who had saved her, who had told her, with steel authority, 'You never met me, I was never here . . . You never saw my face.'

Beth had been eight times to the Wabar site, the ninth largest in the world, with a principal crater four hundred metres across where an iron core mass of three thousand tonnes had impacted. The largest known was in Arizona, fourteen hundred metres in diameter, but to Beth that was a tourist site, boring, and she had not visited it. Nor had she gone to the site at Chicxulub, on Mexico's Yucatan coast, which dated back sixty-five million years: there, a rock said to have been the size of Everest had hit the earth's surface at perhaps six thousand miles an hour and had caused such seismic shocks as to destroy the dinosaur population and shift fractionally the earth's orbit – coachloads went there, utterly boring.

His fingers had been at her throat, and she had felt no fear. Over the years men had tried to impress her, had put on peacock feathers . . . He had not. The men she had known, at university and in her social life in London, and on the field trips, had sought to create an indebtedness, had bought her dinner, taken her to the theatre, carried her bags ostentatiously, tried to insinuate themselves . . . He had not. There were men who had made her laugh, and men who had demonstrated their cleverness with intense and earnest talk . . . He had refused to answer her questions. Men told her their life stories . . . She knew nothing of him.

There was not one person in the world, no one she knew, to whom she would have talked about the encounter in the dunes, not even her mother. He had wanted nothing of her. There had been a serenity about him, a strength, and a gentleness when he had moved her arms to stand and slip away while she pretended to sleep.

What confused her most – at Shaybah she met Arabs from every country in the Middle East, Yemenis, Egyptians, Kuwaitis and Jordanians, and there were labourers from Pakistan, but she could not place or match his accent.

Every aspect of her life was based on certainty, except him. No name, no start point and no destination. She cursed out loud.

Her voice, yelling the obscenity, rolled back at her from the sand wall. Angry, as if he watched her, she flounced back to the Land Rover, snatched up her camera, her samples bag and clipboard. She started to work where no other human had stood before, but she could not escape him.

For the first time, Caleb rode. He would not have done but Ghaffur insisted. Ghaffur made him ride, shouted at him in his high-pitched voice, and showed him. Ghaffur said that if they were to catch the caravan then Caleb must learn, and that if he fell off he should mount again. He had to ride because they must rejoin the caravan by nightfall.

The boy called the camel the Beautiful One.

Caleb rolled, rocked on the hump. The Beautiful One went her own way at her own speed. Caleb had no control over her. He sat on a saddle of sacking and clung to the reins or to her neck and clamped his thighs to her flanks, but he survived, did not fall . . . Again he crossed the chasm. The memory was from far back, rain on his face, darkness and bright lights around him, and the quiet of the Sands was replaced with raucous noise: it was a fairground and he rode a roller-coaster. Boys screamed and girls shrieked . . . but the desert was around him, and the quiet. It had been something from the past, breaking into his memory, and he rode the hump and obliterated it. The Beautiful One crossed the sand with long, weary strides. He had seen the way Rashid treated his camels; foul-tempered to the men he escorted, but sweet with the animals – almost love. The boy turned often, as if expecting to see that he had been pitched off, but there was not the usual mischief on the young face. They made time. Caleb realized that the boy had caught from his father a new suspicion of his resolve, and had caught it, too, from Hosni and Fahd and Tommy: all of them – without his intervention – would have killed Beth Jenkins and would have left her body for the wind and sand to strip, for the sun to rot.

Twice they found the tracks of the caravan, each time close to a gully between the dunes where the sand was sheltered from a brisk wind. Each time they had gone through the gully, the tracks were lost. The surface of the sand seemed to float and it filled the hoof-prints. Caleb marvelled that the boy could go with certainty after the caravan when he, himself, saw no tracks.

They did not stop to rest, eat or drink. He perched on the hump, bounced on it, would not fall. He had forgotten her, she was no part of him, the long night was behind him, and the wind blew the smell of her from his robe.

'I've got a target.' Gonsalves was flushed with excitement at the Ground Control's door. They needed the excitement he peddled: the door hadn't been more than half open, and he'd only had a glimpse of the back of the pilot's head and the profile of the sensor operator's, but the shoulders and back postures told him excitement was in short supply. 'I've got a real target for you.'

He had been strapped into the Cessna for the flight down, had never loosened his belt. Now he paced the tiny space behind their workbench. He thought that the pilot desperately wanted to believe him, that the sensor operator was suspicious of gifts that might be snatched away.

'What I'm telling you is for real. Doesn't come often, but this is HumInt, it is eyewitness. What I told you stands. They are hunted, they are regrouping, they are trying so damned hard to get their shape again. What we have is a camel caravan, and it has crossed the Oman–Saudi border and it has gone into the Rub' al Khālī. By going the hard way, they tell us they have with them at least one man of exceptional value, but they are also carrying sophisticated weapons that we consider to be of lesser but still considerable importance.'

He took from his briefcase a photocopied sheet. He reached forward and slapped it on to the bench between the console the sensor operator used and the joystick that the pilot's fingers were on.

'That is a Stinger box. As it's reported to me, second hand, it is at least similar to the ones the HumInt saw loaded on the camels. Stinger is a shoulder-launched ground-to-air missile, it—'

The woman said, 'I think we know what a Stinger is, Mr Gonsalves.'

Deflated, Gonsalves said, 'There are six of them, loaded in pairs on three camels.'

On the workbench, covered for protection with Cellophane sheeting, was a large-scale map of the Rub' al Khālī. Over the sheeting were the squares they had drawn, and a pitiful few had crosses on them with dates and times.

The woman did the talking for herself and the pilot. 'Where did the caravan cross the border?'

Gonsalves checked his own map, then stabbed with his pencil at theirs. The point rested on the broken line of the international frontier.

'Very good,' she said quietly. 'And when does the HumInt say the caravan crossed?'

'These people are vague. They don't do days of the month like we do.'

'When?' Her question was icy calm.

'More than a week, could be ten days, up to two weeks. We were lucky to get this much.'

Disappointment clouded the pilot's face, his eyes losing hope. Gonsalves could see them through the thick lenses of the spectacles. She talked for him.

'We would have to estimate, Mr Gonsalves, that a camel train can move at twenty-five land miles on a bad day, thirty-five miles on a good day – something between there on an average day.'

She used a black Chinagraph and drew three half-circles on the Cellophane, each covering more of the box squares than the last. He understood. A great segment of the desert was enclosed by the outer half-circle, and its radius from the pencil mark on the border was just short of five hundred land miles.

He said emptily, 'It's the best HumInt I've got. What are you trying to tell me?'

'About needles and haystacks. Take a look, Mr Gonsalves.'

She pointed up to the bank of monitors. He saw the sand, miles of it. Sand that was without an horizon. Flat sand, humped sand, ridged sand and dune sand. He saw true emptiness. Then her finger was on the map, inside the widest of the half-circles.

'We are flying *Carnival Girl* today. Out behind you there's a piss-bucket. We don't leave here when a bird is flying. Marty and I, we're like a fist and glove, we are together. He wants to piss, he stands over the bucket. I want to piss, I squat over the bucket. Why? Because if one of us went out to piss and the other's head was rocking we would miss, on the wide angle, any sort of caravan, let alone a few camels. We get brought sandwiches and we get brought water. We are here as long as the bird is up. We should have at least one more relief shift, but we don't. We should have a stand-by sensor operator, but we don't. Why am I telling you this, Mr Gonsalves? So you appreciate this is a big haystack, and the needle you're giving us – the "best HumInt I've got" – is tiny. Don't take offence. You are trying and we are trying. You are giving it your best shot, and so are we. I hope you have a good flight back.'

He stared at the sand on the screens, stared till the picture distorted his vision. He thought that the pilot and the sensor operator should have relief every two hours if their concentration was to hold, and he thought they were prisoners in the Ground Control for twelve or fifteen hours at a time. The nightmare gathering in his mind: they would fly the UAV, *Carnival Girl,* right over a camel caravan that carried six boxes of importance and at least one man of significance, and they would not see either a trail of beasts or that man.

'Do what you can,' Gonsalves said weakly. For a moment, on his arrival, he had lifted them. Now their shoulders had flopped again.

He went out.

The heat hit him, seemed to stifle his breath.

He walked towards the jeep that would drive him back to the Cessna. It was the life he knew ... A counter-intelligence officer encountered rare highs and frequent troughs. He fought in what was now dubbed in the smart current-affairs magazines back home the War without End. The customers expected goddamn miracles. He remembered what had been said after the Riyadh attacks last year: 'They're saying, "We can get you any time, anywhere." ' It had been good information, but quietly trashed as they had shown him the desert pictures and the half-circles on the map, and all the time his enemy was regrouping . . . Savagely, he kicked a stone from his path to the jeep.

His name was called. He turned, went back, climbed the steps into the Ground Control.

She pointed to a screen.

He saw two tiny shapes. A vehicle roof was at the screen's side and a minuscule figure was in the centre. She played her tricks, the zoom started. He identified the Land Rover, then a woman. The zoom lost the Land Rover as it closed on the woman. She was bending. He could see a clipboard on the sand beside her and bright stones reflected up, then she crouched. Her hair was fair – damn it, he could see the colour of her hair, and of her blouse.

'I just wanted you to know, Mr Gonsalves, what the gear did, if we can find a target.'

'Who the hell do you think she is?'

The sensor operator grinned as she took the picture fractionally closer. 'She's two people. She's a meteorite expert, a scholar. She is also my supplier of tampons. And she's also the only living person, thing, we've seen all day.'

'Won't she wave?'

The pilot said, 'She doesn't know we're up above. We're on loiter at twenty-four thousand feet altitude, that's four point five four five miles. She can't hear us, and if she looked up she couldn't see us. Why we wanted to show her to you, Mr Gonsalves, if there's camels with military crates we can identify them.'

'You got Hellfire on?'

She said they had not.

'Don't ever fly another day without Hellfire on, don't ever.'

'It's riot control they're doing, Mr Wroughton. Five days a week of riot-control training and preparation to counter a breakdown of law and order, that's the truth.'

Wroughton never took a note in the presence of an informer. To have taken a shorthand précis would have made the informer believe his information was interesting, important. His face was a study of disinterest. They were in the lobby of a small hotel that was rarely used by expatriates, and the chairs they used and the table with their juice were shielded by potted plants from the swing door and the reception desk. In any case, his cufflink was a microphone, and the recorder was under his jacket in the small of his back. God, the wretch came cheap.

'Every man and officer in the National Guard who is not on essential priority duties is now being sent on riot-control training. They are crapping in their pants – if you'll excuse me – Mr Wroughton. It's gas and plastic bullets at the moment, but SANG units now have access to live ammunition. I know it's only a little detail, but all the armoured personnel carriers in the National Guard barracks must have full fuel tanks at all times. It's like they know the place is crumbling.'

Some handlers became fond of informants, treated them like wayward children, pretended they were almost a valued part of the intelligence-gathering process. Eddie Wroughton would never make that mistake. Samuel Bartholomew was a creature he despised. Kind words, encouragement, unless laced with a tone of sarcasm, had no place in the relationship.

'I gather it's coming out of the mosques. Not the big ones, the party line rules there, but the small ones whose customers are hard hit by the new austerity. The Americans are gone, their troops have left, but my patient says the poison out of the lesser mosques is now directed at the royals. It's the fall in the standard of living that's doing it, my patient says – oh, yes, the armoured personnel carriers are full-time loaded up with gas and plastics, but they also have heavy machine-guns mounted. They're running scared. I hope this is valuable to you, Mr Wroughton. I've been very dedicated for you, Mr Wroughton, haven't I?'

Wroughton's lip curled. He thought he knew what was coming and he pushed away his near-empty glass with fruit in the bottom. He smiled limply, then stood.

'Please, please, just hear me out.' Then the blurt. 'What I'm thinking, Mr Wroughton, your people can get access to buildings, can't they? And files, can't they?'

They did. 'I'm not following you, Bart.'

'There's files on me. I—'

'Files on all of us, Bart,' Wroughton teased.

'My files at the Devon and Cornwall police and at the BMA, I'm wondering . . .'

Wroughton played the idiot. 'What are you wondering?'

'After all I've done, you know, all the help – well, couldn't they just get lost?'

'Lost,' Wroughton mimicked. '*Lost?* Are you suggesting that we might burgle police premises, and the offices of the British Medical Association, and remove files concerning criminal investigations? Is that what you're suggesting?'

The wretch cringed. 'I think I've done my time. I want out. I want a new start without those bloody files blocking me. That's reasonable, surely that's—'

Always dominate an informant, keep him under a steel-shod shoe. Wroughton said, 'You leave when I say so. Files go walkabout when I decide it – and that's not now. You are going, Bart, nowhere.'

A little dribble of spittle appeared at Bart's mouth.

Anger, Wroughton could have respected. Fight, he could have warmed to.

The doctor caved in. 'Yes, Mr Wroughton.'

There was no spine in the man. He waved him away, watched him cross the lobby and go through the doors. Then he saw her. If he hadn't watched Bartholomew going out of the hotel he would not have seen the woman. Quite elegant – a little plump – well dressed. Silk blouse and skirt. Not young but well cared-for. She turned the pages of a magazine, but her attention was not on the pages. He caught her eye . . . Eddie Wroughton was expert at reading the boredom factor in middle-aged women. She had a wedding ring on her finger. Married women were always the better targets – they were always more bored. She'd caught his eye, and had held it. He thought she matched his own interest. He stood, paused for a decent moment, then eased across the lobby towards her.

A quarter of an hour later, when he had learned she was Belgian, that her husband worked up-country, and her home telephone number, he left her with her magazine.

*

Jed staggered like a drunk. He came off the ferry that linked the accommodation area with Marine Corps administration from the Delta Camp and thought he might fall. He knew that the eyes of every civilian, officer and enlisted man who had sailed on the ferry were locked on him.

A headcold had gone feverish and forced him to his bed. Two whole days, two nights, and part of a third day he had been tossing under the sweat-damp sheet, dosed with pills, twisting, cursing. Then frustration had forced him up and into his work clothes. He was unshaven, unsure whether he could manage a razor with his shaking hand. A lumbering shadow of himself, Jed made his way off the ferry and towards the shuttle bus.

The mission he had set out on hooked him. He had gulped down more pills, dressed haphazardly; the stubble on his face and the unbrushed hair gave him the appearance of a vagrant. He heard titters of laughter. He said nothing, but hauled himself heavily up the bus steps, then flopped on to the nearest seat.

He was dropped off at Camp Delta. He showed his card at the gate. 'You all right, sir?'

'Just fine, thank you, Corporal.' He wasn't 'just fine', he felt god-damn foul. Swaying, he made his way to a store shed, far in the wrong direction from the block where his office was. It was the territory of a giant-built Afro-American sergeant, a man to be treated with respect or steel shutters would block any chance of co-operation.

He gave the name of Fawzi al-Ateh. 'What's the classification, Mr Dietrich?'

He said that the classification was Not to be Continued With, and that the subject had been released. 'You're asking a lot of me, Mr Dietrich – for me to find an NCW who's not even here.'

He asked whether the NCW files had been pulped or shredded and his voice was deferential. He was told where they were, an annexe. He thanked the sergeant. He did not suggest the man put aside his magazine or his two-litre Pepsi bottle, or pull himself up and get himself into the annexe. He said he would be happy to go look himself for what he wanted.

'Don't mind me telling you, Mr Dietrich, but you're not looking your best.'

He went through the door behind the sergeant's desk, and closed it.

Jed passed the racks that held the current files of transcripts, floppy disks and audiotapes. Ahead of him was a wooden door that squealed as he opened it. After more than two years of Camp X-Ray and Camp Delta, the annexe was still under-used. He flicked the switch and a dull ceiling light came on. The Not to be Continued With files and tapes were in sacks on the floor, not separated in any alphabetical system. He shared the annexe with a cockroach, more spiders than he could count and travelling caravans of ants. He had opened fifteen sacks before he found a date on a file that corresponded with that on which Fawzi al-Ateh had been bussed from Camp Delta to the airfield. He had checked nine envelopes, the thin brown pouches used for government service, before he unearthed the transcripts and audiotapes of the taxi-driver. He shoved the envelope under his arm, and left the annexe a little more of a mess than he had found it. It was an effort to walk between the store shed and the office block, and once he had to stop and lean against a fencing post.

He passed an FBI office. Through the open door a voice sang out, 'Hi, Jed, thought you were supposed to be down sick . . .' He smiled at the face behind the shoes on the desk and thanked the agent for his concern. He would shaft them.

In his room, he loaded an audiotape from Fawzi al-Ateh into his cassette-player and slipped on the earphones. He listened, then snapped down on the button. From his desk drawer he took the cassette that carried the voice of the Brit prisoner who claimed to have been nothing more than a religious student in Peshawar, and who had read a translated text in Pashto. Again and again, Jed played snatches of the two voices, till they rang and merged in his mind. His head was supported by his hands, which were clamped over the earphones . . . He was feeling weaker . . . The weight of his head grew . . . He sagged.

He opened his eyes. He knew he had fainted because the tape was finished.

But he had what he wanted.

Caleb and Ghaffur had ridden hard through the heat and caught the caravan in the late afternoon.

When they reached it, Ghaffur left him, urged his camel faster and went past the travellers to join his father at the head. The atmosphere for the last hour of the day, before they halted, was heavy with suspicion and dispute; Caleb was the cause of it. He saw Ghaffur chatter to his father, but Rashid seemed to ignore the boy. When the guide looked round, raked his eyes over those riding behind him, Caleb saw that the malevolence of the glance was not directed at him but fell on the Iraqi. It had been hotter that day than on any other; the heat, Caleb decided, and the lost water were the reasons for Rashid's temper. Because his camel had gone fast, Caleb was stiff, aching, and the sore blisters were growing where his thighs joined his buttocks. Then the Beautiful One speeded up, lengthened her stride, without command. She passed Fahd, who looked away and would not catch Caleb's eye, and two of the bulls, who had the crates, and came level with Hosni's camel.

The Egyptian seemed hardly to see Caleb. His eyes were watery, without brightness and stared down only at the rein and the neck of the camel. The clothes on him hung looser than when they had started out, but even then they had flopped over the spare body. Without shade, exposed to the ferocity of the sun, without sufficient water, Caleb realized how quickly the strength of the elderly Egyptian was waning. His own pains were severe and the blister sores were growing, but Caleb hid them because Hosni's pains and sores would be worse. It must have been his breathing, a little sucked intake as the Beautiful One lurched and the rough saddle sacking expanded the biggest of the sores, that raised the Egyptian's head a fraction.

'Thank you, Fahd, for riding with me. I will not fall, I . . .'

Caleb looked into the dull wet eyes. 'It is me, Hosni, I am back with you.'

'Ah, the noble one. The one with the conscience. What did you achieve?'

'I dug out the wheels, I cleaned the engine.'

'Did she thank you?'

'She thanked me.'

'How did she thank you?' Hosni's voice was mocking.

Caleb said firmly, quietly, 'She told me she was grateful for what I had done.'

The Egyptian, as if it were a great effort, threw his head back and snorted derision, 'She said she was grateful. Are we all now at risk because you dug out her wheels and cleaned her engine?'

'I did not put you at risk, I promise it.'

'Promise? It is a fine word, "promise". I would have killed her, we all would.' From the exhausted weakness of his face his voice came clear and strong. 'You will be asked to stand in a place where great crowds move. A thousand men, women and children will walk in front of you, will jostle behind you, will ignore you or will smile at you. Old men, pretty women and sweet, laughing children will pass by you – and if you carry out your order all are doomed . . . Can we now trust you? I am not sure, Fahd is uncertain, Tommy is certain we should not . . .'

'I will do what is asked of me. I made a judgement, I live by it.'

'If it had been a man, as gross as Tommy, as ugly as Fahd, as old and weak as me, would you have stopped to dig him out and clean his engine, or would he now be dead?'

'I live by my judgement,' Caleb said.

'But it was a pretty woman . . .' Hosni spat into the sand, and the hoofs erased his spittle. The coughing racked his throat. 'Because you ride with me, because you are from outside of us, of great value but new to us, I will tell you of the mistakes made by men of Al Qaeda. Listen well . . . Many mistakes, and all made by men who had faith and commitment but were careless or stupid . . . Ramzi Yousef will die in prison because a colleague left his laptop computer on a table in an apartment in Manila, and the whole of Ramzi's strategy was on the hard drive. Careless and stupid, and a mistake . . . Arab fighters posed for celebration photographs on the armour of destroyed Soviet tanks in Afghanistan, and ten years later one fighter has kept a copy of the photograph and is captured by the CIA. All his closest comrades are identified. Careless and a mistake . . . In Nairobi, approaching the American embassy, needing to get through a guarded barrier to be close to the building, the one chosen to shoot the guard realizes as the lorry bomb brakes that he has forgotten his pistol, has left it in the safe-house. Stupid and a mistake . . . An organizer plans an attack to the last detail, takes months to prepare for the strike, and an hour before the bomb is moved he boards a plane home to Pakistan. By the time he lands the bomb has exploded, security at Karachi is alert. The organizer shows his forged passport at the desk. He is bearded, the photograph in the passport shows a man who is clean-shaven. A mistake . . . A man carries sixty kilos of explosives in the trunk of his car to the Canadian side of the border with America and it is the middle of winter and there is snow on the ground and ice on the road, and he is sweating. A mistake that is stupid and careless . . . A van is driven under the World Trade Center in 1991, the first attack, which did not bring down the towers. In six thousand tonnes of debris, the Americans find the VIN number of the van's engine and trace it to a hire company, and the man who has hired it has given his own name for their records and his own address. A mistake that is careless and stupid . . . Each mistake, the use of the Internet, of a satellite phone, of a mobile phone, costs the freedom of many, and the lives of many. Do you listen to me?'

'I am listening.'

'A week before you came to us I read in an Omani newspaper that, on the Pakistan and Afghan border, the bodies of two men had been found, both dead. Their throats had been cut, and their mouths were filled with dollar notes. They had lost the trust . . . You demanded of us that the woman should live. Was that a mistake?'

Caleb said, 'I did not make a mistake.'

Chapter Ten

It was not the time to break for water, or for prayers. Rashid had halted the march, had put up his hand as a signal to them, had knelt his camel, dismounted, and walked forward alone. The boy had run back on foot and had caught each of the camels' reins; they stood motionless. The sun beat on them, and Caleb swayed on the Beautiful One. The blisters on his thighs, below his buttocks, had calmed in the night but had now reopened in the motion of riding.

'Why have we stopped?' Caleb asked Ghaffur.

The boy shrugged.

'For how long will we stop?'

The boy looked away, would not meet Caleb's eye.

He gazed around him. He sensed the camels were restless, even the Beautiful One, the most placid among them. Some raised their heads high and seemed to sniff, some bellowed, some spat out cud. They were aware, Caleb did not know of what. Around him was a wide plain of sand, unlike any they had crossed before. It seemed crusted under a film of loose sand, and since they had come through a gully between dunes, a harsher sand had caked round the camels' hoofs.

Caleb squinted. Sunlight reflected up from the sand, seemed to burn the lids of his eyes. How long was it, he thought, since he had seen a scorpion or a snake's trail, the little furrowed track of a mouse, a locust hopping or a fly, a living bush or a grass blade? It was as if nothing could survive here. No creatures, no insects, no vegetation. He did not know how far they had come, how far they had yet to travel. It seemed a place of death. It was hard for him to see as far as Rashid. The shape of the guide's body moved, shimmered. But he saw the post.

Caleb blinked.

A pace in front of the guide, and a little to the side of him, a length of old wood, without bark, stuck up from the sand and its snapped-off tip was level with the guide's knee. It could not have been there by any accident of nature. Rashid had his palm to his forehead shading his eyes, and stared out as if searching.

Then they moved. It was abrupt. Up to then, on the march, they had taken straight lines except where dune walls had blocked them and needed to be bypassed. Rashid veered to his right. The boy, behind him, had them all bunched close, and the pack camels, the bulls carrying the crates. When Ghaffur came level with Caleb, he would not look into his face and would not speak, but he slapped the Beautiful One's haunches to make him close up, and Caleb realized the order they took was changed.

He was no longer at the back.

A new order was formed. Rashid, Ghaffur, Caleb. Behind Caleb was Hosni, then Fahd. Caleb's place at the back of the caravan went to the Iraqi, Tommy. Not since they had started out, had crossed the border and moved down into the Sands, had Tommy taken the rear position.

Caleb saw Rashid's face when he turned to check behind him, and saw the face of the boy – felt a gathering tension, but could not place it, could not find a reason for it, but it clawed at him.

The march now was different from any other of the days crossing the desert. There was a second marker. The piece of wood protruded less than half a foot from the sand, and Caleb's burned eyes would have missed it, but at this marker Rashid set a new course to his left. The heat dulled him. Too tired to shout a question at Rashid or at the boy, he clung to the saddle and the Beautiful One followed the camels in front, slow and lethargic, each hoof sinking into the tracks of the ones she followed. The heat was worse, the blister sores were worse. After what he thought was four hundred yards they went to the left and, after what he thought was another two hundred yards, to the right. Then they straightened, and the camels sniffed the warmth of the air and the bulls bellowed, but Caleb thought the sand around them was no different from how it had been every day. The angles that Rashid took confused him, but Caleb could not escape the sense of increasing tension.

He had barely noticed it when Rashid stopped.

Ghaffur took the lead position. Caleb followed the boy. He passed Rashid. He tried to focus on Rashid's face to read it, could not, his eyes wavered and could not lock. No greeting, no explanation, no word. The Beautiful One lumbered on. Behind him were the pack animals, then Hosni and Fahd, and last the Iraqi. He did not understand the tension that now held him.

Caleb turned, twisted on the saddle of sacking. The pain surged in his thighs from the movement: the sores had opened wider. Rashid was now behind Tommy, his camel's neck level with Tommy's camel's haunches. Caleb looked ahead. He took a point for his eyes in the centre of Ghaffur's back. Now the boy swung his camel to the right and the zigzag pattern continued.

His eyes were closed. He yearned for the next stop, for the quarter-mug of water. His eyes were tight against the strength of the sun. His throat was parched. Sand pricked at his face. He rolled, thought he might fall, forgot any concern for whatever happened behind him.

The embassy advised against driving alone.

Bart drove alone and took the shortest route.

Even with a chauffeur, the embassy advised, travel on a Friday in Riyadh should be made with extreme caution.

It was Friday.

Never on a Friday, advised the embassy, should an expatriate go anywhere near the Grand Mosque and the wide pedestrian square between the mosque and the Palace of Justice.

The call had come, it was an emergency and, it being Friday, there was no chauffeur available to drive Bart. He discarded embassy advice, and his mind mapped the most direct way from his compound to that from which the panic phone call had come. He came down Al-Malik Faisal Street, his speedometer needle on the edge of the limit, did not notice the drifting crowds of men, young and old, had no thought of what time prayers would have finished in the Grand Mosque and, when the city's old restored walls were ahead of him, he swung to the right into Al-Imam Torki Ibn Abdulla Street, and had to slow because the crowds thickened and filled the road. Then, crawling, Bart realized where he was.

The pedestrian precinct, bounded on the north by the mosque, on the south by the justice building, on the east by the souvenir shops and on the west by the Souq Deira Shopping and Commercial Centre, was known to expatriates. It was an endless source of fascination, gossip, speculation, and shivering horror. The embassy's security officer advised all expatriates, in the strongest possible terms, that they should never be near that part of the city on a Friday after morning prayers. To the expatriates, the precinct was 'Chop Chop Square'. Without prior announcement in newspapers or on the television-news broadcasts, after Friday-morning prayers the Kingdom's executions were carried out in Chop Chop Square. 'Don't ever want to gawp, don't ever be tempted . . . It is a place of extreme emotions at the time of a beheading . . . Stay clear. Give the place as wide a berth as possible . . . Take no chances there,' the security officer at the embassy advised expatriates. But Bart had been called out on an emergency, and had not been concentrating on the embassy's lectures. Now he had to slow and the crowds flowed around him. He could see, between the moving sea of robes, past the side of the mosque and into the square.

It was an emergency, and emergencies paid well. Friday, no servants in the compound villa: in the main lighting unit of a kitchen a bulb had failed. The tenant, an American lawyer with no servant to do it for him, had put a chair under the unit, had climbed on to it for the purpose of changing the bulb. The chair had toppled, the lawyer had fallen and, with increasing hysteria, his wife had phoned all of the listed American doctors . . . Friday, and they were golfing or tennis-playing or visiting, and Bart's number had been given her. The way she told it, in her panic, her husband's arm was critically damaged. Could he come? Like now. Like half an hour ago. Bart didn't golf, didn't play tennis, didn't do social visiting. He had scooped out a bowlful of food for the cat from a tin, grabbed his bag and hurried out. Expatriates, Americans and Europeans, dreaded accidents and had mortal fear of going alone to a Saudi hospital Accident and Emergency; Bart would be well rewarded for turning out on a Friday in the middle of the day.

The crowds refused to edge out of his way. He twisted among them. Why was he there? Samuel Algernon Laker Bartholomew's road led back directly to the day when he had stumbled from the surgery in Nicosia, and the man had been waiting for him on the pavement and had taken him for a drink. The man, who had so briefly entered his life, was Jimmy: no second name, no address, no telephone number, but a wallet and the minimal generosity of putting, at ten twenty-five in the morning, a double Jameson – no water – on the table in the corner of the bar. 'A man's down, and the whole bloody world gets in a queue to kick him – bloody unfair. This island's dead for you. Look on the bright side, I always say a glass is half full, not half empty. I happen to know where a highly qualified general practitioner, brimming with experience, can do really good work and be appreciated. How I'd put it, the sort of work that would enable a highly qualified and experienced doctor to stuff these unproven allegations down the necks of the bastards making them. Let me run this one by you . . .' Unemployable back home, his bank account drained, marooned in Cyprus, Bart had actually thanked the man for his kindness. It extended to meeting his Nicosia hotel bill, providing petty cash for meals and an airline ticket for the short-hop flight to Tel Aviv. Two days later – and never to see Jimmy again – Bart had been in Israel. God, so naïve, such an innocent.

He hooted impatiently. He looked to the side where the bodies came closer to the vehicle doors. He saw faces that were alive with emotion, and the anger around him seemed to grow. He might have been in an air-conditioned cocoon, but the anger, the emotion, seemed to swell. Shouldn't have bloody hooted. Before he had hooted, the crowd had seemed barely to notice him. Now faces were pressed against the windows and the bodies made a wall in front of the bonnet. Against the noise of the air-conditioning, through the closed windows and locked doors he could detect a slow chant. The interior seemed to darken as the weight of bodies came closer. Then Bart recognized the one word. It came endlessly repeated, with growing force.

'Osama ... Osama ... Osama ... Osama ...'

Now hands were on his vehicle. It shook, they rocked it. The voices matched the faces, anger and emotion. He bounced in his seat. Without the restraint of the belt his head would have hit the ceiling. He felt light-headed, not afraid. He was rolling and the chant reached a new pitch of intensity. Then came the siren.

The crowd melted. As the street cleared, a police wagon drove down it at speed. Extraordinary, but the sun shone through the windows and light bathed Bart. Another few seconds, if the siren had not made the crowds run, he would have felt the fear – he was no hero. He looked to the side, no particular reason, just checking it was clear for him to accelerate away. He could see past the Grand Mosque. A black wagon was pulling away from the square's centre. A man scattered sawdust from a sack, threw it on to the ground, then moved on, chucked more handfuls down and did it again. He thought that the executioner would already have cleaned his sword, would already have gone. He drove away.

Three men's heads had been severed from their bodies. The bodies and the heads would now be in the black wagon. The crowd had chanted an icon's name. The condemned would not have been rapists, murderers or drugs traffickers. The crowd had chanted the name of Osama.

Bart felt, could not hide from it, a creeping sense of excitement. The proximity of death, the name of Osama bin Laden, the power of the crowd made that excitement course in him. He hated the place, the regime, the country, the life he led, the blood now covered with sawdust, the wagon, the chant and the hands that had rocked his vehicle. He was confused and the adrenaline pulsed – gave him a wild message. It thrilled him. Everything he hated he shared with that crowd. He had no loyalties, he identified ... Bart gasped. He drove fast. But the voice echoed in his head: 'You leave when I say so ... You are going, Bart, nowhere.'

He went to see a man who had fallen off a chair while changing a lightbulb.

To Juan Gonsalves, a telephone call was the better medium for a problem than an electronic message. Electronics left a non-erasable trail and settled for eternity in a man's or a woman's records. He called Wilbur Schwarz on a secure line at six thirty in the morning, Washington DC time, and his confidence that Schwarz would be at his desk was justified. Schwarz oversaw the Agency's counter-terrorism operations in the Kingdom from a windowless office at Langley, was close to retirement and his dedication would be missed. Gonsalves trusted him.

'Wilbur, I am not making a complaint. It is off-the-record, and I don't want it to go formal. You shipped in a team with Predators to Shaybah – OK so far? It seems accepted they are doing test flights to examine extreme heat over a desert ... Yeah, yeah, it is some desert. Trouble is, they've been shorted. One pilot and one sensor operator. These kids are great but they're low on fuel and they don't have back-up. They're working round the clock, and then some. I was down yesterday and they were dead on their feet. You have to understand that desert. It didn't get to be called "Empty Quarter" for no reason. It is *empty*. You want sand, you got it. Anything else, you haven't. They spend hours just watching sand. I suppose the first day the sand looks pretty, not after that ... Now, get me right, I am not saying they are already inefficient, that's too big a word. I am saying too much is being asked. Not for me to tell you what sort of help they need, or what is possible in the budget. What I am telling you is that they are liable, in my opinion, to make an error, to miss something. They are searching a hundred thousand square miles of fuck-all ... I don't want to predict disaster here, but in my view that's where we are heading. Wilbur, can we do something here? First thing I had to do when I was down yesterday was lift them, get their morale up – not easy. You got me, Wilbur, will you crunch some numbers and come up with something that eases the load? Try ...'

Caleb knelt. He could not have matched Fahd's cries, or the simple devotion of Hosni, or the dignity and belief in God of Rashid and his son, but he tried. Sapped by exhaustion, burned, suffering the pain of his sores, asking for strength, Caleb felt comfort in his prayers. Only the Iraqi, Tommy, sitting away from them, cross-legged, his back to them, was not a part of them.

When the prayers were finished, when the sun was directly above them and the only shade was between their feet, the guide measured out their midday water ration. It was poured with great care, Ghaffur holding the mug and Rashid tipping the water bag over the mug. There was no line drawn or scratched on the inside of the metal mug, but Caleb sensed the accuracy with which Rashid doled it out. Not a mouthful, more or less, for any of them.

When they had all drunk, the voice burst over the sand.

'You, here, you come here.'

Rashid was beside Tommy's camel. The voice had been a command. Rashid's arm pointed at the Iraqi, who swore, then spat into the sand beside him.

'You obey me, you come here.'

Caleb remembered the tension that the prayers and the water, and his own tiredness, had filtered from his mind. The Iraqi was now the target of the guide's anger.

'You are to obey me, and you are to come to me.'

Tommy pushed himself up, brushed the sand off the seat of his trousers and started a slow, indifferent walk towards Rashid and his camel. Fahd watched him and Hosni, and the boy.

Caleb strained to hear.

The voice of Rashid was quiet, but with poison. 'How many water bags do you carry?'

The surly grudging response. 'I carry four.'

'How many are on the camel?'

'Four, of course.'

'Count them, show me there are four.'

Caleb saw Tommy shrug, as if he dealt with an idiot. He counted aloud as he moved round the camel. 'There is one, there is two . . . here is three, and here is . . .'

The savage interruption. 'Where is four?'

The shoulders crumpled. 'I don't know where is four.'

'You are responsible for the water bags you carry.'

'I am responsible . . . I do not know where it is. All the bindings, before we started, were secure.'

'I show you where is the fourth water bag.'

'I tested all the bindings.' Then defiance. 'If you know where the water bag is then why ask me? I don't know.'

With his arm, Rashid gestured back where they had come. Caleb struggled to follow the line, on their zigzag path, of the arm. The light from the sun bounced back from the sand. He thought he saw a speck, dark against the red of the sand, but could not know at first whether his eyes tricked him. He held his hands over them, shaded them, opened them wider, peered and saw the speck again. The wind moved the surface sand, seemed to make a slight mist over the desert floor. He saw it clearly, held it for a few seconds, but then the brightness in his eyes and the pain in them made him look away. He did not understand how a water bag could have fallen from Tommy's camel four hundred yards back or more. He blinked, screwed his eyes together to cut out the pain.

'There is your fourth water bag.'

'I see it.'

'Go, pick it up, bring it to us.'

The Iraqi had no fight in him. He could not shout or bluster or beg. To have done so would have denied his dignity, destroyed his pride. Caleb saw him reach up and snatch the hair at his camel's neck, lock his fingers in it, then try to drag it down to the kneeling position. Caleb remembered how the order of march that morning had been changed. He had no longer taken back-marker, had been replaced at the tail of the march by the Iraqi. And, he remembered how Rashid had stopped, let the rest of them pass him and dropped back until he rode alongside Tommy, then had come up fast to regain his position at the head of them.

'You don't take the camel.'

The Iraqi spat his answer. 'Am I to walk?'

'You are not to waste the strength of the camel, you walk. The camel did not lose the water bag.'

'Fuck you.'

'It is your responsibility. You walk back and pick up the water bag.'

'I will not.'

'You pick it up and you bring it back to us, and then we will go on.'

The pitch of Tommy's voice rose. 'I am a man of importance. I have a role in this fucking idiotic journey – you are paid to escort me.'

Rashid's voice had quietened, was hard for Caleb to hear. 'If you do not go back, pick up the water bag and bring it to us, then we leave you. We ride the camels and go on. You will run after us for a hundred strides, then you will fall back. We will be gone over a horizon, and you will be alone. Which way do you choose?'

Spinning on his heel, the sand scuffing at his feet, Tommy turned to each of them. Who backed him? None did. Who spoke for him? None did. Not Hosni and not Fahd. Caleb stared back at him. With a brutal kick, Tommy heaved sand up on to Rashid's legs, then started to walk.

He took a straight line, not the zigzag path right and left that Rashid had led them on after finding the first of the two marker posts.

Caleb asked of the boy, 'Would your father leave a man here, walk away from him?'

The boy said, 'If we had no love for him, no trust for him, then, yes, we would leave him.'

The beat of the tension grew. Tommy walked upright and there was a roll in his stride. Hosni ducked his head down as if his eyes could no longer follow him. The heat seared all of them. Fahd seemed to shiver. The sand around Tommy shimmered. They had gone far to the right in the zigzag, and when they had cut back to the left they had not been near the direct line that Tommy took as he tramped, never looking back, towards the speck that was the dropped water bag. Rashid did not look over his shoulder but his face was close to Tommy's camel's head and he murmured soft words in its ear and stroked the hair of its neck. Tommy was half-way to the water bag, the speck. Caleb did not know what would happen, only that the Sands were a place of death, a cruel place, a place with as little mercy as a hangman's shed. Tommy walked the straight line.

He was the only one, Caleb realized it, who did not know what would be the end of it. He had been away from the camp for a whole night, and away from the march for most hours of a day. Through that morning's march, after the marker posts, every turn that Rashid had made had been planned, and he would have gone back to the tail of the caravan and ridden beside the Iraqi, and the Iraqi would have been dead to the world astride the camel with the sun beating on his head and the torpor of the endless vista of the sand sea would have dulled him. The Iraqi would not have known that the guide's fingers released a water bag from the baggage and then tossed it aside, left it to lie on the sand, left it where it could just be seen when the halt was called for water and prayers.

The cry came back to them, carried on the wind.

Caleb thought Tommy a smaller man – shorter, cut off, stunted. There was a little squeal from the boy. For a moment, as Caleb saw it, the Iraqi stood and tried to walk, but could not, and fell. All around him, the sand was clean, unmarked. It was where the zigzag trail had not crossed. The cry became a scream. Caleb remembered: 'Because he hit my father, he is dead . . . Nothing else is possible.' The Iraqi tried to stand, but Caleb could not see his shins or his knees. The arms flailed, and with each struggling movement the Iraqi sank.

The first cry had been shock, then anger. The last cry, the loudest, was terror.

He went to Ghaffur, grabbed the boy's arm, held it so that the boy could not break loose. 'You knew of the quicksand?'

'My father knew.'

'It is not by chance that we came past it?'

'Since he struck my father we changed the route. We came this way for a purpose.'

'To kill a man.'

'He struck my father.'

'How much time have we lost, to kill a man?'

'Perhaps a day – half a day.'

He freed the boy. The cry came again, louder and shriller. There had been bogs in Afghanistan: once he had seen a goat sinking in mud, had heard its bleating, but then the grass carpet covering the bog had been of a deeper, brighter, more treacherous green. Then, one of the Arabs with Caleb had fired a single shot from his assault rifle and the bullet had disintegrated the skull of the goat. It had not been shot to end its misery but to stop the bleating. Caleb would not have thought of quicksands, the same as a bog, in the desert where it might not have rained for ten years, fifteen. To the noses of the camels, there would have been a scent of the buried moisture under the surface of the sand, and the guide had known the purpose of the marker posts . . . it had been a killing as planned and prepared for as any execution.

He saw the chest of the Iraqi and his head and his arms.

The man struggled. Caleb thought Tommy struggled so that he would sink quicker, finish it faster.

He looked around. Rashid had the camels kneeling and was waving to them to join him. Caleb now had his back to Tommy. He walked past Fahd, perched on the hump, as his camel awkwardly stood, and heard the Saudi's sneer. 'Do you want to help him as you helped the woman?' He understood more. He, too, was tested. His strength, or his weakness, was tested. He climbed on to his saddle and gave, gently, the command he had heard the guide use and the Beautiful One rocked him, shook him, and stood.

A scream came on the wind. Tommy's upper shoulders, his neck, head and arms would still be above the sand's level, but Caleb did not turn. The cry was for mercy, and for help, the cry was to him. They rode away. The guide now ruled them. They were in his hands, dependent on his skills. The Iraqi, their brother in arms, had been condemned and none of them – Hosni, Fahd, or Caleb – had fought the guide for his life. He rode beside Rashid.

Caleb asked bleakly, 'When you took the water bag from Tommy's camel, was it full? To kill him, did you waste a bag of water?'

Rashid said, 'It was filled with sand. At that distance, had it not been full, it would not have been seen. I did not waste water.'

The last scream burst behind them, called him, then was stifled and died. There was the sound of the wind against Caleb's robe, the rustle of the loose sand it blew and the thud of the camels' strides. He never looked back.

Camp Delta, Guantanamo Bay.

The guards swaggered behind the orderly who pushed the food trolley along the cell-block corridor. He was at the back of the cell and he wore pathetic gratitude on his face. Earlier, there had been the sounds of a military band playing and singing and cheering had been carried into the block by the wind off the sea. It was the second Fourth of July since he had been brought to the camps. From the scale of the music, singing and cheering, he thought there had been a bigger parade than the previous year when he had been held in X-Ray. Through his dropped eyes, he saw the aggression of the guards, and he thought the music and their love of their country had been primed by the day.

The pathetic gratitude was the act Caleb had mastered.

He had absorbed the routine. The days of his week were governed by his exercise session, two days away, and by his visit to the showers in three days. He had not been interrogated for twenty-nine days, and the only break in the routine would be if he was summoned again. Some men in the block were destroyed by the routine, had their minds turned by it or whimpered because of it, or screamed in the frustration that it brought. He played the part of the model prisoner, whose imprisonment was a mistake.

The plastic food tray was slipped through the hatch at the base of the barred door to the cell. He ducked his head in submissive thanks. The men with red necks and shaven heads, huge in their uniforms, towered in the corridor. Two of the four carried wooden truncheons, and the hand of one, who stood back from the trolley, fidgeted restlessly over a pistol holster. Caleb smiled inanely and waited for them to move on; then he would crawl over the floor to the tray.

A guard said, loud, 'We got Independence Day, son, to celebrate. You got special food today. You, son, enjoy the day as much as we do . . .' The voice dropped to conversational. 'Goddamn gook doesn't understand a single goddamn word. Goddamn pitiful, aren't they? Goddamn pieces of shit.'

Caleb treasured the few hours spent close to the bodyguard and still fed off the strength given him. The guards and the food trolley moved on; he was superior to them, believed it, despised them. The success of the deceit gave him raw pleasure. His head bobbed, he showed his gratitude. They were despised and they were hated.

The strength gave him attention to detail. It might be a year away, or two, or five years – his freedom – but he prepared for it. Word had seeped through the wire mesh sides of the cages that four men, the first, had been released. His life in the cage was consumed by the detail.

Primary in the detail was the removal, the scrubbing clean, of all traces in his mind of an earlier life; the final relegation of nationality, culture, upbringing, work, all gone. Second was the creating of two compartments for his life: in the privacy of his soul he was Abu Khaleb, fighter in the 055 Brigade, and in the eyes of the guards who fed, exercised and escorted him he was Fawzi al-Ateh, taxi-driver. But the detail went deep into the heart of the deceit. He prayed five times a day. When he whispered to the prisoners in the next cells it was about a dead family and a bombed village, and a childhood among orchards; he assumed there would be 'plants', informers, among prisoners rotated round the cages. He assumed also, and the belief bred paranoia, that microphones were buried in the cell back wall and that hidden cameras watched him. He conformed, utterly, to the image he created – the taxi-driver's. If there had been suspicion of him, or if he had *been denounced, he would have been subjected to ferocious interrogation, but he was not. The detail protected him.*

The guards moved on and the trolley squealed to the corridor's end. Then they came back and one whistled cheerfully. They could not see into his heart, could not read the hatred.

He lived the lie, did it well, and the second Fourth of July of his imprisonment faded as the dusk came and the bright lights shone down on the block.

'Something'll turn up,' Lizzy-Jo said, gently. 'You look all stressed out. Something always turns up.'

He was crouched over the workbench and his fingers toyed with the joystick. The muscles in his shoulders were stiff, knotted, and his neck was tight so that the veins and throat tubes stood tall. His eyes behind the thick spectacle lenses had pricks of pain.

Marty said, flat, 'Let's just hope so.'

He used his forearm, wiped the sweat off his forehead. On manual control, *First Lady* quartered a box whose nearest point to the Ground Control at Shaybah was three hundred and twenty land miles. At four and a half miles altitude she crossed the desert floor at eighty-four miles per hour. But when she was up there, silent, secret and fragile, the cross-winds were fierce. The upper-air turbulence dictated that Marty should fly manual, and the extra load of the two Hellfire missiles – two hundred and thirteen pounds weight – one on each of the fragile wings, made her sluggish to commands. If the winds *First Lady* encountered at that altitude had been across or down the runway, she would still be under the awning shelter and grounded. He had to fly her, and each time the high winds tossed her, and the picture rolled, rocked and jerked, Marty heard the sharp intake of Lizzy-Jo's breath, her irritation.

'You know what? – Bosnia and Afghanistan were walks in the park compared to this place.'

'Were they?' His hands were on the joystick, his eyes were locked on the cascade of figures of wind speed, wind direction, wind force in front of him, and the screen above that showed the sand, the damn sand. The sweat ran on his back and over his stomach. 'That is a comfort.'

'But we are here. Here in this goddamned awful place. We have to make it work.'

'You sound, Lizzy-Jo – forgive me – like you're full of shit from Human Resources or Admin. They send you that speech?'

The hardest thing about arguing with or insulting Lizzy-Jo was that she just laughed. She laughed loudly. He always wondered if her man, back now and minding the kid, had ever argued with her or insulted her about her determination to put Agency work in front of rearing the kid and putting his dinner on the table when he came back from selling life-and-death policies. He probably had, and she'd probably laughed at him.

When her laugh subsided, she pulled a face – her serious one. That face made her downright pretty, and the sweat that glistened on it made her prettier. 'We were given a difficult assignment, as difficult as it comes. We are doing our best. What more can we do? What does not help our best is you sulking like a kid without a Krispy Kreme. Lighten up, Marty, lighten up and spit it out.'

'Spit what out?' He knew he was playing awkward. He edged *First Lady* on a gradual turn to port side, and the picture of the sand under the real-time camera blurred. Each time he made an adjustment, dictated by wind speed, and deviated from the straight line of flight a handkerchief of sand below the lens was missed . . . and maybe the handkerchief was big enough for camels with boxes, for men, for a target. But if he did not fly into the wind, when it had mean strength, he risked damaging the bird, like the guys back at Bagram had lost one, and it had been down on the ground, broken and smashed, a sight to make a man's eyes water. An instructor at Nellis had said that the Predator, MQ-1, with Hellfires under the wings, was like a butterfly out in the rain – could fly, but not fly happy. 'What do you want from me?'

'Give me the skinny. Whatever's pissing you off, tell me.'

He gave it to her. 'Well, for one, the head honcho comes down, spiels crappy intelligence, expands the search area . . . We are in a no-hoper, that's my—'

'It's what we got to work with. Next.'

Marty stumbled, stuttered: 'My picture. I shelled out for that. It got sand in it, the storm, it got sand between the glass and the print – and it's got condensation, hot days and cold nights. It's the only picture I ever wanted, and it might just be fucked up.'

She said, sweet and soft, 'I'm sorry. I never had a picture. Maybe when we get out of here it can get repaired . . . I'm sorry. Next.'

He rallied. 'The air-conditioning's going down. It's half strength. We are both dripping wet.'

There was a bleep beside her and a green light blinked.

'Just think about it, if the air-conditioning fails, we're fucked. We're gonna bake.'

She hit keys, made alive a blank screen on which a message flickered.

'The outside temperature is one hundred and twenty degrees, we're gonna cook. We've got an intolerable—'

Lizzy-Jo said curtly, 'What we have got, Marty, is a visitor. I am going to channel eight.'

Against the grinding purr of the failing air-conditioning came a clear, calm voice, brought by satellite from across the world. The voice was Langley's.

'Hi, Marty, and greetings to you, Lizzy-Jo. My call sign is Oscar Golf, that's how you'll know me. You may both feel out on the end of the line, but that is going to change. All the time that *First Lady* and *Carnival Girl* are airborne and transmitting material, from camera and infra-red, we will be monitoring the output. You are not alone, we are right behind you. If you need comfort breaks, meal stops, rest, and the Predators are up, we are here and ready to step in. That's what I wanted to say, over and out.'

The sound feed was cut. Marty slumped. His hands were off the joystick and held his head.

'They don't think we're capable,' he said, his voice a murmur through his fingers. 'Like we're not professional. Shit, and it's all I wanted, to hit, to win—'

'What we both want, Marty, both of us.' Her fingertips brushed against the back of his neck and slipped in the sweat to the tight knot of his shoulder muscles. She was broad Bronx, like she was in a truckers' bar. 'Fuck 'em.'

There was an unused plate, and one portion less of water was poured into the mug.

When they had halted, the boy had searched for an hour but had found neither dead wood, nor roots. When the sun had sunk and the cold came they were without a fire's warmth, and the bread could not be baked. The travellers ate the uncooked dough and dried dates, drank the water in silence, were subdued, but Rashid spoke quietly to his son from the far side of the circle they made and his voice was too indistinct for Caleb to hear. The cool nestled his body, and he seemed to hear the scream of the man whom the quicksand had taken. It pealed in his ears, shrieked for his help.

Caleb broke the quiet. 'That was a game, each move planned. A game was played and Tommy was killed. Why did it have to be a game?'

He heard Fahd's cackle. 'Do you wish to be told? Is it important?'

'It is important to know why one of our family was killed in an entertainment.'

The wind sang around them and Hosni's words were frail against it. 'He struck the guide. That condemned him. After he had hit the Bedu, Tommy was dead ... I negotiated the death. Whatever Tommy's value to us, to Fahd and you and I, he was dead. If we had tried to protect Tommy, the guide with his son would have left us. It is the duty of Fahd and I, and especially of you, to achieve the end of our journey ... you in particular, because of your value. Do you understand?'

'I do not understand why it was a game, an entertainment.'

Again Fahd chuckled, again Hosni answered. 'He was your friend, you talked to him, you heard of the life of a hangman, and you identified with him ... and you stayed with the woman who had seen us and who endangered us, and you helped her. It was not an entertainment, it had a purpose. We watched. Would you go to save him? Would you run across the sand to him? Would you lie on your stomach, where the sand softened, and reach with your hand for his? Very closely, we watched you. You did not look at him. You turned your back on him. He called for you. He faced death and he called for the only one among us whom he thought would help him. It was Tommy's judgement that you were not strong enough for what is asked of you. He called you. You turned your back on him and rode away – you showed us your strength.'

Caleb whispered hoarsely, 'If I had helped him, if I had pulled Tommy from the quicksand, if I had brought him back, what then would have happened?'

Hosni's voice was sharp. 'The guide would have shot you both, but you first. We would have had our answer. Because you would have been of no use to us, the guide would have shot you. It was agreed.'

Caleb sat a long time in the darkness. He saw the patterns of the stars and the moon's mountains, and he felt the freshness of the wind on his body. He shivered, sat hunched with his arms close round him . . . Rashid told a story to his son of a warrior in the history of the Bedouin and the boy was against his knee and rapt in his listening. He thought of a man whose cries he had ignored and the death of that man in the sinking sand. The voices eddied round him and the wind snatched at his robe and the sores below his buttocks itched in pain. He thought of his promise, that he had not made a mistake in helping the woman, and the test set for him.

Hosni leaned across and jabbed his finger into Caleb's chest. 'Tomorrow is a new day. It is the day we start to recall your past, make the old life live.'

Caleb said, 'I killed the old life, forgot it.'

The old body shook. Hosni's voice had the keenness of a knife. 'You breathe on it, reclaim it.'

Chapter Eleven

Caleb could not escape the dream. He was drawn towards the chasm. 'Recall the past ... reclaim it.' The voice was at his back, the chasm was ahead of him. Each time he stared into the chasm, he wavered. Each time he hesitated, the voice behind him was more demanding. The last time he approached the chasm, his stride quickened. He ran, launched, his feet kicking.

He hung in the air. A chill seemed to grip him. He would not reach the far side of the chasm. It seemed to widen. The moon's light hovered on the far rim. He heard his own cry for help. His arms were outstretched, his fingers splayed. He was falling. The chasm widened. He snatched.

The dream played back to him each moment of his jump, then each moment of his fall.

The fingers caught the rim. The tips and nails of his fingers grabbed at grass and loose earth, at rocks and the roots of trees. His feet, bare, had no support. Grass came away in his hands, and earth crumbled. He slipped back. However hard he struggled for a grip, the weight of his body took him further down into the chasm. The rocks that had broken free fell past his face, bruised it, and cannoned against his legs, then dropped. A single root held him. He heard the rocks bounce on the chasm's side. He grasped the root and waited for the noise of the final strike of the rocks against the chasm's floor – nothing, only the fainter noise of the rocks' tumble. The chasm had no floor. He did not know if the root, dry in his fists, would snap. If it snapped, he would fall. He hauled himself up. The root held him. He reached over the rim, one-handed, and the root made a support for his knee, and his fingers grappled in the earth and the grass. He crawled on to the rim. He would never go back. He lay on the grass and his breath sobbed in his throat. He looked behind him, across the chasm, and he could not see Hosni, only a mist. The wind seemed to tug at his clothes. He saw the terrace of houses. He walked through a door, a hall, a kitchen, and he looked out across a yard. Over the low wall was the canal towpath. He knew he would never go back, over the chasm. He wept.

Caleb woke. He did not know where he was, did not know who he was.

The boy stood over him, dark and silhouetted against the stars.

'You screamed.'

'Did I?'

'You made the camels restless and that woke me. Then I heard you scream.'

'I am sorry. It was a dream.'

'What was the dream?'

'Nothing – something about the past.'

'Was it so bad for you to scream?'

'It was only a dream. It was not real . . . How long is it before dawn?'

'Enough time to sleep again.'

'Go away.'

'I hope you sleep again and do not dream.'

'Thank you, Ghaffur.'

'I never dream,' the boy said, and drifted away into the darkness.

Caleb lay on his side and, as if he were now vulnerable, his knees were pulled up against his chest. The images, recalled from the past and reclaimed, played in his mind, but his eyes were open. He was too frightened to sleep. If he slept, he might be pushed again towards the chasm, might have to jump it again, might feel again the grass and earth and rocks breaking away as he clung to them, the emptiness below his feet. He had crossed the chasm, there was no going back, his memory lived.

Caleb lay in the sand and waited for the first light in the east.

Murky pale, the dawn came as Beth finally regained her bungalow, dead tired, hungry and thirsty. Although her headlights had caught the car she did not register it until she had to swerve to miss it. It was parked in the unmade road outside the gates that led up to the carport beside the villa. She knew the Mercedes, top of the range, and she swore. She took her time. Outside her front door, which was ajar, she unloaded the Land Rover. On the patio, she dumped her cold box, her water canisters, which were empty, her sleeping-bag, her clipboard and the filled sample sack. She felt a wreck. Sand was stuck to her face, held there by the sweat, oil streaks were on her hands and her blouse, and grime was caked under her fingernails. She wanted to lie in a bath, gorge herself from the refrigerator, then sleep. What she did not want was a visitor. The exhaustion caught her as she pushed the door wider. For a moment she leaned against the jamb, then went inside to face him.

The deputy governor was sitting on the couch in her living room.

How long had be been there? The answer was in the ashtray on the couch's arm, filled with crushed filters . . . God.

'Hello,' she said, playing natural and failing. 'What a surprise.'

The response was bitter, an attack that the politeness and softness of the voice did not hide. 'Where have you been? I came yesterday in the morning, yesterday in the evening. In the morning the maid told me you had packed food and water as if for the desert, and in the evening the bungalow was still empty. In two hours' time, if you had not returned, I was going to call out the trackers, a search would have been mounted for you . . . I was worried. You left no note, no in-dication of where you had gone. While you were away there was a storm in the Sands. You can easily understand my anxiety.'

'I was on a field survey trip, it took longer,' she said, and knew the explanation was inadequate and hollow.

'There was a storm and you were alone. I am *disappointed*, Miss Bethany, that you declined to take the offer that I have always made to you, that I provide an escort with reliable vehicles for you to go into the Sands – exceptionally disappointed. A person such as yourself, a distinguished scholar ... under my patronage and support – has no need to travel by herself, with all the attendant risks that creates.'

He was indeed, and Beth understood it, her patron and supporter. Without that patronage and support, her visa was worthless. She would be on the next night's flight out of Riyadh.

'I'm sorry, truly sorry,' she said. 'I just didn't think, being selfish, that anyone would worry.'

She could still feel the touch of him. She had thought of him, no name, all through the night as she had bumped, sped and woven, always searching for the hard salt flats ahead, the lights' beams arrowing over the sand and guiding her. He had been with her. He had left her. He had roused feelings in her passionless, loveless life. Yet she had not owned him. She owned everything she wanted, except him. He had gone away from her, gone away into the Sands, gone beyond reach. The deputy governor, prince of the Kingdom, owned her. She was his chattel.

'I sincerely apologize. It was selfishness. What else can I say? I thought only of myself. I very much respect, and am grateful, that you worried for me.'

Well, short of getting down on her knees and ripping off her blouse and exposing her back for a bloody good flogging, there was not much more she could do. At the convent, when in minor trouble, she had learned that the contrite approach softened anger, reduced punishment. Beth hung her head.

'You, better than any foreigner, understand the dangers of the Sands. You know them as the Bedu do. You know them as I know them.'

'I do.'

'It is basic procedure that if you go into the Sands for even half a day, you leave a map of your route.'

'It is.'

'I was fearful for you.'

The ashtray told her he had been on her couch for the whole night. His robe was crumpled, creased, from sitting through the long hours in the quiet of her bungalow ... She wondered where the man without a name was – where a little caravan of camels was. Had he already moved because the dawn had come, along with the men who had wanted to kill her, and him? She owned nothing of him. He was not of the Bedu, not of the Arabs, she did not know where he came from or what was his destination, or the purpose of his journey. He went in secrecy – others, to preserve the secret, would have killed her. Her life was saved by his trust in her . . . She smiled, dreamed.

'You take it lightly, Miss Bethany, my anxiety and your danger?'

'No, no . . . I can only apologize.'

The silken voice hardened. 'The storm, Miss Bethany? The airfield here was closed. I could not come back from Riyadh because of the storm. Nothing moved here. Because of the storm I was concerned for your welfare.'

The lie came easily. 'I missed it, no problem. I saw it coming, hunkered down in shelter. There was some drifting round the wheels but I dug them out.'

When had she last lied? Beth could not remember. It was not in her nature to lie. Everything she had learned at the convent, and at home, had told her that an untruth chased a liar.

The question slithered quietly from him. 'Did you see anybody, Miss Bethany, in the Sands?'

She blustered: 'No . . . Who?'

'Any travellers, any traders?'

'Why do you ask?'

'I merely ask because, if we had had to search for you, Miss Bethany, I wonder if we would have met travellers or traders who had seen you and would have directed us towards where you were.'

'No.' It was the second lie. 'I did not see anybody.'

'These are difficult times . . . there are rumours . . . It is said men travel in the Sands, who are illegal and dangerous . . . only whispers, I do not have evidence of it.'

The lie tripped from her tongue. 'I told you, there was nobody.'

'Promise me, you will not go alone again into the Sands.'

'I saw nobody . . . But I want to tell you what I did see.'

She told the deputy governor about the ejecta field where the iron-ore fragments had come down, and she ran outside. She tipped the sample bag on to the plastic patio table, and the stones and glass pieces rattled and rolled on the table's surface. His hands were cupped and she laid the largest pieces in them. His fingers stroked them. She told him that when she had written her paper, when it was submitted with maps, photographs and samples to the American-based society that collated meteorite finds, she would give the field his name. She saw the pleasure in his face and the joy with which his fingers, hesitant, touched the pieces. He had been frightened for her – he did not own her, she owned him. There was one man whom she did not own.

As he handled the pieces, with love, Beth heard the soft drone in the air and looked down from her patio into the brightness of the low sun. She saw the small aircraft lift from the runway. It did not have the grace she had seen before, but seemed to yaw and struggle clumsily for height. There were khaki tubes, one under each wing . . . The aircraft climbed. She saw that her patron looked up, watched the aircraft's slow, pained climb, then his eyes were back on the stones, bright with fascination for them.

She had lied, she had avoided the promise. She let the deputy governor keep two pieces for his collection, then saw him go.

Beth ran her bath, and stripped . . . She did not recognize how greatly the lies she had spoken had changed her.

High in the control tower beside the runway, the deputy governor was given binoculars. He raised them and studied the tent camp by the far edge of the perimeter fence, and a frown puckered on his forehead. The beauty of the glass and the stones slipped from his mind.

His host passed the glass of Saudi champagne. It was done awkwardly, and the man's heavily strapped wrist restricted any fluency of movement. Bart smiled, took the glass. He thought his host would have preferred a sling, as if it were a Purple Heart ribbon, but Bart had decreed that a tightly wrapped bandage was appropriate. It was only a sprain. By way of reward for coming across Riyadh at the speed appropriate for an emergency, he had been invited to an all-American picnic. It was not permitted to barbecue in the park of the diplomatic quarter, but the host's wife had cooked the beefburgers in her villa kitchen, had wrapped them well in tinfoil, and they were still warm. The talk bustled round him, and Bart thought he was expected to look and feel privileged to be present.

'I don't know where this country is going, except down. I don't see a future here. Once they got it into their thick skulls that they could do without us, without Americans, when they'd got that delusion into their heads, they were going nowhere but down the pan.

'What really sucks is the absence of gratitude. I have spent ten whole years here, eleven come Thanksgiving, and I have never heard a Saudi say that he is grateful for what we have done in their country. All right, they have oil. All right, so we want the oil. At every stage we have shown them how to exploit and market that asset. Up to last year we have posted the finest young men and women in our armed forces here, let them live out there in the desert, for the protection of the regime. I ask you, did you ever hear any thanks? Arabic for "thank you", I'm using it from morning to night, is *shukran*, and I don't hear it said to me much. You know, in 'ninety-one we fought a war to stop this place ending up as an out-station of Baghdad, and we get no gratitude.'

Bart seldom met Americans. They inhabited their own compounds. They used their own Chamber of Commerce, had their own fenced-off section of the grandstand at the races. Insularity was the name of their game. These men, Bart accepted it, were not fools. Bombastic, yes. Arrogant, yes. Stupid, no.

'They are living in denial. Their heads are in the sand. They're the source of Al Qaeda, they bankrolled that gang of fanatics, zealots, psychopaths. I read that think-tank report from back home. Quote: "For years, individuals and charities based in Saudi Arabia have been the most important source of funds for Al Qaeda, and for years Saudi officials have turned a blind eye to the problem." Unquote. You wait till that nine/eleven law case gets up steam. You remember what that Pentagon briefer called this virtuous and God-following Kingdom: he called it a "kernel of evil". What I say – who needs Saudi Arabia? We got Iraq, we don't need these people. We're the power, they're nothing. They sowed the field, let them harvest it.'

His mind drifted. The condemnations and criticisms wafted around the linen tablecloth. Food filled the mouths, the best that could be bought in the supermarkets of the Riyadh shopping malls. He thought they rolled out this talk each time they met, yet still retained a fervour for it. If the place was such shit, why stay? Bart reckoned they stayed because the money was good, and because they were, one and all, too proud to consider that the Al Qaeda crowd – the fanatics, zealots, psychopaths – could make them scuttle for the airport. Why did he stay? Bart half choked on the end of his burger. Maybe it took more courage to run. Bart could have torn up the airline ticket, not caught the flight to Tel Aviv, could have refused to get into the waiting car, could not have checked into the Dan Hotel and settled himself into a room with a beach view. To stand against the wind took more bottle than flowing with it. An Englishman had come first, had thanked him on behalf of a medical charity, whose name and background Bart assumed had been cobbled together in the last week. The Englishman had eczema on his wrists, and the signs of over-high blood pressure – Bart was good on symptoms – and a nasal voice. 'What I heard, you were looking for a route back to respectability, old boy. I can put you on that route, but I promise that travelling on it might be bumpy ... In my sort of work, I trade. I do a friend a favour, and I know I'll get a favour back. Let's call you the favour. You are the favour I'm doing for a friend.' Bart could have walked out then, but it would have taken more guts than he had. An hour after the Englishman had left him, while he'd been watching the swimmers on the beach, there had been a knock on the door. He had met Ariel. Ariel was cheerful, bouncy, had the happy enthusiasm that made problems disappear. It would have taken a better man than Bart to refuse Ariel. After the burgers, flushed down with the bogus champagne, the wives sliced portions of apple pie, crowned them with dollops of soft-scoop vanilla ice cream from the cold box, and the venom gathered strength around him.

'What I can't stand is the corruption – nothing's transparent – the skimmers, the pay-offs, back-handers, and the middle-men's cuts.'

'I can live with that. The stone in my shoe is the waste, the extravagance – you know what it cost the last time the old king went for his summer vacation to Spain? Three million dollars a day, believe me.'

'If they don't learn, and fast, a truckload of humility, one day they'll wake up and find we're gone. Then you'll hear some hollering.'

The host's wife smiled at him, like it was outside church and everyone felt good. 'You haven't said much, Dr Bartholomew.'

There was much he could have said, but Bart chose the easy path, 'Been enjoying myself too much. Wonderful food, fantastic hospitality, couldn't have been bettered.'

*

Al Maz'an village, near Jenin, Occupied West Bank.

He saw the blood drip down and felt the guilt.

The best house in the village, on the central square, was an older build-ing. It would have been constructed before the Second World War, perhaps by a merchant, and it represented a long-gone prosperity in the Palestinian community. Before Bart had arrived to work in the village, the building had been a target for Israeli tank shells during an armoured incursion. Now, extraordinarily, the family that had long ago scattered from the West Bank and had made money in the United States of America had sent funds for the restoration of the building and had pledged it to the village as a centre for local administration, adult education and for a communal meeting-place. The first stage of spending the donated money was to erect scaffolding so that the building could be made safe around the shell holes. Over the weeks he had been in the village, Bart had watched the erection of the scaffolding but had seen precious little work carried out there, and he'd thought the benefactors had only a damn small return to show for their bucks. The body hung from the scaffolding.

He was a doctor who was familiar with the south-west of England, the Torbay district of the county of Devon, the town of Torquay. Where he came from could be summoned by cream teas, rolling fields grazed by cattle, fam-ilies holidaying on beaches, retirement homes for men and women in their twilight years . . . The body of a lynch victim was suspended from the rusted scaffolding poles. The vomit rose in his throat. He understood, knew how far he had fallen.

The legs no longer kicked, but the rope between the poles and the neck twisted in the light wind and the heavy rain; the body spiralled rhythmically. The rain was dragged off the windscreen by the wipers. Bart had a clear view of the victim and of the mob below.

He could not have said whether the knife cuts that loosed the dripping blood had been inflicted before the victim was hanged, or while he was hanging but still alive, or after life had been jerked away. The rain fell hard on the body and the man's T-shirt was soaked against his chest and his back, and the flow of water made the blood run easily. In the dulled light, he saw the brightness of knives and a butcher's cleaver raised above the heads of the chanting crowd. Bart had been driving into the square, had seen the milling mob, had braked. Only when he had stopped had he seen the

222

object of the crowd's fury – the body below the rope and the drip of the blood.

Kids were at his window. They tapped on it. Their faces were alive with excitement. One wore a football shirt from a German team. It was not a game that the kids had watched as spectators, not a goal that had thrilled them: it was a killing by lynching. Their voices jabbered broken English at him, their faces were distorted by the rain running on the driver's window. He did not need to be told.

'He was an informer . . . He was a traitor paid by the Israelis . . . He had his reward for taking their money . . . His information killed a hero of the armed struggle.'

It was necessary for Samuel Bartholomew to play out his part, to stifle the vomit. He took up his medical bag, locked the vehicle and walked forward. He was a Pied Piper – kids ran and skipped after him. Joseph, in the hut at the checkpoint, had told him, 'We take great care of you. You are a jewel to us, so precious. Have no fear . . .' To save him, an informer of lesser importance had been sacrificed. Word would have been passed, a channel of disinformation would have been opened. He had killed an activist, that he could justify. Bart had seen the photographs of the aftermath of the attacks by suicide bombers. He could tell himself that the death of an activist, by his hand, was acceptable – not the death of an informer that he might be protected. The crowd thinned, the knives and the butcher's cleaver were lowered, voices hushed. He walked the middle line: he would not condemn, nor would he condone.

Bart said, a little stammer in his voice, 'I think it would be better if he were taken down. Could you, please, cut him down?'

A man, his face masked, climbed nimbly up the scaffolding, unfastened the rope and the sodden body fell. It crumpled on to the paving near to Bart's feet. He felt weak. He wondered if his knees would buckle . . . He saw the woman who huddled, all in black, at the building's doorway. The crowd had thinned, and the kids. The woman watched Bart, her eyes flitting off the body to his.

In a croaking aged voice through the translation of a youth, the woman said to Bart, 'I am his mother. I came. His wife would not come, his children did not come. His wife said he had shamed her family. His children said he, their father, had betrayed them. When he was taken his wife hit him and his children spat on him. Only I came. Who will bury him?'

Bart bent, felt the neck and wrist of the body, and found no pulse.

'What do I do? Do I bury him alone? . . . What he did was for his family.

*He took the money from the Israelis, but it was to feed his family who had
no food. The Israelis killed him, and I curse them . . . They will not bury him.
Who will?'*

'You have not spoken.' Hosni's voice was coaxing.

'You are like a man who is tortured,' Fahd said.

The Egyptian had dropped back and the Saudi had come forward.
They rode on either side of Caleb. It was the middle of the afternoon,
the sun high, and he did not welcome them.

'Did you find your memory?'

'Did you breathe life on it, as Hosni said you should?'

He stared ahead, watched the guide's back as the man rolled with
the movement of his camel. Each day they went more slowly, and
each hour less ground was covered. He sensed they were either near
to their destination, or the march would fail. He had not asked the
guide how much further they had to travel, but that morning, and at
the midday break, there had been a smaller measure of water in the
mug. The snap was long gone from the camels' stride. They went
heavily, and the crates had had to be taken off them before they
would attempt to climb a slope that a week before they would have
managed without having to be unloaded. If they failed they would
die in the sand. First to die would be the camels, then Hosni and
Fahd, then Caleb. After he had died it would be the turn of Ghaffur,
the boy, and last to die would be the boy's father, the guide. Caleb
had no fear of death in the desert. The fear was of his recalled,
reclaimed memory.

'If you have no memory you are worthless.'

His memory had given him the terrace of red-brick homes, and the
front door, with black paint, the number askew because a screw had
fallen from the base of the second plastic digit. He had walked
through a narrow hall where the wallpaper peeled, where the pattern
of the stair carpet was worn away with age. He had gone through a
kitchen that stank of old frying fat, and through a yard littered with
rubbish. At the back of the yard against the low wall the dumped
washing-machine lay on its side. They were back, the images that
would have betrayed him to the interrogators. He felt weakened.

'You have to have the past, and live with it. You are not an Arab.
We have an army of Arabs . . .'

224

Caleb said, 'Where I come from, no one – not anyone I knew – would have lasted a day in this place. No one would have, not more than a day. I can survive because I have forgotten. The past is nothing to me.'

Would they tell him what was wanted of him? He could not ask. Fahd dropped back and Hosni kicked his camel's sides and went forward. He realized that Hosni had never looked into his face and he wondered how far the blindness affected the elderly Egyptian . . . Then the sand swallowed his thoughts and the pains from the blister sores consumed him.

The caravan moved on.

'This is Oscar Golf . . . Your last turn to starboard, because of wind direction change to north-north-west, meant we missed out. We didn't get picture on the base of that dune. We lost vision of an area we estimate to be zero point nine miles by zero point three miles. Could you go back, please? Could you repeat over that ground, please? Oscar Golf, out.'

It was the third time in the five hours *First Lady* had been up that the voice, always so reasonable, had come seeping into their headphones.

Lizzy-Jo responded, wouldn't have trusted Marty to. 'Roger that, we will make that manoeuvre.'

'This is Oscar Golf. Much appreciated. Looks like flying conditions are not easy. Oscar Golf, out.'

Marty was on the joystick and Lizzy-Jo called the co-ordinates to him of a new backtracking course that would bring *First Lady* on a second run over a stretch of sand that was zero point nine miles in length by zero point three miles in width. She sensed that Marty burned. Everything they did, and said, was now watched and listened to. The feeling, hers and Marty's, was that they were no longer trusted, and each time the voice oozed politeness, the feeling grew. It was not unusual for pictures in real time to be going live to Langley, she'd had that in Bosnia and Afghanistan, but the pitch of the disembodied voice seemed to doubt their skill. Marty took it harder than her. After the second call, he had freed his right hand from the joystick and scribbled on his notepad: 'This feels like three in a bed.' She'd grimaced, no humour, had leaned across and written:

'Worse – like his mother's in my kitchen.' Everything overheard, every move monitored, they were spied on . . . but Lizzy-Jo would have had to admit that the starboard turn had clipped an area of desert. The area was a quarter of a square mile of flat, gold- and red-coloured sand, and they had missed it because of the upper-air turbulence.

They went back over. The camera surveyed empty sand. Lizzy-Jo's eyes ached as she peered at the screen. The voice of Oscar Golf, when it came into the headphones and intruded into their world, could always be justified. To shut the goddamn voice up she strove for per-fection. The sandscape was infinite, limitless, and nothing moved down there. There was a needle pain in her skull from concentration on the real-time images. Out in that wilderness a camel train was loaded with six crates, escorted by perhaps six men. She saw just the sand and the sloping dunes, the high points and the flat expanses. She looked for the camels, the men, for tracks . . . There was nothing.

Lizzy-Jo punched up the forecast. She swore.

Marty's head rocked in exhaustion. His eyes blinked shut, then opened. She mashed her fist into the small of his back. She said, 'Doesn't let up, does it? The forecast is for stronger winds, westerly, tomorrow. If the forecast's right, there's no way we're flying tomorrow . . . '

Lizzy-Jo was only a handful of years older than Marty but she felt, more often since they had come to Shaybah, as if she was his aunt and he was her kid nephew. She was fonder of him, a little more each day, since they had shared the Ground Control, just them together. She hoped the wind speed, up there four miles above the desert, would strengthen, and then the kid could sleep. She cared for him, wanted him to sleep and shed the exhaustion.

He smiled ruefully, and her hand, which had belted him, rested on the skin of his forearm and . . .

The voice said, 'This is Oscar Golf. We fly tomorrow, we fly every day. If you didn't know it, this is priority. We ignore the manual instructions on what is possible. Until that target is found, we fly to the limit. Oscar Golf, out.'

'Are you sure? Are you telling me, man, you are sure?'

'Sure, and no argument. It's tied down.'

His supervisor, Edgar, had been off Guantanamo for two days, back at the Pentagon for sessions on the preparations for retirement. The Pentagon had a good programme for readying long-service men in the Defense Intelligence Agency for the cold-shower shock of waking up on a Monday morning and having no work to go to. Jed watched his superior's eyes twitch and his fingers fidget. He might as well have rolled a hand grenade, pin out, across his supervisor's desk.

Maybe Jed should have felt a tinge of sympathy for the man. The physical reactions were clear enough signs that his supervisor had taken on board the seriousness of Jed's message. Those two days, while the supervisor had been lectured on pension income, the tax implications of part-time employment in the civilian sector, the psychology of switching allegiance from government service to a golf course, had been well spent. The audiotapes of the voices of the supposed taxi-driver and the British 'unlawful combatant' had been edited together and the nasal similarity could not be argued with.

'You are saying . . .' The supervisor's voice eddied away, as if he could not stomach the enormity of a truth now striking him.

Jed said, 'I am saying we freed the wrong man. I am saying that Fawzi al-Ateh, taxi-driver, was a bogus identity. We freed a man who was smart enough, sufficiently intelligent, to deceive us.'

'He was flown back to Afghanistan, so what's the problem? Round him up, bring him back. It's a cakewalk.'

Jed pushed across the desk the signal from Bagram, from Karen Lebed. The eyes scanned it, and the fingers could not hold the paper steady. There was a long sigh, like it was personal pain.

'God Almighty – did we deserve this?'

'Can't say, but it's what we've got. The supposition is that we released a British-origin prisoner who, most likely, never drove an Afghan taxi in his life . . . I suggest you look on the bright side.'

The supervisor was dulled. 'I'd like to but where do I look?'

All the times when the Agency and the Bureau guys had let him know they were the chosen people flashed in Jed's mind. Every little insult, each put-down, every sneer, each patronizing quip floated by him. He might have felt regret at his supervisor's discomfort, but not at any shit that landed on the Agency and the Bureau. Jed grinned. 'I think other guys took that decision. I'd say we're clean.'

The supervisor's gloomy response: 'I sat in.'

'Only to rubber stamp. I don't want to be offensive, but you wouldn't have been in the loop.'

The supervisor brightened. 'It was just a list of names put down in front of me. They'd already done the list . . . Jed, are you aware of the ultimate potential end-game of this?'

'I know it'll be a bad day for the Bureau and the Agency.'

The supervisor's fist tightened on the pencil he held. 'There are bigger things in the world, Jed, than turf wars. Look at it . . . The implications of the release of a man who has gone to that deal of trouble to disguise his identity mean, to me, that he is a dedicated and committed activist. We are not looking at some guy who is just anxious to get himself home. We are talking dedication, commitment. That is a prime man, a man capable of inflicting maximum danger. There could be *consequences*, Jed, real bad consequences.'

'But they're not in our ballpark.'

'Christ, there is a bigger picture.' The supervisor's shoulders dropped as if a burden weighed down on him. 'And that picture is a verified homeland threat. A British-born and -reared fighter, with a shitty little heart filled with hate, can go to places an Arab cannot . . . No name.'

'Then we go find a name.'

The supervisor's pencil was stabbed close to Jed's face. 'I wouldn't want this plastered all over the walls.'

Jed threw his last card, the ace card: 'Shouldn't I get on a plane?'

'Give me time.'

'Thought we don't have much time.'

'Leave me to do this, Jed, and my way. I am not having a situation where my last days here are in a conflict zone with the Bureau and the Agency, I am not.'

Jed scraped his chair back. Between grated teeth, he bit back, 'Don't bury this. If you are going to bury—'

'I am not. I need twenty-four hours of time.'

'After twenty-four hours, I should be on a plane. Don't think this can be buried and don't think I can be bounced off it. It's mine.'

He left the file and the audiotapes on his supervisor's desk. He closed the door and left his man to work a strategy. He walked back to his office and heard the noise of the camp around him; the sun hit on him and he smelt the sea. He did not know where the matched voices would take him, if he was allowed to get on a plane. He felt proud, as if at last in his professional life he had achieved something of value. He strode past the open doors of the Agency team, and past the doors of the Bureau men.

He went into the interrogation block where a prisoner, an escort and an interpreter waited for him, and he thought of the chaos he had let loose. He sat in front of the prisoner, a Yemeni, but another face was there. The Yemeni's features were gone, had merged into those of a taller man with a strong nose and a powerful jaw that the cringing protestations of innocence could not hide, and he thought of the skill of the man who had deceived them all.

The woman was forgotten, as Tommy was. Danger was forgotten. Only survival counted. His mind was deadened and his memory gone.

The sun was in Caleb's eyes. The dried air scraped his throat and the growing wind lifted sand from the hoofs of Hosni's camel, which pricked his face. His eyes were squeezed shut against the grains. If he opened his eyes, blinked, he saw Hosni's back low across his saddle. He rocked on the hump of the Beautiful One, and he thought that only her courage carried her forward. She moved with leaden slow steps over the soft sand. More often than on any other day, he thought he would fall, and he yearned for the evening and the smaller portion of water that his tongue would move round his mouth, and the cold of the night, the uncooked dough, the handful of dates, and then sleep. He had heard Fahd fall behind him and the shouts of the boy, but he had not stopped, had let the boy get Fahd back on to his camel. At the last stop, when the sun had been highest, fiercest, when they had remounted the kneeling camels, Rashid had put a rope round Hosni's waist and had knotted it to the saddle. His survival depended on himself.

The anger billowed in him.

Caleb recognized it, understood it.

The anger came in sharp surges . . . It was the same anger as in the camps. In X-Ray and Delta, the target of the anger had been the guards. The guards imprisoned him . . . Fahd and Hosni were his gaolers. They had the keys and the batons, and they were around him. His mind wandered loose. He was their prisoner. He had the hate for them, as for the guards. His throat, without water, was pricking with the pain, his eyes hurt, the blister sores ate at him. He was the one, supposedly, with the strength, and he was rocking, sliding.

Caleb toppled, lost his hold.

He went down the Beautiful One's flank, was dumped in the sand. He fell face first.

He heard the shrill laughter behind him.

The Beautiful One had stopped and towered over him and the great brown eyes gazed down on him. It was Fahd's laughter.

Fahd reached down and Caleb took his hand. Fahd heaved him up and Caleb caught the reins that hung from the Beautiful One's neck. He climbed, struggled, pulled himself back into the saddle.

'Are you going to fail us? We do not expect the mule to fail us.'

Caleb spat the sand. 'Is that what I am, a mule?'

'A mule is noble, a beast of burden.'

He ran his tongue round his mouth, let it gather the sand, then scraped it with his finger off his tongue. 'Is that what I am to you, a mule?' he repeated.

'What else?' All the laughter had gone from Fahd's face. It was grim, closed. 'A mule is important to us because it carries what we put on its back. It goes where we want it to go, carries what we want it to carry. It is necessary for us to use the mule, but if we thought it would fail us we would shoot it. We would not waste food on it and we would find another mule. You are a mule – a pack animal. You will carry what we put on your back.'

Caleb rode on towards his family.

Instinctively, he looked up around him, ignored the sand blown into his face. He scanned the dunes and the tips of the sand walls, and he looked for danger, and saw nothing. Once, briefly, he looked into the blue sky but then the low sun burned his eyes.

Chapter Twelve

He thought of rain, cooling, healing and sweet, spattering on to the panes of windows.

That last night he had slept, had not dreamed, woken as exhausted as when he had lain down on the sand. In the morning they had set out again. Twice, a bull camel loaded with two of the boxes had stopped, had refused to go forward, and each time Rashid had come back from the front of them, had taken the bull's head in his hands, had put his own face close to it, stroked and soothed its bellowing, and whispered to it. Twice, the bull camel had responded to the kindness of the guide, had shown its loyalty to him, had started again to walk into the strength of the wind.

It was late in the afternoon when they had halted, not to pitch camp. The guide said they would stop for a short time, then go on. Caleb sat against the body of the kneeling Beautiful One and felt the rhythmic panting of the beast against his back.

If he went where his memory took him, he would have stood with his arms outstretched, his head thrown back and his shirt unbuttoned, and he would have let the rain cascade on to him. When it had drenched him, and his clothes had clung to him, he would have danced and sung, gloried in it. He would not have huddled like the woman who pushed her baby in a buggy on the pavement or cringed from it like the man on the towpath who dragged his tiny ratting dog on a lead. He yearned for the rain that would have cooled the heat burning him and soothed the blister sores, that would have dribbled sweet on his lips.

The guide had poured water from the neck of a water bag into a metal mug that Fahd had held. Fahd had carried the mug to Hosni. Perhaps Hosni did not see the mug clearly. Perhaps his eyesight failed him, perhaps he was too confused by exhaustion, by sunstroke. Hosni reached out, snatched at the mug, missed it and caught Fahd's wrist, twisted it. The mug toppled. Water fell from it, like rain.

The water drops from the mug sparkled, jerked Caleb from his fantasy.

'Idiot . . . fool,' Fahd screamed.

Hosni whimpered.

'You wasted water – imbecile.'

Hosni had the mug in his thin claw fingers and tugged for it. More water slurped over the rim. When Fahd released his hold on the mug and Hosni sagged back, more water spilled.

'I bring you water. What do you do? You throw it in the sand.'

Caleb watched, said nothing. The mug would have been a third full when Fahd had offered it to Hosni's stretched-out hands. Now there would only be a wetness at the mug's bottom.

'You don't get any more. You waste water, you go without,' Fahd yelled in his fury and his body quivered. 'We should never have brought you.'

He saw Hosni tilt the mug so that the last drops would run into his mouth, and then run his tongue round the sides and the base of it. Hosni's wet watery eyes seemed to plead with Fahd as he prised the mug back from the fingers.

'There is no more water for you. I am not sharing my water with you.'

Fahd took away the mug. Caleb saw Hosni, his head bent, scrape the film of sand off the place where the water had fallen to retrieve the sand that was darkened. He cupped it into his hands, gobbled it into his mouth, then choked. The guide poured out Fahd's measure and Fahd drank it to the final drop.

'You will learn it for the next time, you do not throw away water,' Fahd shouted.

Without water, they died. The camels could go a maximum of eighteen days without water, the boy had said, then they would die – Caleb had long ago lost count of how many days they had been in the Sands. The men could not go eighteen hours without water. The bags on the Beautiful One were all empty. Caleb was not sure how many bags remained, filled, on the guide's camel; one or two, he hoped . . . Water went again into the mug, and Fahd brought it to him. Caleb took the mug.

He looked down into the water. It was green-coloured, dead. He felt the dryness of his throat, the roughness inside his mouth. He remembered the rain, and the comfort of it. He held the mug carefully as he stood and walked across to Hosni.

He put his finger into Hosni's mouth, worked it round his tongue and the recesses of the man's throat, took out the sand and smeared it on his robe. Then, Caleb held the mug at Hosni's lips and tipped it. When it was empty he carried the mug back to Rashid.

'We are carrying two fools,' Fahd snarled at Caleb, his face contorted with anger.

The heat burning them and burning the sand, and the sky that was clear, blue and without pity, the expanse of the desert, destroyed them. Caleb knew it.

They mounted up, rode away, and the windblown sand covered any trace of their passing.

Another lunchtime, another lecture. The crossword on the back page of Michael Lovejoy's newspaper had not yet been started. The folded page lay across his knee and the pencil was in his hand, but he had read no more than the first question, one across: *A woman who strives to be like a man lacks . . . (Graffito, NY)* eight letters. Lovejoy had his usual seat at the back of the room. He'd come down early, when he'd finished a mid-morning meeting, and had left the newspaper on the favoured chair. Just as well. They were sitting on the aisle steps and standing inside the door.

The speaker had the appearance of an old-fashioned preparatory-school teacher. He was as mild-looking a man as could be imagined – wispy grey hair that had not been combed, a checked shirt with the collar curled up, a woven tie that was not pulled tight, a jacket with leather at the elbows, trousers that hadn't been pressed, and shoes that were scuffed. The man who had filled the lecture room in Thames House, on the north embankment of the river, came with a reputation. Officers from every branch of the Security Service had cut lunch to hear the scientist who was said to be better-informed on his specialized subject than any other man or woman in the United Kingdom. The subject was 'Dirty Bombs'.

'I don't consider there to be a great risk from either microbiological or chemical sources. An explosion that scatters anthrax or smallpox spores or that spreads a nerve gas in aerosol form would have little effect, even in the confined space of an underground-railway system. The evidence from the United States of America, anthrax, and from Japan, nerve gas such as Sarin, tells me the result is bigger in instant headlines than in the reality of damage caused. No, it is the real Dirty Bomb that concerns me, the radioactive bomb. Let us consider, first, the availability of the necessary materials for that bomb . . .'

There was a grated cough from the assistant director of C Branch, otherwise nervous silence. Lovejoy had read the assessments, but the slightness and mildness of the speaker, and the quietness of his voice, gave his message a uniquely chilling quality. He was known to many of his younger colleagues – when they were polite about him – as a 'veteran'. A veteran of the Cold War counter-intelligence work, and the days of the Marxists in the trade unions, and a veteran of the twenty years of Irish guerrilla warfare, he had also learned the earlier history of the Security Service. Already, he thought this the bleakest lecture of a nightmare future he had heard since he had enrolled from Army service. In fact, and his mind roved, the only comparable moment would have been when the Service was told, sixty-four years earlier, of the imminence of a German invasion.

'We start with a suitcase. Any suitcase of a size that a man or woman uses for a week's stay in a hotel. Stand at Heathrow airport, at the arrivals gates of any of the terminals, and you will see passengers flooding through with suitcases of such a size. The wires and timing devices are available at any hardware and electronics shops. The terrorist will need ten pounds of Semtex or military explosives or what's used in quarrying operations, and he'll need detonators – everything so far is readily available. Sadly, and I urge you to believe me, the necessary radioactive material can be found without difficulty. Caesium chloride would be suitable. Vast quantities of it litter the countryside and farm buildings of the former Soviet Union. It was used to blast seeds, in powder form, at high pressure, therefore making them more productive once sown. We do not have to go to the agricultural industries of Belarus or the Ukraine. Radioactive materials govern X-rays. Medical instruments for the treatment of cervical cancer use caesium. The radio isotope caesium 137, which if spilled has a contamination life of thirty years, is widely used in radiotherapy. We are awash with it, but I am going to stay with caesium chloride, what you could hold in one hand, no more – bought in lethal quantities for next to nothing. The caesium chloride is packed round the explosives, and is covered with clothes, books, washing-bags, presents, and only the most awake security man at an airport, monitoring check-in and fresh off a meal break, will see anything suspicious.'

All of them in the room were supposed to be the last line of defence for the tax-payers who coughed up their salaries. He did not know where that defence line could be drawn, and the hushed quiet in the room told him that none of the others, newcomers or old-timers, had a bloody clue . . . and he remembered the young Russian from last week, and the psychologist from the week before, and their messages. He would go home that night to his wife, Mercy, and not stop at the pub – where they thought he worked for Social Security – and he'd talk it through with her, because she was the only shoulder for crying on that he had.

'A man walks with this suitcase, not an onerous burden, into London's Trafalgar Square or New York's Times Square or he approaches a major intersection in central Paris. He puts down the suitcase and walks away, and before the alarm is raised, the suitcase explodes. A big, big bang. On that night's television news, we see burning cars, damaged buildings – all very obvious – and we are told that three people have been killed and thirty injured. We do not see or hear the cloud, the particles of caesium chloride. The cloud climbs in air heated by the detonation, then it moves on the wind. The speed is extraordinary – half a mile in one minute, five miles in thirty minutes. The particles reach cooler air, further from the bomb site, and they drop. They fall on grass, into gardens, on to buildings that are residential and that house thousands of office workers, and they seep into drains and through the air-intake ducts of the underground's ventilation system. Twenty-four hours later, the terrorists use a Middle East originating website to announce that the bomb is dirty, the city is contaminated. Then, ladies and gentlemen, what do you do?'

Go and live in a cave in mid-Wales. Go and rent a farmhouse in the Yorkshire dales. There were no names, no faces, on the files in Library, and Lovejoy doubted that the files of the Federal Bureau of Investigation held anything of value. They groped in the dark. He sensed, in the room, a pent-up desire to be out and looking, hunting, and a matching frustration that there was no target to search for.

'Depending on the proximity to the explosion, the particles could be harmful to human life for up to two hundred years – which is, to most of us, for ever. The risk of fast-developing cancer is small, but in the long-term that risk increases. In theory millions, born and unborn, face the nightmare of being cut down by hideous tumours. In reality, the greater problem for government is the spread of panic. *Panic*. An ugly word for an ugly image. The creation of panic is the terrorist's principal aim, and I guarantee to you that he will have succeeded. Consider the psychological impact, so much worse than the recent SARS outbreak, then imagine panic on a scale never seen before by our western societies, and a commercial shut-down that is unprecedented. You see, ladies and gentlemen, civilians under the weight of the German blitz or the Anglo-American bombing of Hamburg, Berlin or Dresden could see, feel, touch, hear those attacks – but this cloud moves invisibly, at speed, silently. Panic would be total. What response can government make?'

Precious little – it would come out of a clear blue sky. The explosion, the panic would tumble from that sky, probably without warning. And the lead to the identity of such a man who carried a suitcase, that also would come out of the same cloudless sky. The good old clear blue sky was both the hell and the heaven of counter-intelligence officers.

'The clean-up after the spill of one fistful of radioactive material in a Brazilian city, not scattered by explosives and not riding on the wind, necessitated the removal of three and a half thousand cubic metres of earth and rubble. My scenario is a bomb in the heart of a city, and the impossibility of stripping out buildings, tunnels, gardens and parks. It would take years, not months – and where then do you dump this Himalayan heap of dirtied material? The cost would be prohibitive. I venture that the answer is mass evacuation, then the abandonment of an inner city . . . The panic caused would initiate a new Dark Age. I can offer only one fractionally small area of comfort to you.'

Lovejoy decided on the answer to one across.

'If the man who carried the suitcase into that crowded city centre never opened it, never touched the caesium chloride, and was well clear when it exploded, he would survive. I cannot say the same for the bomb-maker. I would estimate that the bomb-maker's un-avoidable contact with the powder would limit his life to a few weeks after the completion of the device. He would die a slow and most unpleasant death. That is the only comfort I can offer you, ladies and gentlemen. Thank you for your attention.'

There was no titter of relieved laughter at the fate of a bomb architect, and no applause when the scientist stepped back from the lectern. No chair moved. Lovejoy wrote: *Ambition*. 'A woman who strives to be like a man lacks ambition'. It would give him a start for three, five and six down. For a moment, the crossword was protection for Michael Lovejoy against the awfulness of the message.

When he reached his office, and his sandwich, there was a note on his desk from his Branch director.

> *Mikey,*
> *Arriving tomorrow, American Airlines 061, from Florida, is Jed Dietrich (Defense Intelligence Agency). His people coy/shy about reason for his travel to UK, but they request co-operation. You, please, meet, escort and wet-nurse.*
> *Boris.*

A clear blue sky – not bloody likely. He looked from his window, out over the Thames. The cloud was low, ashen and carried rain.

The voice was quiet, calm, and eased into Marty's headphones. 'This is Oscar Golf. We appreciate that conditions are adverse, but we think we – you, sorry – are doing well. You have good control and we like what you're doing.'

He acknowledged curtly.

'Unless there is a major deterioration in upper-air wind strength, we believe that we – sorry again – you should keep the bird up. That's the bottom line. We have complete confidence in you, Marty, but if you get too tired, need to rest, then we will take over. We are monitoring all output while Lizzy-Jo sleeps, everything is A number one. This is quality flying in that wind strength, and we go to the range limit. Oscar Golf, out.'

Lizzy-Jo had all the floor space behind him. She had brought in her sleeping-bag, used it as a mattress. Her head was close to a wall and her feet were by the door. George had been in during the afternoon and had driven them both insane with the banging of his hammer and the scrape of his spanner, but he hadn't succeeded in getting the air-conditioning motor going. She wore short shorts and had her blouse unbuttoned, right down. His mother, back in California, would have turned up her lip and said it wasn't decent. If he turned, Marty could see a deep brown birthmark on the white skin of her lower stomach, Lizzy-Jo's breasts and the squashed-down nipples. Back in Langley, where Oscar Golf was, they did Lizzy-Jo's work and monitored the real-time camera images. He wasn't happy with her sleeping. Oscar Golf, and his crowd, were not tuned to the desert – not like she was. Ten more minutes, he'd give her. He sat very still in his chair, only his fingers moving with the joystick. He wondered whether she dreamed of her daughter, and of her husband who sold insurance in North Carolina. The few times he looked at her, Marty thought Lizzy-Jo looked good.

But he didn't look often.

It was hard flying. If it had not been for the order from Langley, *Carnival Girl* would not have been up. He was pressured. Refusal was not an option. In good weather conditions, without upper-air wind speeds that were at the limit or beyond, Oscar Golf and his people could have had control. In good weather, with what the instrumentation told them, *Carnival Girl* could have been flown from Langley, all commands transmitted from – whatever it was – six thousand miles' distance. But the weather was miserable.

And because the weather was miserable, with the high winds,

Marty had done that rare thing, had imposed his will on George. *Carnival Girl* would fly, not *First Lady*. The clapped-out, raddled Predator would be up, not the better aircraft. *First Lady* was too valuable to go down, hit by those winds, a dragonfly with broken wings. He thought that since they'd moved from Bagram he had learned more about adverse-weather flying in a week, or ten days, than he had known in years of piloting before. His hands ached on the little joystick, but he held her steady and she ate the ground and beamed the pictures. Soon the night would come, then they'd go from the real-time camera to the infra-red images . . . No fucking way would he permit Oscar Golf to take over control of *Carnival Girl*. She was his, if she went down it would be his fault, no other asshole's.

He flew her over the emptiness of the sand.

She woke. He heard the floor creak. He felt her hands on his rigid shoulders, on the tightness of the muscles.

She had the sleep still in her voice. 'How is it up there?'

'Like shit,' Marty said.

'Wind still bad?'

'Getting worse – moved to south-south-west, forty knots.'

'What's acceptable?'

'Gone beyond acceptable, the manual says we're grounded . . . We're on the edge.'

She slipped back into her seat. She told Oscar Golf that she was 'on station'. Her blouse still hung open, like that wasn't important. There was a line of sweat dribbling from between her breasts and down to her navel. He could feel, through his fingers on the joystick, the force of the gale winds that hit *Carnival Girl* . . . Then the Predator bounced, and fell. The dial needles jerked in slashed movements. Lights winked. There was a warning howl. She plunged. Lizzy-Jo stayed quiet. Marty had to let her go. She seemed to plummet and the real-time camera's image brought the desert sand leaping up at them. It was what they trained for in the simulator at Nellis, the air pocket – low-air density. He felt, through his fingers, the strain on the wings, already burdened by the Hellfires. She fell for a minute and twelve seconds, and all the time Marty kept the nose cone down and prayed she would not go to tail down and corkscrew. She seemed to hit a floor of air, then he had control. For three land miles he took her on level flight and checked every piece of instrumentation for damage, then climbed her back up and returned into the high thermal winds. Marty sighed. Lizzy-Jo's hand was on his arm, and she squeezed, like that was the way to tell him he'd done well. He was calculating how much fuel had been used in the engine thrust to hold her as she was going down, and how much more had gone with the climb to cruise altitude, and how much flight time had been lost.

She said, face set and jaw jutted, 'We'll get them – whoever they are and wherever – I have the feeling that we'll get them.'

Lizzy-Jo had not done up her blouse and he didn't think she was going to.

The light was failing.

Bart had no alternative. A braver man would have walked away long ago – he was not brave and accepted it. Never had been, never would be – had never stood up to his father, or to his wife. He sat that evening in the outer office of the real-estate rental company, and waited for the little prig inside to be *so kind* as to see him. He had been punctual for the appointment, the prig wasn't.

His business there was to seek an extension to his rental agreement for the villa. In that past week he had failed, again, to stand up to Eddie bloody Wroughton. *'You leave when I say so. Files go walkabout when I decide it – and that's not now. You are going, Bart, nowhere.'* And 'going nowhere' necessitated an extension to the tenancy contract. The only way that he would win his freedom from Eddie bloody Wroughton was when he produced information of such value that it trivialized all the gossip, rumour and innuendo that was the stock-in-trade he peddled. Then he could quit, run for the damned airport.

Nor had he stood up to Ariel. At least Ariel had made him feel wanted, not threatened. One evening in the Dan Hotel on the beach-front, one day shared between a car and an office in Jerusalem, one morning walking in the central streets of Tel Aviv. Ariel had courted him, had been assiduous. For the evening, Ariel had talked of the threat to peace in the whole region that was the work of the three organizations, Hamas, the Al-Aqsa Brigade and Hizbollah. 'They hate peace, they make war on peace,' Ariel had said. He had been driven in Jerusalem by Ariel to a fruit and vegetable market and to a bus station, and he had been told where the suicide bombers had detonated their waistcoats, and he had tried to imagine the carnage at the locations now rebuilt. 'The zealots kill many, but hundreds more who have survived, or have buried their loved ones, will be scarred for the rest of their days by the fanaticism of these murderers,' Ariel had told him. In a bare office, in a building that had no nameplate by the door, he had been shown the books of photographs of the immediate aftermath of the explosions, and he had seen men carrying from the smoke and fire the debris of severed arms, legs, torsos, heads of men, women and children. 'The ones who plan and recruit, then arm the kids with explosives and send them to their deaths are the men we target – they do not "sacrifice" themselves, they do not look to be martyrs, they hide behind the delusions of the kids. They are the murderers who destroy the chance of peace. We target them to kill them,' Ariel had murmured in his ear, as he turned the pages of the books. He had been walked in Tel Aviv down Ben Yehuda and along the seafront, and had seen restaurants, cafés and discothèques with guards outside them. 'If we are lucky, at the last moment, as the bomber hesitates and steels himself, or creates suspicion because he wears a coat to hide his bomb and it is hot, the guard may intervene in time, but we need great luck – if we know the bomb planner, and his movements, and his factory, if we strike him then we do not need luck. More highly than luck, we value intelligence. If you help us, Dr Bartholomew, you would be a proud servant of peace, and honoured,' Ariel had whispered in his ear, as they had threaded between the pavement crowds. He was not a brave man, not then and not now.

When he was called in, forty minutes after the time of his appointment, he did not meet his landlord. The villa was owned by a prince of the blood, and the tacky work of negotiation was done by a hireling, the prig in the white robe and red-checked *ghutrah* who pared his nails with a chrome file and waved him casually to a chair.

That evening Bart surprised himself.

Not bravery but bloody-mindedness ruled. Everything they preached at the embassy and the Chamber of Commerce about patience was abandoned. He launched in with a blatant untruth: 'I don't mind sitting in the waiting room for forty wasted minutes, but my patients mind. I am late for home calls to two patients who are unwell, who need my attention. You are dealing with a busy man. Now, I seek an extension to my tenancy of six months. I note that five of the villas in my compound are currently empty because of the security situation. If a sixth villa is not to join them, bringing in no rent, then I require a discount of twenty per cent for that half-year. I believe that should be acceptable or I will go elsewhere.'

He leaned forward. His expression, carefully nurtured and fraudulent, was of concern and anxiety. 'Have you seen a doctor recently? Your neck looks a bit swollen to me. Had any pain in the glands in your neck, pains or aches? I'm not saying you should be worried, but I really do advise that you book an appointment with your doctor and get him to give you a run-over. Nasty things, when they go wrong, glands. Best caught early.'

Masterful, and the little prig had blanched. His fingers were under the hang of the *ghutrah* and were massaging a naturally plump neck.

'Right, I've two appointments to cover, so I'll be on my way. I'm looking at a six-month extension with a twenty per cent reduction in rent – and, of course, my sincere best wishes to His Royal Highness. I can see myself out.'

He went out into the evening. A harsh wind snatched at his trousers. The chauffeur flashed the headlights. As Bart walked to the waiting vehicle, he reflected that – at long last – he had stood his corner . . . not on anything that mattered, but he felt better for it. There was a spring in his step. The bloody wind caught his tie, snaked it over his shoulder.

Beth heard the wind beat on the windows. Outside, the palm trees' fronds shuddered. She held up the book. 'Everyone got it, Sonnet Eight? I'll start, first two lines, then each of you, to a stop or a colon, from the right. "Shall I compare thee to a summer's day? Thou art more lovely and more temperate." Next . . .'

In front of her, hanging on her words, were her four most advanced pupils. Shakespeare for them, not the technical language of petroleum extraction. Her finger wavered towards the chemist from Pakistan.

It was *risqué* for her to have chosen a sonnet of love: it was at the limit of religious correctness. One day, when she had her flight out booked, confirmed, she might just get round to *The Merchant of Venice*, give them Shylock's lament. For now, *love* was challenge enough, and taught by a woman.

She cued in the pipeline engineer. The man read and stuttered to a halt. 'Miss Bethany, I do not understand it.'

The men laughed, she grinned. She could have done *Lear* with them, or the speeches at Agincourt, or given them *Coriolanus*. She had chosen *love*. A nun, a permanent virgin, at the convent school had made the class learn the sonnet by heart. Not a full hour of the day had gone by when she had not thought of him . . . and the wind outside now whipped the sand and she wondered where he sheltered, huddled, and how hard it went for him.

'You will, when we're through it. OK, on we go . . .' She pointed to the airfield manager.

He had not left her. He had been with her in the shower in the morning, no time for a bath, and as she'd gulped down her breakfast. He was with her now. She heard the beat of his breath as he had dug with the shovel. She saw him stare out the men who would have killed her. His voice was with her, as he had gone away with the boy: 'You never met me, I was never here . . . You never saw my face.' He was never away from her.

The warning of the deputy governor was wrong, she decided. She would not accept it. He had said that illegal and dangerous men travelled in the Sands. She had lied, she had said she met no one, saw no one. But the warning was a saw's blade on a plank nail, and she could not escape it.

'Right, excellent – questions.'

The pipeline engineer asked, 'It is very fine, Miss Bethany, but what is Shakespeare writing of? Is it lust? Is it infatuation? Is it love? How can we read Shakespeare's mind? Is it about love?'

'Read it to your wife when you are next at home, and ask her,' Beth said. 'For myself, I think it is not infatuation or lust. No, it is about love.'

The wind outside was worse, fiercer – where he was.

They were in darkness. Only a thin light washed down from the moon. He thought, was not certain of it, that the route of the march was no longer straight but that it curved along the line of a crescent. His eyes were slitted against the sand the wind pelted him with, and sometimes – against the strongest gusts – he lifted the cloth that covered his mouth and protected his eyes. When he went blind, or when he peered ahead, he could only make out the rump of Ghaffur's camel in front of him. He could not see Rashid, but he sensed that the guide took them on great lengths of quarter-circles, then corrected, then took another curved course.

Was the guide lost?

He thought Fahd slept, and Hosni. Both men were tied to their saddles. Three times, after they had restarted the march, when the moon was highest, Caleb had lost sight of Ghaffur and the boy had gone forward and must have talked with his father, but each time he had dropped back and taken a place again in front of Caleb, and then – each time – the route had swung into another gentle long and arching turn.

What if they were lost?

The guide had no map, no instruments, and in the darkness he could not see the features of the greater dunes – if there were any.

His mind had drifted back into his memory. He had seen a room. There was a bed, unmade, and a green coverlet was crumpled on the floor. The carpet was thin and pale brown and magazines tossed down shared it with the coverlet. Motorcycles and cars were the photographs on the opened magazines. Girls – big hips, small swim-suit bottoms, big breasts – were on the walls. The room was gone from Caleb's mind.

He tried to remember from what direction the sand hit him, didn't know, was too confused, too tired, too thirsty, hungry and bruised by the day's heat, and now chilled by the night. Each of the Beautiful One's strides dragged her closer to collapse. He had set in his mind that they were lost, that they had doubled back on sand covered the previous day, or the day before. He croaked the question: 'Does he know where he's going, Ghaffur, does your father know?'

The boy seemed to hiss for him to be quiet.

'Has your father been here before, ever before?'

The hiss was louder, sharper.

'It is madness to move in darkness . . .'

The hiss whistled at him, cut him.

He could see, faintly, that Ghaffur was high on his saddle. His head was raised. The wind tore at the boy's robe. It was natural to ride into the wind with the body bent low and the target for the wind minimized. It was as though Ghaffur sniffed the wind, or listened.

He strained to see the boy better, could not. 'Ghaffur, tell me – are we lost?'

'My father knows where he is, where we go. He knows everything of the Sands.'

'Why do we not go straight, in a straight line?'

'Only God knows more about the Sands. My father is responsible for you. He decides the route and you follow.'

'Why do you go forward and talk to him, and then each time we turn?'

The boy called back to him, a slight voice beaten by the wind, 'Because of what I hear.'

'I hear nothing.'

'My ears are the best, my father says they are the ears of a leopard, one that lives in the mountains. It is an engine's noise. A long way off, but I thought I heard it.'

'What sort of engine? On the air or on the ground? Where was it?'

'I do not know. Each time you talk I cannot listen.'

Caleb heard only the footfall of the camels, the snoring of Fahd and Hosni, and the darkness closed round him and the wind speared against him.

In the night the wind swerved to come from the north, and greater ferocity came with the change.

In the sands of the Rub' al Khālī, men lay against their camels' bodies to find shelter, and only their guide knew the value of the wind.

Above the sands, rocked, tossed and shaken, a Predator flew and hunted, in secrecy and silence, and under each wing was a Hellfire missile.

The dawn's light nestled on the wings of the Predator and caught the sandcoated backs of the camels.

'In words of one syllable, or two, stop fucking me about.'

'I am sorry, Mr Wroughton, sir, but I do not have authority to admit you.'

'Young man, I am expected.'

'I don't think so, Mr Wroughton, sir.'

'I had a meeting fixed up.'

'Yes, sir, but not here.'

In the half-light, as the city woke, Wroughton had left the bed of an agronomist's wife – Belgian, large and not entirely pretty, but experienced – and had driven to the Gonsalves' compound. Sometimes he went there when Teresa was giving the kids their tea and waited for Juan's return, sometimes it was for breakfast before Juan drove to the embassy. The agronomist was due back in Riyadh from Layla, west of the big desert, that evening. If it had not been for his appointment with Juan, his friend, Wroughton would have enjoyed another three hours, or four if he could last it, in the agronomist's bed – inside the agronomist's wife; the man was down in Layla to examine the possibilities of growing a strawberry crop on the edge of the big desert – bloody fool. Teresa had said, in her night-dress and with the kids howling round her, that Juan had already gone down to the embassy, had been gone an hour.

'Just, please, get on the phone and tell him that I'm downstairs . . . or is that too bloody difficult?'

'He knows you are here, Mr Wroughton, sir.'

Teresa, at her front door, had yawned, then pulled a face and winked. 'Big flap, Eddie. Panic call. He was dressing as he was driving.' The marine on the embassy desk had rung through, and the young man had come down. Wroughton knew him as the number five out of five in the Agency's Riyadh pecking order. The meeting, over breakfast, round the kitchen table, was just routine and the chance to exchange snippets, but it was important for Wroughton. That day of each month he started on his report, regular as his bowels, for Vauxhall Bridge Cross. Much, too much, of his monthly report came from the crumbs off Juan and Teresa's kitchen table. A big flap, a panic call, he needed to know the detail of that. He was blocked, and his temper rose.

Wroughton swung his fist towards the internal phone on the desk in front of the marine guard. 'Just get him on the phone – I'll speak to him.'

He thought this young man had a future in fielding customer complaints in a telephone or electricity company – so calm, and his voice never betrayed anger. 'He said you'd be round. He said, when you came round, I was to come down and tell you that he was too busy – some other time. He'd ring. That's what I was to tell you, Mr Wroughton, sir.'

The young man shrugged, then sidled away, went through the inner gate with a punch-number lock.

Wroughton turned, furious. What price the special fucking relationship? He stamped towards the swing doors where the marines watched him impassively. A big flap, a panic call, and Eddie Wroughton was shut out. He would not have believed it, not of the special relationship, not of his friend. He could still smell the Belgian woman on him, and he went home to change his shirt . . . and his whole damned world was upside-down, was tossed aside.

'How much more time, for God's sake, do they need?'

For five minutes more than an hour, Juan Gonsalves had been watching the screen. He wore a bar microphone and the headset was clamped in his uncombed hair. He paced in the communications area. His shirt hung out of his trousers and his vest had the hand-prints of last night's kids' food – but his eyes, bloodshot and tired, never left the screen. Not often did he show raw stress.

He was not permitted a direct link with the Ground Control at Shaybah. The raised hut on the trailer down at the end of the runway, beside the perimeter fence, was off-limits to Gonsalves. Too fraught down there, he'd been told. What it meant, they didn't need a rubber-necker over their shoulder. Close to him, leaning against the closed door, was Nathan, the new guy out from Langley, and he'd had the signal from the young man that the visitor in the lobby had been sent away. There were things that Gonsalves would share, and things he would not. A live image from four and a half miles over the Rub' al Khālī – with a target – was not to be shared.

The feed on the screen, real time, rolled and bucked, went soft focus, reclaimed the target, lost it, found it again. Nathan had moved to the coffee dispenser. Over the headset, Gonsalves heard the re-assurance of Langley and the increasing tension of the guys down at Shaybah. The talk was coded, technical, and Gonsalves could under-stand only trifles. Why the hell did they not strike? The picture on the screen, beamed off the Predator, wavered off and on to a drawn-out camel train. The effort of the sensor operator was to get clear images of the cargo carried by three of the camels. More times than he had counted, the zoom had gone down on the camels, blurred with magnification, but then the picture had been lost. He had seen the men, five of them, spread out over a length that might have been as much as two hundred metres. They went slowly in long arcs. The camera tried, one more time, to go close-up on a cargo box, but the focus failed. The angle changed. Gonsalves imagined, high above the caravan, kicked by the gale winds, that the Predator circled.

Nathan gave him coffee. He drank, didn't notice the taste. He flung the beaker towards the trash can, missed, and coffee dribbled on to the floor. He picked up off the table the photocopied picture of a crate box, olive green, that could hold a Stinger, the man-portable surface-to-air missile system. He knew the wind had reached new levels at the altitude of the Predator and at the level of the desert, because the picture rocked more severely and there seemed to be a mist over the camels and the men, which he thought to be from driven sand. In his working life, Juan Gonsalves had not known a stress level so high. He depressed the speech button on his headset.

'How much longer – when can we go?'

The voice was massaged, quiet: 'This is Oscar Golf. Interjections from what we regard as spectators interrupt and divert us. Briefly, we do not take out a target until it has been identified with certainty – identification is in process. These are difficult conditions. We're right at the upper altitude where the UAV currently flies, and it's near impossible to get a stable platform. The weather is deteriorating and we are running low on fuel. So, please, no further interruptions. Oscar Golf, out.'

He had been put down, felt like a scolded child. He watched the screen, saw the caravan moving steadily under the real-time camera. He felt weak, sick.

'Four more minutes on station,' Marty said.

'After four more minutes we cannot bring *Carnival Girl* back,' Lizzy-Jo said.

The voice of Oscar Golf came back, so calm. 'Reading you, hearing you.'

Marty worked the joystick, his decision, and brought *Carnival Girl* down a full six thousand feet of height. Each foot of descent made the camera platform less stable. He had backed her away, gone to the west, had lowered the lens angle. Lizzy-Jo followed him. They were like dancers in step. The camera raked along the straggling length of the caravan. He didn't need to speak to her. They moved together, better that day than any other. He ran *Carnival Girl* from the tail of the caravan and on towards the front of it. The computers did the calculations. George flitted at their backs and kept the bottles of water coming. Marty could not drink, did not dare to release his fingers from the joystick. It fascinated him that down below, on the camels, they did not know the eye of the lens watched them. He was halfway along the caravan, and Lizzy-Jo's finger stabbed at the digits playing at the base of the screen – two minutes and forty seconds. Would they pull out, on Oscar Golf's orders, or would they sacrifice *Carnival Girl* and let her crash in the desert with her fuel tanks exhausted? The momentary image was of a big camel, loaded – then the voice in the headphones.

'We have a freeze – wait out. We are looking at a freeze frame.' No excitement in the voice, without passion.

Marty looked up, took in the screen on the right side of the main image. The freeze frame was like a still photograph. The picture held two camels. He saw the clear lines of the crate box. He—

The voice betrayed nothing, no thrill, like it was a machine. 'Hit them. Right now.'

He heard Lizzy-Jo's question. 'One strike or two?'

The answer. 'Give them both. Waste the fuckers.'

He came round, was head on towards the caravan. It was what they trained for, what they practised to achieve. Lizzy-Jo didn't have to tell him what she needed. It would be without warning. Down there, slow moving in the sand, they would have no warning. The cross-winds hammered *Carnival Girl*.

'Port side, missile gone,' Lizzy-Jo murmured.

On the screen, racing from it and diminishing, was the fireball. Twelve seconds or thirteen, at that height, from firing to impact. Again the camera shook at the weight loss.

'Starboard side, missile gone.'

Two concentrated flame masses, burning solid propellant, careered down. Each powered a missile with a warhead of twenty-five pounds weight of explosive, fragmentation quality, on impact fuses. He watched. Lizzy-Jo guided them and he heard little yelps whistle through her teeth. They were nearly down, he was counting silently, when the camels scattered. A few paces, the lens picked up the panic. They were turning, running, and then the flames cut in among them. He saw the camels break the line, then the cloud burst over them, and the fireflash. A ceiling of dust, sand, filled the screen image.

Marty said, flat, into his face microphone. 'I am out of flight time. Do I bring her back or do I lose her?'

'Bring her back – and give her some good loving care. Nothing will live under that. Bring her home. Oscar Golf, out.'

Marty turned her, and the lens lost the cloud.

He heard nothing.

The boy was on a dune's rim, and his hands were cupped together across his mouth, his shoulders heaving with the effort of shouting. Caleb could not hear him.

He did not know how long he had been alone in the Sands with the Beautiful One. She had stampeded in terrified flight. He had clung to her. She had bolted, had run in the few seconds of ear-splitting noise before the first explosion. She had been going at full stride at the moment of the second explosion. He had hung on to her neck. She had gone on until she could run no more, then had stopped, trembling. He did what he had learned from the guide. As he had seen Rashid do it, he snuggled his face against the Beautiful One's mouth, his nose against the foulness of her breath, and he had whispered sweetness to her. He had stilled the trembling. They had meandered on, alone and together. He had not known where he went – the camel had taken the course. His ears were dead and his mind was numbed, and the strength of the sun had grown.

In the distance, high on the dune, the wind made a canopy of the boy's robe. The ears of the Beautiful One lifted, pricked, as if she heard him when Caleb could not . . . They were all his family, the boy and the Beautiful One, and the men who waited for him at the end of his journey. He had no other family. The camel's pace quickened, closing on the boy who had searched for him and found him.

Chapter Thirteen

They rode on.

Many times, Caleb looked up and searched for the danger. There was not a cloud in the brilliant blue of the sky. He gazed up till his eyes ached, saw nothing and heard nothing.

They made a straggling line, their tracks covered by the wind's shift of the sand. Rashid was out in front. On a bull camel, already laden with two crates, was the body of Fahd. Further back was Hosni, then Caleb, then another bull. Last in the line was the boy, Ghaffur. Caleb had not seen them, but left beyond the horizon were the carcasses of Fahd's animal and one that had carried crates and one that had carried food.

He thought of Fahd, the zealot, who had insisted that they stop each time for the necessary prayers, thought of the man who had not had an encouraging word for him, for any of them . . . His eyes had watered but now had no more moisture to secrete, and there was agony in them each time he lifted his head and tried to scan the sky, to search into its blue depths.

The wind dragged at Caleb's robe and tore at the headcloth that covered his mouth, his scalp and his ears. He did not know whether Fahd had been taken by the first explosion or the second, whether he had had a moment to think on Paradise. Had he – for one second or two, or for the half-minute that had separated the explosions – considered the Garden of Paradise? All of the Arabs in the 055 Brigade swore on their Faith that they believed in the Garden where martyrs went, where cool streams ran, where baskets of fresh fruit lay, where girls waited for them. He could see Fahd's corpse, its feet hanging on one side of the camel's flanks, and the head on the other. The back of Fahd's head was gone, but the blood from it and the brain tissue had fallen out long ago and had been trampled into the sand by the following camels. Caleb had looked into the skies, into the clearness of the blue, as the Beautiful One had lumbered through the last of the blood and brain that had dropped from the opened skull. Had Fahd, in the last seconds of his life, welcomed death? Had he believed in the Garden of Paradise? Caleb did not, could not, know. Caleb had crossed the chasm into his old world, rejected before, which muddied the certainty of the Garden of Paradise. Rolling on his saddle, gazing up, Caleb felt a sadness that the last he would remember of Fahd was the anger in the Saudi's face and the screams of his voice . . . The man had been his family too.

He tightened the hold on his reins and he bent and his voice whispered soft words in the ear of the Beautiful One. He slowed her step, and the sight of Fahd's head and feet drifted further away. The sand disturbed by Hosni's camel was no longer lifted into his face, and the pack bull passed him. Caleb waited for the boy to reach him.

'Will you talk to me?'

'My father says that to talk is to waste strength.'

'Does your father also say that to be alone is to be frightened?'

'We are never alone in the Sands. God is with us, my father says.'

'Were you frightened, Ghaffur?'

'No.' The boy shook his head.

He remembered himself at Ghaffur's age, and the kids he'd messed with. Caleb would have been, they would have been, terrified when the flames had come down, fireballs, from the sky, which was clear, blue and empty. He believed the boy.

'Tell me.'

'My father says it is an aircraft without a pilot. It is flown by commands – I do not understand how – that are given it by men who sit far away. They could be a week's camel ride from it, or more. My father heard about it from the Bedouin of the Yemen. There was a man from the town of Marib, he was Qaed Sunian al-Harthi and he was hunted by the Americans, but he was in the desert and he thought himself safe, and he rode in a vehicle towards an oil well where Americans worked. He had made a bomb ... He was betrayed. They knew when he would move and in what vehicle. There was no warning. He was hit from the sky. My father says there are cameras in the aircraft, and the Americans would have watched the vehicle he rode in. He was killed from the sky, and all the men with him. The Bedouin would have believed that the bomb he carried had exploded, but the police told the Bedouin that the Americans had boasted about their aircraft in the sky ... You were frightened?'

Caleb bit at his lip, and the sand stuck at his teeth. 'I hope I am not a coward – I admit I was frightened ... Does your father say how we can run from it?'

'Only with God's help, and He gives us the wind.'

'If the wind is too strong?'

'If that is what He wishes,' the boy said solemnly. 'God spared you – He has a great purpose for you.'

It came in against the gale. From her window, Beth had seen it make the first attempt to land, but that was failure.

She had thought it extraordinary that the aircraft should have flown in those conditions. It had been fifty feet or so above the extreme end of the runway and had seemed to be lifted up, as if by an unseen hand, then thrown sideways. The regular flight from Riyadh had not come in that morning, and that would have been a Boeing 737, heavy and stable. This aircraft was tiny in comparison, a lightweight toy. It had climbed, shaking, as if it was punched, and while it had come round for the second attempt, Beth had gone out on to the patio. It made no sense to her that they should be flying, for evaluation and mapping, in such weather.

It had lined up again over the landing guide lights that were in the sand beyond the perimeter fence. Everything in Beth Jenkins's life, before these last several days, had been based on certainty. She clung to the trunk of the palm, and she saw what was different. There were no tubes under the wings. There had been tubes under the wings the last time she had seen the aircraft lift off.

She was confused, knew no answers, heard only the questions.

It rolled with the wind. It was over the runway, seemed to stop like the hovering *shahin* her patron flew. It lurched clumsily – she remembered the grace of its take-off. A wing went down, its balance was lost. In bad weather, her patron would not have risked the lives of his prized *shahin* or his *hurr*. He had paid – and had told her the money was well spent – a hundred and ten thousand dollars for the trained peregrine, and eighty thousand dollars for the saker falcon, and she thought this bird must have been valued at many millions of dollars. Why would they risk it? It made no sense. Beth thought it was past the point of return, had to come down.

The right wing came up, it levelled, was a crippled bird and fragile. The left wing dipped.

No pilot. The only life in danger was that of the bird itself. The left wing-tip scraped on the Tarmac. It ran on, stopped, then turned. It taxied down the runway and, as if its engine was cut, came to a slow and hesitant halt. A jeep came from the little camp and sped towards it.

She went back into the bungalow and started to work again on her report on the ejecta field, but she could not concentrate . . . Nothing was certain, doubt ruled. He was with her. '*You never met me, I was never here . . . You never saw my face.*' She hit the laptop's keys, but demons danced and she could not lose them. Beth could not make the link between the aircraft and him, but sensed it existed.

She wanted to cry out, to yell a warning, could not and the silence dripped around her.

He saw a man who was tall, athletically built, tanned, and not dressed for that morning's English weather.

Michael Lovejoy strode forward, not with a springing step because the legacy of the winter was increasing pain in his hip joints. The man had Lovejoy's name in big letters on a sheet of paper and held it up. The flight was in early and Lovejoy was late. The man wore heavy shoes, suede, and faded jeans with a brightly checked cotton shirt. There was a grip bag at his feet as he gazed around him, a frown of impatience writ large on a sunburned forehead. Lovejoy played at charm.

'Mr Dietrich – Mr Jed Dietrich? I'm Lovejoy, I was asked to meet you. Sincere apologies for keeping you hanging round. The traffic was awful.'

'Pleased to meet you. I was just beginning to wonder . . .'

His handshake crunched Lovejoy's fingers. 'I'm sure you were. Anyway, all's well that ends well, don't you know? God, this place is a nightmare. Car's outside, bit of a walk, I'm afraid.'

Lovejoy rarely met Americans. Those he did were from the embassy's legal department. They were Federal Bureau of Investigation, men with cropped scalps, polished shoes and bow-ties, or women with flat chests, trouser suits and bobbed hair. As a breed, he was innately suspicious of them. When they came on to his territory it always seemed they expected his immediate and un-divided attention, and when he went on to their ground it always seemed they were busy and uninterested. He was not late because of awful traffic but because Mercy and he had lingered over breakfast. He had brought his own car, a six-year-old Volvo estate that was good for ferrying the grandchildren.

In the multi-storey car park, after walking as fast as his hip joints permitted him, he unlocked the vehicle. He expected the American to comment on the child seats in the back. The cousins from across the water, both sexes, usually liked to talk kids and produce photo-graphs from their wallets. There was no remark on the seats, or on the kids' clutter in the front from the school run Mercy had done the previous week. They pulled out.

'I see you've been in the sunshine, Mr Dietrich. You won't find much of that here . . . So, you've come in from Florida. Is that your workplace, or the end of a vacation?'

There had been no holiday that year for Michael and Mercy Lovejoy. The new conservatory at the back of their home had gulped the spare cash. Lack of funds had denied them the usual two weeks in a rented Cornish cottage and his summer leave had been spent decorating the dining room and the sitting room. When Lovejoy referred to other people's holidays there was often a barb in his tone.

The reply was crisp. 'I work at Guantanamo Bay.'

Last thing before leaving home for the drive to the airport, as Mercy had kissed his cheek, Lovejoy had told her: 'God knows what their Defense Intelligence Agency want from us. What I've always understood, they're the "eternal flames" – you know, never go out. Spend their days stuck in bunkers trying to make sense of radio traffic and – I suppose – looking over aerial pix with a magnifying-glass and searching for an oil drum of anthrax in suburban Baghdad. Feel for me, darling, it's going to be grim.' He was a safe pair of hands. More important, as the trail of Al Qaeda funding grew colder, was iced over, in the City of London, his absence from his desk would matter little. Mercy had grimaced, had kissed him again.

'I am an interrogator at Camp Delta.'

'Oh, are you? Well, that's a rather interesting place.' He hoped the little intake of breath, sharp, went unnoticed. At Thames House there was a desk on the third floor that dealt with Guantanamo Bay and the eight Britons detained there. Five visits had been made to Camps X-Ray and Delta but he had never seen anything remotely relevant coming back, or not, at least, across his desk. He knew that High Court judges refused to denounce the detention without charge and trial of the Britons as illegal under international law; he knew also that the relevant government ministers obdurately declined to make a noise, or waves. The Britons were, as Lovejoy understood it, in a Black Hole.

The whole working life of Michael Lovejoy, twenty-eight years an intelligence officer with the Security Service and before that his fifteen years as an Army officer with the Green Jackets, had been governed by the Bible of Need to Know. Since marriage, only Mercy had needed to know – not the people he met in the pub or other guests at dinner parties and, often enough, not colleagues. Himself, if he had just come off a flight in New York or Washington, Lovejoy would have guarded his secrets closely, said what was necessary and not a damned word more. He listened.

'The only thing fascinating about Camp Delta is that it is bogged down in a rut – that is, one hell of a rut, like a tractor wheel makes in mud. We're just going through the motions. Not even a dozen times in two years – after the first splash of intelligence – have we learned anything new or important. We go to work, we talk to people, we read back the transcripts, and we fall asleep. We don't learn any-thing. Then it happens, and we're shaking. It happens.'

'Out of a clear blue sky is, I believe, the cliché.'

'Out of that clear blue sky comes a thunderbolt. Got me? We

released a man. We're under heavy pressure to find a few innocents and ship them back with a fanfare, the full shebang. We released a man whom we believed to be a taxi-driver, from Afghanistan . . .'

Lovejoy waited – he was rarely impatient.

'I was on holiday, up in Wisconsin with my wife and kid and getting in some fishing before the winter came down. The taxi-driver, he made my list – I wasn't there when they decided to shift him. We have the Joint Task Force 170, which is Bureau, Agency and us, but the Bureau, the Agency run it, we're country cousins. They made that decision. He was flown out. He was being driven into Kabul, asked for a comfort stop and did a runner. If he was just a taxi-driver, who cares?'

'You care.' A further talent of Lovejoy was his ability, with apparent sincerity, to flatter. Sandwiched among the lorries and vans, he drove at a steady pace, anxious always to relax his informant . . . God, what would he do when he retired? What sort of man would he be? He dreaded the day. 'So, you came back from leave and found the taxi-driver gone.'

'I had a Brit in with me. Some creep, a nobody. I asked the questions I was supposed to ask – last week. You know how it is, that gut feeling. You get a match. It was his accent . . . I was a Cold War specialist when I started, then I went to the Balkan desks, now I do Guantanamo. I've heard every goddamn accent there is – Russian, Polish, North Korean, Serb, Bosnian and Croat, Yemeni, Egyptian, Saudi and Kuwaiti. I got accents coming out of my ass. The Brit I had in, he spoke with the same accent as the taxi-driver.'

'Did he now?'

'To me, it was the same accent – then I got sort of scared at what I was looking at . . .'

With good cause. Lovejoy's hands had tightened on the wheel. Little parts of three lunchtime lectures seeped into his mind. A psychologist had said: 'I urge you to look elsewhere. Where? For quality, for ability, for the best – because it is those young men that the lieutenants of bin Laden search for.' A Russian counter-intelligence officer had said: 'Somewhere, in his psyche or his experience, there will be a source of hatred. He hates you and me and the society that we serve.' A scientist had said: 'We start with a suit-case. Any suitcase of a size that a man or woman uses for a week's stay in a hotel . . .' Scared with good cause. He remembered the stunned quiet in that room at Thames House, the day before. A man who had the skill to defeat the interrogation process was a man who was owed respect . . . Funny thing, *respect*. It was often churned out for an old enemy – respect for a Rommel, or for a Vo Nguyen Giap, or for the Argentine pilots in the south Atlantic – but he had never heard respect given to the new enemy. On any floor of Thames House he would not have expected to hear of respect for a suicide bomber, or for a fighter in the new order's army. If an enemy was not shown respect – given only the status of a pest – that enemy presented increasing danger.

'Do you have the tapes of the interrogations, the Brit and the taxi-driver?'

He saw the head nod.

'How long have you got, Mr Dietrich?'

'I got till yesterday – and please call me Jed.'

The rain on the windscreen had come on heavier. 'You travelled light – have you brought winter clothes?'

'I got authorization, and I went out of Gitmo, like a bat out of hell. I know if the Bureau and the Agency had gotten their act together, I'd have been called back. This could bring down empires, could wreck big careers . . . but, for the moment, it's mine and I'm keeping it. I'm going to the end of the road, Mr Lovejoy, and –'

'Michael, please.'

'– and if I'm wrong, I will be fed to the crows. And if I'm right, probably the same. I will not win a popularity contest. I don't give a fuck.'

Lovejoy took his mobile from his suit jacket and rang Mercy. She would have been upstairs, making the beds for the kids, coming that night. He told her he would be away, apologized, then asked her to dig out the sweater his daughter-in-law had given him two Christmases back, a size too large and never worn, and the old green waxed waterproof coat he hadn't used for five years. He said he'd be by for them in an hour, but would not be stopping. Then, steering with one hand and locking the wheel with his knees when he changed gear, he thumbed through the contacts book that was filled with names and numbers. He tapped out the digits on the phone and made the appointment he needed.

After two hearings, the professor of phonetics at King's College, London University said, 'Well, you're wrong. I'm sorry to disabuse you. It's not a matter of argument, but a fact. The accents are not from the same place. What you have called Tape Alpha, the Briton reading Pashto, is quite different to a trained ear from Tape Bravo. I regret any disappointment that may cause you, but facts are facts. Tape Alpha is Birmingham, with only marginal similarities to Tape Bravo. Tape Bravo is the Black Country. Now, you'll have to excuse me, I have a tutorial.'

They were out on the street, hurrying through the sluicing rain across the car park, and the American was struggling into the old waxed waterproof coat.

Lovejoy said, 'Don't look so bloody miserable. The Black Country is not at Kandahar, or Peshawar, or in the Yemen. Forget that pedantic buffoon. The Black Country is on the immediate north-west boundary of the city of Birmingham. You did well. Fifteen miles from Birmingham, maximum. You did very well.'

He stood in the doorway, had pressed the bell and waited for it to be answered.

The maid, a Filipina, faced him.

Eddie Wroughton walked past her, went into the sitting room. The Belgian woman was watching a video in her housecoat and painting her nails in a cerise that matched the lipstick.

He went into the kitchen and poured himself a juice from the fridge. For a man who was rated clever, intelligent and cunning, he had taken a giant risk in returning to the villa in daylight, when spying neighbours and gossiping servants would see him. Three times he had tried to ring Juan Gonsalves and three times he had been told that Mr Gonsalves was 'in a meeting', and would get back to him. Wroughton's mobile had not rung.

From the kitchen, he heard the shopping instructions being given to the maid. There was an officer serving in Riga, Penny, who had his photograph beside her bed. She had told him of the photograph in one of her many unanswered letters. He had no thoughts of Riga, or of the risk, only of the agronomist's wife. He heard the front door close.

If his friend, Gonsalves, had returned his calls Wroughton would not have been in the agronomist's kitchen, would not have been frustrated into taking the risk. He wondered whether the paint on her nails was dry, whether the lipstick on her mouth would smudge and run. His name was called, not from the living room but from the bedroom.

He craved to erase the humiliation of the lobby below the Agency's floor.

His shoes and clothes were scattered over the tiled floors of the kitchen and the living room and he was naked when he reached the bedroom, except for his tinted glasses. He hated his eyes to be seen: they might betray his humiliation.

Between patients, the receptionist brought Bart a printout of the extension contract offered him by the real-estate company.

He had won.

The offer was for an eighteen per cent reduction in monthly payments.

That was victory.

When she'd gone out, as he waited for the next patient, Bart surprised himself: clumsily, he danced a little jig. He hopped from foot to foot, in tune to the whistle from his lips. He had won the victory by his boldness – Christ! He thought, as he skipped, of the many who had walked over him: in particular, Eddie bloody Wroughton – not that he would gain his freedom from Wroughton, but the victory was a moment of success to be savoured.

The German patient spoke shamefacedly of snoring problems; Bart spoke of lymph-node complications, the patient's wife spoke of the disturbance in her night's sleep; Bart spoke of a consultant who was a very decent Greek at the ear, nose and throat section of the King Fahd Medical City. They were relieved and grateful.

'I'll make the appointment, Mr Seitz, I'll take care of everything. Leave it to me. You didn't tell me your business in the Kingdom.'

'I took early retirement from the Luftwaffe. Now, I train air-traffic controllers for the Saudi Air Force.'

Bart wrote up his notes. 'Do you now? That must be fascinating.'

'Complete chaos, it blows my mind.'

Never looking up from the notes, with studied casualness, Bart asked, 'What in particular do you find stressful about your work?'

He was a worm at the core of an apple – victory on his rent or not, he was still Eddie bloody Wroughton's man.

Caleb rode with Hosni. He sensed the wind slackened, but the smell was worse. Fahd's body was bloated by the sun's heat, and the wind carried to him the stench, sweet and sickly. He remembered the smell of the bodies in the trenches after the big bombers had gone over.

The sand grains were plastered round the old Egyptian's eyes. They were dulled as if the life was going from them, and Hosni's head never turned to him. He rode with him for kindness. He thought of how it must have been when the missiles had come down. And how it would have been, in a half-light, when the camels had scattered, when Hosni's own had stampeded, its passenger strapped on, shaken, jolted, deafened, and not knowing. From a past life, a memory surfaced . . . There had been an old man who walked beside the canal, sunshine or rain, with a stick, and the kids had shouted at him and he had flailed the stick around him, but had not seen them. Caleb had been one of the kids. He had thought of the old man beside the canal, his stick and the jeers, and he rode with Hosni. Hosni was so frail, so weak, and Caleb thought his courage was an inspiration.

'What, Hosni, can you see?'

'I see what I need to see. I see the sand, I see the sun.'

'Is there something a doctor can do?'

'A year ago, perhaps there was something. Two years ago, for certain a doctor could do something. We were hunted, first in the Tora Bora, then in caves on the border. I could not go to Quetta or to Kandahar to find a doctor. I was with the Emir General. If I had gone to find a doctor and been taken . . . I knew too much to go to Quetta or Kandahar. In Oman I saw a doctor.'

'Was there nothing he could do?'

The head came up and the smile cracked the face; the caked sand spilled down from it. 'He could do *something*. He could tell me. I have from the doctor a diagnosis. It cannot be treated, it is not reversible, it deteriorates.'

'What?'

'Maybe I washed in dirty water. Maybe I waded a stream that was polluted. It could have been long ago, right back in the days when we fought the Soviets and I was beside the Emir General. The doctor had a fine name for the condition, onchocerciasis, and a finer name for the parasite, *Onchocerca volvulus*. The doctor in Oman was a very educated and well-read man. The parasite is a worm that can live for fourteen years in the body. The female enters the body through any lesion, a scraped knee or cut foot, as you go through dirty and polluted water, and it breeds larvae. Soon your body is the home of many millions of worms and they roam through you. Some, it does not need to be many, make the long journey to the backs of your eyes. They live there, the little worms, eat there and breed there. The diagnosis is eventual blindness.'

'How much time do you have?'

'I have enough time to do what I wish to do. Do not be frightened for me.'

'Tell me.'

'I will not live to go blind.'

'Explain.'

'There is a suitcase or a bag that a brother prepares. In the bag are materials. I handle them, I work with them. I have said I will do it. To touch the materials is to walk away from life. When the bag or case is sealed it can be carried in safety. I dream of it. The dream sustains me in this hell. And I dream of the young man who will carry the case or the bag, and he is my friend.'

'I am your friend, Hosni.'

'Do you hate enough?'

The smell of Fahd's body played in his nose. The noise of the thunder was in Caleb's ears, and he saw the fire exhaust from the missile streaming down from the sky.

'I hate enough. I will carry a case or a bag.'

Camp Delta, Guantanamo Bay.

Exercise day . . . Another week gone by. Exercise, then his shower.

He was escorted into the dirt yard. It was the second time that he had been led into the exercise yard and had seen the new goalposts.

His hands were manacled. A chain led from the manacles to his waist, circled by another chain. More chain link hung down from his waist and reached the shackles on his ankles. The guards let go of his arms. 'Off you go, kid – go get your circuits in.'

The football pitch was in the centre of the yard, with white lines marked out across the dried mud. Around the pitch, a line of men shuffled the circuit, each twenty paces apart, their steps restricted by the length of chain between the shackled ankles, and listened to the shouts from the pitch where twenty or twenty-five prisoners chased a football. The most recent edict at Delta had invited prisoners to apply for extra exercise. Caleb had been confused by it. He had not known whether he should volunteer, whether it would help the deceit, or whether it would compromise him. If he had taken up the invitation would he then be expected to inform on fellow prisoners? He had not put his name forward. He had fifteen minutes of exercise ahead of him, but the football-players had an hour of chasing the ball.

A big American, tracksuited, ruled the pitch with a whistle. He loathed them, all of them, loathed them whether they wore a tracksuit and praised, whether they wore the bright sun shirts and interrogated, whether they had the camouflage uniform and the key bars to the manacles and shackles.

He did his circuits. When a goal was scored, the American blasted his whistle and applauded. He looked at the players, dancing because the ball was in the back netting, and tried to remember the faces. If any were moved to the cell next to his, he would be more careful, would guard against the smallest mistake.

At the end of his last circuit, his escort gestured for him.

His arms were held as he was led out of the yard. He would not exercise for another week.

'You could be doing that, kid, playing soccer. You've only got to ask.'

He did not understand. He smiled nervously at the guard. He had learned his part.

He was taken to the shower block.

With the loathing was contempt. He felt superior to the men who escorted him, unmanacled and unshackled him, who watched him undress, who saw him into the cubicle where the water sluiced down on him. He did not come cheap. They would not turn him with the offer of a game of football. He deceived them. The certainty of his superiority gave him strength.

A towel was thrown to him.

Marty lay on his back on the camp bed. Beside it, propped against the chair on which his clothes hung, was the picture, his only valued possession. Behind the glass, spattered with sand grains and misted with condensation, was Marty's hero; the hero at Gundamuck who had wrapped round his chest the colours of the 44th Regiment. Lieutenant Souter, a hundred and sixty-two years before, had survived the last stand of his troops and gone home, fêted. Marty aspired to heroism, and did not know how he would achieve it.

If he had still been at Bagram, Marty would now have been in the Officers' Club. He would have been a centre of attention. The beers would have kept coming. The Agency people would have been round him, pilots, sensor operators, interrogators and analysts, and the cans would have kept coming for free. He had done a launch, seen the Hellfires go, watched the cloud mushroom up. It would have been his party time, his moment of heroics, if he had been at Bagram.

But he was not, he was in this shit-hole.

At Bagram Marty would have had an audience, with supervisors and ranking agents doing cheer-leading. His praises would have been sung. And the talk would have moved on to him bringing *Carnival Girl* home, with the tanks showing empty and the wind plucking at her as she touched down. He was a goddamn hero but no one was around to tell him.

The wind battered at the tent's sides. The sand came in between the flaps and the ground sheet, and the roof billowed. A solitary beer, given him by George, was half hidden on the chair by his clothes, which were hitched on the back. Marty hadn't pulled the can's ring.

The last thing he'd heard from Oscar Golf was a demand for 'soonest' information on potential damage to the port-side wing-tip of *Carnival Girl* in the touch-down. There had been no hero-gram out of Langley, no congratulation from goddamn Gonsalves, nothing. He had staggered out of the Ground Control, had been close to spilling himself on to the sand at the foot of the trailer steps, and George had given him the beer, which hadn't come from an icebox. George had gone off in the jeep to tow the bird off the runway. Lizzy-Jo had been slumped, dead to the world, over her end of the workbench. He should have slept, but he could not. Again and again, searing in his mind, he saw the lurch of the platform when the first Hellfire went away from *Carnival Girl*, the ball of fire going down, and the camels breaking their line of march, then the cloud – and the second missile going into that cloud. Could not sleep.

The tent's entrance flap was lifted back. The wind came in behind her. The sand spewed round her, spraying on to his legs and body, and over his face.

She dropped the flap.

She sat on the bed. Her hips, in the tight short trousers, were against his knees. He could have covered himself, could have reached for the boxers or his singlet, but he did not. Too tired, too dead, too cheated to care. The bed bent under her weight.

'That's a fine sight,' Lizzy-Jo said, and winked. 'Might frighten a girl in the Carolinas – but not a New Yorker.'

She had not buttoned up her blouse. Her hand rested on the hairs of his chest.

'Did you sleep?'

'No. Tried to, didn't.'

'You want the news?'

Her fingers pulled at the hairs, teased them.

'What's the news?'

'You look like you need a lift-up . . .'

For months, Marty had worked with Lizzy-Jo, had shared a work-bench with her. She'd been good, he was raw. The guys said, at Bagram, that she was assigned to mind him. Half the pilots at Bagram would have given a month's pay to work alongside Lizzy-Jo. He'd wondered often enough whether she'd complained about being put with him because he was new and given the dirty work, hadn't been an Air Force flier, had acne and fat-lensed glasses. He didn't know her – knew about Rick, who sold insurance, and about Clara, who was watched over by Rick's parents during the working day, knew about a marriage that had died, knew about her dedication . . . and nothing of her.

'Langley says that flight out of Shaybah was of the highest quality technical achievement, that it was pressed home in the most adverse conditions, that the video record of the flight and the missile firing will be used for training programmes in the future. It's what Langley said.'

He felt the blood pound in his cheeks.

She was bent over him, her breasts hanging close to his chest where her fingers played in the hairs. 'And Gonsalves came through from Riyadh. He said he was proud of us. If you'd stayed around in the trailer you'd have heard what he said.'

He blushed, felt like a kid. It was like when his high-school grades had come through – and he'd thought he'd flunked when he hadn't.

'I'd say it's party time.'

She leaned over him, reaching for the can. He did not know her, did not know what she felt for him . . . and her finger was into the ring and tugging it. The beer's foam sprayed over him, ran on his belly. She tilted the can for him to drink and the beer spilled from his mouth as he swallowed. He thought he'd drunk half the can, then she put it down. She licked the warm beer off his chest, took the hairs in her mouth, then her tongue was on his stomach.

'You good to party?'

Marty nodded, closed his eyes. She kicked off her flip-flops and wriggled out of the tight short trousers. Her face was serious, set – like the business was important – as she stood and pulled down her panties, then her weight was on him. The condom had been in her pocket, and she ripped the wrapping off with her teeth and peeled it over him.

He turned his head away so that he could not see her face . . . and he did not know why, what she needed from him, whether she had done it like this with the insurance salesman. The sweat ran in rivulets between her breasts and on to him, oiled them and fastened them together. The last time had been with a girl at Nellis, from the management of the base canteen, and she'd had thicker spectacles than him and had weighed more than a hundred and fifty pounds. She'd hoped he'd marry her. Then he'd gone to Bagram and she'd never written.

He had *killed*. The reward for him, for killing, was to get laid twice in a half-hour. Maybe she had done it many times at Bagram, in her own prefabricated quarters or in a pilot's, but it did not matter to him. He gloried in the feel of her and squeezed deeper inside her the second time. He heard her shallow cries and the pace of her breathing, and he hung on to her as if in fear that it would finish. He did not see into her eyes, did not know her. He pushed his hips against hers. At the last moment, he yelled out, gasped, and sobbed his thanks to her. She squealed . . . He wondered how many of the technical guys or Maintenance heard her, if George did. He could go no deeper. His nails gouged her back and the sweat came off her and was in his mouth and he tasted the salt of it, with the beer.

Lizzy-Jo took the second one off him, knotted it, dropped it beside the bed.

She kissed his cheek, like she was his aunt.

She knelt on the bed over him and her head was cocked up. 'You know what's different?'

Marty panted, 'You and me, us? That was fantastic, it was—'

'You dumb ass,' she said, sharp. She showed no passion. Her face was the same, serious and set, as it had been when she'd zoomed the camera for the freeze-frame and when she'd launched. 'It's the wind.'

'I don't hear any wind.'

'You fool. That's what's different.'

He looked at the sides of the tent, then at its roof. The tent shook in the wind but not like it might collapse. He heard the sing of the wind but no longer its scream. She had her panties back on, was dragging up her short tight trousers and slipping on her blouse. The wind was down. Now it was not carrying sand under the flaps and on to the groundsheet. She bent over him and he tried to kiss her, but her face turned away and she only reached down to pick up the two knotted condoms, which went into her pocket . . . He did not understand anything of her. 'Why did you come here, to me?'

'I thought we deserved a party – didn't we?'

She went out through the flap and it dropped back. Marty kicked himself off the bed. He dressed slowly. A clean shirt, boxers and T-shirt from his bag, and the old jeans. His mother and father, up in the cabin overlooking Santa Barbara, had never asked him whether he had a girlfriend, seemed to expect that one day he'd turn up with one; he didn't know how they'd feel about a woman like Lizzy-Jo. He wrote to them once a month, was due to, but he would not tell them about his party. He drank the rest of the beer, stale and flat, and splashed water on his face. He did not go for a shower, did not want to take the smell of her off him.

Outside the tent, the sun hit him.

A small windsock flew from a pole on the far side of the satellite-dish trailer; it was out but not rigid.

A little knot of men worked around the port-side wing of *Carnival Girl*, and George and Lizzy-Jo blocked his view of the forward fuselage. He walked towards them. George faced him, stepped aside and made a mock bow of respect. It was black on the white of the fuselage. Marty gazed at the skull and the cross-bones under it, clenched his fist and raised it above his head. It was a confirmed kill.

Marty felt on top of the world.

She said impassively, like she'd shared nothing with him, 'We're going back up tomorrow. You look like you need some sleep. Take-off an hour before dawn. Get over the strike site, get a damage assessment, then go after any of the bastards we missed. Got it?'

Alive, the body had been thin. Dead, it was swollen and grotesque. When they stopped in the dusk, as the sun sank, they did the burying before taking the share of water.

There were no stones for them to make a cairn to cover Fahd's corpse. Rashid, Ghaffur and Caleb scooped away sand with their fists, used their nails to dig, and made the hole. Hosni said the prayers.

With their feet, they pushed the sand back over him, covered what remained of his head.

After the sand had taken him, the stench of the body stayed with them. Caleb thought it clung to his robe. Then they drank their water, a quarter of a mug each, and moved on.

The wind only flapped their clothes, did not rip them. He knew the growing danger. They were hunted. The boy sat rigid and upright on his camel, rode and listened. The darkness settled on them, and the cool came.

Hosni said, 'I asked you – do you hate enough?'

Caleb whispered his answer. 'I told you, it has not changed – I hate enough.'

'Without hate you will fail.'

'I have the hate. First there was excitement, then there was pride. After the pride came the hate.'

'Explain to me.'

'When I went to Landi Khotal with my friends, everything was strange, was colour, was new. I was tested, then I was chosen. I had never known, where I came from, that excitement. I passed through the training camps, I was accepted into the 055 Brigade, I was made a squad leader. Of course there was pride – I had never been trained or accepted, had never led before. In the camps, X-Ray and Delta, there were two choices, two roads. I could have surrendered, as many have done, and submitted, or I could have fought them and hated them.'

'Where you come from, is there no love of that place?'

'None. All my love is for the family that I go back to at the end of this journey.'

The chuckle was low, choking, beside him. 'Bravely said. What would be your future if you had not gone to the wedding at Landi Khotal?'

'I would never have known excitement, pride and hate,' Caleb said simply, and quietly. 'I would be dead, and without love. I would have nothing. I would be choked to death by boredom . . . That I am alive is because I believe in the love of the family – you and Fahd, even Tommy, and the love of the people who helped me to reach you, and the love of those who wait for us.'

'Great trust is put in you, and what you can achieve.'

Caleb said, 'I hope not to fail that trust.'

'Tell me, those who were your friends, back at your old home, if you have achieved what we ask of you, what will they say of you?'

'They would not understand – they live without living, without love.'

'If they were to spit on your name?'

'They are forgotten, they are dead. I would not care.'

He felt the thin, bony hand touch his thigh. It seemed to crawl up it, then found his fist on the reins. It was held tight, as in a vice. This was his friend, not the boys from school or the kids on the canal towpath or the men in the garage. This was his family, not his mother. He lifted his fist. He kissed Hosni's hand.

Chapter Fourteen

'It is wrong,' Caleb said. 'We have to change.'

He challenged the guide.

Through the dawn, the thought had formed in his mind, as they had started out again, and in the morning's first hours. When the sun was high, convinced that Rashid was wrong, he had pushed the exhausted Beautiful One forward, faster. They had been in a long line, the guide far in front and the boy far to the back. He had come to the guide's shoulder. The Beautiful One stumbled from the effort.

'It is wrong because we make too big a target. We have to change.'

He spoke in the language he had learned from the Arabs in the 055 Brigade – what he had learned when they laughed and when they shouted in anger and when they cried in fear. He had been with them in good times, and in the hell when the bombers had been over them.

'We have to believe that it fired, then was recalled because of the wind. The wind has gone. We have to believe it will return to search for us.'

He could not have counted how many days it was since the great storm and the girl, and since Tommy had gone down into the sand. In all of those days it was the first time he had ridden at the head of the caravan, been beside the guide.

'If we are so spread out we make it easier for them, for the camera, to see one man or one camel, than to see us all.'

The desert had changed, the formations were now small hills of reddened sand. Some were twice his height as he rode the Beautiful One. Here, the wind had made perfect circles of the hills, and between them were the flat areas where sand had been scraped away. But the formation of the caravan had concerned him. In all the days, uncounted, he had not thought to challenge the guide.

'We have to close up, be tight together. We have to make the smallest target possible. We have to make it hard for them.'

Now the guide turned. He had not spoken, had not used his rein to slow his camel. His face was a loose, uncut beard, thin lips that were dried and cracked, a strong, jutted nose, narrowed eyes that gleamed, and the deep cuts of the lines at his forehead. He was a man to fear. At his waist was the curved sheath and the dulled worn handle of his knife. Close to his hands, which held the camel reins, fastened to his saddle, was the rifle. The brightness shone in his eyes.

'If they go over us, they have five chances of seeing us, or six. We should make it one chance only.'

Caleb had spoken quietly, with patience. But his mind was made up, the decision was taken. He had led a section of the 055 Brigade. The decision was as clear to him as when he had squatted in the cages of X-Ray and Delta and had promised himself that he would fight. The Chechen, with the dead eye behind the patch, had seen the quality of a leader – the interrogators, guards and escorts had not. If he had needed it, the proof of his ability to think on his feet was on his wrist: the plastic bracelet with the reference number: US8AF-000593DP. He did not discuss, did not talk it through with the guide, did not ask the guide's opinion. He spoke it as if he were giving an order, but did so with politeness. He would not argue, he would lead.

'You will say that if we are close and they find us that one missile kills us all. I say if we are close the chance of them finding us is smaller. I respect you as my brother, but please do it.'

Caleb showed his patience. He dropped back and for half an hour he rode alongside the leading bull camel. He could read the batch number of the manufacturer, the stencilled name of the factory from which it had come, and the designation of the weapon, in the language he had thought he had lost, on the wooden crate it carried. In half an hour, the guide rose on his saddle and waved for Hosni to come forward, for his son too, for them to bring the camels close. They were together. The heat burned them. The sun's light, reflected up from the sands, was cruel in their eyes. The shadows were tiny beneath the lumbering hoofs. Caleb did not look up. To search the skies would have brought a weakening of his determination. Each could touch the other. He was strong.

Bart spoke and Wroughton listened.

'The pilots are all right, that's what he's saying. The pilots are fine, very professional, but they're not trusted. They know it and resent it. Of course they know it, and it hurts. Morale is poor throughout the Air Force, he says, but especially so among the pilots. He was told – one of them spilled it all out for him – that the lack of trust stems from their training. They go to California or Arizona, they're off to the land of the free where they get their introduction to what I think is called "fast jets". They live among Americans and that marks them down, in the regime's eyes, as potential for contamination. They are beyond the reach of the great theocratic state during the training, are exposed to influences. Good pilots, yes – but how reliable? Is this useful?'

Wroughton nodded, but Bart thought his attention was far away. They were on familiar territory, on the low seats behind the palms in the corner of the hotel lobby. Normally Wroughton varied their meeting-place, did not create a pattern, and it had puzzled Bart when this location was named. It was the first time Bart had ever reported on the Air Force and he'd expected a keener reaction ... it was the first time that Bart had seen Wroughton appear haggard – tired, drawn, his tie not over his collar button, and his shoes not immaculately polished.

'Useful, but I think we've heard all this before.'

'Have you now? Well, what about this? Armaments. I suppose it follows on from what I told you I'd had from the National Guard man – you remember, the chap training them in riot control, yes? If they do practice bomb runs, then they fly up north. Up north, they load the bombs, but they have fuel restrictions. They don't carry enough fuel to fly back down to Riyadh with a bomb, only to get to the range and let it go. Then they have to land again, but up north.'

'I expect our air attaché would have known that.'

'Would he? I can only offer, Mr Wroughton, what I'm told. When they are flying within range of the palaces they are not armed. Sorry if you already knew that. The fear, of course, is that a pilot may have been poisoned psychologically while training in America. Two sorts of poison, my patient says. Could be that exposure to America, its culture – McDonald's, Coca-Cola and pornography – has driven him into the fundamentalists' arms ... Could be that he realizes the Kingdom is backward, living in an aged mind-set and that a bomb down the chimney of the King's palace would get the place going forward. Whichever, no armaments.'

'As I said, nothing there that's new.'

Wroughton had eased up from his seat. Bart wondered what had happened in the bastard's life. He was pleased he'd come, delayed two appointments, and had seen his tormentor fazed. Wroughton dropped a banknote on the bill.

'I just try to help, Mr Wroughton.'

'Keep in touch.'

Left alone, Bart finished his juice, gulped down what Wroughton had left, then sauntered across the lobby. At the swing doors, he realized that the banknote left to cover the price of their two juices would have paid for five and a handsome tip. Extraordinary. Through the doors, he stood on the step and looked for his driver. A red Toyota saloon was parked in front of him, its engine idling and a European at the wheel. Wroughton drove out fast in his Discovery with the CD plates, and – Bart would have sworn to it – the red saloon accelerated, followed him out, then nestled into a lane two vehicles behind Wroughton. It could have overtaken and did not.

Bloody hell, a tail on Eddie bloody Wroughton. Bart was certain of it.

In Bart's past there had been briefings on how to recognize surveillance and a tail.

Al Maz'an village, near Jenin, Occupied West Bank.

'God, if only there were more people like you Bart. If only.'
He walked at the end of the little column into the central square. She was

Austrian. She would only be in Al Maz'an for twenty minutes, en route between Jenin and Nablus. The column was peopled by these representatives of a Munich-based medical charity and their Palestinian escorts. When Bart had heard that they were to come to Jenin for a morning's study, then drive on to Nablus, he had suggested to the organizing committee that a visit to the village, however brief, would be welcome.

'I do what I can. Sadly, I can do very little.'

'Tell me again what are the principal complaints of your patients?'

'Well, their overwhelming complaint is the savagery of the military occupation. All the hardship stems from it. Obstruction at every turn by the Israeli Defence Force, refusal to allow the entry of medical supplies, harassment of doctors and nurses and ambulance crews, even me . . . but that is not what you meant.'

She was pretty, earnest, and her face was a study of concern. Two Palestinian doctors were behind them, within earshot. An official of the Palestine Authority was in front. Her colleagues in the delegation were further ahead, fanning out into the square.

'I have here rampant bacterial diseases. E. coli, salmonella, typhoid, the constant threat of a cholera outbreak – you name it. I treat amoebic dysentery and toxoplasmosis. There is hepatitis A and B. Then I have the insect-vectored illnesses that you will have been told about in Jenin – dengue fever, filariasis and a particularly powerful strain of schistosomiasis where the parasites settle in the bowels, rectum and liver. Here, in the Occupied West Bank, Miss Hardenberger, we're looking at what your ancestors would have encountered in fifteenth-century Vienna. It is so unnecessary. Without the brutality of the Occupation all of them would be eradicated.'

Every word he said was heard, was meant to be. The scaffolding was still up. In the seven weeks that had passed he had not seen again the woman whose son had been hanged from that upper cross pole. In the seven weeks he had been three times to the hut at the checkpoint and had played out his charade of abusing the troops who searched his car. He had had nothing to report to Joseph and had sensed, the last time, a frisson of impatience.

'I don't think I know, Dr Bartholomew, about schistosomiasis – I specialize in midwifery. You understand?'

'Of course, of course. All I am trying to say to you, Miss Hardenberger, is that when you get back to Vienna, please, stand on a rooftop and let the whole of that city know what you have seen. Please do that.'

'I will. God's truth, I will.'

It happened quickly. He was looking into her face, a little taken by the scrubbed cleanliness of her skin, no cosmetics, when the car came by. It was driven fast and the two men behind them, the doctors, quite roughly, with urgency, pushed Bart and the Austrian woman from the middle of the street. At that moment, as the car – a rusted lime-green Fiat – passed them, the back-seat passenger looked their way. A face from a photograph.

'Tell me, Dr Bartholomew, because your commitment and dedication humble me, what did you give up back in England to come here?'

His mind wandered. All of the photographs were good. They were not standard police photographs, front and profile, but unguarded surveillance pictures. They had a naturalness, were recognizable. In Joseph's hut, the photographs were ranked in order of sensitivity and the most sensitive were shown to him most often. He knew the face of the man in the back seat of the Fiat. The car sped across the square.

'A normal practice.' Bart grinned. 'You know, hernias and hips, pregnancy and prostates.'

'You gave up so much.'

'I tell you, Miss Hardenberger, if you are here and you are tempted to drift into self-pity, you have only to look around you. Here, self-pity is not an option.'

'I hope God watches over you,' she said softly.

He smiled at her . . . More importantly, he thought, did the rapid-reaction unit stationed up on the hill at the checkpoint watch over him? Everything he said was listened to. They went past the scaffolding where children waited in line to give flowers to the delegation, and there was a shout from the front that they must hurry if they were to visit the medical centre, a Portakabin shed.

He let her go ahead, said something about not wanting to hog her. She walked with the man from the Palestine Authority. Alone, without the distraction of her chatter, he could look better for another sighting of the Fiat.

He saw it down a side alley, barely wide enough for it to have parked and for another vehicle to pass. The alley was on the right-hand side of the wider street that led to the medical centre in the yard of the village school. Opposite the alley he spotted a good marker, a collapsed telephone pole, felled by a manoeuvring tank months earlier and not raised again.

Back at their vehicles, as the delegation loaded up, the Austrian woman came to Bart, stretched up on her toes and kissed his cheek. He could smell the soft scent of the flowers she held.

Two hours later, in the hut at the checkpoint, over a mug of coffee and a sweet seed cake, he told Joseph of the lime-green Fiat, and the photograph was on the second page – at the top – among the most sensitive fugitives, and he described the flattened telephone pole at the top of the alley.

'You are sure?'

'Certain.'

'There is no possibility of an error?'

'None.'

Joseph said, 'I think to utilize this we have little time. Not time enough to make a complicated separation of you from the target. I don't wish to frighten you – be very careful, be exceptionally careful.'

Bart drove home. He fed the cat. He sat in his favourite chair, the sun beat on the windows and he shivered.

The class finished.

'Shu-ismak?' What is your name?

'Min wayn inta?' Where are you from?

That morning of the week, the last before the lunch-break, Beth had her biggest class. No history, no literature, and not the detailed language of the petroleum-extraction manuals. It was for basics.

'Ana af-ham.' I understand.

'Ureed mutarjem.' I want an interpreter.

The class catered for workers from every section of the Shaybah complex, was always full. Each time she read out the Arabic phrase, there followed a choir of voices struggling with the English translation.

'Mish mushkila.' No problem.

'Wayn al-funduq?' Where is the hotel?

In any other week she would have enjoyed the class for its enthusiasm. She did not think that any of them, as she spoke the Arabic and they replied in English, had realized that her heart was not with them, her concentration was gone. The class drifted towards the door with a cacophony of conversation and scraped chairs. One of the last to leave, gathering up the photocopied sheets she gave them for private study, was the head of Security. She was wiping clean her blackboard.

276

She called his name. She asked, please, if he could stay a moment. The room cleared.

'Yes, Miss Bethany?'

She hesitated, then blurted, 'There is something I do not understand.'

'If I can be of help.'

She felt stupid. She should have backed off – but she never did. It was not her way. She tried to master a fraudulent casualness in her question. 'Someone told me that the Rub' al Khālī around us is a place of danger. Is that true?'

He glanced down at his watch, as if unwilling to be delayed. 'True, and you know that. Extreme heat, dehydration, remoteness, it is very harsh.'

'Sorry, I don't explain myself – danger because of the people who move in the Sands.'

'False.' Again his eye slipped to his watch and a puzzled frown settled over his eyes. 'In your language you call it the Empty Quarter. That is what it is. Only the Bedouin are there. An old culture of trading has given them the knowledge of the Sands. They can survive there, nobody else. The Bedouin are not thieves, they have a tradition of kindness and generosity. I know you go into the Sands, Miss Bethany, when you search for the meteorites, and you should be fearful of the conditions of nature, but not of criminals. Only the Bedouin are there, no other man can survive such a place. A stranger who tries to walk in the Sands, he condemns himself – he is dead.'

'Thank you.' She dropped her head.

He lightened. 'Now, I understand ... You have heard, Miss Bethany, the rumours – what they would gossip about in a camel market – of terrorists in the Sands. No, no. Those people are in Riyadh, Jedda and Ad Dammam, not in the desert. They would die there. Excuse me, please.'

She was left in the emptied room.

She wiped out the last lines on her blackboard. *Min wayn inta*? and *Shu-ismak*? She smeared out the chalked words.

Where are you from? Who are you?

'In the boxes are the Stinger missiles. Do you know about the Stinger missiles?' Hosni was laid across the neck of his camel and his voice was a reedy, frail whisper.

Caleb crouched in his saddle to hear him. 'Once I saw one, but not close.'

'They are old. We do not know whether they are affected by the age. But they are important.'

They moved in a tightened knot, man close to man, camel brushing against camel, and he smelt the sweat on the guide and the boy, on the Egyptian and himself, the foul breath panted by the camels. His knee bumped against a box's edge on the flank of a pack bull.

'I saw one when we tried to hold a line beyond Kabul, but the bombers were too high,' Caleb said. 'It was not fired.'

'The Stinger turned the war for us against the Soviets. The Soviets had a great fear of them.' Hosni coughed, tried to spit, as if the old memory of an enemy required it.

'I was never taught to fire one.'

'We bring them across the desert, deliver them, then they will be moved on, taken to where there is a target . . . but we do not know whether they will operate. Tommy opened the boxes, and there were manuals inside. They were written for Americans and Tommy could not read American.'

'Should we leave them behind?' Caleb had changed the order of the march. He expected to be listened to. 'Will the weight of them kill the camels?'

'You are the Outsider to us. I am told to escort you. I am told to bring you to the heart of the family. I do not know where you have come from, who you were. I do not ask. Two are already lost, but four remain. If I ask whether you can read the American manual of the Stinger, then you tell me something of yourself. My ignorance is your protection.'

'I am asking you, is their weight worth the life of the camels, do they slow us? What is more important? You and me or the Stingers?' He knew the answer, expected to be told what he knew. 'Tell me.'

He did not know what the pale, watering eyes saw, but they speared at him and the voice grew in its pitch. 'I think you show ignorance. Perhaps it is only the Stingers, if they work, that will get us, you and me, through to those who wait for us.'

'The next time we stop, I will open a box, take the manual . . .'

'And read it?'

'. . . and read it. I will, because of my importance,' Caleb said.

For a moment, Hosni struggled to rise in his saddle, but the pinions held him. Caleb saw the man who had fought the Soviets, who had given his life to the struggle of the Emir General, saw the controlled anger.

'I warn you, ignorance you will learn from – vanity will destroy you. With vanity comes arrogance, with arrogance comes failure . . . Imagine. Caravans move, columns of men move, mule trains move. Men struggle not only through this desert but through mountains, through passes, through streets and through the alleyways of *souks*, they come from the doorways of mosques and from the entrances to caves. You are only one man. Do you believe the organization of the Emir General depends on one man, whose past gives him importance? We are many. A hundred men move – some will be stopped, some captured, some will be killed – and they will be replaced by another thousand. In an engine, you are one tooth in one cog. I ask of you, never again show me your vanity.'

Caleb flinched. The boy close behind him would have heard the attack, and the guide in front. It was as if he had been struck. He felt small, a pygmy dwarfed by this needle-thin old man whose hand he had kissed in love.

'The next time we stop I will read the manual.'

A dozen men and women sat in two lines, divided by computers. Two lines of six, facing each other, separated by the screens and keyboards.

The raindrops, from their run between the car park and the Library entrance, were on the shoulders of Lovejoy's coat and the waxed waterproof loaned to the American. The skies outside were ashen and the forecast was for rain all day, then an unsettled week – no clear blue skies on the horizon.

He spoke quietly to the chief librarian. He'd telephoned her in the morning and been told at what time the Internet class was scheduled to finish. He didn't do tourist trips. They'd stayed in a hotel just outside the centre of Wolverhampton, gone early to bed because the American seemed exhausted from his overnight flight. Over breakfast Lovejoy had made his calls, which had culminated in a less than frank conversation with the chief librarian. This was the first step. He had not taken the American for a drive round the sights of Wolverhampton, but had killed time in the hotel lobby. The first step always made Michael Lovejoy nervous, and his justification for going to the Library had been brief and terse.

The Library was three miles south-west of Wolverhampton, nine miles north-east of the Birmingham city plazas. After eight phone calls, Lovejoy had spoken to the chief librarian and had heard what he wanted. She was a middle-aged woman who introduced herself as Aggie, who was careful in her appearance and had the brightness of enthusiasm. To her, Lovejoy was a lecturer from the University of Birmingham. The American, a complication to the cover story, was not introduced, had been told not to speak, just smile.

'Right, well done, everybody, the hour's up . . .' Aggie's voice boomed in the Library's quiet.

It reflected her endeavour. The interior was bright, cheerful and clean. It had a section at the far end for magazine reading, and the newspapers. There was an annexe for children, surrounded by shelved picture books and boxes of toys. Away, against the end wall, was the double bank of computers. She might have been speaking to juveniles, but those she addressed were in their twilight years: 'If you could, please, switch off, close down. You're making great progress, I'm very pleased.'

Lovejoy held the audio-cassette player, and the American had the tape in his pocket.

'I'm going to ask you to meet Michael – he's from Birmingham University and he's needing some guinea-pigs for a social-awareness project.' She spoke slowly as if she might not be understood, and loudly because the majority of them wore hearing-aids. She'd explained on the phone earlier that her Internet Familiarization class for Senior Citizens, starting at eleven, offered him a chance to meet older community members in a group. That day, and he'd checked it out, there was no specified gathering of the elderly at either the working-men's club or at the British Legion. It was, in his opinion, the best chance of meeting men and women whose lives were embedded in the area, born and reared there, worked and retired there. They looked up at him, tired eyes magnified by spectacles, and he thought he saw an expectation of interest after the struggle to master the computers' intricacies, and the Internet that was now forced on them. 'I ask you to listen very thoroughly to what Michael says, and then help him. He's relying on you.'

She waved for them to leave their blank screens and follow her to the chairs in the magazine reading section. They straggled after her, five men and seven women, all ethnic white, all with pale, aged faces; two used wooden walking-sticks and one had a metal hospital stick. She arranged the chairs so they made a half-circle behind a table, and they sat. Lovejoy put the cassette player on the table and reached out for the American to pass him the tape; he slotted it into the player. He sensed the scepticism of the American behind him. They hadn't spoken much so far. It was a long journey from the Caribbean sunshine of Guantanamo Bay to a public library three miles south-west of Wolverhampton.

He lifted his voice: 'Ladies and gentlemen, I'm very grateful for your time. You are the experts and you can help me. Aggie tells me that all of you have lived here all your lives. You'll know accents, you'll be able to place one. For my social-awareness project, I need to test your knowledge of where an accent comes from, which community it originates from. I'm going to play you a tape. You won't understand the language used on the tape, and that must not bother you, but I want to see if you recognize from what area that voice comes. Please, don't guess. I need you to be certain.'

He used his winning smile. Mercy Lovejoy liked to say that that smile, cultivated over more than two decades as a counter-intelligence officer, would calm an enraged bull in a china shop, would allow him access into the secrets of any life. The smile, deprecating and almost shy, always charmed.

'You will hear a voice in American, ignore it – then a voice, a woman's, in a language you won't understand, ignore that as well. Then you will hear a male voice, and that's the one my project is interested in.'

His finger hovered over the 'play' button. Only very rarely did Michael Lovejoy, officer of the Security Service charged with Defence of the Realm – the safety of these elderly men and women and their children and their grandchildren – meet *ordinary* people. His work days were spent roving in the electronic and cyber world of National Health Service records, National Insurance contribution numbers and the statistics of personal bank accounts. To confront ordinary people, who knew nothing of his world, challenged his mettle. He felt a small shiver of excitement. He pressed the 'play' button.

The American's voice was muffled, as if distant from the microphone.

'The people in your village, Fawzi, what do they think about Americans?' the voice of the man behind him drawled, bored. Lovejoy had been told the tape was from one of the last interrogations, when hope of live intelligence was dead, fulfilling a schedule that said prisoners must be questioned once a month. 'Can you tell me how the people in your village regard Americans?'

In a pretty poor light, Lovejoy thought. He had read the file in his room last night, and the file said that the family of Fawzi al-Ateh, taxi-driver, had supposedly been pulverized by the bombs from a B-52 aircraft . . . except that the taxi-driver was bogus and came not from a God-forsaken village in Afghanistan but from here. The woman's translation was similarly distorted.

The voice played in the hushed area of the library. They strained to hear it. They leaned forward, and one reached inside his jacket to tweak the control of his hearing-aid. He thought them all humble, decent, generous people. Their new clothes would have come from charity shops and their old clothes would have been repaired with needle and thread. He depended on them. The voice was the target of the microphone, was sharp. One woman, deep in fierce concentration, reached out over the table and made a twisting gesture, and Lovejoy turned up the volume dial. Camp Delta swamped the section of the library. The voice died away.

The question came. 'Before the accident, Fawzi, and we very much regret accidents – accidents are inevitable in modern high-technology warfare – did your village people welcome the intervention of the United States against the repression of the Taliban, and against the terrorism of Al Qaeda? Did they . . . ?' He switched off the machine, had been concentrating on the faces and had not intended the tape should run into the second question.

'Ladies and gentlemen, that's a first playing and I can play it as many times as you want. Where's he from? Where's that young man from?'

Some were certain of where he was not from.

'He's not from Moxley.'

' 'Tisn't Ocker, I'd swear on that.'

'Not from Dudley.'

'And I'll tell you something else – he's speaking Asian, but he isn't. May speak Asian, but he's not.'

'Right, Alf – Asians can't do the V, can't get their tongues round it. Asians say "wehicles", they say "wery", can't do V . . . And it isn't Tipton, or Upper Gornal.'

'Not Lower Gornal, neither – you're right about what Asians can't say, Alf.'

'But it's south from Wolverhampton.'

Lovejoy, so quietly that it was barely noticed, intervened. He'd reckoned – taken the gamble that he was not wasting his morning – that the elderly whose lives were lived south-west of Wolverhampton, stuck in the concrete of their streets, immured in their communities, would have a knife-sharp recognition of strangers. They would know where the stranger came from. He interrupted: 'Let me play it again to you. Can you tell me where you think he comes from?'

They listened, transfixed, to the voice, and he sensed the start of recognition.

'It's more like Deepfield.'

'Don't you mean Woodcross?'

'I think it's sort of Ettingshall.'

'What about Lanesfield? What you reckon, Alf?'

There was always a leader in any group. In the Internet Familiarization group, the leader was Alf. A heavy man, bald, his trousers held under his gut by a broad leather belt. 'It's not Ettingshall and not Lanesfield, but that's close. I'm reckoning it's up Spring Road from Coseley, but not as far as Ettingshall. It's where your cousin is, Edna, the one with the pigeons.'

'Wonderful birds, champions – ever so many rosettes.'

'He doesn't want to know about pigeons, Edna. He wants to know where that young chappie's from. I'm saying he's from between Coseley and Ettingshall.'

'I think you're right, Alf, between Coseley and Ettingshall.'

'You've got it, Alf – funny, him speaking Asian but not being. That's it, between Coseley and Ettingshall. Definite.'

Lovejoy picked up the cassette player, took out the tape and passed it to the American. He smiled his thanks, then told them how much they had helped his project. He shook Aggie's hand, and left them chattering happily about Edna's cousin's racing pigeons.

The American trailed after him and out into the car park. They ran in the rain, dived into the Volvo, and Lovejoy snatched the newly purchased map from the glove-box and began to spill through the pages.

'Was that scientific?'

'No,' Lovejoy said. 'It was better than science could give you. If they say it, I believe it. White and not Asian.'

'Which is going to blow the roof off Delta – Jesus Christ.'

Lovejoy's finger found the page, then pointed to and rapped down on the names. 'Ettingshall and Coseley, about a mile and a half apart. That's where your man's from. Bet your pension on it.'

'I can only tell you, Eddie, what he told me.' Teresa leaned against the door and two of her kids, the youngest, hung from her skirt. The other two were shouting inside. 'He wasn't proud of it, you getting the turnaround in the lobby, but there were things – what he told me – that were too grand to cut you in on.'

'I see.'

'For God's sake, Eddie, surely there are things you wouldn't share with the Agency, even with Juan.'

'Maybe.'

'He's sleeping down there. Nathan, his sidekick, came round for his spares. When Juan rings, shall I tell him you called by?'

Wroughton said evenly, 'I wouldn't want to bother him, wouldn't want to disturb him.'

She couldn't see behind his tinted glasses but she fancied his eyes would have blazed. 'Come on, Eddie, you know what it's like.'

He seemed not to hear her, had already turned his back. She watched him walk briskly away across the lawn and past the Pakistani garden boy. She was not prepared to incubate a feud so she stayed in the doorway and waved to him, to a friend, as he drove off, aggressively fast. She was still in the doorway when he went through the guarded entrance gates and pulled out into the traffic. She saw a red Toyota car come up behind him, brake, then follow him away. She watched and waved until Eddie was gone.

Inside, the kids' shouting had become screaming. She closed the front door and went into the kitchen to play peacemaker – it upset her that there was not peace between her husband and his best friend, and she did not know what was too critical for sharing between them.

He heard the voice in his headphones, like it caressed him. 'No better time than the present. At your own pace, guys. Oscar Golf, out.'

It was fourteen minutes since the camera slung to the belly of *First Lady* had found them. Inside the Ground Control the heat baked them. The desultory conversations between Marty and Lizzy-Jo had died. George was behind them with the water. The screens were in front of them and their focus was on the central picture beamed down to them.

The tactic of the target had changed.

From an altitude of twenty-three thousand feet and a ground speed of seventy-one knots, the picture was transmitted to the middle screen, the largest. Marty held her steady – optimum weather conditions – on figure-eight passes over the target, and she went through the programmes that changed surveillance to target acquisition. The water George had poured on to his head, which ran down his back and stomach, had cooled him. He felt good, had the right to. Marty could stand alongside the former Air Force pilots who flew for the Agency out of Bagram. Because he had killed, he thought himself a veteran.

She had not spoken about the sex, hadn't touched him, hadn't brushed against him – like she'd distanced herself from him. Her blouse was undone again to her waist and he'd seen the water run down to the flesh folds of her stomach . . . She had the target on camera, followed it and never let it go while he made the figure-eight passes and thought she seemed older than before, more clinical than he'd known her.

'When you going to go?'

'Next pass,' she said. 'I don't have a problem.'

His fingers were softer on the joystick than the last time. Then he had had the wind to fight. She had it on the wide angle. The camera caught the target as it moved, a little wriggling beetle, over the expanse of sand. What had changed, the target was closed up. It was now the ninth hour since he had taken *First Lady* up. Two hours into the flight they had circled over the first missile strike and he had seen the twin blackened craters and the carcass of the camel, and then they had started to hunt. He had taken *First Lady* on a criss-cross of patterns over the desert floor. A pursuit that was relentless after fugitives who could have no hope, that was what he'd thought. Inevitable. He had not doubted that Lizzy-Jo's camera would find them. Nothing shrill in her voice when she had, no blurt of excitement – only the gesture of her hand, then the finger pointing to the right upper quarter of the screen. She'd worked the camera and the target had gone to the screen's centre. Fourteen minutes later he brought *First Lady* back on the figure-eight curves, and Lizzy-Jo was going through the procedures for firing.

The beetle moved so slowly. They were tight together. He wondered whether they searched the skies, gazed up at the sun and burned out their eyes. They would fail. The heat haze came up off the sand round them, distorted the picture, but it remained clear enough for him to see them, to watch their crawling progress. He saw four men. He did not know them, they had no identity for him. He remembered what Gonsalves had said. It echoed in his mind: *'The hardest man, the strongest. The man they need. The man that can hurt us most. A man without fear.'* He saw four men, saw no threat, no danger, no chance of risk – four men, on camels, in the desert.

She said, 'When you turn behind them, I'm launching.'

Marty wished he knew them, wished he saw the threat, the danger they made.

'What are they thinking?'

She darted a glance at him. 'God, I don't know.'

'Doesn't that matter – what they're thinking?'

'Thinking about water, about chow, thinking about a shower – I don't know. Thinking about us.'

'What are they thinking about us?'

'Whether we've found them, I suppose – how the hell should I know? – whether we're over them.'

He saw them on the screen, worked the joystick and banked *First Lady* so that she would line up behind them for the strike. 'That's not an answer – what do they think about *us*?'

'About hating us, about having contempt for us . . . you want to be their shrink, Marty? Forget it. Think of your duty to our country and do your job. Forget that shit – I don't know what they're thinking and I don't care.'

Marty said softly, 'We are flying west-north-west, wind speed eight knots, our air speed is—'

'I got all that . . . Going in five.'

He did not know about them and that hurt in his mind.

The whisper, 'Port side gone.'

His fingers tightened on the joystick and he compensated for the lurch of *First Lady*. She was thrown up at an angle, starboard side dipping. He heard the little gasp of annoyance from beside him: he'd been slow in making the commands that held her steady. On the central screen, the fireball seemed to loiter before it started to race away on its guided descent. He had her steady, and he waited for the next leap of *First Lady* – which didn't come.

'You shooting?'

'I'm holding . . . Look at them, Marty, look at them run.'

On the big screen, the central one, the beetle below the fireball broke up.

'Bastards.'

Marty saw the panic scattering of the camels. They went in crazy lines, like they'd broken the knot that held them.

At that height, and with the oblique firing angle, the Hellfire would fly for seventeen seconds . . . Half-way down . . . He saw, from the fireball, the little adjustments she made as she guided it, and he watched the camels career together and apart. He watched their panic. He was the voyeur. He was the hard-breathing youth in the shadows of the car park above the ocean where the university students brought their girls. He rubbernecked the stampede of the camels. The missile went into the sand.

The Hellfire was for a tank. Firing a Hellfire at Nellis, the sensor operator should get an armour-piercing warhead up against a tank turret from twenty-four thousand feet, should get a hit on the range within one yard of the aimed point. Instructors liked to reckon they could hit within half a foot on a stationary tank turret . . . Nobody at Nellis had ever thought of a target of running camels for an impact of a fragmentation warhead. The dustcloud rose.

The cloud came up towards the camera lens. Marty lost the camels, did not know whether they were under it, or had escaped it. There was a darkness at the core of the cloud, then a fire flash in its heart. Red flame blossomed from the cloud. They had hit ordnance. The new fire burst through the cloud and climbed, then guttered. Smoke, dark and poisonous black, replaced the fire.

The voice came in his ear, massaged him like her fingers had. 'Good work, guys. Secondary explosions would prove you've hit gold. Please look at your screens, extreme left. I see empty camels on the right side, ten o'clock, but you should be looking extreme left, four o'clock. Centre on that target, and take it. Oscar Golf, out.'

Alone in the desert, a single camel ran. Marty had been to ten o'clock, four camels together – like they were tied – no riders. Then Lizzy-Jo was raking the picture across, going to four o'clock, and zooming. The picture was tugged to close-up, and she tweaked the lost focus. A single camel ran in the sand, wove between the hills. Marty came over it. The camel stumbled, like it had no more running left in it, tried again, then stopped. The screen was filled with the camel. It stopped, like its spirit was broken. It sank. The knees went from under it. The technology that Marty watched, that Lizzy-Jo worked, showed a camel run to exhaustion and crumpling. He saw the weight that the camel could no longer run with.

The vomit was in his throat.

He was the representative of a master race. Four point five four – recurring – miles below the camera an old man was laid out on the back of the camel.

Beside him, Lizzy-Jo trilled amazement. 'This is just wonderful gear, incredible – like he's just down under us.'

Eight million dollars of Predator, at factory-gate prices, circled an old man on a camel and lining up against him was a hundred thousand dollars of Hellfire with a fragmentation warhead. He could see the old man's face and a blur of greying hair, and the old man seemed to twist his head and look up, and he would have seen nothing and would have heard nothing. Marty did not know why the old man had not jumped clear of the knelt camel, why he had not gone away from it. He was stretched across the camel from the hump to the neck. Did he know? Must have. His arm came up. First, Marty thought it was like a salute. Wrong. The arm was outstretched, pointed upwards towards *First Lady*: 'Fuck you.' He thought the arm, raised, said, 'Fuck you,' to him.

Lizzy-Jo let the second Hellfire go.

For a dozen of the sixteen seconds of its fireball flight, Marty watched the screen, then turned away, his eyes closed. He did not watch its hit.

He spun his chair and ripped off his headset. He pushed away George's hand and went to the door. He heard Lizzy-Jo murmur to her mouth microphone that her pilot had gone off station. He stood in the door, above the steps.

The vomit cascaded from his bowed head.

When he was conscious, he could feel the warm wetness of the blood. But Caleb drifted.

When he came back to consciousness, he could feel the pain. It was deep waves.

Conscious, he did not know how they had made the litter, and how they clung to the undersides of the camel's bellies, hanging from the hidden saddle straps.

The litter, three sacks, was suspended low down between the Beautiful One and Rashid's camel. He was belted by the animal's legs and rocked from the motion of their walk. On the far side of him was the boy. Father and son, gasping, held themselves against the stomachs of the camels, and behind them was the last of the bulls.

When the pain came, and the scent of the blood, he could remember. The boy had howled the warning. The fire had come down on them. The blow, with the hot wind and the clap of the thunder, had felled him. They had snatched him up, father and son.

He was hidden, as were Rashid and Ghaffur.

The last sight he had seen was the one camel, Hosni strapped across it, fleeing from them.

He prayed to sleep, to lose the pain.

Chapter Fifteen

The cloth against his head was wet and cold. It stank with stale odour. The voice said, 'Do not try to speak.' With great gentleness, the cloth was wiped on his forehead, round his eyes and on his cheeks. A little of the dribble from it rested on his lips – it stung his eyes.

He tried to move, to shift the weight on his back, but the effort brought the pain – he gasped – and for a moment the cloth was across his mouth.

'You must not cry out.'

How long he had been unconscious, asleep, dead, he did not know.

The pain was in his leg and at the side of his head. When he tried to shift, the pain was agony in his leg and his head throbbed.

'If you are seen, heard, it will have been for nothing. You must not be found.'

The cloth over his face calmed him.

His eyes moved, not his head.

The night was around them. Rashid crouched over him, laid the cloth in a bucket, lifted it, squeezed the water from it, then spread it, cool and bringing life back, across his throat and his upper chest. He lay on the same sacks that had made the litter and in his nose was the smell of shit and urine – his. Flies buzzed him. Close to him were the hoofs of the camels. As if she were alerted by his faint movements, or the guide's murmured voice, the Beautiful One arched her neck down and her nostrils nudged against him. Beyond the camels, fires burned. He heard roaming voices, laughter and the scrape of harnesses. He smelt cooking meat, carried on the wind, and spices mixed with boiling rice, could recognize them through the stench of the camels and his own excreta. He squinted to see better, and shadows passed across the fires – when a shadow approached closer to them, Rashid reached for his rifle and was alert, but the shadow ignored them and went on. They were separated by thornbushes from a great gathering of men and animals. When it reached his lips and he sucked at it, the water was foul, old. He retched, could not bring anything up, and the choking in his throat and gut brought back the agony in his leg and the hammer in his head. Rashid cradled him.

'I thought you were dead, I praise God.' The voice guttered in his ear. 'For three days and three nights, I thought you were the scrape of a fingernail from death. Only God could have saved you . . . I sent Ghaffur for help. I asked him to go alone into the Sands, and his life is with God . . . All the water we had was for you, and one day back, and one night, it was finished. Now we are at a well-head. It is bad water, it has not rained here for many years, but it is the water that God has given us. If you are found here there will be people who will see your wounds and will know you are an Outsider to the Sands, and they will seek to sell you to the government, or they will kill you and take your head to the government and ask money for it. We came in the night and we will leave in the night, with God's protection. You should rest. Death is still close to you. If God forgets you then you are dead.'

The words croaked in Caleb's throat. 'You sent your son?'

'I sent my son into the Sands, that you might live. We are just two men. That we are alive is because of the Egyptian. He rode away from us. He took the eye in the sky from us. The eye went after him. I heard the explosion as we fled. He gave his life for us, for you. You have to live, it is owed to him.'

'And to your son . . .'

His eyes closed. His hold on what was around him slackened. So tired, so weak. He did not have the strength to think of the wound in his leg or the wound in the side of his head. He drifted. He was by the canal, on the pavement close to the black-painted door, was kicking the ball in the yard and aiming at the glass in the hatch of the overturned washing-machine . . . He was nothing, nobody. He lost the pain, lost the cool, healing touch of the wet cloth. He lost the image of the boy, his bright mischief eyes, sent by his father and alone in the Sands.

In the Hummer, they played Willie Nelson loud. Will drove and Pete did the satellite navigation. 'Help Me Make It Through The Night' came out of the CD system. Two more Hummers, with the Arabs, followed them. Will never trusted an Arab to drive him, and Pete never reckoned anyone else but himself could do better on navigation. Both rated the Hummer, the civilian version of the Army's Humvee, as the best there was on wheels, and capable of taking them where a helicopter – screwed up with the density altitude barrier from the heat – could not. They were the same age, had been through the same Galveston education line, lived on adjacent plots in the Houston suburbs, and did the same work. They were two gas-extraction field surveyors. Blood brothers. The trip, never a snide word between them, had already taken them across in excess of six hundred miles of sand – but the mapping now was complete. That night, if the Hummer with three tonnes loaded on her held up – and the Hummers with the Arabs behind them – they would be on a late plane back to Riyadh. They were on the Exxon-Mobil books, earned good money – and the world, because of where they were, owed them it.

Time had slipped away, two and a half weeks of it. For eighteen days they had driven, camped, worked in the Empty Quarter, without sight of human company other than the Arabs who travelled behind them; top temperature out there was a confirmed 124° Fahrenheit. The Hummer took them anywhere they fancied going, up dunes and down them, through loose sand.

'Well, well, lookey-here . . .'

Will was imagining the juicy burger he'd have on their return to the Riyadh hotel.

'Hey, no foolin', take a look.'

Will said, 'Well, I'll be. You got some hawk eyes on you. I'd have driven right on by.'

'I don't reckon we should. Look it, he's just a kid.'

A hundred yards, a little more, to the right of where they came down off the dune, were a child and a camel. The camel stood and the boy sat in its shade. At that distance, through the sealed sand-sprayed windows, they could see, each of them, the gaunt resignation on the boy's face. The camel, dead on its feet, didn't even turn towards them as they edged closer.

'Like they're jus' waitin' to die.'

'This is one evil fucking place.'

'I reckon the camel's just stopped, won't go another step. You're gonna go and git yourself a rosette, Pete, that's one good deed for the day.'

Fifteen minutes later, they moved on. The kid was stowed on top of the luggage mountain on the second Hummer. The camel was dead, shot with a bullet to the head by their camp manager. They were two hard men, away from home in Houston for eight months of every year, played hard and drove themselves hard. Neither spoke. Pete had a wet eye and Will would have choked on any words. The kid had held the camel, soft hands round its neck as the rifle barrel had gone against its head, and the big dopey brown eyes had been on the kid. Blood had spattered when the bullet had been fired – new blood on old across the kid's robe. Old caked blood covered the kid's robe . . . He wouldn't talk of it. The camp manager had tried, hadn't gotten an answer – it wasn't the kid's blood. What the kid said, translated by the camp manager, he had to get to Miss Bethany at Shaybah, and nothin' else.

Will thought of the fruit machines he played when he could find them – thought he had a better chance of a once-a-year jackpot than the kid had had of being spotted out there in the sand.

Pete reckoned that Someone, up there in the clear blue sky, must have cared for the kid, must have watched out for him, because if he'd come down the dunes heading left they'd never have seen him.

The Hummer powered towards Shaybah, the late-night flight out and burgers in Riyadh.

*

The deputy governor was ushered out by Gennifer.

Before the outer door had closed, the ambassador had the internal phone against his face.

'Gonsalves, that you? The ambassador here. Get yourself down to me, please, with a degree of urgency.'

He reflected. Power had shifted from his desk. The evacuation of military personnel from the big airbase south of the capital had grievously wounded his status. The war in Iraq had further damaged it. The pending lawsuits – where legal men back in New York talked billions of dollars in prohibitive damages on behalf of the victims of the Twin Towers – against members of the ruling élite, the Royal Family, had caused a breakdown in precious trust. The compound attacks in Riyadh had been a coffin nail. Before the evacuation, the war, the filed suit, and the suicide bombers' assault, he would have told – with exquisite politeness – the deputy governor to go stuff himself. The world marched on, and the Kingdom was no longer his fiefdom. Another year and he would be teaching at Yale.

The door opened after a knock, and Gennifer showed the Agency man inside.

He launched: 'Gonsalves, this is not a criticism. I have no complaint about the liaison you have had with me. You told me, and I acknowledge it, that you were bringing a Predator team into the Shaybah Field base for, as I remember it, surveillance of the Rub' al Khālī – under a pretence of mapping and also the testing of performance in extreme heat. Well, we have a problem.'

The ambassador was a man for whom personal appearances mattered. He changed his shirt twice in a day, and three times if he had an important evening function. He always wore a tie, never dragged the knot down or loosened his collar button. Opposite him, lounging and appearing at the edge of sleep Gonsalves wore jeans, a grubby vest and an open shirt. His face was stubbled, his hair uncombed, like some damned Fed in deep cover in Little Italy, the right gear for lamp-post leaning.

'The local authorities here are increasingly suspicious of us. There is growing obstruction. It comes down to a desire to derail us. Just out of my office is the deputy governor, the province that includes that big block of sand, and Shaybah. We are not welcome. No longer are Predator aircraft welcome at Shaybah. We have little prying eyes watching us, you'd know that better than me, seeking to flex long-unused muscles. I suppose there's other places you can go – Djibouti or Dohar – but the door at Shaybah is closed. Two alternatives: ship out and smile, cut them in and tell them what you're doing . . . I know which I would go for. Personally, I would not trust the last live rat in the Kingdom with detail of any anti-Al Qaeda operation of sensitivity. I think you should talk to your people. I bought you some time, probably about three days, but no more.'

Not too many clouds passed over the Riyadh sun. A cloud flitted across Gonsalves' face. He was up and heading for the door, like he'd a bayonet under his backside.

'It was surveillance, wasn't it, Gonsalves? Just surveillance?'

From the door, a child's smile spread across the Agency man's face. 'Yes, we were watching them. Right down to the time the Hellfires hit. We watched them when the secondary explosions, ordnance, blew. If you ever get tired of TV movies just call me, and I'll send you down a video.'

'Three days.'

The smile was gone. 'It's a prime route to where they are.'

It was like they were wary of each other.

There were areas that were off-limits.

The light had gone out for him, Lizzy-Jo thought.

Three days and three nights back, George had thrown a bucket of water on to the Ground Control steps but there were still scrapes on the treads of his dried-out vomit. He'd brought her in, had made a good landing for *First Lady*, then had gone to his tent. He had not studied the video the morning after, not like the first time, had not seen a second time the zoomed lens image of the old man bent across the camel's neck. He had not gone out to see the handiwork of George on the fuselage of *First Lady*, the new skull-and-crossbones stencil. Had not eaten with her, had not talked with her. What did he think it was all for? A teen game in an arcade? Staying in for computer warfare because it was raining outside? There hadn't been fun between them, or laughter.

Three days and three nights. That was enough.

She looked away from her screen, flipped off the switch that gave voice contact to Oscar Golf. 'OK, so he looked like your damn granpa

– so what? You think Al Qaeda pensions them out, don't do granpas? Don't be a wuss – you're a kid who wants to play with the big boys' toys. Grow up. Next time you want to go soft I'm making certain the whole world's going to hear and you'll be dead in a junkyard.'

She slipped the switch back, regained voice contact with Langley.

The sand slipped across her screen as it had done for most of the hours of three days and three nights, all the time that *First Lady* had flown. When they landed her, seven more hours and into the night, she would be grounded for maintenance. The next day they would take up *Carnival Girl*, the old lady. She was beginning to hate the fucking sand. On the screen it was empty, had been in all their flying hours spread over three days and three nights, and the real-time camera in the day and the electro-optic/infra-red in the darkness had shown up nothing.

The teleprinter started up.

They were on new boxes. They'd circled where the old man had been, lying across the kneeling camel, before the Hellfire pulverized him, and they'd stayed up there on station till the smoke dust had cleared. When the cloud had gone, after they'd seen the small crater, he'd brought her back over the first hit and the larger crater. Then they'd gone searching. Four camels, no riders, in the screen. Four camels tied together, no men, followed for a half-hour, then allowed to go on. If they'd searched again, hard enough, she thought they'd have found one camel down and the rest standing and unable to drag them-selves clear, or two camels down . . . dying in the sand, under the sun. Best that they'd been given a new set of boxes to work over.

Lizzy-Jo tore the sheet off the teleprinter. She felt bad at the verbal abuse she'd given him but did not know an alternative.

'Listen,' she said. 'Just less than seventy hours and we're out of here. The Saudis have closed us down. If that's what Bagram is, we're going home. Hey, you shoot, you score – we wiped out bad people, and their granpa, wasted them.'

He came out of the supermarket. He loathed the place, a little corner of London or New York, but it was fast and quick. Faster and quicker because so many of the expatriates it was designed to serve had checked out from the Kingdom, gone back where they'd come from. He would have liked to browse in a street market, buy what was local, but the security situation forbade it.

In two plastic bags Eddie Wroughton carried a sliced loaf of bread, two litres of milk and three chilled meals-for-one that would go into his microwave, a kilo of New Zealand-grown apples and two containers of water allegedly bottled in Scotland. That evening, had it been normal – but it was not – he should have eaten at the Gonsalves' kitchen table, then chucked a softball in their backyard.

He crossed the car park. There were high lights, sufficient to show him his own vehicle, but they threw down shadows. He did not see the red Toyota, or the man who loitered close to it. The lights fell, for a moment, on his linen suit and his laundered white shirt; the silk of his tie glistened and made stars on the darkness of his glasses. His mind unravelled an old memory. The family Sunday lunch, and the next day he was going to Century House for the start of his recruits' induction course. His father there, his grandfather and his great-uncle – old warriors of intelligence – and the talk had gone on from how he should conduct himself with his examiners and had eddied to comfortable nostalgia. Old campaigns refought – and port passed, cigars lit, and the bone had been the favourite one for chewing . . . the *Americans*.

'Never trust them, Eddie, never ever.'

'The greatest sin for an American is to lose – don't forget that, Eddie, don't. Make certain you're on a different planet if they're losing, don't be up close.'

'A chap once said: "America is a big happy dog in a small room, and each time it wags its tail it breaks something." They don't even notice, Eddie, the damage they do. Be your own man, not their poodle.'

He had thought Juan Gonsalves was his friend . . . He reached his vehicle, zapped his lock, then the shadow was across him. He opened the back door, to dump the bags.

'Is that Mr Wroughton, Mr Eddie Wroughton?' the voice, English language and foreign accent, whined.

He turned. The man came from the shadows, tall and wiry, middle-aged, with a sharpness in his eyes.

He said curtly, 'Yes, that's me.'

'Is that the bastard who fucks my wife?'

Nowhere to back off to. His vehicle was behind him. The man was in front of him. From the high lights, he saw the clenched fists and the stone-bruised, sand-scraped boots, and the loathing at the mouth. Wroughton stiffened, felt the deadness in his legs and arms, couldn't have run. Could have shouted out, could have yelled for Security at the main doors, but his throat had tightened: nothing would have come from it. He saw the right boot swing back. The kick came into his shin, against the bone and the pain ran rivers. He crumpled. His head went down and the clenched fist hit him on the side of the jaw, the edge of his cheek. More kicks, some on the thigh and the target was his groin. More fist blows and his head was a punchball. He was down. Men from the Royal Military Police came to the fort on the south coast – outside Portsmouth – and taught self-defence. Last time he'd been on the course was seven years back, before the posting to Riga. He tried to protect his head – could not protect head and testicles. One or the other. It was done cold. Iced venom. Not frantic or flailing. It was the attack of a street-fighter. Where had a bloody Belgian agronomist learned the tactics of a street-fighter? Nothing said, not a word. The man did not even pant. Wroughton felt the blood in his mouth. He was not going to die, he knew that. The man was too calm to kill him, intended only to humiliate. The tinted spectacles had gone and he heard the crunch of the boot on them, then a hand snatched at his tie, grasped the silk and pulled up his head with it. Twice, as he choked on the tightened knot, the fist hit his face, once the lower lip, once the bridge of his nose. The man spat in his face. The tie was let go. Wroughton fell back. The shadow moved away from him. The blood was on his chin and in his mouth. It washed round his teeth and ran in his throat. As the clatter of the boots left him, he managed in a supreme effort to lift himself on one elbow.

Through a spew of blood, Wroughton shouted, 'Pity you couldn't satisfy her – she said you were a lousy screw.'

The boots went away, the stride never breaking.

He pulled himself up, using the door-handle, and sagged into the seat, then drove out of the car park.

Wroughton knew enough of personal medicine to realize that if any of his ribs had been broken, or his wrist or his jaw, the pain would have been too great for him to drive. What was hurt was his pride. He went through deserted streets. What was kicked and punched, blown away, was his prized self-esteem. He reached the compound and held up his ID for the guard to see, his face turned away.

Inside, he stripped off his clothes, moaning at the struggle to loosen the belt, the zip and the buttons. His linen suit was torn at the knees and elbows and smeared with the car park's dirt; his shirt was blood-stained. When he had binned the suit, shirt, socks, shoes and underclothes, he crawled across the floor, dragged out the telephone plug, then switched off his mobile. Eddie Wroughton could not face the world. Naked, he sat in his chair and let the darkened room close around him.

She lay on the stone patio. She thought of love.

Far in the distance, below the bungalow, she heard the high-pitched roar of a powered engine.

For Bethany Jenkins, love was alive.

Infatuation, no. Lust, no. Love, yes – damnit. It consumed her. Love was the skin, could be pinched, scratched, scraped, but could not be shed – the hard skin on her legs and arms, the soft skin below the hair on her thighs, the tanned skin on her face. She could not forget him.

Her mother had said to her once, on a third gin and Italian, that she'd seen her father across a crowded box at Newbury races – before they'd met, before they'd spoken – and known, when their eyes had met, through the shoulders and between the heads, that he was the man with whom she would live her life.

Love was not, as Beth reckoned it, the product of introductions made by grandmothers, aunts and best friends. Wasn't about bloody suitability. Love was not sensible. Love happened, and fuck the consequences.

Love was the chance meeting on the upper deck of a late-night London bus, in a carriage on a train out of King's Cross going north ... Love was not about earning prospects in the City, nor about decent families and fat inheritances.

It was beyond control. Did not have an agenda. A rifle was raised, a knife was grasped, and a man held her life in his hand. She didn't know him, he didn't know her. He had put aside the rifle, had shielded her from the knife – had protected her. She had not believed him. She'd said: 'Are you going to try to rape me ... are you going to kill me?' She'd held the little opened penknife with the two-inch blade. He'd said: 'No ... I am going to dig you out.' He had. And she had loved him.

'Well, I can't bloody help it,' she said to the moths. 'It's not my fault, blame the bloody hormones.'

The beams came up the track towards her bungalow.

Beth would have said that she remembered him with more clarity now, on the patio, than an hour after he had disappeared over the crest of the dune . . . Would her mother understand? It would take more than three gin and Italians – if Beth ever met him again – for her mother to take her daughter into her arms and gush, 'Oh, that's wonderful, darling, I'm so happy for you.' Love came out of a sky that was clear blue . . .

The big vehicle stopped on the track in front of her small green watered garden and more moths danced in its headlights. A window lowered.

A voice called to her, 'Is this the residence of Miss Bethany? Are you Miss Bethany, ma'am?'

'It is. I am.'

The door nearest her opened. She saw the bundle lifted with big hands over the passenger's body, like it had been over the gear lever, then it was dropped down. She saw the boy.

Blood was caked on his robe.

'You'll forgive the intrusion, ma'am. We found him out in the Sands. His camel was finished and he was damned near gone. We filled him up with water. He gave us your name. Where he's come from, I don't know. I don't have time to play with, ma'am, we've a plane to catch. He's not hurt. Nothing wrong with him, 'cept his tongue. All I know is, he gave your name. So, I can take him back to Security at the gate and dump him, or I can leave him here – and we're running late for our plane. Ma'am, it's your decision.'

'Leave him here,' she said.

The boy was part of him. She remembered the boy's whistle, sharp, through the fingers at the small mouth, telling him it was time to leave her. She saw the dark bloodstain on his robe, and the lighter spatter that surrounded it. She felt so bloody weak.

The boy came from him, she knew it, and she knew the dark bloodstain was his.

'Don't you ever listen, Mum? Don't you ever care about what I'm saying, what I want? What's it to you?'

300

He did not hear his own voice, its anger.

'It's only money. I want the money for the fare and the money for spending. Is that such a big deal? I want money, got it? I want money to get out of this shit-hole. It's crap here, *crap*. It's the end of the bloody world here. All my life, do you want me here? Bloody wonderful life living here – oh, yes, oh, yes. Top of the bloody world, isn't it? What's the boundaries of the world? Ettingshall and Coseley, Woodcross and Bradley? Rookery Road and bloody Daisy Street? Is that as far as the world goes? Don't go over the railway line, best not to cross the canal bridge – might bloody fall off the end of the world. I want more in my life than this heap of shit's got. I mean, what is there here? Bingo, chips and work, cinema and last bus, girls who want to be hairdressers – what is there here? I want some excitement, I want to bloody live – not locked up here, not in this bloody cage.'

He did not know, as he cried out the anger of it, that the old language ruled, had come back from across the chasm.

'You got the money. What do you have to do? Just get yourself down to the building society, draw it. What's money for? "For a rainy day, Caleb." It rains here every bloody day. I want something to remember. I don't want to grow old in this bloody place, no bloody excitement. When else am I going to get that sort of a chance? Look at this place, it's full of the walking dead. When did you last hear anyone laugh? I want laughter and sunshine and, Mum, I want *excitement*. I want to breathe . . . I'm dying here, I'm going to be walking dead . . . I have this chance and I have to take it.'

He did not see that a Bedouin guide crouched over him and used a wet cloth to try to still the confused rambling.

'They're good guys. They get away, out of here, every two years. They're my best mates. It's a proper invitation, Mum. All I have to do is find the fare. You got anything against them, my best mates? So they're Pakis – is that your problem, Mum? My best mates are Pakistanis. Well, it's where you bloody live, isn't it? You – we – live among Asians. That's your choice. They're all right, doing a bloody sight better than us. Farooq and Amin are my best mates. They'll look after me. I'll be with their families . . . Just once, two weeks, I'll get to a place I've never been. And I'll get some bloody excitement. Cop on, Mum. Please.'

He did not feel the cool of the cloth or the heat of the fever that caught him.

'Get me straight, Mum, I'm going. I want it. Mum, if I have to take you down to the building society, half break your bloody arm doing it, I will. I'm going. It'll be like freedom, two weeks of being bloody free, shot of this place. You going to miss me, Mum? You going to cry on your pillow, Mum? Are you fuck. No, you'll go to the bingo. Mum, have you ever heard of the Khyber Pass? It's history. You ever heard of the North West Frontier? I was down the library, it's fantastic. I want to be there, breathe it, feel it . . . Then I'll be home, and the bloody door'll lock behind me. Mum, don't cry. Mum, I hate it when you bloody cry . . . You shouldn't have said that, shouldn't have. I'm not arrogant, greedy. Don't ever say that again, Mum. I want to have been somewhere. I want to be someone.'

He did not taste the cloth over his mouth, but it quietened him.

She felt strangely calmed. She had the telephone in her hand, had dialled, and she heard it ring out. An age before it was answered.

'Yes?' She heard a stifled yawn. 'Samuel Bartholomew – who's that?'

She swallowed hard. 'You may remember me, Beth Jenkins.'

'I remember you – fit as a flea.'

'Sorry about the time.'

'Not a problem. What can I do for you?'

A line was drawn in front of her. The boy was behind her, gorged with food and water from her fridge. She had questioned him, a mix of brusque interrogation and of gentle probing. She knew what had happened and that he was wounded . . . The boy had described a gash to the head and a slashed leg, and the blood of proof was on the boy's robe. With simplicity, the boy had described the injuries, the weakness, the loss of consciousness. He might already be dead. Lost and gone, *dead*. And the boy had described a track, and she had taken the big-scale map down from a shelf above her desk, spread it on the tiled floor and knelt beside it with the telephone. The line was drawn in front of her. It was like the deep indentation made by the tyres of an earth-moving Caterpillar tractor. It could not be missed, or avoided. It stretched, either way, in front of her. The line blocked her. She recognized the moment, did not delude herself: the moment would define her life. She could step over it, she could turn her back on it.

'Are you still there? I asked what I can do for you, Miss Jenkins.'

She did not know who else she could have turned to, only this slug-fat man at the end of a long-distance phone line – not the doctor at the Shaybah clinic, from the Emirates . . . She took the step, crossed the line.

'I need you down here, in the desert.'

'Excuse me, but I'm in Riyadh. Don't you have medical staff where you are?'

'I need you, I'm afraid.'

'I think it reasonable of me, Miss Jenkins, to request an explanation.'

He was the only doctor she could have called.

'It's a friend . . .'

'Yes.'

'. . . who is hurt out in the Sands.'

'Then get a helicopter, Miss Jenkins. Get a helicopter to lift him out.'

'That is not possible,' she said, and the calm had not deserted her.

'I'm not following you. What's he done – turned his vehicle over?'

She sensed the boy standing motionless behind her, eyes on her, not understanding her. The boy had been in the desert for three days and three nights. He had hazarded his life to come to her.

Beth said crisply, 'I can't send for a helicopter, I cannot use a local doctor. My friend has been wounded in military action.'

'God! Military action? Am I really hearing this?'

'From a missile attack, Dr Bartholomew, my friend has a head wound and a leg wound. I think he has very little time.'

'Do you have any comprehension of what you're asking of me?'

'I do – because I'm asking it of myself.'

'An enemy of the regime, is that your friend?'

'He is just my friend.'

'I lead an easy life, Miss Jenkins – what you request is—'

She heard only the wheeze of his breathing. She thought of him in turmoil and the sweat running on his neck. She was across the line. She waited, did not help him. She let the silence hang.

'God help me – why am I doing this? Where did you say you were? Where do I come to?'

When she'd told him, when she'd ended the call, Beth took the boy out on to her patio. She pointed. She showed him the distant lights in the compound. Under one awning, brightly lit, were the fuselage and the extended wings of an aircraft, but the space under the nearer awning was empty. The boy called it the 'eye in the sky'. He told her of the Predator, which carried two missiles, could not be heard, could not be seen and had found them twice. She had her hand on the boy's shoulder and it rested on the darker bloodstain. Mapping. Evaluation of performance under conditions of extreme heat. The *bitch*.

The lying bitch.

She went inside, the boy following her, and she emptied cupboards of what she would need to take.

'I don't think I'm going to be able to help you.' The headteacher leaned back in his swivel chair. Jed watched him. 'Don't get me wrong, Mr Lovejoy, I'm not being obstructive here. Of course, I will do everything I can to help, everything within my ability – and I quite understand that, on a matter of national security, you are vague to the point of opacity on the reasons for your visit – but, and I don't wish to obstruct, I am just not able to help.'

Beside Jed's feet was a bucket into which leaking rainwater dripped with monotony every fifteen seconds. The walls were damp, too, and posters peeled off them. He did not think that the head-teacher, his face pale from the drudgery of work, lied. The photograph he had brought from Guantanamo lay on the cluttered desk.

'You'll deserve an explanation for my negative response. You believe the man whose photograph you have shown me is approxi-mately twenty-four years old, and therefore left the Adelaide a minimum of six years ago. I have been here two years, and I doubt you'll find a single member of my staff who has taught here for more than four years. Put brutally, we don't last. Adelaide Comprehensive is a sink school. Believe me, it's hard work. It sucks the enthusiasm from you – I'm not ashamed to say it. We burn out here, and quickly. If we're lucky, we move on somewhere else where the stress is less acute. If we're unlucky we sign on with a doctor and accept our failure. We try to prepare our students for adult life, to give them a smattering of education – occasionally we even hit the heights of an exam pass – but the future of the majority is car theft, petty burglary, drug-dealing, under-age pregnancy, vandalism ... The truth is, youthful ambition – other than for criminality – is rare indeed.'

Jed saw a sudden smile crease the headteacher's face.

'I have to say that the vision of a past pupil of Adelaide Comprehensive rising to be a serious player against the security of the state appears to me to be almost ludicrous. Ambition is rare, boredom is endemic, fatalism is contagious. They see no hope. What do they look for, the ultimate? Good benefits, a hotted-up car with anti-social speakers at full blast, not the destruction of the United Kingdom. Look, this area from which my school feeds is listed in the dozen most deprived parts of Britain.'

Jed took the cue. Lovejoy had stood and picked up the photograph. The headteacher shrugged. There was nothing more to be said.

They saw themselves out, left the beaten man behind them.

The rain still fell. Not a cleansing rain, Jed thought, but a dirtied, contaminating rain. He had taken Michael Lovejoy on trust. All of the elation he had felt at unravelling a God Almighty-sized error at Guantanamo was being scrubbed out of him in the English rain. Behind them was an avenue of closed classrooms, now darkened, where nothing had been learned that day or would be learned the next. They were at the Volvo, in the black evening, when he heard the piped shout.

Water ran on the shirtsleeved shoulders of the headteacher and on the sheet of paper he held.

'I was wrong. We might just be able to help you. Try Eric Parsons. He's retired, but a bit of an icon at the Adelaide. He went two years before I arrived but – don't ask me how – he lasted sixteen years here. Taught maths, but did the football team and drama. He might just be your man. I've his address and his number for you. Eric's worth a try.'

The paper was given to Lovejoy.

In the Volvo, Lovejoy used his mobile. It rang until the answer-machine responded, a tinny voice: 'Eric and Violet cannot take your call, please leave a message after the tone.' He didn't, he cut it.

Jed slumped. 'Probably on vacation – God, just what I needed. Damn . . . damn . . .'

Lovejoy said grimly, 'My wife always tells me that shouting at a kettle never made it boil faster.'

They drove out through heavy gates that were set in a high barricade of close-set steel posts with mesh slung between them and coils of barbed wire over the top. It didn't add up to Jed. They went away down streets lit by dull lights, where windows had plywood hammered over them, where the sodden grass was knee high in front gardens, where there were old industrial chimneys – silhouetted against the night – with no smoke and factories whose roofs had collapsed. It didn't add up – in the conventional thinking of the Defense Intelligence Agency at the Pentagon – that this was where a fighter had come from who was clever enough to have fucked the system at Camps X-Ray and Delta. Jed Dietrich didn't know if he was capable of eccentric thinking but reckoned it was time to start trying.

'What are you thinking?'

Lovejoy said, eyes never off the road, and face in shadow, 'I'm thinking that our target fits a pattern – and the pattern makes him a headache.'

Unobtainable on the landline, and a voice message on the mobile. Bart swore. He had never known Wroughton's twin phones, home and mobile, to be unobtainable and switched off. But he prepared himself to travel. A bag of intravenous drips, two multi-packs of lint field dressings, his suture kit, the plastic box that held the debridement gear of scalpels, scissors, clips, forceps and swabs, the wound-cleaning agents, the antibiotics and the local anaesthetics went into a neat pile on the floor. He checked each one off against his list. Last was the morphine, the painkiller.

When they were all laid out, he tried the numbers again. No answer.

For fuck's sake, it was his freedom, but the damn phones were unobtainable and on the answer-machine. He left no message. It was the damned big one. It was the chance to wipe all of the indifference off Eddie bloody Wroughton's face, to shove the sneer down his throat. It was the reason he had told the daft cow that he would drive through the night into the damn emptiness of the desert.

Bart went to the lock-up room off the utility room – where his maid washed and ironed his clothes and kept her buckets – for the big water bottles and the plastic petrol containers. All expatriates had such a supply, had done since the attacks in the city. Water and fuel would be needed, if civil disturbance broke out and the airport was closed, for an escape north to Tabūk or Sakākah or Ar'ar and then on to the Jordanian frontier – eight hundred kilometres from Riyadh.

He ferried the medical bags, packets and boxes to the Mitsubishi outside, then the water and the fuel. Inside again, he studied the map. The journey would take him down the main highway, 513, to Al Kharj and on to the metalled road, Route 10, to Harad. Then he was directed to use the dirt surface track south into the Rub' al Khālī. It was the only way into the desert, and he would be on it for a minimum of three hundred and fifty kilometres ... Bloody hell, madness.

But – perhaps – out of madness came freedom.

He tried a last time to call Wroughton. He yearned to tell his tormentor of a man wounded in the desert – close to death – by military action.

He picked up his cat, kissed it, put it into its quilted basket. He closed his front door behind him.

He thought he should be there by dawn, where she'd said she'd meet him.

They came up off the sand and crossed the raised track.

Because Rashid made the camels go fast, and the sack litter jolted him, Caleb saw the distant lights between the animal's legs. Half a dozen small lights as far away as he could see, as far as the horizon was. Then they were gone.

He rolled on the sack litter. The flies droned in his ears, made their circuits, came back to his head and his leg. Nothing to keep the flies off. Had no strength and could not swat them.

They were over the raised track, and headed away from the lights.

Caleb knew he was slipping. The heat, the flies and the dirt in the wounds doomed him. He knew it ... He was back across the chasm, where he had come from and where he had not known of a God to pray to. The camels stank around him, but he had a new smell in his nose, meat that was decayed, flesh that rotted – where the flies laid the eggs. Himself.

Thanks to the water, and the fodder at the well-head, the camels' stride was faster now, and each jolt made Caleb slip further.

It was charity for him when he drifted, unconscious.

Chapter Sixteen

Still talking, a murmur in the old language, but weaker. He no longer saw the guide. He did not know that Rashid sat apart from him, that he was alone under an awning spread between two kneeling camels.

'I was nothing before I met the Chechen – nobody. A man looks at you, strips you, reads right through you. You know he's judging you. Are you shit or are you useful? To anybody else who'd ever looked at me, I was shit. Not looking at me like I was a piece of meat, and hung up, but like I was a person. I went up that hill, it was all live rounds they fired. It was his test. If I had failed it, I'd have been on that plane home the next day – and I'd be back in that shit-heap, and I'd be nobody.'

He had not the strength to swipe away the flies at his leg wound, or to push himself up and see the darker flesh ringing the wound.

'The Chechen's a fighter. He didn't tell me but I heard it – he was one of those who lay in trenches and let the tanks come over the trench, then came out, was behind them where they were soft and broke the tracks with grenades, or put grenades down the hatches. He did that – bloody tanks. He was under tanks, fifty tons of them, and he wasn't scared. He was my hero, and he cared about me – like he was my father.'

On his back, the flies buzzing about him, he did not know that the guide had sent his son – his only son – out into the desert to bring help. He was beyond that corner of his memory.

'The Chechen made me someone. Back in that crap-heap. "You want to come down the canal? You got enough for the chipper? Heh, you met that bird out of Prince's Road, who'll do you a suck for a fiver? Get your arse moving, 'cos there's a Beemer in the station park and the radio's a Blaupunkt – you want it?" There, they never knew a man like the Chechen. He made me feel important, no one else ever had . . . wanted.'

He did not know that, in the heat and with his blood oozing away, he was on the road to death.

'Among those kids – none of them'd ever met anyone like the Chechen, because they live in a crap-heap. I owe everything to him. I make you a promise, Chechen – you won't ever regret picking me. But you're dead, aren't you? Out in all that fucking dirt, you're buried . . . Can you hear me, Chechen, can you? I'm your man . . . God, it bloody hurts, Chechen.'

Still talking, but fading.

In the slack dawn light, the spread cloud of dust reached the settlement. He approached, Bart thought, the back end of nowhere – the only stop for food or fuel on the only track running south into the desert. On his map, 'nowhere' was given the name of Bir Faysal.

Back up north – at Al Kharj, and again at Harad – where there was still a metalled road, he had pulled into the side and had used his mobile. In both towns, high in the darkness of the night, there were antennae on towers to relay his signal, but there had still been no answer from either of Wroughton's phones, both switched off. Three times, in seven hours of driving on the track after Harad, he had had to swerve on to the bedded stones at the verge to avoid collision with lorries – bastards, coming straight at him, not giving way to him, using the centre of the track – and once he had gone right off the track and the stones, nodding off to sleep, and had manoeuvred his way back on to the track by crossing packed sand. To keep himself awake, he had found a station on the radio, but it had static across it. No phone signal, no radio – only his thoughts to keep him company.

Excited thoughts. Thoughts of liberation. Freedom to go to the airport, with his cat box, in the knowledge that he had paid his debt and that the files were shredded. Thoughts of what he would tell Eddie bloody Wroughton.

The tyres of the Mitsubishi threw up a dustcloud behind him. Scattered grey concrete buildings were in front of him. He slowed. He had not thought, alone in his vehicle and struggling with tiredness, of what he had – by his own volition – edged himself into. Now he did. The thought clamoured in his mind as he drove carefully past the building over which a flag hung limply against its post. In front of the police station, one man in khaki drill lounged on a chair and watched him go by. It would have taken some wriggling if the policeman had been alert, had jumped up from his chair, had waved him down, would have taken a bloody good story. After the police station he came to a fuel forecourt, then a cluster of low buildings surrounded by thorn hedges . . . The policeman might not have been, but Bart was alert. He had his window down, the air-conditioner switched off, and he heard clearly the bleat of goats behind the hedges. The desert was ahead. Where was she? He went past the last of the buildings. A woman in scalp-to-toe black ducked away and a child waved enthusiastically and . . . the flashed headlights caught the side of his Mitsubishi.

It was madness.

The lights speared into his face from a gully beyond the last building.

It would not have been madness if he had been able to speak to the landline phone or to the mobile. He had not spoken to Eddie bloody Wroughton. Perhaps he should never have started out from his compound.

He saw the Land Rover come up from the gully, straining for traction. She drove. There was a boy beside her. She came past him, spewing sand, then he saw the wave of her hand, the instruction that he follow. Like a damned hired hand, wasn't he? He followed her for a mile, until the settlement was lost behind them, then she braked the Land Rover and pulled on to the stones He stopped behind her. Her door snapped open and she walked towards him. What to tell her? He remembered the brightness in her face at the party, its lustre in his surgery, and it was all gone. She was drawn, pale, and she seemed to rock as though exhaustion was near to beating her. The sand coated her, was in her hair, on her face and round her eyes; it lay on her blouse and across her trousers. He framed in his mind what he would say.

She leaned on his door. 'Thank you for coming. Thank you very much.'

He had intended a response of cutting sarcasm. Then he saw the genuineness of the gratitude on her face, and in her eyes, reddened by tiredness, strain and sand grit. Oh, God, that sort of genuineness came from one source, one alone. Bloody hell, that was *love*. The world threw up enough problems in Bart's life without the intrusion of love . . . a lucky man he'd be, the subject of her love.

He said, matter-of-fact, 'Good morning, Miss Jenkins – it looks like you're about to spill a load of trouble on to my shoes.'

'Probably, I have . . .'

It was another of the moments, fleeting, when he could have – should have – turned back.

'Did you bring your gear?'

'Yes . . . If it's not presumptuous, who is my mystery patient who has suffered injuries in military action?'

'I don't know. Honestly, I don't know his name or where he's come from or where he's going to. That's the truth.'

He believed her. It was the last time he could have turned back. At the end of the day he would have been in Riyadh, and in his compound. And he would not have forgiven himself. He looked into her face. It was all madness. Bart's life was a story of being trapped and never turning.

'Right, then, we'd better get moving.'

She told him to follow her. She said the Bedouin boy with her would guide them. She walked away, lurched back to her Land Rover.

He kept close to her. She led him another mile down the track, then swung right and went west. He went down off the track and the wheels ground on the chip stones, then sagged on to sand. He used the low gears for cross-country. He had never driven on sand before. He sensed that the boy – who had stared back at him from the Land Rover, his face riddled with suspicion – guided her. Many times they stopped and the sand in front of the Land Rover and Bart's Mitsubishi seemed without features, endless ochre hillocks that had no bushes, no trees, no cliffs, nothing to Bart that was recognizable or could be caught by memory; they would halt for a few seconds, then veer to the right or the left. He found his steering was sluggish and unresponsive. No one that Bart knew, back in Riyadh, went into the desert, even with their vast four-by-fours. The wildlife park, a few kilometres beyond the city limits, was enough. A trip by tarmacadam road cutting into a desert on the way to Jedda or Ad Dammam was sufficient for anyone he knew to believe they had experienced a survival ordeal. Other than the straining engines of the Land Rover and the Mitsubishi there was silence around them. He saw nothing that lived. By the end of the second hour, off the track and twenty-eight miles covered, he felt a crawling fear. He could not turn back: he had lost his sense of direction. Wouldn't have known whether he drove towards the safety of the track, went parallel to it or away from it . . . worse than fear, and he sweated. His mind played games with him, mocked him. He remembered a school play. His father and mother in the audience. Its setting was a First World War dug-out. He was the coward among the officers waiting for the Big Push. The hero asked, musing, whether a worm knew, when it tunnelled in the earth, whether it was going up or down and speculated on the worm's bad luck if it went down when it thought it was coming up. His father had said that he should not have allowed himself to be cast as a coward. He clung to the tyremarks left by the Land Rover, and he saw that, behind him from the mirror, the brisk wind lifted the sand and covered the tyres' ruts. The fear made him shiver.

It looked at first, through the haze thrown up by the Land Rover, like a stunted needle. At the start of the third hour, Bart realized their target was a column of stone, weathered and sculpted by the wind, with a sharpened tip.

Beth watched.

'He's pretty far down the road.'

Behind Beth, the boy squatted beside his father, whose hands loosely held a rifle across his lap.

'I think I'm just in time but I can't promise anything. By rights he should have died yesterday. Extraordinary resilience.' The doctor spoke as if a commentary were needed from him. The needle was in a forearm vein, and he was hooking the bag, connected by a tube to the needle, on to the cross-rope that supported the awning. Then he crouched over the leg wound. 'First things first. Do the dehydration, get as much from an intravenous drip into him as quickly as possible, saline. You see, there's a big blood loss. It's all about liquids in the body. First, to counter dehydration loss, the body steals from the blood supply, then from extra-cellular space, and the last reserve is from intra-cellular space. When that's exhausted it's death by de-hydration. I'm surprised he's still with us.'

She wanted to throw up. The doctor took the other arm, without the drip in it, and firmly pinched the skin just above a bandage of dirty cloth on the wrist. When his fingers let go, the pinched flesh still stood erect.

'It would have gone down, where I pinched, if there was enough liquid in the body. It hasn't fallen back because there's no liquid there. It's an old trick.'

Beth thought the doctor talked because of his fear.

He reached for the cloth on the wrist and started to unravel it. 'We're hardly going to make a sterile area, but at least we can try – let's get shot of this filth for starters.'

Beth saw the plastic bracelet. In the sand, in the night, she had found it, had tried to examine it. His strength had prevented her. She saw the doctor peer down at it. She leaned closer and made out the printed reference number. The photograph was clear to her. Alongside it, under the number and the filled-in spaces for height and weight, below sex, was 'Issued by: Delta'. She gagged.

The doctor turned to her. 'Did you know about this?'

'No, I didn't. No.'

'Do you know what Delta is?'

'I think so.'

'*Think*, Miss Jenkins? Can't you do better than *think*? Let me help you. Delta is the name of the camp at Guantanamo Bay, the camp for terrorists. Good God, what have I got into?'

'I didn't know.'

The doctor seemed to gasp, to drag in a great gulp of air. 'For help-ing this man, I – and you, Miss Jenkins – could go to Chop Chop Square. May I assume your ignorance stops short of not knowing what Chop Chop Square is?'

She seemed to shudder, could not help herself. 'I know what Chop Chop Square is.'

The doctor went on – as if he had cut the square and the ritual of public execution after Friday prayers from his mind – in a flat monotone. 'You see, his tongue, and his mouth, they'll be dried out. It's not a worry because the drip will fix that. He will have had an extreme shock from the effect of the missile detonation and that will have surged his adrenaline, further aggravating the dehydration process. First appearances, the head wound will have caused severe concussion but not much else. The leg is the greater problem, and the resulting blood loss. There are ten pints of blood in the body and it is my estimate that—'

'Are you going to save him?'

'My estimate is that he's lost at least two pints – I make no promises. There is blood loss and there are signs of advancing gangrene. Do you want him saved?'

She looked down. He lay on old sacks. His eyes were closed and his breathing was a slow, shallow struggle. The head wound was a long slice, below his forehead and above his right ear, and the hair had been cut back from it by the guide. As soon as they had arrived, the doctor had barked questions to her, for translation: What had been done for him? What, if anything, had he been given? What had been the patient's reaction? The guide had used a knife to cut away hair from the head wound, then had anointed it. He had wiped the gum from *murr* on to the wound's edges. Beth translated this as 'myrrh', and the doctor had muttered, '*Commiphora molmol*', and had not criticized the Bedouin's use of the ancient healing resin. She saw the first drip bag draining steadily into his arm. A cloth lay across his groin. The leg wound was on the left side – there were flies around it. It was shorter in length than that on the skull, but wider, deeper, and the flesh around it had already blackened. He did not look, to Beth, like a threat. He seemed to her to rest in exhausted peace. She crawled closer to him and took his hand, both fists covering his fingers.

The doctor made room for her, then stood and changed the drip bag. 'I can't do anything about the leg until he has more strength. It's the leg that worries me. Maybe in an hour I can start on it.'

What did she want of him? Everything. How far would she go to help him? To the end of the road, to the square. What did she know of him? Nothing.

She sat and held his hand. The father and son stared at her, eyes never off her. A camel pushed its head against her arm, competed with her to touch him. The doctor now knelt at his bags and packages and checked an inventory. She did not look into his leg wound, but at his face. Never before had Beth held a man's hand with such caring softness. The drip worked. She thought of a dried-out flower that was watered and straightened. She felt his fingers stir in her grip. The breathing quickened. The doctor broke off, came closer. Lips moved. The doctor crouched to listen. The eyes opened. She saw the eyes fastening on the doctor's as he strained to listen.

The voice came weak but clear: 'Don't look into my face, don't.' The fingers tightened in her fists. 'Don't see my face, don't ever.' He seemed to sink back. 'Don't . . .'

She reeled, clung to his fingers but shook.

'That's all I bloody need,' the doctor wheezed beside her. 'He's English – as English as you or me. He spoke English like I do, like you. Well done, Miss Jenkins – this just keeps getting better and better.'

'You can stand there as long as you like but until I see identification you're not coming in,' Eric Perkins had said. He'd been behind his door, opened to the extent that the security chain would permit, and his wife had been behind him. 'You can stay on my step all the hours that God gives but you're not coming in till I see who you are.'

The retired maths teacher was wizened, small, and his cheek was cut from shaving, but he seemed to have the obstinacy that came with age and bloodymindedness, and he had been behind his front door, as if it was the portcullis of his castle. The door had been closed on them, and for ten minutes the rain had dripped on them. It went against Lovejoy's grain to show his card. He'd rung the bell again. He'd shown the identification card that gained entry through the electronic barriers at Thames House, and the American had shown what was good enough for Camp Delta, far away on Cuba.

'Eh, wasn't so difficult, was it?' Eric Perkins had said, then had turned. 'Violet, love, we have visitors from the Security Service in London and what's called the Defense Intelligence Agency in

America – and they're half drowned, not that it's my fault. They'd like a cup of tea, love, and I think some cake might see them right.'

The chain had come off the lock. Their coats had been hung in the hall and yesterday's newspaper was under them to protect the carpet.

They sat in the front room.

Maybe, Lovejoy thought, they should have taken off their shoes. The room was pristine. Perkins held up the photograph in front of his face. He'd demanded to hold it, handle it, and Dietrich had shown ill-concealed reluctance to pass it to him. Dietrich had covered the top of the head and the whole of the body with his hands, but the retired teacher had insisted.

Perkins chuckled. The photograph was close to his eyes. The prisoner's camp reference number was stamped at the bottom. He chuckled till he coughed. The light of his eyes danced. 'I used to do mathematics. The basis of mathematics is solving problems. I'm wondering if your problem, gentlemen, that needs solving, is that you don't know who he is.'

'I don't think you need explanations, sir,' Dietrich said sourly. 'We are merely investigating background to—'

The wife, Violet, was in the doorway, holding the tray. Her husband's arm was up, like an old-time traffic policeman's. 'Sorry, love, waste of your time and effort. They won't be staying. They don't trust me, love.'

Lovejoy playing his winning smile, and said, 'Just so we have no misunderstandings, and I remind you, Mr Perkins, of the strictures of the Official Secrets Act, this man was a prisoner, designated as an unlawful combatant in Afghanistan, at Guantanamo Bay. He was released, because the authorities there thought him a taxi-driver from Herat in that country. While he was being transferred from the airbase to Kabul, he ran away. We don't know who he is, but believe him to be from this area. If he is from here he would most likely have gone to Adelaide Comprehensive. Mr Perkins, we are looking for your help.'

His face had lit as each morsel of trust was given him, and he'd laughed till his cheeks flushed.

'I was wrong again, Violet, they're staying. A late run for the post, getting by on the rails. Tell Violet whether you'd like sugar, gentlemen. Yes, I know him.'

Tea was poured and cakes were passed.

'Not that he was any good at mathematics. If I was judging him solely by the ability to multiply and divide, add and subtract, I'd have little to say. I digress. Most of the boys going through my final-year classes would have competency to add up profits from drug-pushing, or to subtract the days of a sentence remaining to be served in a young offenders' institution. That's about it. Adelaide Comprehensive isn't a school known for its shining successes but, over my time, I did have a couple of them. For this lad, well, I was able to provide something – call it motivation. Yes, there are little victories to be won, even at Adelaide Comprehensive.'

He broke off. He called to the kitchen to thank his wife for the tea. Lovejoy saw the impatience building in the American: the shaking hands rattled the cup and saucer and the cake on the plate on his knees had gone untouched. He caught him with a glance: bide your time, man.

'There was a boy who was being bullied, an Asian child. There were two problems with the boy: a stutter and a wealthy father, cash in the child's hip pocket. You'll have learned a little of the area from which the school draws pupils. The money and the speech impediment made this pupil a predictable target – that's the real world. I induced your man here to become the pupil's friend. He did, and no doubt was paid for it, and the bullying was a thing of the past. The motivation was more complex. He sided naturally with the minority. He went against the majority – not, I fancy, for any altruistic reason, not for any defence of the handicapped in a cruel world, but because it gave him pleasure to run against the tide. Are you with me? Are you beginning to see him?'

'Just getting a glimpse,' Lovejoy said drily.

'Second time around was more interesting. Our then esteemed headteacher, before he fled to the quieter world of local-education-authority inspections, wanted a competition launched for public recitation. Pupils standing on a stage and declaiming to their peers, such was the headteacher's plan. Most of the males could barely communicate, other than to demand their rights in a police station on a Friday night. The headteacher was very keen. I was given the job of organizing it. Was it a fiasco? It was not. Why not? Because this boy agreed to participate. What did I choose for him? I'd been to a funeral that week, in West Bromwich. There had been a reading from the First Epistle of Paul to the Corinthians, chapter fifteen, starting at verse fifty-four. Do you know it, gentlemen?'

Lovejoy did not, but he saw beside him the American's lips move. They kept time with the recitation.

'He stood on the stage, in front of the school, and he silenced the chatter, stilled the movement. "So when this corruptible shall have put on incorruption, and this mortal shall have put on immortality, then shall be brought to pass the saying that is written, Death is swallowed up in Victory. O death, where is thy sting? O grave, where is thy victory?" He did it, did it well. You see, by doing it he showed he could stand alone. It was nothing to do with the spirituality of the words, their uniqueness. Again, he just needed to run against the tide . . . Would you like more tea, or another cake?'

Lovejoy shook his head patiently, and the American followed suit.

'I liked him enough to make a small effort to find him work when he left us – a garage, Harrison's Auto Repair Unit, on the industrial estate behind the high street. I don't know whether he lasted there. Sometimes I see pupils I taught, on the street and hanging about, sometimes I read their names in the paper, remanded in custody or remanded on bail. I haven't seen him since the day he left school. What was different about him was a desperate, unsatisfied restlessness, and nothing here that could satisfy it, and the response to my trivial efforts was a minimal answer to the symptoms. I have to believe, because you have come to see me, that he is now considered a danger to society. I suppose trained men will seek to kill him before he can kill others – and I'd not argue with that. Where would he have learned the hate? Probably from your camp at Guantanamo Bay, Mr American. No, I won't argue with you, nor will I cheer you on – I rather liked the boy. You'll have to excuse me because Violet has a dentist's appointment.'

He stood. He looked a last time at the photograph. 'Oh, yes. What you came for. His name. I presume that with his name it will be easier to find and kill him.'

The American said, 'It will be easier to find him and stop him in his tracks before he can murder innocents.'

'Of course, of course . . . He's from that estate near the school, by the canal. Perhaps I sell him short, perhaps he's more than I've painted him.' His jaw jutted and his fists clenched. 'Always interesting to hear how former pupils have progressed. He is Caleb Hunt.'

Caleb did not know that a third bag dripped saline solution through the tube and the needle into his arm.

'They'll hear my name, won't they? The bastards'll hear it. Hear it loud. They're walking dead, got nothing – all they got is radios out of Beemers and sucks and smokes, got nothing. They're not really living. I live. Everyone will hear my name.'

Caleb did not know that Beth stared bleak-faced at him.

'Guys, where are you? What you doing? I did something else. You'll live, fucking die, no one will know, you're nothing. What you got? You got fuck-all.'

Caleb did not know as he rambled, as the drip gave him strength, that Bart prepared a scalpel, scissors, clips, forceps and sterile swabs, and listened, or that Beth bit her lip.

'It's the biggest desert in the world, it's got worse heat than anywhere in the world. I'm walking in it. I'm barefoot in it. You wouldn't have lasted in it a day, not half a day. I'm going through it because my family's waiting for me . . . That's a proper family. I belong to my family.'

Bart loaded a syringe with Lignocaine, the local anaesthetic.

'When you hear my name, all of you bastards, it'll be because I've done what my family wants of me. Anything . . .'

Caleb exposed his mind, made his mind as bare as the wound on his leg.

Camp Delta, Guantanamo Bay.

'This is him?'

'This is al-Ateh, the taxi-driver.'

'Have we done him?'

'No, the Agency haven't interrogated him. The Bureau have but not for eight months. The DIA done him since eight months back. These are their transcripts.'

He stood with his head bowed in docility. In front of him were two men he had not seen before. He had learned well to give no sign that he understood what they said.

'Who did him last, from the DIA, which of those creeps?'

'Dietrich. You know Dietrich, Jed Dietrich?'

'I know him. What does he say, Harry?'

'He doesn't say anything – he's on vacation. And won't say anything – not back till after the due date, if this jerk goes.'

The chain manacles bit at his wrist, and the shackles at his ankles. He stared at the floor, made a target of his feet and did not watch them as they shuffled paper between them. The interpreter stood beside them, an Arab, and his respect for them told Caleb of their importance.

'It's the quota, that's what matters. Two old guys, a middle-aged guy and a young guy to make up a quota minimum of four – if they're clean.'

'Too many of them are clean.'

'I hear you, Wallace. Try not to think about it . . . You going to the club tonight, that concert?'

'Marine brass band – wouldn't miss . . . OK, let's go process this guy.'

The interpreter translated. The one called Harry told him that the United States of America had no grievance against the innocent, the United States of America valued the freedom of the individual, the United States of America was committed only to rooting out the guilty. The one called Wallace told him that he was going home, back to Afghanistan, to his family – then had checked as if a paragraph in the file about the wiping out of the family by B-52 bomber had been, for a moment, forgotten. He was going back to the chance of making a new life with his taxi.

Through the interpreter, Harry asked, 'I hope, young man, back in Afghanistan you won't come out with any lies about torture?'

The meek answer. 'No, sir. I am grateful, sir.'

Through the interpreter, Wallace queried, 'You have no complaints about your treatment here?'

'No, sir. I have been treated well, sir.'

Through the interpreter, both of them: 'You take good care, young man, of the opportunity given you . . . You help to build a new Afghanistan . . . Good luck . . . Yes, good luck.'

The guards' hands were on his arms, and the waist chain was tugged back.

He heard Harry say, 'Pathetic, aren't they, these jerks? He's lucky to be out. I reckon the lid's going to come off this place.'

He was being led out through the door. Wallace said, 'Too right – discipline's cracking, more suicide tries and more defiance. When the *tribunals start up and when that execution chamber comes on line, the lid could come off big-time. What time is the concert?'*

He was shuffled away, the chains clanking on his ankles.

He had contempt of them, had beaten them. He would hear them scream, wherever he was. When he had returned to his family, he would hear them scream in shrill terror.

'I think I'm going to ask you to help me.'

'Of course.'

'And it's best if I educate you to my equipment.'

'Yes.'

She followed Bart out from under the low awning, stretched and stood tall. 'What should I know?'

He hissed, 'Not what you should know, what about me knowing something? When did you realize this man was a fully fledged terrorist, and British? May we begin there?'

'What do you want? A confessional?'

'The truth would help.'

'What he is and what I knew, does that determine what treatment you give him?'

'My decision, Miss Jenkins, not yours.'

She told him, haltingly, what had brought her to this unmapped corner of the greatest desert in the world and what she owed this man. He thought, himself, he owed nothing. 'That's it – are you going to walk away?'

Whatever he was, Bart was not an idiot. If he walked away, went back to the awning, collected up his boxes and packages, carted them to the Mitsubishi and loaded them, the rifle on the older Bedouin's lap would be up to the shoulder and would be aimed. The eye behind the sight would be brilliant with hatred, and he'd hear the clatter of it arming; he would die in the sand. He pondered on all those who had wrecked his life, had walked over him.

'In about half an hour,' Bart said, 'I'll start to work on the leg wound.'

'I trust you.'

From the sky, the heat cascaded on him, and the sweat ran on his body and collected in the folds of his stomach. 'That's good, because you have to.'

*

Gonsalves rang the bell.

Wroughton checked him in the spy-hole then opened the door. He held his hands across his privates.

Gonsalves walked inside, had half skirted the black bin-bag, then stopped at it, put down his briefcase and tipped the bloodstained clothes on to the floor.

'Your people, when I called them, they said you had a flu dose. When I asked if a remedy for flu was taking a phone off the hook, your people didn't know.'

Wroughton said, 'It seemed easier to say flu than that I'd walked into a door.'

He hadn't washed. The bruises on his body, thickest at his groin, were a technicolour parade of black, mauve and yellow. The blood had dried around his nose and at the split in his lower lip. He dropped his hands away from his privates, away from where he was shrivelled up, because modesty didn't seem to matter.

'You could help me, Eddie, you could tell me where to look on your face for an imprint of a door handle, because I don't see it. Did the door handle have a wife?'

'I'm not expecting flowers or an apology – my father used to tell me, never explain and never apologize – but I expect to be cut in.'

'Where's your maid?'

'When she came to the door I told her to get lost.'

'I'll make some tea.'

Gonsalves went to the kitchen and Wroughton slumped into his chair. The voice boomed through the rattle of the mugs and the opening and closing of cupboard doors. 'I think I heard you right. "Cut in?" You hear me. You are a junior partner in our endeavour. We use you when we need you, we ignore you when we don't. Did you get big ideas because Teresa does pizza for you, and you're Uncle Eddie to the kids? Shouldn't have done. It's a tough world out there. You're a taker, Eddie, but you don't have much to give. It's why I cut you out. We were running a secure operation down in the Rub' al Khālī.'

'I think you told me you had "big boys' toys" there.'

'In the Rub' al Khālī we had something special going, and –'

'And I told you – "not much to give", I'm sure – about a caravan going out of Oman and a direction route.'

'– and we had Predator UAVs up, with Hellfires loaded. And we'd done a con-job on the Saudis – which is why it was secure and why you weren't cut in, and—'

'Fuck you.'

'That what the door handle said? We did two hits and we couldn't keep it secure and now the Saudis have chucked us out. We got a day and a half left in there, then fatter cats than me have to decide whether to fly UAVs out of Yemen, Djibouti or Dohar and take the risk of violating Saudi air space. We're out in a day and a half.'

Gonsalves carried in the tray, put it down, poured tea, gave a mug to Wroughton.

When he'd sipped his tea, Gonsalves reached into his briefcase. 'Want to see the tricks the "big boys' toys" can do?'

'I don't beg, not a damn poodle and dribbling.'

'Why I love you, Eddie . . .' Gonsalves had a file of photographs in his hand and spread them over the coffee table around Wroughton's mug.

He couldn't help himself, felt his excitement quicken. Three pictures, colour, eight-by-six, showed black-circled craters in the ochre sand. They were the raw, only dreamed-of currency of an intelligence officer. Centred on one was a dead, keeled-over camel. Not electronic intercepts, not analysis of radio traffic pulled down by the dishes. He snatched up the crucial picture, peered at it and lingered over it.

'Don't get a hard-on, Eddie – do me a favour. OK, it's before the first strike. Three men travelling. Two guides leading them. Three pack camels carrying crates, and Stingers is as good a guess as any. Now, look at the close-ups on the three . . . Is this not as sexy as it gets?'

Wroughton held the three photographs, felt in awe of the technology that had magnified them to a point of recognition from four miles of altitude.

'That one.' Gonsalves' finger stabbed at a photograph. 'We identify him as Gibran al-Wafa, aged twenty-seven, involved in the Riyadh compound bombs, Saudi citizen.' The finger moved on. 'Him, he is Muhammad Sherif, aged fifty-nine, was in Afghanistan in the Soviet war, with bin Laden in the Sudan exile, with him back in Kabul, but disappeared before Enduring Freedom, now a strategist. Egyptian national and sentenced to death in his absence.' The finger loitered. 'This one, we don't have him. The computers can't chuck anything up.'

Wroughton gazed at the photograph. He saw the body of the young man upright on the camel, the head high. He strained to make out the features, but the pixels confused him. He thought he saw a strong chin but . . . 'So what? Isn't he dead?'

Gonsalves said that the sensor operator had aimed twice for specific and individual targets as the camels had scattered. The two targets in the two strikes had been the Saudi and the Egyptian.

'So, you may have missed him, for all your damn technology . . . And I get cut in because you don't know who he is, right?'

'Succinctly put, Eddie. I'll see you.'

After Gonsalves had gone, Eddie Wroughton sat in his chair, held the photograph in front of him, and tried to read the face.

Lizzy-Jo cursed. George's message was pithy, without embellishment. The needs of maintenance ruled his life. Maintenance was obligatory, not optional. The Predator, *First Lady*, was now beyond all limits set for maintenance. Flying hours in optimum conditions had been exceeded, but she had also been up in worst-status conditions. She was grounded – no argument – confirmation of what he'd said the afternoon before. She needed a sanitized hangar for the necessary maintenance, and the only sanitized hangar she would see was back at Bagram. He went out of the Ground Control, went heavily down the steps, as if unsettled by Lizzy-Jo's curse.

Beside her, Marty flew *Carnival Girl*, did the new boxes. When they'd brought her back in the small hours, while she and Marty had stolen sleep, the bird's tanks had been filled so that fuel had spilled out.

Carnival Girl, the old warhorse, the fighter from Bosnia and Kosovo, from Afghanistan – with a first skull-and-crossbones stencilled on her fuselage – had gone up twenty minutes after midday for her final run out of Shaybah, not her prettiest chase down the runway, with the fuel load and the burden of the Hellfires under the wings.

The boxes on the map were on the east side of a track. They had tasked themselves, and Oscar Golf had not argued it over the link, to have her up for the full twenty-four hours of her endurance at four miles altitude and at loiter speed. Late on in the flight, tomorrow, they would do a small section of the map boxes on the west side of the track. They had not yet reached the track, but it would be good when they did, would make a diversion from watching goddamn sand.

He was hunched over the joystick. She had tried to jolt him, but he spoke when he had to, not otherwise. She had wanted to bring the life back to him. He flew *Carnival Girl* without error but as if he sleep-walked.

She lied . . .

Lizzy-Jo said, 'Last time I was in New York, I was in a bar – been to see my mom and was going down to North Carolina for the last spat, but had time to kill. The bar was behind Fifth Avenue. I was alone, this guy was alone. What did I do? Wasn't much of a chat-up line. I was in Afghanistan. Was I hurting those bastards? Real venom in his question. I was trying. He told me why he hoped I was.'

She had gone straight from her mom's apartment, in a taxi, out to the airport for the flight. She had never been in a bar behind Fifth Avenue.

'His partner worked up high in the North Tower. It was a day like any other. Nothing different about the eleventh of September. Himself, he didn't go to work because of an optician's appointment. He was in the waiting room, was next in line to be called. The TV was on. Where his partner worked was above the hit point of the American Airlines plane. It was all on the TV in front of him, and he could see the window nearest to his partner's desk. I listened.'

She talked without emotion, didn't play to a gallery, watched her screens.

'Twenty minutes later, as he sees it on TV, the United plane goes into the South Tower. What he's telling me, he's not watching the South Tower, only the North Tower and the window nearest his partner's desk. You know what he sees – there's smoke and fire. You want to know what he sees from the window nearest his partner's desk? They jump. People start to jump. They got the fire coming up under them and they got nowhere to go, and some of them jump. They are ninety floors up, and they jump. He sees people jump from that floor, from those windows. He sees tiny, ant figures falling. It's all on the TV. Did his partner jump? There's a lot of people jumped. Now, sudden but late, he starts to get active. Goes to the desk, rings his partner's phone. It's not picked up. He wants to think his partner jumped, that falling ninety floors, arms and legs out, was a quicker death than waiting for the fire to get up there – or the collapse. He said his partner was the only love of his life, and he thinks he saw his partner jump from ninety floors up . . . That's a horrible way to die. That's bad people that make you die like that. I bought him a drink, and I told him we went hard as we could after the people that made his partner jump, to hurt them. Then I headed out to catch my flight.'

She saw, from the side of her eye, the tears stream from under Marty's spectacles and run on his cheeks. She had no shame for the saccharine emotion of the lie, daytime talk-show stuff. She went brusque. 'How's she doing?'

'She's doing well,' he choked. '*Carnival Girl*'s flying great. She's the bomb.'

Caleb felt the strength back in him, but the pain was agony and it rolled down in waves to his foot and came up through his hips and stomach. Lifting his right arm brought the pain in a torrent. He gestured for Rashid to come to him. When the guide was close to him, ear bent to mouth, Caleb whispered what he wanted brought to him. He heard other voices, indistinct – a man's and a woman's – but could not make out what they said. The camels chewed cud on either side of him and slung between them was the awning that made shade for him. A blow hammered down on metal. Wood screamed as it was broken and hinges whined. He was brought the manual.

The pages were grey, dry and crackled in his hand, and the large print on the cover had faded.

There was a needle attached to a tube that dangled over him, in his left arm, inserted immediately above the plastic bracelet, which was no longer covered. He tried to push himself up to look around, but that was beyond his strength.

The voice was in the old language. 'Don't do that – please, don't. Now, let's set down the ground rules. I am a British-born doctor, sir, I am here at the request of your friend, Miss Jenkins. I do not speak Arabic, nor do I need to. When you were in, sir, a confused state –

natural following the traumatic experience of your wounds – you talked English. You were incoherent and rambling, and I understood nothing of it. Got me? But as far as I am concerned you are as British as I am ... I call you "sir" not as a mark of respect, but because neither Miss Jenkins nor I knows your identity, and we have no interest in it.'

On the cover page of the manual was printed: *Raytheon Electronic Systems FIM-92 Stinger low-altitude surface-to-air system family*. The man materialized above him.

A pudgy fat-filled face. A shirt stuck with sweat to a vest. Trousers held up by a narrow belt. He saw the man. The woman was behind the man.

'You should not have come,' Caleb said faintly.

'I said, remember it, "If it is ever possible, I will repay you." It was possible. I brought a doctor who is going—'

'Who saw my face.'

'Who is going to help you – don't be so damn stupid. He's a doctor, not a bloody policeman.'

'Why did you come?' Caleb grated.

'The boy was sent to find me. Why?'

'I had forgotten you – you should have forgotten me.'

He saw her head shake, as if in personal crisis. 'It doesn't matter why. I'm here and he's here. That'll have to be good enough.'

The doctor said, 'All very charming, but hardly relevant. I think we should get on with it, or I won't be cleaning your leg, sir, I'll be taking it off. Now, do you want me here or do you want me to bugger off?'

Caleb felt the smile wreathe his face and he heard his own soft-spoken voice: 'I'm very grateful to you. Don't look at my face. I thank you for coming. Lose my face from your mind. I appreciate what you do for me.'

'I'm going to talk you through it, each stage of it. Your head wound is clean, a direct shrapnel strike, but below your headcloth. Not so the leg wound. It is dirty, infected, with the early stages of gangrene. In the wound is sand grit, probably small stones, maybe missile fragments, certainly pieces from your robe will be buried deep in it. It has to be cleaned and all of the detritus has to come out. I intend to use Cetrimide as a cleaning agent, and I will inject a local anaesthetic –

Lignocaine – into the muscle around the wound. Its location is good, too low for nerve damage and the wrong side of your leg for the principal arteries, and the muscle has protected the bones from splintering. Later, when I've worked on the wound, I will inject you with antibiotics, Ampicillin is what I carry. I see you have reading material. I advise you to use it. In spite of the Lignocaine, this is going to hurt like hell. Are you ready?'

The question must have been in Caleb's eyes.

'What's worrying me most – not who or what you are, sir – is that bloody item up in the sky, hunting and searching. We've her vehicle and mine and no cover for them, which is a good enough reason for getting on with it. Do I make a start?'

Caleb nodded. He lifted the manual, the words on the page dancing in his eyes, and he felt the first needle plunge into his flesh.

Chapter Seventeen

The face above Caleb was impassive. He saw it above the manual held tight in his hands. He tried to read. To read, he thought, was to escape from the pain and – what was worse than the pain – his dependence on the doctor.

He read of the launcher assembly with a missile, the grip stock, the IFF interrogator and the argon gas battery coolant unit. Words played across his eyes, which blurred. Target adaptive guidance circuit, azimuth coverage ... it was their world. Their technology, their skill, their power ... He was a man who had fought from ditches and trenches, from caves and scraped holes in the dirt, from the cages of a cell block. Their technology, their skill dwarfed him, and their power could crush him. The face hovered over him, and the pain sought out each nerve in his body. He could only fight, nothing more was left to him: fight or die, fight or be forgotten. His eyes, watering, fastened on the caption line: 'Engagement Procedure'. The moisture in his eyes blinded him and he looked away from the page. The last thing he had read, before the mist closed on his vision, was 'Training requires 136 hours of instruction before weapon qualification is given.' He did not have the hours, did not have the instructor, did not have the knowledge. He looked up.

'What is your name?'

'Samuel Bartholomew – I would not claim to have friends, but acquaintances call me Bart. Won't be long, the Lignocaine works quickly.'

'Have you looked long enough at my face to remember it?'

He saw the doctor flinch.

'I never remember a face – whatever that bloody book is, just read it.'

Behind the doctor, squatting at the edge of the awning's shade, the woman bit her lip. He understood so little, not why the doctor had come, not why she had cared enough to bring him. They were no part of him, either of them.

'Can you wipe my eyes?'

She did.

Caleb read again. First the system was shouldered, then the battery coolant unit was slotted into the grip stock, then the IFF antenna was unfolded. The target, if visible, was interrogated by the AN-PPX-1 system. The IFF switch is depressed and locks on the target. Depress the impulse-generator switch, and 6000 PSI pressurized argon gas flows to the IR detector. Did it bloody matter? Did it matter to him how their technology worked? What mattered was whether the bloody thing fired. Again he stared into the doctor's face. 'What am I to you?'

He saw a slow smile settle at the doctor's mouth.

A third time, the needle was raised. The manual was all he had. If the aircraft came back – hunted for them and found them – and the boy heard it, he must use the weapon and know the manual's procedures. He started again to read the close print below the caption – shoulder the system, insert the battery coolant unit, unfold the IFF antenna, depress the impulse-generator switch, listen for the audio signal telling of target acquisition. He felt the growing deadness in his leg and the dulling of the pain. Chubby white fingers gripped the syringe, held it poised.

He could see, beyond the doctor, beyond her and behind the guide, that the boy sat alone, his head cocked. He thought the boy listened: he was cross-legged with his back straight and his chin raised. If the aircraft hunted for them and found them, the boy was the first line of defence. If Caleb was to reach his family, he needed the boy as much as he depended on the doctor.

Caleb did not know if the weapon would fire, if it had passed its shelf life. His family waited for him. In a single-storey building of concrete blocks, or in a cave, they waited. He seemed to see men rise up and their arms were outstretched and they held him and hugged him; they gave him the welcome that was the heart of a family. He tried to cry out, as if to tell his family that he came, but had no voice . . . He walked away from the family that he cared for, that he was a part of. He wore a suit and a clean shirt, with a tie, and his shoes were polished, and he came through a great concourse of people – none of them saw him as they flowed around him – and he carried a suitcase or a grip or had a traveller's rucksack hitched on his shoulder, and he yearned for the praise of his family, and he prayed to hear the screamed terror of those his family hated.

He read the pages, memorized them. The needle came down. The woman tried to hold his hand but it would not free itself from the manual's pages. He felt the pain of the needle.

The total dose of local anaesthetic, split between three injections, was – and Bart had carefully measured it – twenty millilitres of one per cent of Lignocaine.

He could, so easily, have killed him.

As a rabid dog was shot, so Bart could have ended the life of the man whose face he had looked into, whose name he did not know. He could have said that the brute was a violent fanatic, raging with a desire to murder. He eased the needle into the left side flesh of the wound, where the blackened gangrene had taken deepest hold. A total dose of forty millilitres of two per cent Lignocaine would have put down the rabid brute. The dog would have gone into spasm, then been on the irreversible process towards death. Instead, Bart had measured out what was necessary to spare the dog pain. Too many had walked over Bart. He was not their servant. He thought the young man handsome. There was a quality about him, Bart thought, that the stubble on his face, the tangle of hair above his eyes, their brightness, and the dirt encrusted round his mouth did not mask. Flitting into his mind was his own boy. The boy who loved his mother, loved Ann. The boy who had taken the owner of the Saab franchise to be a proxy father. The boy who had never looked into his face after the dawn visit of the police. He could justify himself.

He used the cleaning agent, Cetrimide, slopped it into the wound, and began to dab with the lint. 'This is going to hurt, going to hurt worse as I go on. I've used all the painkiller that's possible.'

He sensed that the head nodded behind the manual. He did not think that the man would cry out. Perhaps an intake of hissed breath, maybe a gasp, stifled . . . He cut deeper into the wound pit, poured more of the Cetrimide into it, swabbed, then manoeuvred the forceps over the first pieces of grit and stone, and took them out. The woman's hand was over the man's fist but his eyes never left the printed page. Bart went deeper. He cut, swabbed, retrieved. He knelt beside his patient and the sweat slaked off him. He thought it extra-ordinary that the man did not cry out, but had known he would not. She held the hand tight. Bart could have told her she served no purpose, that the man did not need her as comforter. He found the pieces of cotton, embedded, and lifted each of them out, had to cut again to find their root. Any other man that Bart had known would have fainted. Himself, probably his heart would have stopped . . . Debridement was from the battlefield surgery of the Napoleonic wars, with patients either insensible from shock or dosed with brandy or biting on a peg of wood or leather. No gasp, no hiss for breath. He searched for more cotton fibre, stone, grit, a fragment of the missile, and heard the rustle of a page turned. No man that Bart had ever met could have endured it without protest. Bart had reckoned he might have to kneel on his patient's ankles and have the woman hold down one arm and the older Bedouin the other arm, grip him so that he could not struggle as the scalpel went in and the forceps probed. Not necessary.

'You're doing well,' he murmured. 'We're getting there.' He was sodden with sweat.

He went to work on the gangrene. It was neither pretty nor delicate work. Not at medical school, certainly not in the practice at Torquay, not even in the villages around Jenin had he performed such primitive surgery before. He was guided by old memories of books read long ago, and his instincts. Bart sliced at the flesh, cut slivers from it, then flicked the scalpel blade to the side, ditched it behind him. The woman flushed. A section of flesh, poorly dis-carded, had fallen on to her ankle. Her eyes were screwed up at the sight of it. She would have felt its diseased wetness on her skin. He cut again. Still there was no cry and no hiss of breath. Closest to the wound the flesh was black. Away from the wound it was darkened. Layer upon layer of it he sliced away. He reached out, took the piece from her ankle and threw it further. The flesh, scattered behind him, brought flies in a feeding frenzy. He cut to pink, rosy flesh, and to clean skin.

He was weak when he finished. 'Well done.'

The whispered response through clenched teeth: 'I didn't do anything.'

'Well done for not thrashing around.'

'Would have made it slower, more pain for me and more difficult for you.'

Bart did what was forbidden, looked into the face. It was ravaged. The eyes stared out, great lines furrowed the forehead and the muscles bulged on the neck. He thought that whatever this man, terrorist, rabid dog or freedom-fighter, set out to achieve he would succeed in it.

'I can't give you any more Lignocaine because that would kill you. I'm going to close it up, not totally. Superficial sutures to hold the skin's edges, but it has to be open so that any further pus can get clear. Later we'll do an antibiotic injection, and if the pain is unmanageable by this evening I'll try a morphine jab.'

'Why am I still alive?'

Bart grimaced. 'Why indeed . . .'

Al Maz'an village, near Jenin, Occupied West Bank.

The helicopter belched the rocket. It had made one pass, a slow circle above the village, then steadied and fired. The flame creased behind the rocket, was vivid against the cloud. He had been locking his vehicle when he heard and saw it. He had watched its circle and known what would follow. The flame speared towards the village roofs.

Bart could not see its target, but knew it. The rocket – then another, then a third – dived, exploded, devastated, and threw up a mushroom cloud of dirt, dust and rubble.

He ran. It was expected of him that he should run. His cover demanded of him that he run.

He ran across the square and into a wide street, went towards the medical centre in the yard of the village's school. He knew what he would find in the alley, opposite the collapsed telephone pole. He did not look up, did not see the helicopter turn away. He would find a hole that smoked and burned, and around it would be collapsed rubble. The hole would be like the black gap when a tooth fell out. The rockets from the helicopter were always fired with precision. The crowd spilled from the alley, a wasp storm. A fist, where the crowd was densest, held up a mobile telephone. The scream of the crowd reached him. He saw her . . . tens of arms held her and snatched at her. She was supine and did not struggle. He thought of her as thirtyish, no more than forty. The hands had dislodged the scarf from her head. He did not know whether she was an agent, of lesser importance than himself, or whether she was merely an innocent who had used her mobile telephone while the helicopter had made its first circling pass. An agent or an innocent, she was doomed. Hysteria would kill her. He did not know whether she was a wife, a mother. She went with the crowd and Bart was pushed aside, half crushed into a doorway. She was taken towards the square. Bart saw her eyes. She was condemned but her eyes had peace. He thanked his God for it. He thought the shock of her capture had destroyed the fear. The moment that their eyes met was a split second, then she was gone, at the core of the baying crowd.

He went on.

At the collapsed telephone pole, Bart turned into the alley. The missing tooth had been a home, was now a crater, and the two floors of the homes on either side of it were exposed. Sleeping rooms were opened up. Beds hung angled over the crater, and more rubble had fallen in the alley. Dust had coated the lime-green Fiat. Men dug and crawled in the crater. He heard the low, keening moan and knew there was no work for a doctor here.

First two children were carried out.

A woman's corpse followed them.

With reverence, a man's body was lifted clear.

He saw the frozen face of the man who had sat in the rear seat of the Fiat. It had been on the second page, at the top rank, of the most sensitive fugitives. Now the face was like a circus clown's, coated with the white dust of the plaster of the interior walls. The dust made a mask for the face and death had distorted none of the features. No wound disturbed it: strength was written on it, and he fancied there was honesty. Bart turned away, and pressed his hand against his throat to suppress vomit.

He did not dare to walk back through the square. He had not the courage to go past the scaffolding erected in front of the square's principal building.

An hour later, Bart sagged from the chair.

He went down on to the hut floor and the coffee he'd held spilled on to the boards.

He wept.

Only Joseph saw him.

On his knees and on his elbows, his body quivering from the tears, he heard the beat of Joseph's words. 'You did well. For us you are a jewel. A man who was a murderer was liquidated because of your bravery. You are responsible for the saving of many lives. Listen, Bart, we regret the deaths of two children and a woman in the house. We regret also that a lynch mob has killed a woman they believe guilty of treachery to their society. Two children and two women are set on the scales against the lives of many. You are a hero to us. I tell you, Bart, beside Jerusalem's Mount Herzl is the Yad Vashem memorial where we remember our own and their suffering, and also remembered there are the honoured foreigners who have helped our survival, and your name—'

'I don't want that fucking crap,' Bart sobbed. 'I am gone. I'm finished.'

'I thank you for what you have done.'

Back at his home, he packed. One suitcase for his clothes, a medical bag, a cardboard box for the cat and a plastic bag of tinned food for it. He wrote the note and pinned it to the door. 'Mother seriously ill in England. Returning there. God watch over you. Your friend, Samuel Bartholomew.' He had arrived on an untruth, had lived on an untruth, and left on an untruth. He was gone before dusk fell on the village, driving with wet eyes, and two patrol vehicles discreetly escorted him down tracks and along roads and he was only clear of them when he had gone through the check-point. All the way to Tel Aviv, blazoned in his mind, was the image of the dust-coated face, at peace, of the fighter he had killed.

The book dropped from his hands. Beth saw the pain break over him. She looked around. If he had cried out it would have helped her, yet he did not. He lay on his back and gasped. At a distance, beside the knelt camels, the guide watched, and close to him was the broken-open crate from which the manual had been retrieved. The face was in shadow and she could not see the eyes or the mouth and did not know what he thought. If a spotlight had been shone on his face she doubted she would know what he thought. Further back, erect and statue still, was the boy.

Did it matter what anyone thought? Beth, as teenager and adult, had never cared for advice, counsel, guidance. She knew her mind: it did not tax her if a road or a street flowed past her and mouthed disapproval, if the crowds of a town, a city, condemned her judgement. She was her own person and the innate stubbornness of character brooked no criticism. She was beside a killer whose eyes had closed.

She slipped away from him, out from under the awning, and went towards the drone of the snoring.

At his vehicle, where the doctor lay on the seat depressed to its full extent, she snapped open the door. His mouth was open, gaped wide, and the snoring brought spittle to his mouth. The shirt clung to his body and on his lap was a chocolate-bar wrapping, not shared with the rest of them. She punched his arm. He snorted, convulsed and then was awake.

'God – what did you do that for?'

'He's in pain,' Beth said.

The arm smeared the sweat off his face. 'Of course he's in pain. A bloody great hole like that, the flesh I took out of it and its depth – what do you expect if not pain?'

'You talked about morphine.'

'Talked about morphine this evening. My experience, Miss Jenkins, pain seldom kills. Morphine does, often.'

'He doesn't cry out,' she said, a trill of bewilderment.

'And further experience tells me, Miss Jenkins, that the reaction to pain explains more about the patient than about the injury.'

'I don't understand what you're saying.' She was unsure, her voice was small, her guard was down.

He attacked. 'That's rich – like my favourite Christmas present. I am introduced by you to a war casualty who talks in delirium and confusion about mass murder. By you, I am nagged to save this creature's life. And you don't know who he is, don't know what mayhem he plans to inflict – don't know anything except you've an itch you want to scratch. What do you think he's going to do when I've got him up on his feet and hobbling forward? Is he going to give you a loving kiss? Get you to wrap your thighs round his neck? Or walk away from you like you never existed?'

She trembled. 'How much morphine would you give him?'

He clutched her hand and she felt the slithering wet of his palm.

'None, if I can get away with it. If I decide that he must sleep, cannot because of the pain, then I will inject between ten and twenty milligrams.'

'Not more, if the pain's bad?'

'It's an equation, Miss Jenkins – it's about getting the sums right. Too little, and the pain continues. Too much, and respiration is fatally slowed and the myocardium, that's the heart muscle, is depressed, ceases to operate and death follows.'

'Yes.'

'It is not my intention to overdose him on morphine.'

'No.'

'If it's not a problem to you, I would like to resume my rest.'

His eyes had closed and his head was averted, his chin sagged and his mouth opened. She left him. She went past the boy, who did not look at her, stayed intent on his concentration. She looked up and saw only the clearness of the sky, blue, and she raked it till her eyes burned on the sun. The boy's father ducked out from under the awning, but did not meet her gaze. She realized it: she was alone. She skirted the camels and bent to go under the awning. He was propped up and had the pieces on his lap, and the manual. When he saw her, he waved her away – like she was flotsam.

He had the manual and the pieces. Across his lap was the launch tube with a missile inserted, and the battery coolant unit; he looked for the slot into which it would be inserted. Beside him, on the sacking, was the beltpack that housed the IFF interrogator unit, and next he would find the plug in the grip stock where its cable went.

He beat the pain.

The wound oozed but did not bleed.

He had seen the disappointment cloud her face. He had no interest in her. He did not see where she went, where she sat. He had no need of her.

When Caleb had found the slot and the plug socket, he rehearsed the firing procedure. His eyes flitted between the grip stock and the manual.

His finger rested on the impulse-generator switch, then the button controlling the seeker uncage bar. Then it rested gently on the trigger. He read of the less-than-two-second response time between the trigger pull and the missile's launch. He imagined the fire flash and the lurched first stage of the missile's ejection from the tube, then the blast of the second stage, then the climbing hunt for the target.

Again and again, his pain controlled and his finger steady, Caleb rehearsed the preparations for firing. Without the missile he would not reach his family ... but he did not know whether its time wrapped in an oiled covering had decayed it.

Getting to his family was his goal, his reason for survival.

The courier had been and had gone. The sentry, low down in the rocks in front of the cave's entrance, scanned the desert's expanse. The courier had reached the cave after the first prayers at dawn and had left before the prayers at midday. He had brought with him a sealed, lead-encased container – the size of a water bucket – and had taken away with him finely rolled cigarette papers on which coded messages were written in minute script.

The heat shimmered the sands in front of the sentry, but he squinted, looked ahead and watched for them.

For midday prayers, men had emerged blinking from the cave, and one had held up the compass so that the direction of Makkah would be exact and not an estimation. They had prayed, then returned to the dark recesses.

The sentry had watched the courier in, had watched him out and away over the emptiness of the sands, and had not prayed. He had stayed hidden among the rocks with the rifle always in his hand and with the machine-gun, loaded with belt ammunition, close against his knee. During prayers, an eagle had wheeled high over the escarpment where the cave was. The sentry's eyes ached as he looked for a sign of their coming.

If they came in daylight he would have long warning of them. He would see a speck of movement, then the shape of a small caravan would materialize. If they came in darkness he would see them, from three or four kilometres away, on the night vision glasses, Russian military, that hung from his neck. They were late.

They were late by four days.

But four days mattered little to the sentry and to the men inside the cave whom he guarded. The war was without end. He did not doubt that they would come, but he hoped fervently that they would come during his long watch, not after he was relieved. His eyes scraped over the sands and little images danced in his mind, small hallucinations, but he did not see the caravan. Their importance was to be measured by the ordeal they endured, crossing the Empty Quarter for secrecy and the preservation of their security. He wanted to be the first to greet and welcome them.

He watched for them, as he had watched for each of the four days since they had been due. He searched the sands that were without limit for the caravan. But he saw only the desert and the dunes, heard only the silence . . . They would come, he was sure of it. Their importance, in the war without end was too great for them to fail the journey . . . and the one of greatest importance, he had heard it whispered while he rested in the cave's depths, was the one who would carry the suitcase when it was loaded with the content of the container the courier had brought that morning. That was a man to be greeted and welcomed.

Billy Boy said, 'He was all right when the boss brought him in. He was OK then, but he changed. Then he was shit. When he changed he hadn't the time of day for us. Don't expect me to care, not if Caleb Hunt's got trouble on his doorstep.'

Half a pace behind Lovejoy, Jed stood and absorbed. Lovejoy's way, as lectured in the Volvo, was to begin at the bottom and work up. It was the explanation as to why they were not knocking at a front door and interviewing a family, but instead were in the workshop of a grimy car-repair business. He had seen a derelict gasworks to the right side of the complex built in a passed-over factory, and a once-fine church on the left side with graffiti sprayed over the plywood covering the windows. Jed thought the place reeked of failure. But flesh now stretched on the skeleton that was Caleb Hunt – and on the taxi-driver, Fawzi al-Ateh, who had sat across a table from him at Delta, in his interrogation room, and who had screwed him.

Vinnie said, 'We helped him when he started. When he didn't know a carburettor from a clutch, we covered for him and treated him like he was one of us. He was learning, he was good, then it all went sour. One day he was fine, then it was like we weren't good enough for him.'

They came forward in turn, called out from under a bodywork

chassis and from the examination pit, and they talked with what he believed to be utter honesty – and confusion – and almost a trace of sadness. It was as if they had been rejected and still wore the marks of it. Each, his name called, came and shuffled awkwardly and spoke of the man who had duped Camp Delta's finest, and him. It made hard listening for Jed.

Wayne said, 'He told us, at the end, the day he left, that the work bored him and that the boss bored him, and that *we* bored him. You know, I'd shared sandwiches with him and my towel, shared bloody everything with him, but we were crap – we were beneath him. He let us know, not laughing at us but arrogant-like, we were second-rate and he wasn't.'

They moved into the inner office. Files and worksheets were dumped off chairs for them. He remembered the docile, humble young man – light skinned, but so were many Afghans – who had been a taxi-driver and he thought it remarkable that the lie had been sustained against all the pressure that Camp Delta had thrown at him. Jed had never before been on a field investigation: his life had been spent behind a desk, a suspect in front of him or a computer screen. He admired the quietly spoken expertise of Lovejoy, who started men talking and never interrupted them. A kettle whistled, instant coffee was doled into mugs, the water was poured and milk added from a bottle. Jed knew flesh on the skeleton would now become features.

The boss said, 'I gave him the chance because Perkins asked it of me. Perkins taught me and my wife and taught our girl. Perkins got him the chance. It's not the top of the tree, but it's a start. If a lad wants to work, and to learn, then I'll give him a damn good apprenticeship. Won't pay him much, but a start's a start, and a trained engine mechanic is in work for life. For two and a half years he was good as gold and it had got to the stage where I'd give him my best customers, my regulars, for services and MOTs, and he'd do all God's hours ... Don't quote me, but I was going to put him in charge of that lot. He had what it takes, the leadership thing. He could take responsibility, seemed to enjoy it. Good with customers. They liked him because he told them it straight – you know, "Your motor's a wreck, sir, and us fixing it is just chucking good money after bad," or "No, we can do that, sir, do it over the weekend – I'll come in Saturday and Sunday and do it." People had started to ask for him. Whether it was an engine strip or knocking out a front-wing dent from a shunt, people used to say, "I'd like Caleb to do it." Then it all went pear-shaped. There was two lads started to hang around for him. First they'd be outside, then they used to drift in and sit around, talk to him while he was working. I should have told them to piss off, but I didn't – suppose I thought Caleb would walk out on me. Shouldn't have bothered. He did. They were Pakistani boys. Don't go getting me wrong. I'm not a racial nut – plenty round here that are, but I'm not one of them. They had a hold on him. At the end, they'd show up and he'd just down tools – whatever he was doing – and he'd be gone. No more weekends and no more Sundays either, and half the Fridays he was gone. There was this Tuesday, and they came in for him. I was going to fire him that evening anyway, would have done it a month earlier if it hadn't been for old Perkins. They came in late morning, and he went off and wiped his hands – and we were busy as sin – and he told me, like my problems didn't matter to him, that he'd be gone for a couple of weeks. I told him he could be gone for a couple of months or a couple of years because there wouldn't be a job here when he came back. Both the Pakistanis were laughing at me, but not Caleb. I turned my back on him and I went in the office. He followed me. Nobody else saw it. He'd this spanner in his hand and his fingers were all white round it. God's my witness, I thought he was going to belt me, I reckoned he'd lost it – then he put the spanner down. You know what it was? I'd said he was sacked. He was not in control, and he couldn't take it. What I saw in his eyes, when he had that spanner, he'd have killed me and just walked like nothing had happened . . . I don't know why you're interested in Caleb Hunt, and don't suppose you'd tell me if I asked. No, of course . . . Oh, the lads who used to come round for him, one's called Farooq, and his dad's got a restaurant down on their estate. Amin is the name of the other one, don't know what he does. You see, there's very few white boys are close to Asians, but they all come from the same street. Sorry, gents, but I've got a business to run.'

They went outside where the sky seemed to merge with the grime of the old brickwork.

'It was the capital of the country's old engineering industry,' Lovejoy said.

'What have we got?' Jed asked.

'And it's all gone, the engineering industry. You know, just down the road from here they made the *Titanic*'s anchor chains . . . What have we got? I'd say we've got enough to lose sleep over.'

'Much sleep?'

'Persuasive leadership and pride, violence and vanity, commitment and courage – doesn't that stack up to a sleepless night? Come on, I'm hungry.'

They walked briskly towards the car, but Jed wasn't done. 'I can see him, clear as yesterday, in my room.'

'But he's not there, is he? He's lost and he needs killing. He's not in your room. Do you eat curry?'

Marty flew the map boxes. The chart on the work-surface lay between his joystick and her console keyboard. Each time they'd covered a box, she'd reach across with her Chinagraph pen and make a black cross on it. There were guys at Bagram who did mine clearance and they used map boxes, not of a mile square but of ten yards square, and they crossed out the sections of the map they believed they'd cleared. The guys said that the sections wouldn't be a place to take a picnic because they could never be certain they'd not missed one. It was like that with the boxes on the chart: they could have missed a target and flown on. Below the new line of black crosses were the red exclamation marks she'd made, four in two boxes, one mark for each firing of a Hellfire. He thought that when he brought *Carnival Girl* back for the last time – the late morning of tomorrow – he'd route her over the exclaimers and give himself a last look at the craters, freshen his memory of them before he climbed up into the big transport aircraft.

The wind made for good flying conditions; the one problem was the thermals coming up off the sand, which made *Carnival Girl* sluggish to commands. What he'd learned and what he'd tell them at the Bagram debrief, the heat from the ground killed the infra-red, but the real-time camera showed acceptable pictures for her to look at . . . They were alone.

For once, they did not have Langley with them. Two hours before, Oscar Golf had signed off, telling them he was going for a shower and food. Could they manage on their own? He'd seen Lizzy-Jo smile and heard the clear rasp of her voice. Yes, they could manage on their own.

Maybe Marty's hand slipped, sweat on the joystick. Maybe his fingers were numbed from holding the stick. *Carnival Girl*'s picture jolted, and she swore, and the picture dived.

'You OK?'

'I'm fine.'

'What I mean is, are you really OK?'

'I'm really fine.'

'No kidding?'

'I'm good and fine and I'm grateful – can't say more.'

She stretched, touched his hand on the joystick and her nails indented on the veins at the back of his hand, which shook a moment, and *Carnival Girl* plunged another two hundred feet. She was giggling like a girl and Marty felt the smile fill his face. He was grateful because he had blipped, grateful because she had kicked the blip hard. He owed her his thanks. It was between them. He had certainty that the collapse of his morale after he had flown in pursuit of the old man was a story she would never tell. And he would never tell that she had come to his tent and had bedded him on his cot. He would go back to Bagram and the coffins off the transporter would be unpacked and technicians and ground crew would stand around and admire the skull-and-crossbones symbols adorning *First Lady* and *Carnival Girl*, and his own crew and his own technicians would recite stories of the killing, wasting, of Al Qaeda men in the desert of the Rub' al Khālī. He might even let them know, at Bagram, it had not been easy flying.

Languidly, that was how she flew. *Carnival Girl* climbed in response to the joystick's command, without enthusiasm. Alongside him, like she recognized he had come through the depression, she had the blouse unbuttoned and she hung loose, but he didn't look at her a lot, more at the screen above the stick. If he had found something in the Sands she would have alerted him and zoomed on it and he would have done a figure eight over it, but she didn't, and there was only the pure windblown shapes of the dunes on the screen, and the emptiness – utter emptiness. A couple of hours back, when Oscar Golf had gone for his shower and food, she'd asked him if he'd need a pill to keep him going till he brought *Carnival Girl* back the next midday. He hadn't wanted a pill, he could last.

He thought they might, because she was old and ancient, put *Carnival Girl* in a museum. Useful life gone, stripped of what was valuable but put on show. Schoolkids might come round her with teachers, and hold maps of Kosovo, Afghanistan and Saudi Arabia. The kids would gather at the forward fuselage, where the skull-and-crossbones was stencilled on it, and the teacher would talk about the men and women who defended the United States of America and about the hunting down of the country's enemies. He dreamed . . .

'So, are we flying or not?'

On the screen he saw the dive, and arrested it – then grimaced. 'Sorry.'

'Stop playing deadhead. I'm telling you, we're flying until the last hour, the last minute, of fuel. We're keeping her up all night and through tomorrow morning. We're going till the tanks are dry. It's the way it is. Always there's one more map box – it's Murphy's law, always the next box where the action is. We're with this until the end.'

'Got you.'

He thought of the man she had drunk with in the bar behind Fifth Avenue, and of the phone ringing out unanswered on the high floor of the North Tower, and of the bodies of the jumpers that seemed to float but came on down. Then he wiped his mind clear and flew *Carnival Girl* on towards the next map box. When the day died, they would reach the boxes alongside the track marked on the chart, do the east side of it in the night, and by dawn they would be over the track. Then time for the west side of it, and one last line of boxes over desert, before he turned her for home.

Far from him, but under his command, the Predator's lens ate the Sands.

He had waited an hour in the car park, but the bastard hadn't shown. It was the first time that the weasel, Bartholomew, had stood him up. For an hour he had sat in his car, in the far corner of the car park, and the wait had been fruitless.

He had driven to the surgery, had stamped through an empty waiting room and confronted the receptionist. Where was he? There had been a message on the answerphone the previous morning telling her to cancel all existing appointments for three days, but she had not known where he was. And, staring at the scars on his face, she had told him that he could either go in the book for three days' time, when there was a window, or she could give him the name of another doctor if his complaints were urgent. He had stormed out. Never before had Bartholomew left town without warning.

His finger on the doorbell, Eddie Wroughton stood on the step at the villa's front door beside the empty carport. The maid came.

He pushed past her. A cat, obviously a stray, stood its ground in the hallway, arched its back and hissed defiance. He kicked at it, missed.

Where was he? The maid scowled, hostile as the cat, then shrugged. She did not know.

He was trained to check over a room, a villa. The maid followed him, but did not watch what he did – only stared at his face.

'Something wrong with me, is there?' Wroughton snarled.

She broke away, fled for the kitchen.

In his mind was an inventory, not of what he found but of what was not there.

Bartholomew's medical bag – gone. He forced open the drugs cabinet in the bedroom – the lower shelf was half emptied. He broke into the cupboard beside the cabinet – no operating kit there, and the packets of lint and bandages had been rifled through, as if some had been taken hurriedly. From the kitchen, stepping over the treacherously wet floor that the maid had mopped, he went into the utility room; he remembered from the one time he had been to the villa that Bartholomew kept water and fuel there. No water canister and no fuel can.

Back in the living room, alongside the chair where the cat had taken refuge, Wroughton lifted the phone and dialled the call back. The answer came in Arabic digits for the last number that had called. He was about to write it on the pad beside the phone when he checked himself and scrawled it on the back of his hand around an abrasion that was now scabbed. He tore off the top sheet and slipped it carefully into the breast pocket of his last linen suit.

He rang his office in the embassy, gave his instructions to his assistant, told her the telephone number. Where had that call originated from?

Wroughton looked around him, saw the bareness of Bartholomew's life. Nothing there that was personal. Rented furniture, hired fittings – as if his soul had been eradicated. How could it have been different? It came to him like a jolting blow, as violent as any of the agronomist's kicks and punches: he himself had pulled his telephone plug from the wall socket, he had switched off his mobile while he had sat naked in his own room, among his own rented furniture and hired fittings.

On his way out of the living room, going past the settee beside the door, he lifted a cushion and threw it at the chair where the cat was, but when it landed the cat had gone.

Wroughton slammed the front door shut after him.

He asked, in the new language of his life, 'How long?' The dark had settled under the awning. He could barely see the doctor's face.

The voice from the shadowed mouth was crisp. 'Let's not fuck about. You speak the Queen's English as well as I do. I haven't the faintest idea what you're asking me. In your condition, and if you want my further help, I would suggest you end the charade. You're English – if you want answers you will speak in English. So, let's start again.'

Caleb shook. He thought the doctor knelt on the manual and that his thigh pressed the launcher against Caleb's good leg. As he remembered, he had last spoken English in the taxi on his way to the wedding. Through the dusty streets of Landi Khotal, bumping in the back of the taxi, squashed between his friends and nervous, he had spoken English – but not since.

As if he walked a new road, he spoke with soft hesitation: 'How long before I can move?'

'That's better, wasn't so difficult, eh? You spoke English when you were in extreme pain. How long? Depends what you want to achieve. If you want to get off these stinking unhygienic sacks and go have a piss, because you've drained out four saline drip bags, you could probably manage that now. I'm sure Miss Jenkins will support your arm while you do it.'

'How long before I can move away?'

'If you're going in Miss Jenkins's vehicle, I suppose you could move straight after you've had your piss.'

'By camel?'

'Still the adventurer. I believe I could have you hobbling around in the morning. If it was imperative, and you've slept, you could mount up and head for where the sunset will be – yes, in the morning . . . Is the pain bad?'

'I accept the pain.'

'I can give you morphine for it.'

'No. When I spoke, what did I say?'

'If you're intent on riding a camel tomorrow I suggest I inject you now intravenously with Ampicillin, an antibiotic, then another dose at midnight, another at dawn and one more when you head off. In addition I will give you what syringes I have, because you should take four a day for three days.'

'What did I say?'

'After that, because your arm will be a pincushion, you can take it orally – again it's five hundred milligrams a dose, four times a day.'

'You saw my face?'

'Difficult not to have, young man, when I'm bent over you and scraping that crap out of your leg – difficult not to have seen your face, and difficult not to have heard what you said. Right, let's get it into you.'

His arm was lifted and the fingers held his wrist just below the plastic bracelet. He felt the cool damp of the swab, then saw the movement, felt the prick of the needle.

The needle was withdrawn. He heard the grunting as the man pushed himself heavily up.

'You have to sleep. I'll jab you again at midnight, but you must sleep through it. Sweet dreams, my nameless friend.'

Caleb heard his shoes scuff away in the sand. He would not sleep and would not dream. He did not know what he had said, knew only that the doctor had seen his face. He tossed and the pain in his leg surged. He remembered the men who had seen his face, and all were gone. To see his face was to die. And he remembered the old man who had ridden the donkey, who had brought him to the opium smugglers – who was blind and had not seen his face – and he thought the lifeless eyes might have saved the old man.

To have seen his face was to be condemned. The doctor had.

Caleb shuddered and the pain racked him. So had the woman.

Chapter Eighteen

It was the start of the last day. Caleb was jolted from his sleep. A hand lifted his arm. It had been a fitful sleep, without calm. The swab wetted the skin. From instinct, because he was touched, he flinched and tried to break the grip.

'Easy, young man, easy. Don't fight me.'

The doctor's voice was soft in his ear. Then the needle went in. He gazed up and saw the outline of the man's face and above it the dark ceiling of the awning.

'Had you slept long?'

Caleb nodded.

'That's good. Funny, but sleep is a better healer than any drug. It's good that you slept and you must sleep again.'

The needle was withdrawn. His arm was lowered gently. He remembered what he had thought before the sleep had caught him.

'Why do you help me?'

The shape towered above him. 'The question, young man, is becoming repetitive. You care not to tell me your name, and I care not to burden you with reasoning for my actions. You get your next injection at dawn. Go back to sleep.'

Caleb started up, tried to push himself higher on his elbows, to raise his back. 'That's not good enough.'

'It isn't good enough that I don't know your name, don't know where you come from, don't know where you're going and what your intentions are when you get there. Don't tell me, young man, what's "good enough" and what's not.'

He was gone. Caleb sagged. The body of the launcher was against his leg. When he had slept he had forgotten it and the pain in his leg, and he had forgotten that to see his face was to be condemned.

The kindness of the doctor and the devotion of the woman who had brought help to him did not compete with the demand of and his obligation to the family. It would be weakness if he did not destroy them. He lay on his back under the awning and felt the throb in his leg and the hammer of the pulse from the antibiotic injection. The doctor and the woman were trifles when set against the importance of the family: they had seen his face. They were condemned. They stood between him and his duty. He let his hand fall beside him, and beyond the edge of the sacking bed, his fingers lifted a pinch of sand grains and he held his hand above his chest and the sand ran from it, fell on him – not one grain of sand but a thousand. A great crowd, not one person but a thousand, passed him and among them were the doctor who was kind and the woman who was devoted. He could not cherry-pick among the crowd he walked through with a suitcase or a grip bag or a rucksack, could not say that some were his enemy and some were not – could not extricate the doctor and the woman from the crowd. To do so would be a betrayal of the family, would show weakness.

In the morning, when the doctor had given him the strength to stand and when the woman had supported his first hobbling steps – as hesitant as when the chain shackles had been on his ankles at Camp Delta – he would go to the guide, take the rifle from him, arm it, and do what was necessary to prove to the dead, to Hosni, Fahd and Tommy, that he was not weak.

He drifted back towards sleep.

He was at peace, because the strength had not deserted him. He felt no shame because he would not have recognized the man he had been before. He was his family's man.

*

'Tell me about him.' It was not a request from Lovejoy but an instruction.

They were at the table alongside the one at which Lovejoy and the American had eaten. Farooq's father had taken their order and Farooq had served them. They had eaten slowly, then lingered over their coffee as, around them, the restaurant had cleared, and father, son and other waiters had wiped down the tables and tilted the chairs. The shadows had closed on them and only their tablecloth, cups and empty glasses were lit. Lovejoy could play polite and could play domination. When the last customers had paid up and gone out into the wet night, when only they were there, Lovejoy had raised his hand and snapped his fingers imperiously for attention. The father had hurried to them. Lovejoy had said, 'We can do this here or we can do it down the road at the police station under anti-terrorist legislation. We can do it comfortably here or we can do it after they have spent a night in the cells. I want to talk to your son and to your son's friend, Amin. If you try to bluster me with lawyers sitting in, it will be straight down to the police station. You do it the straightforward way or you do it the difficult way . . . and my colleague and I would like more coffee. Thank you.' The friend had been sent for, looked as though he had been roused from his bed.

The young men, Farooq and Amin, had shivered as they sat at the table beside them, and Farooq's father had hovered at the edge of the light before Lovejoy had waved him away. He played domination. He was brusque to the point of rudeness because that was the tactic he had decided on. He could hear, very faintly, the slight squealing howl of the turning tape that was on the American's knee, hidden by the tablecloth. His companion's arm was stretched out, lying, apparently casually, on the cloth but close to where the young men sat. The microphone would be inside his cuff.

Lovejoy said, 'I want only the truth. If you lie you'll be going straight to the cells. If you are honest with me you will sleep in your own beds after I've finished with you . . . I start with you, Amin. Tell me about Caleb Hunt, tell me about him before you went to Pakistan, everything about him.'

The response was hesitant and frightened.

He learned about the jubilee estate of houses built to commemorate the first fifty years of Queen Victoria's reign and how

Asian families lived in all the homes of ten streets, but there was one street of terraced houses where four white families lived. He heard about a white schoolkid who had first walked to school with Asian schoolkids, and moved on with them to the Adelaide Comprehensive.

'Caleb was our friend. We didn't have other white friends, just him. But, then, he didn't have white friends – we were his friends. He stood by Farooq when he was bullied. Didn't make any difference, skin colour. Most of the kids at the Adelaide didn't have Asian friends. We kept to ourselves, but Caleb was with us.'

Lovejoy felt that he peeled away layers of skin.

'We had scrapes, nothing much,' Amin said. 'We had trouble – graffiti and sometimes a car radio, and there'd be fights – but he was with us, not the skinhead bastards. We did everything together. Yes, we messed about, we had fun – but not bad trouble. We didn't go into his house. He wasn't happy with that, or his ma wasn't, but he came to our house. We left school and it was different then.'

Lovejoy probed. How was it different?

'I went to college, to get the A levels for a law course. Farooq came here to work for his dad, and Caleb went to the garage. It started about a year later, after I'd got the A levels and I was waiting to go on and do the law bit. We started up again, but we were older, more aware. I mean, you go to the mosque and sometimes there are guest *imams* and they tell you about Afghanistan and about Chechnya, about all the places where Islam is and where it's fighting against oppression, and he used to take Fridays off. He wasn't a Muslim, no. If we went to a mosque in Birmingham, where he wasn't known, then all he had to do was follow us, do what we did and listen. You see, we'd changed. I suppose when we were kids, Farooq and me, we'd rebelled against the Faith. We smoked and drank alcohol, thieved a bit – but we finished that. He came on board with us, did what we did. We were the only friends he had and it was like we were his family, not his ma. We did the evenings together, and if there was a big *imam* speaking in Birmingham we'd collect him from work and we'd drive down in Farooq's car. We heard about the war in Afghanistan, and saw videos of it, and there were more videos of Chechnya and what the Russians were doing to Muslims. Please, you have to believe me, Farooq and me just listened and tried to be better

352

Muslims and have more faith – but he'd come out of the mosque, Caleb would, and he'd be all tensed up. He was most tensed when he'd seen a video of fighting.'

As each layer of skin came away, Lovejoy thought he came nearer to the hidden, reddened mass that held the poison.

'He used to say he was so bored, used to say that was real excitement, doing fighting. Yes, we'd talk about it, but didn't take it serious. He hated it here, that's what he told us. He was coming from nowhere and going to nowhere. It all happened quick. We'd heard this *imam* speak about Afghanistan and the need for fighters there, and a couple of guys had gone up, gone forward, at the end of the talk. They weren't boys we knew, and afterwards Caleb said they were the lucky ones, because they were going to get real excitement. I didn't think anything of it, what he'd said. A couple of days later my father had the invitation to this wedding. I suppose we talked about it. We must have told him that Farooq and me were going, and he was all crestfallen, like he was shut out of something he wanted. I suppose we talked about where we were going, the mountains and a wild place . . . Farooq said that he could come with us, why not? Farooq said he could carry our bags, joked it. It was just two weeks. He really wanted to come.'

Lovejoy said, 'Thank you, Amin. Take it up, Farooq, and only the truth.'

'I never saw him so happy. One day he'd wear his own clothes, next day he'd borrow ours – my top and Amin's pants. He liked to walk with us round the street-markets in Landi Khotal. It's chaos there. It's noisy, dirty and smelly, and Caleb said it was fantastic. People knew who he was. Family people knew he wasn't Muslim and knew he was white – didn't seem to make a difference because he wasn't white, not strong white. He merged, he blended. Best thing about him was that he was humble. He said we were lucky, luckier than we knew, to have family like we had – he'd sit down with our family at meals and eat what was put in front of him, and he struggled to learn words, to say how grateful he was. I'd never seen him smile so much, be so happy. But it was coming to an end.'

'The wedding, and then the flight home – then back here?'

'The day after the wedding we were due to get the bus to Islamabad, then the evening flight out. That last day, the wedding, he

353

was all subdued. He wore a suit, a clean shirt and a tie; it was like he was making a statement that he was going home, and we talked a bit in the taxi going to the wedding, but he hadn't much to say – I remember that. At the wedding, inside our family there, all the men knew that Caleb was a stranger, that he didn't belong to our family – however much he'd been welcomed, he was outside our family. I didn't see it at first, the interest in him. It was only when he was called over . . .'

'He was spotted, he was picked out,' Lovejoy nudged.

'A part of the family is from across the border, from Jalalabad in Afghanistan. We think now, Amin and me, that word of Caleb in Landi Khotal had reached Jalalabad before the wedding day. A man was watching him. I have never forgotten that man. Late in the wedding party, the man had Caleb called to him. We believe he was already chosen, but a test was given him. It is a wild place on that frontier, a place of guns and fighters . . . I tell you, sir, I am prepared to go to a mosque in Birmingham and to listen to the fire of an *imam*, but I would not be prepared to go into those mountains and to fight. The test was that he should shoot a rifle and then that he should climb a hill and use the cover of the bushes and rocks on it while men fired live ammunition at him. He shot well and he reached the top of the hill – but he had already been chosen. The test confirmed the choice. It was the decision of the man who had called him forward. We were told what we should say.'

'What were you told?'

'We were to go home, come back here to the jubilee estate, and we were to say that Caleb had decided to travel on. Thailand was mentioned, then a final destination of Australia. That is what we were told to say. He had passed the test set for him, had been chosen. He was with the man. His suit was taken from him, and his shoes and shirt. I saw him being given the clothes of a tribesman, then his clothes and shoes went on to the fire. I saw them burn and I saw Caleb's face in the firelight. It had a happiness that I had not seen before. He left soon after that. He went away in the back of a pickup and he never turned to look for us, to wave goodbye to us. We left the next morning, by bus, for the flight home. I have nothing more to tell you.'

'Who was the man who chose him?'

'A brute, a man who made fear.'

'How did he create fear?'

Amin took up Lovejoy's question. 'What he did, and his appearance, they made fear.'

Four years, less a month, before, and Lovejoy saw that the fear still ruled as sharp as on that day. 'Tell me.'

'When Caleb went up that hill, using the cover of the scrub and the rocks, he did not only fire in the air. He *aimed* when he fired. He tried to shoot Caleb. He tried to kill Caleb. He was from Chechnya, he had an eyepatch and a claw, he was a brute. He took our friend away from us.'

Across the table from him, Lovejoy had seen the American stiffen.

The American spoke: 'Thank you, gentlemen, I think we've heard all we need to hear.'

Lovejoy paid the bill, gave a decent but not generous tip, and pocketed the receipt. They left the darkened restaurant and went out into the rain-drenched night. They walked, not quickly, up the street to where the Volvo was parked. Dietrich told Lovejoy of the link now made. Many of those questioned at Camps X-Ray and Delta had spoken of the Chechen, who was recognizable by his eyepatch and the artificial hand. He had been killed in an ambush set by American troops of the 10th Mountain division, had died in a commandeered taxi-cab. The taxi had been driven by Fawzi al-Ateh, recently freed from Guantanamo Bay.

'We reckon anyone associated with the Chechen, certainly anyone who was chosen by the Chechen, to be of élite quality,' Dietrich said. 'Jesus, man, are you following me? That is the scale of the disaster.'

It was past one in the morning of a new day. On his mobile, with the scrambler attached, Lovejoy rang Thames House, spoke to the operations room. He was an old warhorse, a veteran of the Service, but it was hard for him as he made his report to stifle the tremor in his voice. He felt exhilaration briefly, then a burdening, nagging apprehension. He thought he walked with the fugitive but did not know on what road or where he was led.

'Will you get a citation for this?' Dietrich asked.

'I wouldn't have thought so – more likely get kicked. In my experience, few of our masters regard a messenger bearing bad tidings favourably – about as bad as it can get, wouldn't you agree? As – I say with confidence, Jed – you'll find out at first hand.'

In the small hours of the night, a signal passed electronically from Thames House on the north side of the river to the sister service's headquarters at Vauxhall Bridge Cross on the south side.

The night duty officer chewed his sandwich, sipped his coffee and rang the home number of an assistant director, woke him, smiled grimly at the stuttered response, and thought: You may not be awake now, you old fart, but in fifteen seconds you'll be active as a ten-year-old with a tantrum. He knew all assistant directors had a loathing for the bombshell careering down from a clear blue sky, except that the night skies over London were cloud-laden and spewed rain.

He spoke the name, the history and pedigree of Caleb Hunt.

The dream soaked him in sweat but he could not wake, could not lose it. Sprawled across the front seats of his Mitsubishi, Bart rolled in his sleep and pleaded – pleaded for escape. Not even the thudding blow of his chin against the steering-wheel, jarring him, was enough to break the sleep and the dream.

Abandoned by his embassy, forgotten by Eddie Wroughton, the doctor of medicine – Samuel Algernon Laker Bartholomew – was lifted down through the back doors of the black van. His bladder was going, his sphincter was loosening. His hands were tied behind his back and just before the back doors had opened they had blindfolded him. But the cloth across his face had slipped and he was aware of fierce sunlight replacing the gloom of the van's interior. He stumbled but the hands held him and he did not fall. Like the waves on the pebbles of Torquay beaches came the murmur of a host of voices. He wore a prison robe, not the Austin Reed slacks that were his usual dress in the consulting room or the shirt from the same brand that his maid starched and ironed, and the robe was pressed against his body by the breeze that carried the voices. No man spoke for him, he had no friend. The heat blistered his face, above and below the headcloth. He walked – sandalled feet scraping the ground but held up – a dozen paces, then was stopped in his tracks. He felt the weight of the hands pressing him down —not so that he should lie prostrate but so that he should kneel. His weight pressed down on the skin of his knees, the voices were stilled and he heard the silence.

The dream slipped back in time, but Bart did not wake.

Departures at the airport of Riyadh. He stood in the queue. Around him there were families, adults grumbling and complaining, children sulking and whining. He edged towards the desk and used his toe to push forward his bag. The flight non-stop home was fully booked, and Bart queued for the KLM aircraft to Amsterdam. He thought only of escape, and the slow progress of the line towards the desk fuelled his fear and impatience. A woman behind him, bowed down by a lifestyle of bags, tried to tell him how her servants had wept before she'd left for the airport, but he ignored her. The desk came imperceptibly closer, and beyond the desk was the departure gate, then the lounge, the walkway, the aircraft cabin's door. He was sweating, could not hide the mounting fear . . . It was almost a relief. Men came behind him. Nasally, in accented English, he was asked his name, and hands lifted up his bag, other hands were at his arms. He was out of the queue. He was gone. The escape had failed.

The dream was without mercy.

He cringed. There was the slither of feet on the concrete of the corridor floor beyond the steel-faced door. Low sun threw from the barred window dark shadows the length of the cell. They always came for him in the early evening. When the sun went down, the beatings began. They were late for him: already he could hear screams that pierced his head. He had seen a man, two days before, through an open door as he was led to his own interrogation, suspended from a pole by his wrists and ankles – like a pig on a spit – and had heard the man shriek as he was hustled further down the corridor. The door opened. Bart was taken down the corridor, but not to an interrogation room. A brightly lit room with easy chairs and a polished desk, and Eddie bloody Wroughton: 'You confessed, nothing we can do, you told them everything. You went down into the desert. You made your own bed, Bart, and now there's nothing we can do to stop you lying on it. They'll try you, closed court, condemn you, and then they'll execute you. You're beyond our help. When it comes to the end, try to put up a good show, try to walk tall, try to have a bit of dignity . . . It'll be quick. What I don't understand, Bart, is why you were so incredibly stupid.' Taken back to his cell, and listening to the screams and shrieks of others.

The dream was a circle that was routed from the square to the airport concourse, to the cell block, and back to the square.

He knelt in the silence. He imagined that a thousand throats gasped in anticipation. He smelt the fresh sawdust. He seemed to see the machine that shredded wood and made the sawdust that spilled from the machine into a sack's mouth. He could not see the sack but the scent of the sawdust was in his nose. He hunched. The sun and a gentle breeze were on the skin at the back of his neck. He tried to make the space, the skin between the back of his head and the top of his shoulders, so small that the executioner would find no place that his sword could strike. He buried his neck in his shoulders. He had not slept in the night. The dawn had come after an endless wait. Before he had been walked to the black van, he had been stripped of his prison uniform and dressed in a robe that was stiff from many washings and, in spite of them, was stained. The back of his head nestled against the top of his shoulders and he made no target for the executioner. He felt the pinprick at the base of his spine, where it merged with his buttocks. The prick was sharp pain, the executioner's trick with the sword point. Bart could not help himself. He jerked forward. His neck extended.

The dream ended.

He was not on the seats of the Mitsubishi but on the floor, his face squashed against the accelerator and brake pedals.

Above him, the chrome lit by the moon, the keys were in the ignition.

Bart could have pushed himself up, could have sat in his seat, wiped the sweat off his face and from his eyes, could – in one movement – have turned the ignition key and driven away into the sand in the hope of finding the track, might have been back in Riyadh by the late afternoon. Possibly, he would have lifted a telephone, have said: 'Mr Wroughton, it's Bart here, I've something really rather extraordinary to tell you. When and where can we meet?' Should have saved himself.

'Fuck you,' Bart murmured. 'Fuck you all. I hope he, whoever *he* is and whatever *he* does, hurts you.'

Bart looked at his watch. Three more hours of night before the next injection.

He had purged the dream. He slept.

It was a risk, but necessary.

First Caleb slotted the battery coolant unit into the grip stock, then he depressed the impulse-generator switch – as the manual told him to. He was in darkness, could not see, could only feel and hear. The manual said – he had read it and memorized it – that 6000 PSI pressurized argon gas coolant ... He did not have to remember a scientist's jargon, but had to listen and watch. The whine grew, but the red light winked at him. The manual said that a red light's sporadic winking indicated low battery power. When it was exhausted the red light would be continuous. The manual recommended that the battery coolant unit be recharged or replaced when the red light winked – only in circumstances of exceptional combat conditions should an attempt be made to fire a Stinger at a hostile target when the red light was winking. He killed the switch, the whine faded and the red light died. Caleb might have used the last of the battery's power when he made the test: the final chance of firing might have gone.

He fell back, the launcher resting on his body.

It all depended on the boy, on the freshness and youth of Ghaffur's ears. Without his hearing – if the Predator's eye was above him – he would not succeed in the last leg of his journey back to his family.

He had had to know that the missile would fire, would eject from the launch tube, would seek out a target.

Caleb lay on his spine. The exertion of lifting the Stinger's tube had brought back the throbbing pain to his leg.

He rested, was relaxed. What had disturbed him was not what he would do in the morning after the light came when he would stand and hobble to the guide, Rashid, and take his rifle: what had churned in his mind was that the battery powering the Stinger had lost its life.

They had *Carnival Girl* up over the track that ran north to south. On the map boxes, she would fly from Al Ubayiah at the northern point and down above Bir Faysal and At Turayqa to Qalamat Khawr al Juhaysh in the south.

Because they tracked a lorry they were both awake. Marty brought *Carnival Girl* down to the low limits of loiter speed and they kept pace with the lorry and its trailer. The infra-red real-time picture had the lorry as a clean dark shape on the screen. They might have been ready to doze, might have needed more caffeine to keep them upright, but the lorry diverted them from drooping. It wasn't the first lorry on the track, but all of the others had been going south to north, which was pretty much a straight line running through the centre of the map boxes. What was a lorry with a trailer carrying?

Marty said, 'It's refrigerated and it's got a load of iced root beer.'

'I wish.'

'Or it's got Big Macs, and ketchup and chillies and fries.'

'Dumb-ass.'

Marty said, 'My last go, it's got fans and air-conditioning units.'

'I tell you what it's got,' Lizzy-Jo chuckled, 'it's got sand. There's not enough sand here so they're hauling it down from the north – what you think?'

In the dulled light inside the Ground Control – easier to see the screens – George's entry was not noticed. They were both laughing: Lizzy-Jo thought they needed laughter as a distraction to stay awake, keep working.

George said, 'What you got is a visitor.'

He told them. The laughter went cold. She snapped upright, listened to all of it, then she called up Langley. Oscar Golf was on the headsets. George hadn't the authority to challenge a visitor. Marty was flying *Carnival Girl*. Lizzy-Jo said she'd do it, the challenge, and Oscar Golf would take over the sensor operator's controls via the satellite link. Effortless transition. Oscar Golf told her to take the guy on the perimeter-gate bar with her.

'Lizzy-Jo, go careful. Don't start a war, and don't give a yard.'

'Hearing you, Oscar Golf. Out.'

She took a swig from the water bottle, did up a couple of the lower buttons of her blouse and followed George down the steps, into the night. He'd been working on *First Lady*. The wings were off, and the engine was being stripped, the camera units already taken out. By the time it was daylight, *First Lady* would be ready for her coffin. The transport plane was due in at ten hundred and was scheduled for lift-off at twelve ten hours, and for *Carnival Girl* to be stashed and loaded in time for lift-off, then her sister craft had to be packed and crated in the coffin. George's people swarmed round *First Lady*. George left her when they reached the armourer, who had a stubby rifle hanging across his spine from a strap, but his hand was hooked back and had hold of it.

The armourer pointed up past the gate in the razor wire, then handed Lizzy-Jo his night-sights. The binoculars were heavy in her hand, and she took a moment to get the focus right. A Mercedes was parked two hundred yards up from the gate bar, with a chair by the front passenger door. On it sat an Arab. He was middle-aged, had an austere, thin face and trimmed moustache, wore a dark outer robe, an under-robe of white brilliant enough to flood her glasses, and a headcloth held in place with woven rope. Around his neck, hanging from straps, were his own binoculars. Behind his chair the Mercedes' rear doors were open and three men stood close to the body of it. She gave the night-sight glasses back to the armourer.

'You reckon they've got hardware?'

'In the back – yes, Miss. An arm's reach away.'

'What you got?'

'An M4A1. We call it a close-quarters battle weapon, Miss. It uses ball ammunition and it has an attached M203 grenade launcher. And I got—'

'Jesus, is this going to be fucking Dodge City?'

'It's their call, Miss, what it gets to be.'

'Where are you going to stand?'

'I'll be, Miss, right behind you.'

'Don't mind me saying it, but I'd prefer you a yard to the right or to the left. Wouldn't want to be in the way of a close-quarters battle weapon,' Lizzy-Jo said, dry.

The armourer lifted the bar for her. She walked forward. Lizzy-Jo was a sensor operator, not a diplomat, a negotiator or a soldier. She felt the cool of the night air, a little wafting wind, on her bared thighs and shins, on her arms and face. The man stood as she approached and the guys with him seemed to inch closer to the open doors. She heard, against the tread of her footsteps, very soft, the click of oiled metal behind her and knew the armourer's weapon was armed. The man moved a little aside from his chair and motioned that she should sit.

'No, thank you, sir.'

'Would you like water?'

'Sir, no, thank you. What I would like to know is why, at seventeen minutes past three in the morning, you have binoculars on us.'

'You should button your blouse. In the night cold it is possible to contract influenza or a headcold if one is insufficiently covered. I am a prince of the Kingdom, I am the deputy governor of this province. Each time I am in Shaybah, since you came, I watch you, but before from a distance. I have a question for you too: why are you flying at seventeen minutes past three in the morning?'

She said, parrot-like, 'We're doing mapping and evaluation of flying performance over desert lands, as we stated when permission was granted us.'

She heard the mockery in his voice. 'With a military aircraft?'

Lizzy-Jo might have been a corporate recorded message. 'The General Atomics MQ-1 Predator has dual purpose military or civilian use.'

'For mapping and for evaluation of performance do you need to carry, without the Kingdom's authorization, air-to-ground missiles?'

In the darkness he would not have seen her rock. 'I think you must have mistaken the additional fuel tanks carried under the wings for missiles.'

'When you came the fuselages of your two aircraft were without markings. Yet the one being dismantled now carries a skull-and-crossbones – once the symbol of a pirate, now a warning of death or danger – on the forward fuselage. I ask, why would such a symbol be on an aircraft preparing maps and evaluations?'

'Sir, I can only refer you to our embassy in Riyadh.'

'Of course.'

'And I am sure that, inside office hours, any query you have will be answered. Actually, sir, we will be gone in less than nine hours.'

'With your mapping finished, your performance evaluation completed?'

'No, sir,' Lizzy-Jo flared – should not have done, but did. 'Not completed – because some jerk shoved his nose in, and screwed things for us.'

He stared at her. She heard the hiss of his breath between his lips. In the darkness, his body seemed to shake.

The words were chill. 'Maybe you are from the Air Force, maybe from Defense Intelligence, maybe from the Central Intelligence – maybe you were never taught to dress with correctness and decency, were never drilled in the virtues of truthfulness and the values of humility . . . but you are American, and how could it be different? You lie to us because you do not trust us. You have no humility because you believe in your superiority over us. When you have been expelled, in less than nine hours, take this message back. We fight terrorism. Al Qaeda is our enemy. We are not the wet-nurse to the fanaticism of bin Laden. Together, and with trust, you would have been able to fulfil your mission. Your arrogance destroys that possibility. It is why you are hated and why you are despised, and why your money cannot buy affection or respect. Take that message home with you.'

She bit her lip. Anyone who knew Lizzy-Jo – knew her in New York or at Bagram base – would not have believed that she could resist a response. She turned on her heel. She walked back to the armourer and kept going. She went past George and his team, who were struggling to crate the engine of *First Lady*, and past her tent, which was now folded with her possessions stacked, and past Marty's tent – and past the boxes of the Hellfires that would not now be needed. Alone untouched, because *Carnival Girl* still flew, were the Ground Control and the trailer attached to it that carried the satellite dish. She climbed the steps.

Flopped beside Marty, she called Oscar Golf. 'Lizzy-Jo here. It was just some local rubbernecker, it was nothing. I'm taking over, but thanks for helping out.'

Marty said, smiling, 'I got bored watching that lorry. Wasn't sand it was carrying. I reckon it was pretzels.'

She snapped, 'Just watch your fucking screen – watch it till we finish.'

It was as if he was building a wall of information. Eddie Wroughton's way, when trying to make sense of intelligence, was always to pretend that he was building a wall of coloured bricks. He sat cross-legged on the floor, had pushed aside the rug to give himself a firm surface and spread out sheets of paper. He had used his highlighter pens to ring each of the sheets – red and green, white and blue, and yellow.

He had started to build the wall.

In the *red* brick was the telephone number that had called Bartholomew's home. The number's code identified it as coming from the extreme south-east of the Kingdom, and his assistant's unpraised work had found that it was listed in the name of Bethany

Jenkins. He remembered her from a party – tall, a picture of healthy endeavour, well muscled, tanned – and from a casual meeting at the embassy. Something about meteorites and something about the oil-extraction plant at Shaybah. She had called Bartholomew late in the evening, and he'd gone, disappeared.

He had run the fine dark sand granules across the indented sheet that he had taken from Bartholomew's notepad beside the phone. Pretty basic, what they taught on the recruits' induction courses, about as sophisticated as invisible ink pens – and they still lectured on the use of them. Scribbled words came to life after the granules were tipped from the indent marks. 'Military action . . . missile attack . . . head wound and a leg wound . . . Highway 513. Route 10. Harad, south. To Bir Faysal (petrol station).' That was the *green* brick.

The *white* brick was Shaybah, from where Gonsalves' people flew Predator unmanned aerial vehicles that were armed with twin pods for Hellfire missiles.

The *blue* brick built the wall higher. Wroughton reached behind him for the photographs taken by the Predator's real-time camera. With a magnifying-glass – could have done it on the computer with the zoom, but preferred old ways and trusted practices – he studied those who were identified as dead, and the one who was not accounted for. A young man, head up and erect, and the magnifying-glass – at the blurred edge of its power – seemed to show a strong chin. He laid the photographs on the blue sheet.

Two and two did not make five. The worst sin of an intelligence officer was to leap to untested conclusions. Conclusions must always have foundations, his father used to say, as any wall must. What he knew . . . Bethany Jenkins had rung Samuel Bartholomew from Shaybah. At Shaybah there was an Agency search-and-destroy operation, which had searched and destroyed, but there was a target still not accounted for. Bartholomew had driven away in the night, with fuel and medical supplies, after being told of a patient injured in 'military action'. The stupidity of the woman – Jenkins – astonished him. The involvement of Bartholomew bewildered him – and then his own guilt swelled around him. It came back to him as the scabs on his face and body itched. A phone plug pulled out, a mobile switched off. But Bartholomew could still have left a message on the voice mail. His head sank. Why had no message been left?

There was a knock.

Wroughton called sullenly, 'Come.'

His assistant always had a nervous twitch in his presence, as if expecting a rebuke. He had not known she was still there. Thirty-five minutes past four in the morning. What was she staring at? She was staring at nothing. Hadn't she ever seen the scrapes from walking into a door? She hadn't noticed any scrapes. What did she want? Had thought Mr Wroughton might need coffee and a hot beef sandwich – and she put the mug and the plate on the table in front of him.

As Wroughton growled an acknowledgement, without grace, she said cautiously, 'Oh, and this just came through – it's a general notification, to all stations. It's probably not worth you looking at right now but . . .'

'I am trying, if you didn't know it, to work.'

Papers and photographs were laid on the table alongside the mug and the plate, and she fled.

On his hands and knees, Wroughton went to the table, lifted down the mug and slurped from it, then the plate and took a coarse bite of the sandwich. In putting back the plate he dislodged the papers and the photographs. They fell at his knees. He started to read.

Caleb Hunt. 24 years. Description, *ethnic Caucasian but sallow-skinned, and no distinguishing marks,* and his height and weight. The address, *20, Albert Parade,* and the name of a town sandwiched between the conurbations of Birmingham and Wolverhampton; the address of his place of work as a trainee garage mechanic. The recruitment, *Landi Khotal, North West Frontier of Pakistan, April 2000 by known Al Qaeda talent-spotter.* The arrest, *captured by US military personnel in ambush south of Kabul, December 2001.* The deception, *assumed the name and identity of Fawzi al-Ateh, with profession of taxi-driver.* The detention, *held at Camps X-Ray and Delta, Guantanamo Bay, under category of 'unlawful combatant' until release back to Afghanistan in programme for freeing those believed innocent of terrorist involvement.* The escape, *during comfort stop en route from Bagram to Kabul City for lodge-ment and processing with Afghan intelligence, ran, and was not subsequently recaptured.* Status, *extremely dangerous, exceptionally professional and highly motivated. His success at duping interrogators at Guantanamo marks him out as* . . . His laughter split across the room and broke the night's quiet. *More detail to follow.* He pushed the papers away across the floor, looked again at the bricks – and the upper photograph caught his eye.

Wroughton breathed hard.

The upper photograph was a school group, a leavers' picture, with a circle drawn round one face. The lower photograph was a compilation of a prisoner, full face, left profile and right profile.

He laid the papers from Vauxhall Bridge Cross on the yellow-bordered sheet, then the photographs. The image of the lost fugitive taken before the Predator's strike did not match Guantanamo, humble and cowed. He gazed down at the school photograph – the boy was taller than the others, straight-backed and head held high. The face, Wroughton thought, showed a mind that was detached and restless, and the eyes looked through him and beyond. It was where Caleb Hunt would be, in the wilderness of the Rub' al Khālī. He was injured, and Samuel Bartholomew had been idiot enough to be persuaded to minister to him. He went to the door, leaned through it. 'I'd like to say thank you for the coffee and the sandwich. I much appreciate that you've worked through the night.'

It was the first decent thing he had said to his assistant in months and he saw her gape.

Back on the floor, peering down at the papers and photographs, he realized there was one area of doubt among the many certainties. Why was she involved? Why was Bethany Jenkins – quality, with class, wealth and education – in the desert and helping the man? Why . . . ? The doubt was erased.

'Because, Miss Jenkins, you are naïve, self-centred, and you have let the world pass you by.' The photographs and printouts, the imagined bricks, were Wroughton's witnesses as he spoke. 'You cut yourself off from the real world, and scrabbled in the sand after meteorites and did not listen to the radio, didn't watch the satellite TV and didn't read newspapers. You did not concern yourself with the Twin Towers or with Bali or Nairobi or a hundred bombs around the world. You did not care about rows of coffins and about the weeping of victims' loved ones. You did not know about the hatred because you'd closed your mind to everything other than your own demands. It'll take some getting out of, Miss Jenkins, where you've put yourself. Unless you're very smart – smarter than you've ever been – you are destined to end up as a casualty, and you'll call for people to help you but they'll not come running.'

Through a pane of glass, she saw them. She dreamed. They were together and she rode beside him, rocking on the camel hump, and the emptiness of the desert stretched away in front of her. She did not feel the heat, or the dryness in her throat, or exhaustion, and she was aware only of her happiness to be with him in a place of beauty, and free, and it was her future and his.

A shot was fired. She heard the rifle's crack, then the breaking of the glass.

She no longer saw herself clearly, and did not see him.

The voice was in her ear, replaced the ring of the shot.

Beth woke, blinked in the darkness.

The boy was above her, his face was silhouetted against the sunken moon.

'Please, Miss Bethany, do not make any sound.'

'What . . . what?' She lay on the sand, a single blanket wrapped round her, beside the Land Rover's wheel.

'What my father says . . .'

'What does your father say?'

'My father says you should go.'

'Go?' Beth stammered. 'Go? Where to?'

'My father says you should go, and leave, drive away.'

'Yes, in the morning. More injections. When he can stand, ride, when he leaves . . .'

'Go, my father says, go now.'

'I made a promise,' Beth said bleakly. 'I gave my word. I cannot break my word.'

'My father says you should go.'

The boy slipped away. She heard the rustle of the camels' harnesses, their endless grinding chewing, and Bart's snores. She felt small, frightened, and she knew by how far she had overreached herself. She had given her word, had made her promise.

She would not sleep again, would not dream again . . . There would be no happiness, no place of beauty, and she thought the simplicity of love was snatched.

Beth rolled in her blanket, swore, lay on her stomach, swore again, and beat her fists down against the sand.

He slept. He heard nothing, saw no movements. The great body of the Beautiful One, beside him and close to him, soothed his sleep.

Caleb slept because the pain had been beaten back, slept as the first light of dawn broke.

Chapter Nineteen

'Do you want morphine?'

'No.'

He had taken the injection in his arm. Caleb had lain on his back while the doctor had examined the leg wound, then replaced the lint dressing.

'You can have morphine either intravenously or by ampoule, for the pain.'

'I don't want morphine.'

'It's a free world.' The doctor smiled grimly. 'You take it or leave it.'

He did not want morphine because he thought the drug would cloud his mind. Back at home, in the old world that he sought to forget, there had been heroin addicts – the world came back more often to him, nestled with him, disturbed him – and in the summer they went down the canal towpath to the bridge that carried the rail link between Birmingham and Wolverhampton, and they huddled in the gloom below the bridge's arches and injected themselves. To feed it, they stole, mugged and burgled. Going to school, going to the garage, going in the car to Birmingham for the mosque, he had seen them shambling, pale, their minds lost. He needed control, that day above all others.

The doctor hovered over him, rubbing his eyes as if tiredness overwhelmed him. Caleb had slept. The sweat ran from the doctor's forehead and down into the stubble on his cheeks . . . The doctor had saved him, but had seen his face.

'Actually, I'm rather pleased with it.'

The low light seeped under the awning that swung and jerked from the growing restlessness of the hobbled camels. In an hour he and Rashid and Ghaffur would be gone, the ropes would be unfastened and the animals would be loaded, and they would move. Morphine would derange his mind when he needed clarity.

'It's clean, there are no indications of infection. Oozing, that's expected, but no pus. It's what's going to happen next that you have to think about.'

Only the high-flying eye could find the vehicles, and then by chance. They might not be found for weeks, months, a year. If a storm came, at any time in the weeks or months, the contours of the dunes would shift and the vehicles would be buried – and the bodies.

'What you've got now is temporary. With clean dressings, it'll last three or four days, but then – if you've kept the infection out – you'll have to have it stitched tight. I'll be frank with you. The speed of your recovery, from trauma and dehydration, astonishes me. You've done well, or been lucky. But you will need a professional for the stitches.'

He would not bury the bodies. He would abandon them to rot in the sun and decay, and the clothes would degrade, and the flesh would be burned off the bones, but the first storm would bury them. His strength would be safeguarded.

'I'm going to do you some extra dressings, and I'll leave eight Ampicillin syringes, enough for two days, and then the same in tablets – just swallow them. Twenty pills will keep you going for another five days. You'll need proper care in a week. I'll put out some morphine as well, and two syringes of Lignocaine anaesthetic if you have to take a penknife to the wound – I don't think you will. There's not much more I can do for you, but you've had my best effort.'

'Why?' Caleb asked.

The doctor giggled at him, then wiped the smile. 'I don't think we need to talk about that. I'll get it all ready and packaged up. No sudden movements, no exertions, no walking unaided, and when you ride one of those bloody creatures you should keep the pace steady and slow. You, my friend, are a fragile petal.'

He watched the doctor walk away. There was, for a brief moment, a shiver of anger in him that his question had not been answered. A brief moment. It did not matter. He bent his body, levered his back up and looked out from under the awning. He saw the doctor head towards his vehicle. The woman was sitting against the wheel of the Land Rover, her knees drawn up to her chest and her head down on them, sitting against the wheel where he had laboured to dig out the sand. Beyond the guide, who was hunched down with his rifle laid across his lap, the boy stood with his head still and listened. He brushed his hand against the furred skin above the nose, and the Beautiful One nuzzled his arm. He caught her harness and dragged himself up. The pain shimmered through his body. He stood, his head against the awning's ceiling, used the launcher as a crutch, his hand tight on the grip stock.

He went, slow step by slow step, out from under the awning and towards the guide.

Camp Delta, Guantanamo Bay.

They sat on the bus. They were all blindfolded, and the chains were on their wrists and ankles and round their waists. He heard guards' voices from out-side the bus windows and the hammering of construction workers and the churning of cement mixers. The sun beat on the bus roof, minutes passed. Maybe there was shade from a tree or a building, but the guards outside the bus came nearer, and Caleb could listen. It was drawled, slow talk.

'Me, I wouldn't have let any of them out. Me, I'd have kept them all here, here for the shed.'

'Three weeks, so I heard, ready for when the tribunals start up.'

'Are we going to hang them, inject them or fry them in the shed?'

'Each of them's too good for these bastards.'

'Do that and there's no chance for regrets, kind of final . . . I mean, who says those jerks are innocent and should be sent home?'

'I reckon the high and mighty said it, and as usual their talk is probable shit.'

The engine started up and he no longer heard the voices. Birds sang, and there was the waft of salted air through the open door of the bus, and he heard gates open in front of them, then scrape shut after them. On his knee was a little plastic bag, compliments of the Joint Task Force, Guantanamo. It contained a change of underpants, fresh socks, a bar of soap, a toothbrush and a small tube of paste. He did not know that beside the gate now closed behind them was the big board that said, 'Honor Bound to Defend Freedom.' They drove for the ferry and the airfield on the far side of the bay. He wanted nothing of them, would carry with him only the bracelet on his wrist that gave his name, Fawzi al-Ateh. As the bus bumped through more checkpoints, past more guards, he put the plastic bag on the bus floor and kicked it back under the seat. He wanted nothing of them but that they should be hurt, by his hand.

The fly came back, settled on her lip. Beth swiped at it again with savagery. She saw him.

With short stumbled strides, his weight on the weapon, he came clear of the shelter and headed out over the sand. His robe was hooked into his waist, the sun caught the whiteness of the new dressing and his shadow stretched away in front of him. The guide's boy had come to her, told her she should leave in the night, and she had spoken of her bloody promise. She should have gone in the night to the snoring, tossing Bartholomew, and told him, ordered him, to load up the big dose to burn away the dream. She had not had the courage. He reached the guide.

At that distance Beth could not have heard words spoken between them. She screwed her eyes to see better and did not think words were spoken. He let his weight settle on the weapon that supported him, reached down to the guide's lap and lifted the rifle. There was no protest from the guide, no struggle for the rifle. He stood over the guide, the weapon as his crutch, and both his hands held it. She heard – as an echoed sound across the sand – the scrape of metal on metal as he cocked it.

He held the rifle in one hand and turned, with his weight on the weapon and the length of its tube, so that he faced vaguely towards her. He moved. She leaned her weight against the tyre and watched him. His face was contorted. The veins stood out on his neck and the lines cut his forehead, and his eyes were near closed as if that might hold back the pain. She saw the first blood trickle from his lip where he bit it. He came nearer to her and the sand scuffed out from under his bare feet. The guide still sat and she could not read his thought, and further back and higher the boy was on the shallow dune. She wriggled back against the tyre, but it was ungiving. Then she realized. He was not coming towards her. His target was at a shallow angle from her.

Beth swung her head.

The tail of the Mitsubishi was past the Land Rover's front fender. Bart had his back to him, had not seen him, was stuffing packeted syringes, rolled dressings and tablet bottles into a plastic bag. He did not know that he was stalked.

The rifle was held out, but Beth saw the way the barrel wavered, wobbled, as if caught by the wind.

Bart had a small refrigerated box and unzipped it. He put the plastic bag into it. He reached into the tail of the Mitsubishi and lifted out a water bottle. First he mopped a handkerchief across his face, then he swigged from the bottle.

The rifle was raised. Its barrel seemed to shake. She thought he struggled to hold it steady, and to aim. He was a dozen yards behind Bart.

Beth screamed. No words of warning, only an anguished cry that pierced the quiet.

She saw Bart start up, saw his shock, saw him stare at her, then follow her line of sight. He fixed his gaze on the rifle barrel, then seemed to shrivel.

She heard Bart's voice. 'You don't have to do that, my friend. No cause for you to be worried by me. Snitch on you? No . . . no. Turn in a fighter? Been there. I've seen your face – it doesn't matter. Sort of made the decision last night. I'd go to my grave rather than turn in another fighter, done that long ago . . . I'm grateful to you. Coming down here and getting you on your feet has been kind of important to me – like the chains are off, my friend. What I'm saying is . . .'

She saw that the barrel of the rifle was steady. She pulled herself up against the tyre. She saw the finger slide from the guard to the trigger. She gulped in a breath, and ran.

Beth saw his head lift from the sight. Her boots ground and kicked in the sand as she slithered nearer to Bart.

For the slightest moment, there was irresolution on his face.

The rifle dropped.

Beth reached Bart. She stood in front of him, panted, felt the heave of his chest against her back. She was a shield for him.

'You don't have to,' Bart's voice quavered in her ear.

'I do.'

Images cascaded in Beth's mind. His control over the men who would have killed her, his sweat dripping as he dug out the sand-locked wheels, his smile of gratitude as she passed him water, his frown of concern and patience as he cleaned the engine, his peace as he slept in the sand beside her, the stars and moon above him . . . The barrel was up, aimed. She looked into his face and searched for passion, loathing, madness, and saw only a strange calm. She thought his eyes had the emptiness of death, as if the light had gone from them.

'I've seen your face. I remember it. Be a hero, be a killer. Isn't that what you want? . . . Do you know what you said before the drip worked? I'll tell you: "They'll hear my name, they'll know it . . . Everyone will hear my name . . . When you hear my name, all of you bastards, it'll be because I've done what my family wants of me." Your family, big deal, have made an animal of you. Common Brit scum is what you are, always will be – and vain as a fucking peacock . . . I've seen your face and I will not forget it.'

She stared back at the barrel of the rifle and she knew. Through the sights he must look into her eyes. She held her gaze steady, never lost his eyes. The finger was on the trigger.

She hadn't seen him come. One moment she faced the barrel, the next – the boy was in front of her. The boy protected her.

She felt the trembling of his slight sinewy body against her stomach, and against her back was Bart. Could he shoot? To save him, the boy had been near to death in the desert. To save him, the boy had trekked to her. Over the boy's head, she saw now the pain in his face, and it was not the pain from the wound. The sun caught the bracelet on his wrist, and she thought that when it had been put on him he had not weakened. Now he did. More movement from the corner of her eye. The boy's father walked past the long-flung shadow, and past him, never looked at him, and past the raised barrel. The boy's father spat into the sand, then turned and stood in front of his son. Beth knew he would not shoot. They made their untidy line, body to body, and faced him.

She did not taunt him again, did not need to.

At that moment, as Beth saw it, there was a vulnerability about him, and loneliness, and—

In snapped movements, those of a trained man, the rifle barrel was raised towards the brightened skies, there was the clatter of the mechanism as it was wrenched back and the bullet ejected. The bullet, its case gleaming, arched from the rifle and fell, and his finger was off the trigger. There was the click of the safety lever. The rifle was held out, and the guide went a dozen paces and took it. She wondered if he was broken – if she had isolated him, had killed him.

He walked away from them, using the weapon to lean on, struggling to walk.

Bart said softly, behind her, 'How's he going to get his name up in lights, murder half a city, if he can't blow us away?'

The guide was at the trumpeting camels, knelt to loosen their hobble ropes, and the boy trudged to the high ground to resume his watch. Beth clung to Bart, held the gross, sweaty man in her arms, felt him quiver against her.

'I'm not taking blame. Not any way I'm not. I done everything for him, he never wanted. One quick shag – excuse me – and it's with you the rest of your life. Might as well have hung a rock round my neck. Want to hear about it?'

Jed Dietrich thought himself privileged to be at a master-class as taught by Michael Lovejoy. He knew the woman to be aged forty-three, but appearance gave her fifteen years more, minimum.

'Well, you're going to . . . Me and Lucy Winthrop and Di Mackie, we're all eighteen, all in work at a packager, and it's Friday night. Twenty-five years ago, and it's like yesterday – would be because it screwed my life. We were in the Crown and Anchor, that's Wolverhampton, but it's a car park now. Hot night, summer night, too much booze. Three guys . . . They were Italians, all the soft talk. Italians in Wolverhampton to put in a new printing press or something. Closing time, chucking out. Christ, they'd hands like bloody octopuses, the lot of them. We're down an alley and it's a knee-trembler job. I'm in the middle and we're all going at it – and we're pissed. Mine's called himself Pier-Luigi, and he's from Sicily. What else do I know about him? Not much. Oh, yes – he was big and it hurt. They did their zips and we pulled our knickers up. We went home, they went wherever. . . . Di's OK and Lucy's OK, but I'm in the club. Trouble is, I don't know it till it's too late to dump it. My dad tried to trace him but it was a brick wall. We called him Caleb – don't ask me why, it was Dad's choice. Five years later, Dad and Mum moved down south, bought a bungalow. Truth was, they wanted to be shot of us. So I was left behind with the little bastard. They hated him, said he'd ruined their lives. They're dead now, both of them. We didn't go to the funerals. They wouldn't have wanted us there, neither of them. As a baby and a child he was dark, he was different.'

They'd been at the door early. In her housecoat, she'd answered Lovejoy's knock. He had been so charming, so gentle. Inside the hall he'd remarked on the wallpaper – 'What a pretty pattern, Miss Hunt, what a nice choice' – and he'd edged into the kitchen, and not seemed to notice the filled sink and last night's plate, and he'd fixed on a dying plant in a pot – 'Always did like that one, Miss Hunt, in fact I'd say it's my favourite' – and he'd put the kettle on.

'I was lucky to get this place. Dad had a friend in the town hall, housing. It was his price to me for moving south. Dad got my file moved up, then he could go and wash his hands of me. We're here, like an island, all Asians around us. I'm not complaining – some people would, not me – they're good people and good neighbours, so all his friends were Asians, had to be. He got to blaming me that I wasn't Asian, and hadn't a family like his friends had – but I'm not taking any blame. Nothing's my fault.'

Said so quietly and with a smile that won: 'Miss Hunt, you seem like a woman who looks after herself. I'm hesitating – will you have sugar if I do?' Lovejoy had poured the tea into cups he'd taken from the cupboard, and she'd almost purred. Dietrich reflected that the woman had no idea of the devastation about to hit her shabby, damp little home, and Lovejoy wasn't about to tell her; effortlessly it was established that the room upstairs was untouched, uncleared, from the day the 'little bastard' had left – the room would be the centre of the storm, but only when Lovejoy was finished.

'I tell you who I blame most . . . that Perkins at the school. Made too much of a fuss of Caleb, made him do things that weren't natural to him. Speaking in front of the class, being special, marking him out. Caleb got so that nothing satisfied him. I was dirt. No respect for me, his mother. No respect for the people in the job he had. Always dreaming of something he couldn't have. Why couldn't he have a family like Farooq, like Amin? Why couldn't he belong? He only wanted the Asians – didn't even have a nice white girlfriend. Could have had Tracey Moore or Debbi Binns. Truth to be told, girls scared him and he ran a bloody mile from them. Then the offer came. Nag, nag, nag, money, money, money. He never came back, nor did my money.'

Looking out through the kitchen window – and Dietrich didn't think it had been cleaned that year – he saw a rubbish-filled yard, a washing-machine tipped on its side against a low wall, and above it, the walkway that he knew from the map was beside the canal. A group of loafing kids wandered along it, and he saw an old man with a bent back, who had a terrier straining on a leash, move aside to give them passage. He seemed to understand it was a place to escape from. Lovejoy had driven him through the estate on their way to the early-morning knock. Little streets, little terraced homes, little food shops, and everywhere the little bright-painted boxes of security systems. The only buildings of stature on the estate were the new mosque and the new Muslim community centre. It was a ghetto, not a place where Caleb Hunt could have belonged, and Jed understood why it had failed to provide the man with what he needed. All so different from the scrubbed-down interrogation rooms of Camp Delta where he met the enemy – but he learned more here than there.

'They came round to see me, Farooq did and Amin, and they weren't straight up with me but they stuck to it – Caleb had gone travelling. I'd hear from him, they said, but he'd gone travelling. He's a grown-up, and I got on with my life. Two postcards came, one after two months and one after five. The Opera House in Sydney, and that big rock in the middle. It's more than three and a half years since the last one came. Nothing at my birthday, nothing at Christmas. I suppose he's forgotten me.'

Tears ran down her lined, prematurely aged cheeks. She looked up, past Dietrich, towards Lovejoy.

'Who did you say you were from?'

'I didn't.' Lovejoy stood. 'Thank you for the tea, Miss Hunt.'

They went out of the front door, on to the pavement.

Two big vans, smoked-glass windows, were parked, one at each end of the short street. They walked past the van at the top, and Lovejoy rapped on its window with the palm of his hand. They went on, round the corner, to where the Volvo was parked. Lovejoy wasn't a man to linger for the uglier side of his work. They would be well gone, speeding on the road south, when the detectives spilled from the vans, elbowed inside, tore apart the terraced house for evidence of the life, times and motivations of Caleb Hunt. Not that Dietrich thought there was anything left to know.

They reached the car.

Lovejoy asked brusquely, 'You happy, ready to call it a day?'

Dietrich said, 'Ready to wrap, yes. Happy, no.'

'The postcards?'

'The postcards say that right from the start they marked him down as high potential for infiltration, created a cover. They reckoned they'd their hands on high-grade material. We did well but I don't feel like cheering or breaking out a bottle – I suppose it's because I think I know him.'

'I'll get you on the afternoon flight – my granddaughter's birthday today, and I'll catch the end of the party, which'll please Mercy. I find there's not often cause, in our work, for cheering . . . Never seems quite appropriate.'

They drove away, out of the estate, over the canal and left behind the place that had fashioned the past, present and future of Caleb Hunt.

The file was under his arm. On it was written the name.

'I want Mr Gonsalves on the phone, and I want him now. Please.'

The marine guard and the receptionist stared at the scars on Eddie Wroughton's face.

'You should tell him I am in possession of information he'd give his right ball for, and if you obstruct me I guarantee to flay the skin off your backs. You want to sit comfortably again, then do it.'

A call was made. The receptionist murmured into the phone and fixed Wroughton with a glance of sincere hostility. Somebody would be with him soon. Would he like to sit down? He paced and held tight to the file.

The young man came down the stairs, went through the security barrier, and tracked towards him. 'I'm sorry, Mr Wroughton, but Mr

Gonsalves is in conference, and I am deputed to take whatever message you have for him.'

Wroughton saw his curled lip, the sneer.

'Get me up to Gonsalves, if he wants to see this.' Theatrically, Wroughton held the file in front of the young man's spectacles.

'Wait here.'

He waved the file again, taunting with it, as the desk telephone was lifted.

'Excuse me, guys, bottom right of screen, wasn't that? We lost it.'

The serene voice of Oscar Golf broke into their headsets, the intervention from Langley.

'No, it's not there now. We've gone past . . . Did you see anything? Bottom right of screen for four or five seconds.'

It was a little short of two hours since they had last heard from Oscar Golf. Marty had stiffened. It was like they were watched, tested, spied on. He saw Lizzy-Jo's mouth move as she swore under her breath.

'Our calculations give you fourteen minutes more time over your current box. Let's use the time, guys, by going back. How does that sound?'

He looked at Lizzy-Jo. She'd her tongue stuck out, like she was a kid in contempt of an adult. Then her forefinger waved across her lips – not a time to fight.

'I'll bring her back. We'll work back.'

Oscar Golf, lounging in a swivel chair in the darkened room at Langley, was not a target to pick for a scrap. Maybe Oscar Golf had six pairs of eyes alongside to help him. Marty grimaced at Lizzy-Jo and she shrugged. He'd seen nothing, bottom right of the screen, neither had she, and . . . He heard a thundering roar, piercing into his headset, billowing through the open door. Where he sat, he couldn't see the window of Ground Control, and the door was at the wrong angle. She leaned close, slipped his headset up off his ear and whispered that it was the transporter landing, their freedom bird.

'Oscar Golf, I am going into a figure eight, and let's hope we find what you think you saw.'

'Appreciate that. Oscar Golf, out.'

There was just sand on the screen – from top left to bottom right.

Red sand and yellow sand, ochre sand and gold sand, and there were sand hills, sand mountains and flat sand. The track was out of sight, too far to the east of the last map boxes they flew. Tiredness ached in Marty. The previous day, at the start of the last flight and before the weariness had settled on him, he would have resented any request to go back and look again. With the joystick, he banked *Carnival Girl* and swung her to starboard before the correction to port. Dust came in a storm through the Ground Control open door and he did not need Lizzy-Jo to tell him that the transporter had taxied off the runway and come on to the compacted dirt beside the compound gate. The dust filled the Ground Control Centre, settled on his head and his shoulders and spread over the chart of map boxes. She choked. He heard her gulp and then she had hold of his hand.

'Heh, Marty, see that? What are we looking at?'

Wroughton was led into Gonsalves' empire.

All the desks were deserted. All the screens in the open-plan flickered, but were not watched. He went past a conference annexe, and through the door saw briefcases dumped and files left open.

Wroughton was brought to a technology and electronic control centre. He went in. Over shoulders, backs and heads there was a bank of screens. He saw Gonsalves in a Godawful floral shirt.

He said, 'I've hit a jackpot, Juan, and I'm sharing it with you.'

It should have been a moment of triumph for Eddie Wroughton. In the throne room of the empire, he held up the file and was ready to boast of what he had achieved. He won no reaction, except that Gonsalves waved a hand at him without turning, gestured for him to shut his mouth. He looked at the screen they all watched. And he heard the voice, metallic and distant, from the high speakers.

'That's good, Marty, and well done for bringing us back. You have eleven minutes more flying time on station . . . Lizzy-Jo, please, could you give me a zoom, right in close? I reckon it's a target . . . Good flying, guys. Oscar Golf, out.'

Bart carried the coolbox from the tail of his Mitsubishi, walked well and steadily. The vehicle was fuelled up and he'd discarded the empty cans by the tail.

He felt almost a slight disappointment in the young man: *How's he going to get his name up in lights, murder half a city, if he can't blow us away?* Not that he wanted to be dead, his thorax blasted, his spinal cord broken, lungs and heart punctured by bullets fired on semi-automatic, not that he wanted his blood coagulating in the sand and the flies clustering. He recognized the scale of the failure and it left him with a trace of sadness . . . The two men in the village, fingered by Bart, they would have shot him, would not have failed. He saw, to his right, that the guide and the boy had their animals loaded. He was not sure whose life had tipped the balance, had won his survival. He walked over to the young man who had the launcher on his shoulder and seemed to wait irresolutely by his camel, as if expecting help to mount it.

He reached him, put down the coolbox that held the drugs, syringes and dressings, and looked into the face.

'Can I pay you?'

Bart shook his head. There was, because of the traced smile, a charm about the face he had not registered before. The pain that had twisted it was gone. The shake of Bart's head was expansive, as if mere mention of remuneration cheapened him. He saw the cut of the chin, the delicate shape of the nose, and the brightness seemed back in the eyes. To Bart there was, in that short moment, an image of wildness, of freedom, of magnificence. Rambling, old boy, he thought. Rambling and getting bloody stupid. The bugger should have ended you . . . And it was what she had seen, little Miss Bethany Jenkins.

He turned away. He saw, fleetingly, that the guide's boy had moved a few paces from his father and a frown laced the young skin of his forehead.

She intercepted him, came towards him, and the sand kicked from her boots with the urgency of her stride. Nothing sweet about her, and her mouth was puckered in a suppressed anger. She stood in front of him, blocked him. 'You could have put him down.'

A sheepish smile, a shrug.

'He wouldn't have known – you could have squirted half a gallon of morphine into him.'

But he hadn't. He had patched him up, had brought him to his feet – and had faced his rifle.

'Why didn't you?'

He snapped at her, 'Miss Jenkins, don't ever presume to look into a man's mind, search it and strip it. The exercise might cause you to put your delicate head between your knees and vomit.'

'That is pathetic.'

'It's what you're going to get and—'

The shout came, shrill, keened across the sand, rooted him. He saw the boy, one hand cupping an ear and the other pointed up. Bart's head jolted up to the sky, clear blue, and he saw nothing. He heard nothing. The boy howled the warning.

Bart stammered, 'What does he say – saying what – what?'

'The aircraft, up there – scatter – get clear.'

The guide's arms flailed. Right and left, in front of him and behind. Now the boy ran, and the guide, and she had ducked her head and charged for open sand, and the camels caught the panic, except one. The man, his patient, knelt beside his camel and held tight to its strained harness, had the launcher at his shoulder. Bart was alone. He looked a last time into the sky, and then the sun was in his eyes and he was blinking, blinded. He was alone and stumbling towards his vehicle, groping towards it. He had no cover. He seemed to see himself grotesquely magnified, trapped by a hovering eye. He blundered towards the vehicle's cab, reached it, threw open the door.

Fumbling, grasping for the keys, twisting them, stamping on the clutch, then the accelerator – crying out in fear. He felt the power under him. The wheels spun, whined, then caught. He did not know whether he faced the track and headed for it, or went away from it. He did not consider whether he could, lumbering across the desert, escape the aircraft's eye. He did not look at the speedometer, which would have told him that his pace over shifting sand was not more than twenty-five miles in an hour. Bart went in little surges on caked sand, then slowed in loose drifts. His eyes were misted from the sweat and the sun's power bounced at him from the Mitsubishi's bonnet. He could not see where he went, what was in front of him. Clinging to the wheel, he drove away, jerking the gear lever, and never looked back, never glanced in his mirror at the sandcloud behind him, never thought of the trail he left for the high eye.

He had no idea of distance, might have gone a mile . . . He was in the drift.

Not a wall, not a barrier, but a steady sinking movement. The engine raced, whined, and the needle on the speedometer dial sagged from twenty to ten, to five. Going slower . . . He stamped harder on the accelerator, swung the wheel, went to the clutch and changed down, stamped again, and the loose sand of the drift settled round the tyres.

What to do? Bart did not know.

He did not know whether to claw his way out of the vehicle and try, in the scorched heat, to run. Did not know whether to go into reverse. He did not know whether to get out, go to the back, take the shovel and dig.

'He's got in a drift. Line him up, guys. In your own time, take him. Oscar Golf, out.'

It was like driftwood washed up on a beach. Marty had flown the figure eights tighter as he had gone after the vehicle. Didn't know, not with *Carnival Girl* at altitude and on loiter thrust, how – down there on the sand – they had suddenly been aware of the Predator presence. Two vehicles, camels, and people had been on the screen. Then they'd broken. His concentration had been on the flying, not the detail of the screen. Beside him, Lizzy-Jo hadn't had the zoom in focus and close until the smoke had started spilling from the back end of the vehicle. Of course, that was the target. At first the vehicle had done well, had gone clear of the group, and the screen had shown only the roof of its cabin and the tail of dust spat out behind it. It was the sort of target they did at Nellis for training recruits, slow and easily visible, then it had gotten easy – too easy. It had stopped. He wondered if the guy would get out and run. He half hoped the guy would run. What he had was a vehicle, marooned and going nowhere.

'How long we got?'

She said they had a clear four minutes on station.

'How do you want me to come in?'

She wanted him on the driver's side, and said she'd take the Hellfire in through the driver's door.

Marty had no thoughts of grandfathers – not his own with whom he'd gone out duck-shooting, and not the old man strapped down on the back of a camel and laid out over the hump. He had not seen the man on the screen, as the man had run for the vehicle. He did not see a face and did not care to look for a mind . . . but he had the target.

The end of his figure eight brought him on to the passenger side of the vehicle, and he banked her, dipped the wing, for the half-circle to take him to a firing point against the driver's door. He did not understand why the guy did not run.

He heard Lizzy-Jo recite the check questions to herself, and give herself the check answers for readiness to launch.

Marty held *Carnival Girl* steady, and the camera image was flush on the driver's door. It was as if she hovered, a hawk, in the moment before the dive on the prey. Beside him, Lizzy-Jo whispered the command, then her finger hit the lit button. The screen shook, as if *Carnival Girl* had been punched by turbulence. Marty clenched his fist on the joystick, and watched the flame veer away. The ball of fire dived, like a hawk falling.

In the seconds before the Hellfire hit, Marty said, 'We'll go take a look at what's left behind, the rest of them, then we'll bring her back.'

'Yes, take her home.'

'She done us proud.'

'She's a great girl – then it's turn for home.'

The hit was on the driver's door. A flash of flame, then the first smoke, the climbing cloud of debris that obscured the target.

Around him there was, to Wroughton, an ejaculation of excitement. He could have told them that the chosen target was not Caleb Hunt, terrorist or adventurer or fighter, could have told them that the vehicle belonged to a pathetic doctor of medicine, that the driver was pitiful and harmless. Gonsalves' people whooped and screamed and stamped applause. They hung on each other, clung to each other. He thought the death of Samuel Bartholomew, gossip and spy, made a Mardi Gras day for them. He knew that if his telephone had not been unplugged, and if he had not tapped in the code on his mobile that prevented messages being recorded, Bart, his puppet, would have called him. He held the file, and the noise of celebration hit the low ceiling of the control centre, and Wroughton knew he would not be heard.

Ignored, he said softly, 'Idiots, you killed a nobody. You took out the wrong target.'

*

The fire flash, the Hellfire's launch, gave Caleb his aim point.

He stood, he was alone. The Beautiful One had gone, and the other camels. In the distance, clear to see against the sands and the sky, was the cloud of smoke. He did not know where the guide and the boy, Ghaffur, were, where she was, and he did not look for them. His memory held the point in the blue stretched sky where the flash had come from.

He did it as he had learned it from the manual.

The guidance antenna at the muzzle end of the tube was unfolded. The covering cap of the tube was discarded, lay by his bare and sand-worn feet. The open sight was raised and the belt pack hung on his waist. The impulse-generator switch was depressed by his finger. Caleb did it as the manual told him, without the one hundred and thirty-six hours of instruction that the manual demanded. He heard the whine of the audio signal, struggled to hold up the weight of the launcher, and stood – solid and square – with his two legs taking equally the strain of it: no support, no crutch. The pain throbbed in the wound, which was raw and not closed by stitches. He pulled the trigger in the grip stock. The manual said it was one point seven seconds from trigger depression to motor ignition. The missile lurched from the tube and fire scorched the sand behind him. He saw it so sharply, the clumsy flight from the tube mouth, and, for a moment, he thought it would fall back and roll in front of him on the sand. The tail fins opened out and – as the manual had said – the ejector motor dropped away. A flash as the second-stage engine bit, and she was away.

He sank to his knees. The sand behind him, burned from the exhaust fire and the ignition fumes, stank acrid in his nose. He would have fallen, had he not had the tube to support him.

It was gone fast above the low horizon line. He watched the fire that powered it ebb from him, diminish from him against the sky's blue.

He depended on *their* technology, *their* electronics, *their* magic and wizardry.

It flew free, beyond his control. Twice it meandered, as if it had lost sight of the target, and it hunted to find it again, and twice it locked back. He peered up to where its path took it, close to the sun, but he saw nothing. He did not know where the men would be who flew it, but he imagined the ever-increasing chaos around them as they dived the craft or climbed it, or threw it to the side, tried to lose the closing spurt of fire. The hit was so sudden. It darted, bent its course, sharp, as if its last command was late. High, near to the sun where his eyes burned, a little flash of brightness, but small against the sun's light.

It was not a clean strike. There was no explosion. The little flash, and then the fire moved on, soared higher and burst.

For a long time, Caleb looked up. He looked until his eyes had watered, until he blinked, until he could no longer stare up close to the sun, and the heat burdened him and the flies clustered on the dressing on his leg, and the pain washed in him, and he was alone. It was a speck, falling, and he thought he heard the voice of a child, singing.

It was a swan's song. The far edge of the left wing had been hit, a great destabilizing hole punched in it.

The Predator, brilliant white from nose tip to tail, from port wing to left wing, was spinning down.

Control was gone, death inevitable, falling, with the wind streaming against its wings – until the debris scattered in the sand, until the fire became a pyre.

If he had spoken someone would have hit him. They had all watched the Predator go down. If he had spoken, had pointed out that he had warned of the crates the camels carried, he would have been hit. The silence was like life arrested. The picture on the screen, untouched, was a white-out snowstorm. They had still been in noisy celebration, without shame and not a thought of the incinerated corpse in the vehicle, as the camera had tracked back over the sand, and there had been the flash from far below. At first, a little winnow of confusion: 'What's that? . . . What we got?' The one called Oscar Golf, on the loudspeakers, had never lost his calm. There had been a woman's voice, merged with Oscar Golf's, a flat monotone, as if it were merely a training exercise and instructors had thrown up a problem. The aircraft had swerved, made violent manoeuvres, but the fireball – shown by the lens – had closed. She'd gone down, spinning and spiralling, and the lens had shown a mad image of yellow reddened sand racing to meet her. The voice of Oscar Golf was gone, cut off in mid-sentence – a switch thrown. Who wanted an inquest on failure? Hell, it was only a piece of metal junk, off a factory floor – not the death of a friend. As the audience slouched out, as Gonsalves in that hideous shirt came to him and punched him on the upper chest, Wroughton opened the file and held up the photographs of Caleb Hunt, schoolboy, Camp Delta prisoner and Rub' al Khālī fugitive.

'That's who you didn't get, that's your target.' Wroughton chuckled.

'What is it with you people? So goddamn patronizing. You keep a notebook on points scored?'

They were both laughing, hugging and hanging on to each other, and laughing, like they didn't care it was the waiting room of a funeral parlour, laughing till it hurt . . . and it did hurt because a target of importance had been missed.

He did not look back at her.

The last he saw of her, she was sitting on the sand on a dune and her head was down.

If he had gone to her – confused and tongue-tied and deafened by the launcher's blast – he did not know what he would have said to her.

Neither the guide, Rashid, nor the boy, Ghaffur, had helped him mount the saddle on the hump of the Beautiful One. He was beyond feeling the pain of the wound. He had struggled to drag himself up, then to swing the leg across the saddle.

They were ahead of him and she was behind him, and far beyond her were the last wisps of two columns of smoke. Caleb did not look back, did not wave, did not – at the last moment when his voice would have carried to her – shout his farewell.

He rode away, followed the guide and the boy into the sand that stretched to a far horizon. All that mattered to him, he thought, was that he was close now to his family, to their love.

Chapter Twenty

She stood. She shaded her eyes. Riding away from her were three ant-sized dots almost swallowed by the desert.

She watched them as they diminished, disappeared into the far haze.

The smoke had gone from the downed aircraft and the destroyed vehicle. Her dream of him was downed too. She was glad that he had not spoken to her. There had been no contact between them when he had gone. She had not wanted to hear his voice, see his face: she had feared they would break her resolve. He had not looked back – it was as if he did not acknowledge that he had come into her life, had passed her in the night.

She walked to her Land Rover. The quiet of the place, its beauty and emptiness, washed over her. She took from the Land Rover the two towels she had packed, a spare blouse she had brought, and a bright red blanket she had thought she might need in the night's cold but which she had not used. She carried them back to the dune she had watched him from.

The haze had thickened round them.

She made the arrowhead so that it pointed to him, and the tiny specks on either side of him. There was no wind. The sand was still.

She bent the blanket for the point, blood scarlet on the sand. At each end, to lengthen the arrowhead, she laid the towels. He had gone into the haze, was swallowed in it, but she marked the route he had taken. Beyond the point, as if to sharpen it, she rolled her blouse, put it on the sand.

She marked him.

Beth would never again hear his voice, see him, feel the touch of him. She would not have justified her betrayal of him as having been for the greater good of humanity: she marked him as a piece of personal vengeance. Planes would come, or helicopters, and they would see the arrow she had fashioned. They would hunt him till they killed him . . . Love was dead.

As an afterthought, she stripped off her blouse – exposed the whiteness of her skin to the sun's beat – and that, too, she rolled tightly and used it to make the point of the arrowhead more distinct, more exact.

She walked down off the high ground, left the arrow behind her.

She passed the abandoned tube, the emptied box and the dropped manual. She saw the insect column that carried away the slivers of flesh from his wound. At the Land Rover, she threw a scarf over her shoulders, and gunned the engine.

The sun hammered at him, and the pain surged. Sometimes his eyes were closed and sometimes they could see nothing more than the reins in his hand and the fur of the Beautiful One's neck. The heat was without mercy, and Caleb did not know for how long he had ridden alone.

He stopped, dragged on the rein and whispered to the Beautiful One what he had heard the boy say. They had been in front of him, but were no longer there. He looked to his right and left, and saw only the expanse of the sand and the gentle rise of the dunes. He gasped, forced himself to turn further, to look behind.

Their camels knelt. They stood in front of them and the father's arm was round his son's shoulders. Caleb did not know whether it was for protection or if it was to comfort the boy. He could not see them clearly, was not able to read them, because the tiredness and pain played tricks with his sight.

He realized their intention.

He would have gone on, reeling in his dreams and his fantasies, burned by the sun, half dead and half alive, and would not have known that they had fallen back, had left him. Now, they were a hundred yards, less, from him. In an hour he would not have been able to see them.

He realized they wanted no more part of him.

'I need you,' Caleb shouted.

They would head for their village. The guide would spin a story. The boy would go to a desert grave rather than gainsay his father's lie. Back in their village they would tell of the deaths from the eye in the sky, and of the demand of the wounded traveller, without a name and without a home, that he go on alone. They would return to their village and no man would be able to contradict their story.

His shout burst over the sand: 'I need you to take me to my family.'

For answer, the guide pointed far ahead, far beyond Caleb, towards the haze and the horizon.

'Do you want money? I can give you money.' His fingers scrabbled at the belt at his waist. He loosened the fastening and held up the pouch. 'I will pay you to lead me.'

They gave no sign that they had heard him. He saw them straddle the saddles, then the camels rose. The guide pulled at his camel's head and moved away at a right angle to the route they had led Caleb on. The boy followed him. The money in the pouch would buy a well for the village, pickup trucks for the villagers, was wealth to a degree they could not have dreamed of. As they went away, they did not look at him. Caleb threw the pouch towards them.

He threw it high. It arched in flight and the neck fell open. The coins glittered as they dropped.

'I will get there without you.'

Gold coins lay on the sand, were scattered round the pouch.

They walked under the raised bar, through the gap in the coiled razor wire.

The bags were hooked on their shoulders and Marty carried his picture.

From the tail ramp of the aircraft, George called, 'Come on, guys, you're busting the take-off schedule.'

But they did not hurry. The place was a part of them, where they had lived and where they had killed. Behind them was the emptiness of the compound. Dumped boxes of cardboard and plastic bags bulged with rubbish. Torn-up paper scraps hung from the barbs of the wire. She reached out and took his free hand. They went together. Marty felt a shyness but did not pull away his hand. They went at their own pace, as if the schedule for take-off was not important to them.

At the bottom of the ramp, watched by George and his people, Lizzy-Jo grinned, then tilted up her head, and kissed his cheek – there were cat-calls and whistles through fingers, and feet stamped applause. Marty blushed. They went on up the ramp and into the gloom of the stowage area. Two coffins were being brought back to Bagram, one loaded and one empty, except for boxed spares and maintenance toolkits. Marty blushed because he thought he had failed. *First Lady* was in her coffin, but *Carnival Girl* was out in the desert, broken and lost. While the camp was torn apart, and he had packed his bag, Lizzy-Jo had lectured him on the success of the mission. One more chance to hurt the man who had brought down *Carnival Girl* was all he could have asked for, but it was denied him.

Marty edged up the side of the fuselage, over the legs and knees of George's people, past the coffins and satellite kit, the stowed tents and cookhouse gear, and they found little canvas seats where their feet would be against the wheels of the Ground Control trailer. They were near to the bulkhead, close to the hatch door to the cockpit. He settled, fastened the restraining harness. He was not thinking of Lizzy-Jo and a future, but of *Carnival Girl* who was down and mourned and alone . . .

The Texan drawl cut through his thoughts. 'Good to see you, folks.'

He was far away, where *Carnival Girl* was, in the sand. He looked up and scratched in his clouded memory.

'You don't remember me? I brought you in here – you look rough. You not slept? How did it go?'

'It went OK,' Marty said.

Lizzy-Jo cut in. 'He flew well, way beyond the limits. We lost one but we got good kills – we got Al Qaeda kills.'

The pilot said, smile beaming, 'Right on. You should be glad we're flying out today, forecast is nasty tomorrow – storms and winds that'll gust to seventy knots – good that we got the window today. I'll come and talk after we've lifted off.'

The request welled in Marty's throat as he unfastened the harness clasp. The pilot was half gone through the hatch door, and the ramp was already up. The second pilot had started up the heavy engines. Marty had to yell: 'Excuse me, sir, but could I ask you a favour? Means a lot to me.'

He explained, shouted it in the pilot's ear above the growing howl as the power gathered.

The transporter, laden to the maximum, used the length of the runway, and even then the undercarriage seemed to skim the airfield's perimeter. The pilot should have done an immediate starboard turn for a plotted flight path to the Omani border, then the crossing of the Jabal Akhdar mountains but instead banked to port on lift-off. Marty gave him the map co-ordinates, which were passed on to the navigator, lines were pencil-drawn on the map and the diversion course was set. He clung to the back of the pilot's seat and the transporter shook and bumped as it gained height. Lizzy-Jo was crouched beside him, her hand over his fingers clamped on the seat. He thought that she understood his need. They crossed plateau sand and dunes, and the mountains of the desert. They went over the track – a traffic-control tower queried them, and the pilot said, dry, that navigation equipment had gone faulty, was being worked on, would be rectified in the near future – left it behind them. The navigator did well.

She lay two miles below them. Spread out, fractured, dead. The pilot took them on a tilting circuit. Marty had his nose pressed against the glass of the cockpit side window. He saw the twenty-foot length of one white wing, and the broken pieces of the fuselage. He did not know how to say a prayer, but words of respect choked at the back of his mouth. Lizzy-Jo held his shoulder tight, but it was his moment. He grieved . . . Her fingernails cut down through his T-shirt and then she rapped the pilot's arm and gestured beyond the wreckage.

They saw the arrow. It was on raised ground and pointed across open sand. It seemed, to Marty, as if the arrowhead of bright colours was laid out to be seen from the air. The navigator made calculations, then scribbled on his pad the exact compass bearing in which the arrowhead faced.

Lizzy-Jo said, 'Someone left a marker – someone wants them fucked over. Thanks for the diversion, sir. Let's get on home now.'

As they climbed, headed for the Omani border, for the mountain range of Jabal Akhdar and for the wide sea of the Gulf of Oman, Lizzy-Jo used the communications and broadcast the co-ordinate reference points and the compass bearing – and they went back to their canvas seats.

Marty slept, his head on her shoulder.

The winds rose and they went into the teeth, the mouth of the storm. His eyes were closed against the spat pricks of the sand. Had his eyes been open he would have been blinded. Waves came across him, beat on him, threatened to drag him down off the saddle, to pitch him on to the desert's floor. The Beautiful One led him. Caleb could not have directed her. He let the reins hang loose and clung to the saddle, and when the fiercest gusts hit him he dropped his arms on to her neck and held the long hair. He knew that if they stopped, found a dune that protected them and huddled for shelter behind it, they would never regain the direction of their path. And, if the Beautiful One flinched from the storm, turned away from it, they were dead. The force of the storm brought the hot, scalding air against him, flattened his robe against his body. The sand was in his closed eyes, his pinched nostrils and his mouth, and it beat into the wound, lifted the lint dressing and lay in the cavity that was not stitched closed. He could not drink, could not eat. His throat was raw, dry – his stomach was aching, empty. Stubborn, as he had always been, Caleb clung to life.

Again and again – his mouth closed because to open it would let in the storm's sand – he shouted in his mind that he had not lived to fail now. Obstinacy gave him strength. If he went down, on to the sand and against the Beautiful One's body, his life was wasted . . . before it had begun. He did not see skeletons in the sand, the whitened bones of a man and a camel, rotted clothing and the frayed sacking leather of a saddle. He did not know how fast the Beautiful One carried him, or how far she could take him against the lash of the wind.

He was alone with his God, with his purpose.

*

A day had passed. The shuttle bus waited at the end of the ferry pier. It took Jed to Camp Delta. He showed his card and the guard let him through the turnstile gate. He'd had a good flight to Miami, then a feeder to Puerto Rico, then a military ride to Guantanamo. He had left his bag at the reception of Officers' Quarters, had not checked back in but had gone for the ferry, taking with him only the filled file.

Jed thought the guard looked at him strangely as he presented himself at the gate for Administration, but his ID, swiped, took him through. Maybe the guard was new, hauled out of the reserve, taken off a civilian street, and didn't know him. And he did not see, as he walked towards Administration with the sunshine, the light and the perfect breeze off the sea on him, the guard pick up the telephone in his box. The sun and the feel of the wind made him feel good. If he had not had the file under his arm, Jed might have forgotten, fast, where he had been; might have forgotten the rain of that place and its darkness, the grime on the streets and the sort of despair of it.

He went up the steps into the block, and the guys on the desk looked away from him, like they hadn't seen him. He went down the corridor and headed for his office, wanted to get the file secure in his safe. He went past closed doors, did not look at them. At the end of the corridor, as he walked along it, he saw the big plastic bag, filled. It was by his door. He reached the door. His name wasn't on it. It had been typed on a sticky paper strip, but the strip had been scraped off, as if with a penknife blade. He had his key out of his pocket and into the lock, but the key did not fit the changed lock. He unknotted the top of the plastic bag and saw the photograph in its frame of Brigitte, Arnie Junior and himself on a lake boat in Wisconsin.

He turned, stamped back up the corridor towards his supervisor's room.

Two doors, now, were open – one to a room the Bureau used and one to an Agency room. It was done as if it were synchronized. The Agency man was in front of him and the Bureau man was behind. Their voices rattled round him.

'You looking for Edgar, your supervisor? You won't find him.'

'Edgar went sick yesterday, got flown off Guantanamo.'

Jed thought he understood, thought he knew what their business would be in blocking him.

The Agency man, in front of him, said, 'And he wasn't alone

on the flight. Wallace went with him – except Wallace wasn't sick.'

The man behind him, from the Bureau door, said, 'And Harry was on the same plane – and Harry, too, wasn't sick.'

Jed remembered Lovejoy. The droll and laid-back quip: *In my experience, few of our masters regard a messenger bearing bad tidings favourably – about as bad as it can get, wouldn't you agree?* Lovejoy had told him he would find it at first hand – in front of him and behind him.

'Suppose you think you're clever and a hero – not an utter asshole. You fucked Wallace, and Wallace was a good man.'

'What I think, you motherfucker, you're not fit to wipe Harry's boots. You destroyed his life's service, disgraced him.'

He thought of Lovejoy and his kindness, and of the back roads he'd taken . . . thought of old people in a library and a headteacher and a man who'd seen the potential of a kid, the guys in a repair workshop who weren't good enough to satisfy the kid's ambition to be somebody . . . thought of two Asian youths who'd walked away when the kid hadn't . . . thought of a woman, a mother, on whom the kid had turned his back . . . thought of what it added up to, and the danger that was the kid, Caleb Hunt.

'Wallace, most likely – because of you – will face a disciplinary board, might lose his pension.'

'Those gatherings of senior men, gone off the payroll but honoured – Harry won't ever be there. You disgraced him, snapped him like a fucking twig. For what?'

'For your ego, asshole?'

'To trample on good men's reputations and belittle them?'

'So a mistake was made – big deal.'

'Should have been kept close. You fish, Dietrich, don't you? Good. You've got yourself all the months of the year for fishing.' The Bureau man behind him sidled back to his door.

The Agency man eased to the corridor's side. 'You broke two fine men. We'll break you.'

Jed turned, went back and picked up the black plastic bag. He dumped the file in the top of it, covered the picture of Brigitte, Arnie Junior and himself. He carried the bag down the corridor, past the closed doors. He thought of the panic that caught a city and the screams welled in his ears. Through tears, he saw bloodstains on pavements . . . and he wondered where was Caleb Hunt who could make the panic.

A week had gone . . . The pilot of the big Chinook double-rotor helicopter had told them, in their headsets, that it was unusual, not exceptional, for the Rub' al Khālī desert to be hit by a storm of that intensity and duration, but flight was now possible, though uncomfortable. He had added that ground temperature was currently at 134° Fahrenheit, 56.7° centigrade, and he'd wished them well.

All the time they had been up, Wroughton had felt sick and Gonsalves had twice used the paper bags offered them.

The Chinook carried a platoon of the National Guard, the deputy governor of the province, Gonsalves and Wroughton. The weather had cleared sufficiently for two F-15 bombers, Saudi piloted, to strike the cave complex the previous afternoon; the Chinook flew to confirm the success or failure of the strike.

Wroughton knew he was lucky to be on board. Gonsalves, the ally, had the right to be there. Wroughton was on sufferance, on the manifest because he had the file and the name on the file. Gonsalves had supplied the map co-ordinates where the marker had been left, and the compass-bearing of the arrow.

In a direct line from the compass-bearing, forty-eight land miles from the map co-ordinates, the bombers had found a steep rock escarpment, and among stones they had seen a flash of light, sun upon chrome metal, and on their third pass the cave entrance had been seen. It had been hit. Six laser-guided five-hundred-pound high-explosive bombs had been dropped on the cave entrance.

Wroughton had said it, Gonsalves had believed him, that the cave would have been the destination of Caleb Hunt.

They went, feeling sick and being sick, in search of the body – and the bodies of the commanders that he had crossed the desert to rejoin.

At the map co-ordinates, the Chinook had gone low. They had sensed, both of them, that the pilot struggled to keep the helicopter up. They had seen, faces pressed against porthole windows, clothes, a blanket and towels scattered over a half-mile. The scorchmarks where a vehicle had been burned out were covered by a sand carpet, and only the roof protruded. Of the downed Predator, all they saw was the section of the tail wings and the push-propellor, the rest of it submerged by sand.

On the compass-bearing, they looked for bodies and the carcasses of camels, but the desert below them was clean, wind-scoured sand.

They landed at the base of the escarpment.

Ears ringing, his step unsteady from the Chinook's turbulent flight, Wroughton walked towards the pile of rock rubble. Gonsalves, sweating and complaining, followed him. He could smell the death. The sweet, sickly scent of the dead came on the gusted wind. He heard Gonsalves throw up again, didn't know how the man had any-thing left to vomit. He had felt at ease with himself. The previous night, using the full weight of his embassy authority, he had escorted Bethany Jenkins to the airport, to the check-in counter, to the departure gate and had got her out safely, gratitude for services rendered, before questions had closed around her, hadn't even asked for her London phone number. She could have gone to gaol, or to Chop Chop Square . . . He had felt comfortable, until the smell soaked him.

Wroughton stepped among the stones at the base of the escarp-ment, and held his handkerchief to his nose. A little of the cave's entrance was clear but it was high above him; no way that Wroughton would scramble up over the fractured rocks when he wore his last linen suit. The light caught it. He bent and picked up the tin box – what the sunlight had struck, what the bombers' pilots had seen – and opened it gingerly. Ash and cigarette butts spilled out. His handkerchief was insufficient. Wroughton gagged. Buried by the rocks, only the head, arm and rifle barrel visible, the sentry stank.

Wroughton said quietly, 'Bad luck, sir. You did it all carefully, kept a tin for your fag ends. You were nice and tidy and professional. Except that a flier at ten thousand feet, four hundred miles an hour, can't see fag ends but *can* see a metal tin when the sun hits it. It wasn't me who ever said life was fair, sir.'

The National Guard troops had crawled – like ferrets, Wroughton thought – into the cave entrance. The bodies were lowered down the escarpment, or dropped. They had not yet swollen, but he reckoned the stench worse than anything he'd encountered in Bosnia, at the mass graves. He knew the stench of death.

The troops lined the bodies up, six of them.

Duty beckoned. It could not be avoided.

He worked the collar of his suit jacket over the handkerchief at his nose.

Gonsalves had a camera up to his eye, worked along the line and photographed the dead.

Unmarked. All of the corpses were without wound, scratch or abrasion. He imagined them all cowering at the back of the cave, and the blast funnelling in, finding and killing them. Wroughton had the picture from Guantanamo and the one of the school group. He looked down on them. All at peace, rag-doll men.

'Kind of look harmless, don't they? Like everybody's neighbour, would you not say?'

'I'd say, Juan, that you should change your street.'

'Fuck you. Your man's not here. Likely the storm took him, and the sand buried him. You saw that stuff we flew over . . .'

Now, the troops brought down from the cave boxes of blankets, books, saucepans and plates, files, a typewriter and filled sacks.

Wroughton said quietly, 'What are you standing in, Juan?'

'What we flew over was just impossible. He was hurt bad, had been through all kind of shit. Who'd last out there who wasn't a Bedouin? No one. That place is evil. No one from outside could live in it. He would have to be incredible to survive. Good riddance, I'm betting he didn't. You saw the place . . .'

A box was carried past Wroughton, and maybe his body made a point round which the wind blew, and a slip of bright laminated cardboard blew out of it and guttered down by Wroughton's polished shoes.

'Juan, you are standing in camel dung – not old dung, fresh dung. Have you seen a camel's corpse? Have you seen bits of camel? I have not.'

He picked up the cardboard slip. He went to the platoon officer, broke his deep conversation with the deputy governor, showed him the slip and asked his question. It was denied. Was he sure? It was certain. He went back to Gonsalves.

'Look at it. It's a sales tag. It's for a Samsonite case. The case is called an Executive Traveller, and that'll be a hard-sided case. It's not been brought out. The slip is new, not old rubbish. The case is not there. I'm telling you, Juan, that a man came by camel and the camel crapped and the camel's gone, and a suitcase is gone, and Caleb Hunt is not here.'

Gonsalves was using a chip stone to scrape the dung out of his trainer's treads.

'As I see it, Juan, the situation's gone beyond our reach already. A suitcase is a weapon. What's inside a suitcase is what we fight against. A suitcase, its contents, frightens us half to death, but when a suitcase is missing it's beyond our reach, already . . . The future is out of our hands. The future is with the alertness of a Customs official at the end of a ten-hour shift, or an immigration girl with a queue stretching fifty paces in front of her, or the suspicion of a probationer police officer. We depend on them, they are our future, it's in their hands – whether the suitcase goes past them, whether they stop it, whether they wave it through or whether they ask for it to be opened. If not that case, then another – and another . . . That's the damn future and it sort of crushes you when you see it up close.'

They stared at each other, each burdened by the enormity of it, each searching the future for comfort and not finding it.

'You're leaping, making too many conclusions, going too fast for me.'

'I know I am, but I feel them in my gut.'

The bodies in bags were going into the belly of the Chinook with the boxes and sacks. The deputy governor waved for them, as if he was a tour guide and an outing was running late. Wroughton thought Gonsalves was thinking of his kids and whether they'd ever walk past a suitcase set down in the street with an activated fuse running, or that he was thinking of everyone's kids. In Bosnia he had met young men, handsome and full of friendship, who had cleansed by atrocity. In Latvia he had met old men, who had dignity and charm and who leaned on sticks, and it was rumoured they had worked in concentration camps. In Wroughton's expectation, Caleb Hunt would be handsome and dignified, friendly and charming . . . He felt, as never before, a desperate sense of shame because he had once allowed himself, in a perversion of jealousy, to cheer on the young man who would carry a suitcase. He was wearied, and thought himself dirtied, inadequate.

'Do you want to come by tonight, Eddie, have some pizza, then throw some softball?'

'Thank you.'

The desert of the Rub' al Khālī seldom offered up its secrets.

For a millennium, only the stupid, the brave or the fanatical – Outsiders and strangers – have gone into the wilderness of sand, dunes and shallow mountains that cover a quarter of a million square miles of emptiness. They walked through the fire of the sun's heat, unwelcomed and unwanted. Around them were the bones of lost men and lost beasts, and the wreckage of vehicles and aircraft used by those who believed technology offered safety, and were wrong. Only the lucky survived the desert's enmity. It was said by the few Outsiders and strangers who had known luck and who had come through the fire that the Rub' al Khālī had scarred them for the rest of their lives: they were changed men. They had no need of possessions or of any ideology, no need of friends or of money, no need of love or of belonging. Like the desert's winds, the scars stripped everything from them except the determination to exist – to take another step forward, and another, to reach a distant, hidden goal. But the Outsider or the stranger who had the luck to emerge from the sands had proven his worth.

The desert of the Rub' al Khālī, the home of bones and wreckage, gave a great and humble strength to the few who survived its hardships, set them apart from their brothers and family. They had gone beyond death and it held no fear for them.